"WHAT IS IT, RICHKA?"

He sighed, struggling for words. She stared into his face, as though she would read his mind.

"You mustn't be afraid for me," she said, divining his thoughts more clearly than he did himself. "It's what I want, truly want. . . ."

She pressed her body urgently against him. There was nothing but the touch of her lips beneath his and the feel of her body trembling against him. He held all the girls of paradise in his arms.

"Natasha, my dearest Natashenka . . ."

Shocked, humbled, grateful, tormented—and then inescapably caught up in her reckless mood—his arms tightened about her. Lifting her, he strode across the room to lay her gently upon the red velvet sofa. She lay there, calmly beautiful, eyes closed, at once receptive and mysterious. . . .

"Don't be afraid," he whispered.

She shook her head, beyond words, caught up in the mystery of the moment.

Arabesque

Rae Butler

Paradise Press, Inc.

Plantation, Florida

This novel is a work of historical fiction. Names, characters, places and incidents relating to non-historical figures are either the product of the author's imagination or are used fictitiously, and any resemblance of such non-historical figures, places or incidents to actual persons, living or dead, events or locales is entirely coincidental.

EXCLUSIVE DISTRIBUTION BY
PARADISE PRESS, INC.

Copyright © 1981 by Raymond Ragan Butler

ISBN #1-57657-089-4

Printed in the U.S.A.

To
Kenyon Lilley

Arabesque

CHAPTER

ONE

Natasha touched her velvet cap nervously, setting it more firmly on her dark hair. Her action covered a sudden spasm of stage fright. The hat was perfectly in place, she knew. Her dresser had seen to that, fussing with it endlessly as Natasha stood regarding herself in the long gaslit mirror in the huge communal dressing room. Reflected there was a small slight figure in a knee-length ballet skirt, its silver tissue billowing above her pink maillot. Her long hair fell in smooth wings beneath the Juliet cap, framing an oval face that was unnaturally pale. The unsteady gaslight accentuated the high cheekbones and fascinating slanted eyes of soft dark gray that gleamed with dreamy excitement.

In a few moments she would be making her first appearance as a soloist on the huge and awe-inspiring stage of the Maryinsky Theatre. True, it was only in a divertissement in the opera *Romeo and Juliet*, but . . .

She smiled uncertainly to herself. February 25, 1876—not a date to make theatrical history. Yet somewhere, please God, her performance would not go unnoticed.

Standing in the wings, she could sense the mood of the audience. They seemed more sullen and stiff than usual. She had long ago learned that fashionable audiences in St. Petersburg were always difficult, but she had the impression that tonight they were particularly hard. Or was she being unduly sensitive?

No, there had been a definite atmosphere all through the first two acts of the opera. It was rumored backstage that the tzar's mistress, the Princess Catherine Dolguruky, was in the theatre. That could explain it. The princess was the most hated woman in society, possibly in all Russia. The people in

1

the audience were expressing their disapproval of her pres-. ence by withholding their applause.

Suddenly the footlights looked like a formidable barrier to Natasha. The rows of dim faces beyond were enemies to be conquered. From the moment she danced into the lights, it was going to be Natasha Ivanovna against *them*. She shivered with apprehension, feeling frail and vulnerable. She tried again to control her hands from trembling, smoothing the folds of her skirt, fussing with the jeweled girdle at her hip.

Her partner, Oleg, grabbed her hand, enfolding it in his own. "Courage," he whispered. "Don't worry. We'll breathe some life into 'em!" He winked conspiratorially.

Unlike her, Oleg was dressed in something approaching the period of the story—resplendent in a blue and gold patterned tunic that was trimmed with fur. His muscular legs were covered with dark blue hose. His handsome face looked ghastly in the flaring lights of the gas jets, his eyes abnormally huge and black, his grinning mouth diabolical yet clownlike. Natasha found herself smiling back at him.

She liked Oleg Mikhailovich. More importantly, she trusted him. He had made things easier for her. They had rehearsed this pas de deux for days. Practicing the minor details laboriously, linking up one step to another by degrees. They were second nature to her now. Technically she had little to worry about, at least when she was partnered by Oleg.

The real danger would come in her solo, when she could not rely on his strong arms and precise timing. She knew her major weakness—she could not come down with the music because she became so entranced with her own bodily rhythm that she could lose herself in the dance, holding a pose much longer than the music warranted it. Those were the moments she must guard against.

To her side, the corps de ballet was lining up for its entrance. Turning, she saw that the dancers were watching her. She was startled by the animosity that flared in their kohl-darkened eyes.

Again the sickening wave of fear passed over her, bringing a light sweat to her palms. They all thought it was too soon for her to be singled out . . . and in an adagio pas de deux, however unimportant. They resented even this small amount of glory. She felt dizzy, unsteady. Her legs shook. She could not hold her balance. She wanted desperately to turn and flee.

Steady, she told herself, hold on to Oleg's hand. She mustn't think of failure. Once the idea took shape in her mind it would destroy self-confidence. She must concentrate. It was only minutes to her entrance. Forget the girls. Forget their accusing eyes. Of what was she guilty? She had worked long and hard for this opportunity. She owed it to herself to dance well. She owed it to Oleg Mikhailovich. Above all she owed it to Gerdt, the *premier danseur*.

She owed everything to him. But for Gerdt she would never have been accepted for training at such a late stage in her development. She would now be working in some dreary touring company, playing small parts in the tedious French melodramas that her mother specialized in. Or, worse, playing the vapid ingenue in her father's harlequinade. Had Gerdt not noticed her talent, encouraged her and brought his influence to bear on the school examiners, she would never have seen Theatre Street—except as a gawking tourist. God! how she had hated her life as a "child-actress." She had only to close her eyes to be able to smell those sour dirty theatres, those shabby hotel rooms. Gerdt had saved her from that. He had opened the gate of success to her. She had to repay his faith.

Natasha could understand the feelings of the girls around her, she might have felt the same were she in their place. Her advancement had been extraordinary . . . amazing, almost miraculous. She had spent less than three months as a member of the corps de ballet, and she had never been in the last row. She had been promoted to coryphée at the end of the last season, had led the second mazurka in *A Life for the Tzar*—and now this! A real solo in the ballet scene of *Romeo and Juliet*.

Soon she could look forward to being a second *soliste*, then a first, then a *première danseuse*. She could even be raised to the grandeur of the Imperial Ballet, away from the trashy divertissements of the opera.

No, it wasn't hard to understand their reproachful eyes. She had never been really popular, even before the small successes. In class she had been an outcast—despised for being a provincial, a late starter, a cuckoo in the imperial nest. She was the only girl present who had not been through the spartan, almost military regime of the ballet school from the age of ten. In a sense, she had been foisted upon them. No wonder they felt resentful.

Forget them, she told herself, but she found it impossible.

She could feel fifteen pairs of eyes trained on the small of her back. She clenched her hands together. . . . Only Tamara Krupenskaya seemed unaffected by her promotion. Tamara's pale blue eyes glittered as brilliantly as the diamonds that starred her costume, and she smiled at Natasha now, as the corps glided onto the stage. Apart from a passion for collecting diamonds, Tamara seemed devoid of ambition.

She had always been friendly though, overriding the others. In fact, over the past few days she had gone out of her way to be friendly, sensing Natasha's isolation. Tonight she had insisted that they go off together after the performance "to celebrate." A dance, she had said.

At first Natasha had been reluctant to go. She knew how Tamara had acquired her diamonds, and Natasha had no wish to start her own collection. But when she had been told that a number of other girls would also be going, she had changed her mind. It might make life easier.

"We're on!" Oleg hissed, breaking into her thoughts.

She heard the music for their entrance. She nerved herself for the effort, drawing herself to her full height, taking a deep breath, moistening lips grown suddenly dry. She crossed herself—a magic ritual to banish the flesh-and-blood Natasha and summon her spirit.

Then she was dancing onto the stage, her fears carried miraculously away, the world forgotten—a small bright figure endlessly turning and leaping. She forgot the cold faces in the auditorium. She was there to entertain the guests at old Capulet's ball, who were massed at the back of the stage in their silks and brocades, a fantastic background for her to be displayed against. She knew nothing but the sheerest ecstasy, borne up on the easy familiar rhythms, each movement submerged into the succeeding one.

Twirling with drifting arms, swooping about the stage, giving a touching personal beauty to each pose by her elegant feet and long line of leg, the poised head on the slim stem of her neck, the varied and expressive movements of her hands. She posed *en arabesque penchée,* hands crossed on breast; she ran forward on tiptoe, hand to ear, listening to some distant sound. Then, with swirling arms, on full pointe, springing up, rising with the music . . . up . . . up . . . up . . . she paused to hold an arabesque before running off, to stand panting in the wings.

The pas de deux matched the music very closely. Natasha

ran lightly ahead of Oleg, he following her yearningly. She danced with soft and delicately hesitant movements. He flew across the stage to her. Then he was lifting her through the air, supporting her *en arabesque*, turning her *en attitude*, kneeling to receive her hand on his shoulder. He sprang to his feet, dancing quickly about her, jumping and turning as she pattered after him, then lifting her from one side to the other, posing her beautifully, balanced on one leg, the other stretched behind her, one arm reaching up, the other arm behind. It was a simple arabesque, but visual harmony. An unbroken line seemed to be drawn through their bodies, joining them miraculously together. Only at the end of the coda, when the applause broke in on her, was she aware that everything had gone perfectly.

Richard Greville leaned forward, his arm resting on the plush balustrade of the British embassy box. He was a tall, broad-shouldered man, Viking fair, with the misted blue eyes of a seafarer and the finely chiseled features of a medieval knight-at-arms.

As instructed, he had tapped the British ambassador on the arm whenever his snores threatened to blast through the music; now Richard awakened him for the ballet. Lord Loftus always revived during the ballet. In fact, he preferred a full evening of it. He enjoyed the stage tricks and preposterous scenic effects. Opera was tame stuff by comparison.

He murmured appreciatively as the stage was transformed into the grand hall of the Capulets' palace where the guests arrived for Juliet's wedding to Count Paris, and he applauded vigorously throughout the divertissement, staring at the girls appraisingly, delighting in the lines of dancing figures, their gleaming arms and swelling bosoms, pink undergarments and transparent muslin skirts. They looked like exotic umbrellas, corsetted and bejeweled.

The dark slender girl who danced in the pas de deux was a real beauty. She seemed to waft about the stage, turning the conventional movements into phrases of pure poetry. She was like a piece of living sculpture, constantly changing the line of her body.

The ballet ended to crashing applause. Then the ambassador tried to remain awake during the interminable aria in which the mountainous Juliet drained the phial of opiate, and fell as if dead. He must hold himself in readiness. If the tzar was to call for him, it would be now, in the interval between the last two acts.

The tzar did not send for him. Her majesty's government was still in disfavor—no uncommon thing in the St. Petersburg of 1876.

Richard, walking through the mirrored hall during the last interval, was hailed by Count Scavronsky. Dapper and urbane, Scavronsky was a dark slight man. A white scar on his cheek ran into his small pointed beard—a fencing wound from his student days. He was a man of intense if rather conscious charm. The count, whose sole interest in the opera was the corps de ballet, had arrived in time to see the dancing.

"Must you stay?" he asked.

"His excellency might need me," Richard responded in perfect Russian. "He's waiting for the tzar to send for him."

Scavronsky shrugged. "What a bore!" He took out his gold repeating watch. "He'll hardly send for him now. The curtain will rise in three minutes."

"Nevertheless, I should be on hand."

Scavronsky gestured comically. "As you wish. I shall wait for you, since I have something planned for us. And if you insist on condemning me to this maudlin piece . . ."

"Don't you like it?" Richard asked, smiling.

"It's not at all to my taste. French opera is more esteemed in France than elsewhere, I think." He grimaced. "I've never seen the play, though it translates very well into Russian, I'm told."

"Well, it's all quite preposterous in any language," Richard said, still smiling, "though very lyrical."

"Ah, yes," the count exclaimed, misquoting, "the sweetest music to lovers is the sound of each other's tongue in the night."

Richard laughed. "I think you've been misinformed, Kolya! It apparently translates very badly."

"But there is truth in the line," Scavronsky said, smiling. "And I shall prove it so tonight."

"You have an assignation?"

"No, *mon ami*. 'We' have an assignation. The two of us. We are invited to a very unique entertainment."

"Oh? Where?"

"That must be a surprise."

Richard looked at his watch. It was almost time to return to his box. "Well, I may not be able to get away . . ."

"Nonsense, Richard. You must. It will be a night to remember, I promise you."

The curtain bell rang and Richard returned to his seat, having arranged to meet the count in the grand foyer.

As the auditorium lights were lowered the ambassador hunched forward, watching the figure of the tzar in the imperial loge. Tzar Alexander II sat alone, well forward from the rest of his party. It was his habit, despite the fears of his police that he would make too conspicuous a target for any would-be assassin. He wore a full-dress uniform of white, frogged with gold and trimmed at neck and wrists with blue Siberian fox. His chest glittered like a breastplate, heavy with medals and orders. The once handsome face—"as perfect as the cast for a bronze medallion"—was thin and drawn. He looked infinitely careworn, sad and old beyond his sixty years.

As Richard took his seat, the ambassador murmured, "He'll not send for us tonight. *She* is here."

"The Princess Catherine?"

"Yes. It explains the absence of the rest of the royal family. I had wondered."

Richard leaned out into the auditorium, looking for the princess. In the reflected lights of the stage, the jewels of the women sparkled and the orders of the men gleamed. The whole curve of the theater looked like a vast cluster of tiny stars, a human galaxy.

He could just make out the profile of the tzar's mistress as she sat half concealed by the huge guardsman at her side. The light gleamed wanly on her ivory skin and magnificent chestnut hair. Unlike most women present she wore no jewels, and the neckline of her gown reached to her neck in a froth of lace. Her dress was amber satin trimmed in brown silk ribbons and bows, with sleeves of lace. Her hair was free of any ornament, swept up at the sides and dressed in gleaming coils. It was as though she wished to prove by the modesty of her dress that she was the most respectable woman present.

What an unusual favorite she is, Richard thought. What a dull "scarlet woman."

It was true. Beautiful though she was, the tzar's fascination with her was a very private thing, totally incomprehensible to St. Petersburg society. She shunned the fashionable world, living an enclosed life with her children by the tzar. In her strange nunlike way, she was almost as remote as the empress in her sickroom. She seemed unaware of her power over the tzar, her power over the country. She cared little for clothes or jewels, and only appeared at court when the tzar begged her to do so. She appeared to be utterly without friends, rarely entertained, and then never lavishly. This was her first appearance at the opera this season.

Thinking about her set Richard to musing about his own love affair. Physically the princess bore some resemblance to the Countess Kreuger. Glaphira possessed the same wide eyes and burnished hair, a flawless profile and a Madonna-like smile. But, beyond that, how different they were! Glasha shone in society, cared mainly for power—especially over men—and had a passion for clothes and jewels. She was filled with vanity and a stony pride. Moreover, unlike the princess, who had abandoned all for love, Glasha would never make the smallest sacrifice. She enjoyed her pampered life, she adored St. Petersburg. She would never exchange it for any other city—not even Paris, as she explained to Richard a dozen times a week. She had no intention of taking on the unstable life of a professional diplomat's wife, to end her days in some dreary outpost of the British empire. The idea was too *drôle*.

Richard, who was sincerely convinced that he loved the countess, understood her completely. He could never condemn her for refusing him. He was, he knew, a damned bad catch. The eldest son of the second son of an English baron was no match for the daughter of a Baltic millionaire, a countess in her own right. Unless his cousin Freddie died very suddenly—and soon—he had no hopes of inheriting the title. And, although Lord Eyam was busily sowing his wild oats in every available furrow in London and had shown not the least desire to settle down, Richard could not gamble on him not doing so eventually. He was, after all, not much older than Richard's twenty-nine years.

Richard gave his attention to the stage.

Juliet—not yet aware that Romeo had taken poison—and Romeo—forgetting for a moment that death's cold hand was already reaching out for him—vigorously urged each other to fly to the ends of the earth.

Richard felt slightly nauseated by the sickly music, with its hint of rotting flowers. The sight of the elephantine soprano and the dwarfish tenor counterfeiting "young love" was risible when it was not obscene. The singers had not the least knowledge of acting, and their performances destroyed any illusion of drama. His thoughts fluctuated between the artificial business on the stage, his own abortive desire for Glaphira, and the contrast between their relationship and the tzar's consuming passion for the Princess Catherine.

It was, he supposed, as grand a passion in its way as that of the lovers on the stage. It had set the tzar's family against him and divided St. Petersburg society. Only the dying empress seemed untouched by the scandal.

I'm no more capable of such a grand passion than I am of singing this interminable duet, Richard thought. I could never *wallow* in such romantic excesses. He grinned in the darkness. I suppose I'm just too damned English!

Romeo and Juliet warbled lustily in their death-throes. Richard stifled a yawn. The ambassador, too, sat musing. The opera had set off a train of thought. To his fancy, the English and Russian royal families seemed much like the Montagues and Capulets. There was an old quarrel between them. Russian ambitions were a threat to British interests in the East. Turkey was their Verona. Well, like Friar Lawrence in the play, he had done his best to bury the old strife, though without success.

On stage, at least, the enmity between the two families was ended. The corpses were taking their bows. Lord Loftus breathed a sigh of relief when the curtain finally fell. He left the theater in the wake of the emperor's party, disappointed at not being called to see the tzar.

The great theatre curtain had been down for half an hour, but backstage everything was still confusion. An army of stagehands stripped the stage, carpenters hammered at the huge sets. The working lights were harsh and dismal, thin shafts from the fly-gallery and a few lamps in the wings at the side. The air was heavy with dust, the smell of gas and musty cloth.

Prince Verchinin walked through the stage entrance, past the immense machines for changing the scenery, and found a place beside a winch where he stood waiting. The prince loved to visit the backstage world. It never failed to give him an almost childlike thrill. He loved to be among the gaily dressed people, and the women as nearly naked as might be.

He was, in fact, entering a forbidden world, being one of the
few people outside the royal family who was allowed through
the stage door. He was well known there. Many people
nodded and smiled, claiming his acquaintance. They were
mostly women.

He was waiting for two in particular. Within a few minutes
the first of them appeared. Tamara picked her way delicately
through the confusion. She was an open-faced woman, a
Nordic blonde. Her eyes were of the palest blue, strangely
shallow and yet as unfathomable as mountain lakes. Prince
Verchinin, watching her approach, wondered whether such
eyes could ever reflect truthfully anything at all. For all the
openness and candor of her looks, Krupenskaya was one of
the most devious women he had ever known. Yet, he smiled
amiably. He disliked her and distrusted her, but recognized
his need of her.

The dancer was warmly dressed in a smart, wine-colored
skating dress trimmed with gray fur. Her blue eyes gazed at
the prince unwaveringly from behind the veil of a green silk
hat, tipped on her upswept hair like a saucy plate.

The prince himself was an old man, terribly square and
heavy looking. He had a great forked beard, brows that fell
over his eyes, and tufts of hair that jutted from nose and ears.
His hair was pomaded, his moustache perfumed. His thick
body was tightly corseted, the flesh straining against the
elegant cut of a military tunic; the stiff braided collar cut into
his jowls; a jeweled order twinkled on his dark blue chest; a
brilliant orange sash slashed from shoulder to waist.

He regarded Tamara keenly, the hint of a leer haunting his
lined face. "Well, Tamara Fyodorovna? What is her answer?"
he asked, with all the eagerness of a man thirty years
younger.

Tamara smiled complacently. "She's most obliged to your
excellency."

"Then she is coming tonight?"

"She'll come tonight, yes. I've persuaded her to do that
much." Tamara shrugged, pouting attractively. "But beyond
that . . ."

The old man beat one glove upon the other fretfully. The
heavy rings on his gnarled hands glittered. "What must I do
to please her?"

Tamara smiled knowingly as the prince searched in an inner
pocket and withdrew a small but expensively wrapped box.
He gave it to her and she opened it with a gushing cry. Inside,

on a velvet cushion, rested an exquisite brooch with a clear emerald on silver filigree. Tamara's enthusiasm faded noticeably as she evaluated the price of the brooch to a kopeck.

"It's delightful, prince," she said coolly. *"Small* brooches are all the rage this season."

"It's not intended for Mademoiselle Natalia," Verchinin explained anxiously. "It's a small token of my gratitude to you—for your efforts on my behalf . . . so far. Should my suit be entirely successful, I shall, of course, prove more grateful . . ."

He extracted another box from his pocket and opened it. Tamara's eyes gleamed appreciatively at the sight of a single string of diamonds, glitteringly white, and sapphires, transparently blue, sparkling as they shook in the prince's hand.

"I shall certainly match this gift," Verchinin said. *"If* I have cause for gratitude." He winked coarsely. "These are for Natalia Ivanovna."

Tamara's hand reached out to grasp the necklace while at the same time appearing to wave it away dismissively. "My dear prince, you misunderstand my friend entirely. You'll not win her over with jewels alone . . . however splendid."

Verchinin stared, his pale eyes bulging, incredulous. In his long lifetime of philandering, no woman had ever said this to him before.

Tamara explained, as though to a child. "Natasha has *ambitions.* You must help her to attain them if you want her affection."

"Ambitions? What sort of ambitions?"

Tamara smiled. She had a small wet mouth in which her teeth were scattered like seed-pearls. "She *aches* to be a soloist of His Imperial Majesty," she said.

The old man blinked, thinking of the imperial *solistes,* their stage costumes heavy with the jewels showered upon them by an ardent public. They had no need to depend upon the generosity of individual lovers—even if many of them did so.

He smiled skeptically. "Do you mean that she'll refuse my gift outright?"

"Well, I don't say that she'll refuse it . . . eventually. If, say, the gift were to be given to her *tactfully* . . ."

Verchinin had the impression that Tamara was saying that the gift should be passed through an intermediary—her hands, perhaps. But Tamara waved the exquisite necklace away airily, as though it was nothing but a paste replica.

"She's not to be caught so easily, Excellency. She's not to be *bought*."

The old man looked nonplussed.

"She has to be appreciated," Tamara said gently.

"But I could not appreciate her more!"

"As a *talent*, Prince. Not as a . . . a . . ." Tamara waved expressive hands. The prince still failed to take her meaning. "Not as a desirable young woman," Tamara said finally.

The prince was still confused.

"You must indulge her," Tamara said.

The prince protested, "But, my dear, I'm ready to indulge her every whim. *Anxious* to do so."

The prince's bewilderment almost caused Tamara to laugh aloud. She felt the familiar surge of power. What fatuous beasts such men were. "Then you must take an interest in her career."

"But how, exactly, does she expect me to help her?" Verchinin asked.

"By bringing your influence to bear in certain quarters, Excellency."

He still looked perplexed.

"You are, I believe, acquainted with Khudekov, the editor of the *Gazette?*" Tamara asked.

"Yes, Khudekov and I are moderately good friends."

Tamara leaned toward the prince, resting her hand on his arm. "Ballet-master Petipa is very much influenced by Khudekov," she explained. "They are working on a new ballet together. . . . Well, it is Natasha's dearest wish to be taken out of the Opera Ballet and be given a place in the Imperial Company. If Khudekov were to speak to Petipa on her behalf . . ."

The old prince was still puzzled. "But will she not graduate to the Imperial Ballet in time?"

Tamara's blue eyes veiled with malice. "Ah, of course. In time. She stands a better chance than anybody. She has . . . *something*."

Verchinin nodded. It was true. Even he could recognize it. Tonight the girl had seemed almost inhumanly perfect.

"Natasha yearns for recognition *now*," Tamara went on. "She is very ambitious. Not for fame, or great wealth, you understand, but for the great roles . . ."

"But, surely, she is already rising fast?" the prince asked. "The pas de deux she danced tonight?"

Tamara gestured disparagingly. "A trifle, prince. Truly, she only got the chance—if one can call it that—because two others were away with injuries."

The prince did not really understand Tamara's drift. It was all new ground to him. Despite forty years of wooing ballerinas, he knew very little of the world they inhabited. He despised the ballet itself, its chief charm for him being that it was morally suspect. Otherwise, he thought it a sheer waste of imperial money. Yet some of his most delicious moments had been spent in the pliant embraces of the dancers. Thinking of the girls' smooth white bodies, soft as silk, tensile as steel, made him weak with desire.

Seeing this, Tamara smiled disdainfully. "A dancer needs more than luck. To shine among our dancers one needs genius." The smile changed shape. For a moment she looked almost sad. "One certainly needs influence. Much as I love Natasha, I can't think she has genius. So you see, without her 'chance,' poor Natasha will be left to blush unseen in the opera, filling out the Grand Ballets occasionally . . ."

"And if I can persuade Khudekov to persuade Petipa to take her into the new ballet?"

"You'll have earned her full devotion, I can promise you."

The old man snapped the clasp on the lid of the box. He sighed. "Well, *ma chère*, a necklace is much easier to arrange. Khudekov is a fanatical balletomane, you know, quite puritanical on the matter. He won't be easily persuaded."

Tamara shrugged her shoulders, pouting again. "Well, prince, I can promise you nothing—unless you can increase her chances with Petipa." She smoothed her fur. "For tonight, she's prepared to let you escort her to the ice masquerade."

Tamara spoke quite sharply, with an air of freezing hauteur. She was used to arranging such delicate matters for her more modest sisters in the company, and the prince—the complete picture of a lascivious old goat—was easy enough to manage. He had always been so in the past. Now, he bowed submissively.

"She is coming," Tamara said, and the prince looked up.

A young woman stepped lightly across the stage, picking her way between the discarded scenery, heading toward them. Like most dancers she was a touching mixture of grace and gaucherie offstage. Her fur-trimmed gray jacket was open at the neck to give a glimpse of a dress of dusty-pink cashmere. The long, tightly-molded line of her gown, swathed below the hips, revealed the natural beauty of her figure. Her clothes—her whole style—showed great personal charm, simplicity, a refined eye. The prince was enchanted with her.

She came to where they stood, and the prince bowed low over her hand, in an exaggerated gesture of courtesy. Her small white hand lay in his for a moment, then slipped away. She gazed at him with huge velvety eyes, the eyes of a dreamy child.

There's no ruin in her, Verchinin thought sentimentally.

Yet in some way, it was true. Her face, with its high cheekbones and slightly slanting eyes, was curiously open and trusting, fawnlike. Natasha appeared to be totally lacking in sophistication. He thought it possible that she was sexually untried. At the ripe age of twenty she appeared to have renounced the world. There was nothing of the cocotte in her. Yet at the same time there was some mystery about her. The dark gray eyes had a look half-sensual, half-scornful hidden deep in them. Her smile, when it came, pierced him like an arrow.

He gave an arm to each woman and they walked slowly through the stage door, to where the prince's sleigh waited to carry them to the ball on the ice.

CHAPTER
TWO

Richard could never grow used to the two worlds of the St. Petersburg winter—the outside world of freezing monotony and the inside world of sybaritic hibernation, a world of luxurious wealth and brilliant light. All Russian society danced, ate and gambled away the ice-bound months. But the outside world was another matter. The cold penetrated the thickness of three furs. "Four-coat weather" it was called.

As they made their way through the mournful streets,

huddled beneath their rugs and wraps in the cheerfully
painted sleigh, Richard asked again where they were heading.

Scavronsky laughed. "To a masquerade."

"Where?"

"In a very unusual place. You'll enjoy it, Richard."

They drove on through the empty streets. An icy wind blew
from the sea. Street lamps flickered dimly, making a feeble
impression on the night. Even the houses seemed barricaded
against the cold. The great palaces stood like haunted buildings in an enchanted silence. They sped along the broad
avenues and turned into a maze of narrow streets, crossing
the canals on bridges that hung mistily above the frozen
water.

Scavronsky laughed again when Richard accused him of
traveling in circles. "Of course. It adds to *la mystère.*"

They came out onto the Nevsky Prospekt, and went along
the embankment to Senate Square. The coachman brought
the horses to a halt beside the statue of the bronze horseman.

"Are we finally here?" Richard asked, looking around the
huge square dubiously. The massive buildings were dim
silhouettes beyond the frosted trees. In the distance he could
hear the sound of music and laughter, a clear sound carrying
across the crisp night air.

"Yes, we are arrived," Scavronsky said, amused by Richard's continuing bafflement. He walked to the wall at the
river's edge, beckoning Richard to follow. They looked over
the parapet.

The River Neva stretched before them, still and frozen,
mist-enshrouded and ghostly. Three huge bonfires blazed in
large iron braziers, and the light of a hundred torches made
golden rings upon the expanse of glistening ice. Brilliantly
colored tents and gaily painted booths were grouped around
the fires. Between them danced the skaters. A military band
blared out the latest waltzes. Within the ring of flame it was
all color and whirling life.

Where the river widened, a great wall of ice had been
erected, as though to protect the revelers from the terrors of
the gulf. Beyond it, the mouth of the Neva loomed—vast and
mysterious, a waste of darkness. But the great wall was a
shimmering barrier of whiteness, strung with lanterns and
hung about with flags and draperies of silk and satin. The
whole scene was an oasis of light in the desert of winter.

"Welcome to the ice masquerade," Scavronsky cried,
clapping Richard on the back. "Come!" He led the way down

the broad steps of the steep embankment. Richard followed, the snow crackling beneath his feet.

At the river's edge, Scavronsky's valet met them, carrying two pairs of ice skates. The blades strapped to their shoes, the two men sped across the ice toward the glittering radiance of the ball. Once inside the enchanted circle of light, the banks of the river seemed to recede. They could have been in some vast celestial room. The wall of ice shone with iridescent light, against which blazed the uniforms of white and gold, blue and scarlet. The women's costumes glowed more darkly against the magical shimmer.

"Do you prefer champagne or vodka?" Scavronsky asked, leading Richard into a marquee and then to a table laden with bottles and sparkling glassware. There was the usual extravagant invitation to gluttony—everything from pressed caviar to suckling pig.

Richard hesitated. In Russia, vodka called for food to smother the fire of the liquid, and food then called for more vodka. From one small glass to another he knew how the night would go, in a haze of impressions.

"You won't need vodka to keep out the cold, if that's what you're thinking," the count said. "In twenty minutes you'll be steaming like a samovar, I can assure you."

"In that case, I'll have champagne."

Glasses in hand, they made a tour of the frozen dance floor. "We must find an ice maiden," Scavronsky said.

Richard smiled wryly. "I've already found mine. Her name is Glasha Kreuger."

Scavronsky laughed. "Well, I wish to break her spell, old friend. Look around you at the diversity of females here. Russia doesn't lack for ice maidens. Though these, you'll find, are the more easily melted down!"

Richard, looking around, was struck by the youth and freshness of the women there. He had, so far, not seen a familiar face. "Who are they?" he asked.

"Some girls from the ballet, some dancers from the cafés. Perhaps one or two *ladies*—but not the sort that you'll meet at court, church or in the British embassy." He grinned. "Particularly there!"

Richard looked again, with added interest. So they were all whores. Amazing. Used as he was to the rouge-caked drabs of London's Haymarket and the dashing "equestriennes" of Rotton Row, he had never before seen whores of this description. The few girls from the ballet were at once distinguishable by their suppleness and grace as they sped over the ice, but the "ladies" were of a type unknown to him. He had not seen their like in any Russian brothel.

"Ah, there's our matchmaker!" Scavronsky cried, skating off toward a Nordic blonde in a wine-colored dress.

But Richard remained where he stood, staring after a slender figure who had danced by. He followed her movements with pleasure. She was a ballet-girl, by the look of the soft and sinuous grace of her movements. She looked more like a lovely bird than a human being against the enormous bulk of the man who held her arm.

Richard skated after her, without thought. He stayed at a distance, but always kept her in sight as she skated in and out of the light of the torches. She was a harmony of gray and dusty pink, the veil of her pearl-gray hat lifting in the breeze like wings of gauze. Her head was thrown back to show the long smooth column of her throat, her mouth was open in a kind of ecstasy. She looked as if caught up in some private dream.

Her veil hid everything but the lower part of her face, the pointed chin and gently curving mouth. From her high cheekbones he imagined that her eyes must have a slanted Tartar look. Behind the veil they were as mysterious as a cat's. The man whose arm she held loomed over her ponderously, but to Richard it seemed that it was she who led him through the intricate movements of the dance, without being aware that she was doing so. She was a quick, gay, yet curiously absorbed figure, a keeper in charge of a great lumbering bear.

Richard followed after her like a bewitched dog, until . . .

"Richard!" Scavronsky's voice broke into Richard's trance. He had come level with the count and his matchmaker. Richard stopped by their side. He became aware of two pale blue eyes examining him with interest, touched with a hint of mockery.

"This is Mademoiselle Krupenskaya of the Opera Ballet," Scavronsky said.

Richard bowed, the image of the other girl still hovering at the fringes of his mind. *"Enchanté, mademoiselle."*

Tamara inclined her head.

"Mademoiselle would like you to meet a good friend of hers," the count said. "Mademoiselle Marie Antonova."

Tamara turned to where a slim dark figure stood in blurred outline against the blaze of a fire. She murmured something in a hoarse voice. The girl came forward shyly and curtsied. With a sense of disappointment Richard looked down into a pretty but vapid face. Not even the veil could add a touch of mystery to it. Her small mouth was molded into an uncertainly coquettish smile.

The girl looks like a waxwork, Richard thought, remembering the dark beauty of the other dancer. But, nevertheless, after a few polite banalities, he took her hand and dutifully led her in a dance on the ice.

Later, while he stood by the refreshment tent, listening inattentively to the laughter and chatter of the company, Tamara skated to his side with a rustle of silk petticoats. She touched him gently on the shoulder and he turned so abruptly that he caught her arm and the champagne in his goblet frothed and bubbled.

"Mademoiselle?"

She smiled, looking at him boldly. "You are not very happy with our little doll?" she asked.

"She's charming," Richard said stiffly.

"But your heart is not with her. Certainly your eyes are not!"

Richard made no answer, and Tamara laughed. She had a harsh, grating laugh, "You have eyes for only one woman here, m'sieur. Such devotion is rather unsettling. Delightful in its way, and very flattering to the lady in question, but definitely unsettling—for us others."

Richard still said nothing, his face darkened.

"The lady you so admire is one of my dearest friends," Tamara said. The way that she underlined the word "friend" was unmistakable, as was her expression. Richard knew a bawd when he met one.

"Can you introduce me?" he asked bluntly.

Tamara smiled superciliously. "The lady already has an admirer."

Richard looked down at the ice. "I would be very *grateful*," he said.

Tamara touched his arm again, and shook her head. "Impossible, m'sieur. Her admirer is a very powerful man."

"So you won't introduce me?"

"It would not be in her best interest. I have her welfare at heart."

And her virtue in your pocket, Richard thought. He bowed, very correctly. "Still, mademoiselle," he said. "This is a public entertainment. If the young lady is free, and willing, she may make up her own mind."

He skated swiftly away and glided to a halt beside the girl, who was now standing by a bonfire, sipping champagne. The bearded man at her side glared at Richard as he bowed.

"Mademoiselle, may I have the pleasure?"

She paused for a moment, looking startled. At first he thought that she was going to refuse him, or seek permission from the older man, but she suddenly nodded, smiling shyly. She handed her glass to a passing attendant and took his arm, gliding away from her partner with a backward nod and a smile. Richard had the feeling that she was glad to be free of the old man for a few minutes. Yet it was impossible to tell what she actually felt. Her face was solemn as a child's as they took their places with the other dancers.

The music ended. As the last chord died away, Natasha drew back from Richard's embrace. A distant look came into her face as awareness returned. Richard wondered if she had been conscious of him as they danced. The music had seemed to cast a spell over her; it was as though she moved into a new dimension.

Yet they had skated perfectly together. She had followed him without hesitation, molding her body to his in the elaborate figures he chose to execute. He was aware of a need to impress her, to cut a dash. But she had taken his ability for granted after the opening movements of the dance.

He had been intensely aware of her—his hand resting on her left shoulder blade, her left arm resting on his right, the elbows touching. He felt the soft strength of her. She had drawn into him as closely as possible, pushing against him gently as he pulled her toward him, establishing a degree of stability, all very pleasant, very intimate, yet correct and formal. She instinctively understood the rules of waltzing on the ice. Once sure of him, she had abandoned herself to sheer pleasure, gliding and turning at his slightest pressure. Now, the sensuous trance of the music broken, she gazed at him as though he was an intruder—an impertinent stranger who had no right to have his arm about her or his head bent so intimately toward her.

"Thank you," she said politely, dropping a small curtsey.

"Do you want to continue?" Richard asked, as the band sounded the first notes of a polka.

She almost said yes. She was tempted. Then she shook her

head, looking back toward her friends. Tamara beckoned. She had been watching them with fierce vigilance.

"Natasha!" she called. "Natasha Ivanovna! Come now!"

"I'm sorry," Natasha said. "I'd like to dance, but . . ."

"I understand," Richard said. "Perhaps I can claim another dance later? Or we could take a glass of champagne together?"

For the first time she regarded him directly. Her eyes behind the veil looked interested. Her cheeks flamed. "Tamara Fyodorovna said you are a foreigner—an Englishman."

Richard felt a thrill of pleasure. So they had discussed him. She had asked about him. "Yes, I'm English," he said. "Richard Greville. Second secretary at the British embassy."

"But you speak Russian so well!" she exclaimed. "Like a Russian!"

Richard laughed. "Well, I've studied long and hard. And I love your language. It is so beautiful." He leaned forward, his eyes absorbing her. "I saw you dance tonight, Miss Petrova. You were enchanting." He smiled, risking a quotation. "You have dancing shoes with nimble soles!"

His translation of Shakespeare flowed more smoothly than the count's. After a brief pucker of doubt, he saw that she recognized the passage. Her eyes looked amused, she gave him a piercing smile.

"Well, I am *not* yet past my dancing days," she said.

She looked suddenly alarmed as Tamara glided to them, looking furious. "This is too bad," she hissed, with a venomous look for Richard. "The prince is waiting. He wants the next dance. Come!"

She clasped Natasha firmly by the arm and carried her away. Natasha looked back with an apologetic smile and a little shrug of helplessness. As they went, Tamara's voice carried clearly back to Richard—as it was undoubtedly meant to. "Don't bother with him, my dear. He's a nobody."

Richard watched them go with a sense of baffled anger.

Scavronsky's voice, at his elbow, said, "I think that you're greatly taken with her, Richard. But I'm afraid that you're wasting your time in pursuing her. Such 'virginal' creatures fetch a high price, and are perhaps a little beyond our means. You'll have to wait until she's a little 'shop-soiled.'"

Richard turned away, feigning indifference. "It's of no consequence, Kolya."

The girl was, after all, no more than a high-class whore. He skated away to find Marie Antonova, the "little doll."

To his surprise, Marie proved very accommodating once she had overcome her initial shyness. He resigned himself to the simple pleasures. Richard was a skillful lover, and she matched his skill with spirit once they were tucked up together in bed at Klee's Hotel. There was something almost bestial in her ardor beneath his striking loins. Yet at the height of their pleasure, buried deep in the flower of her sex, Richard was suddenly shattered by a feeling of utter futility. The image of Natasha, which he had banished from his mind, returned with startling clarity. The bright, dreamy face, the wind-whipped cheeks and gleaming gray eyes. The line of her body, the feel of her back gently resisting the pressure of his hands, his intrusive hands. Her quick feet cutting a swath on the ice, the hem of her skirt swirling, petticoats rustling . . .

The wriggling and panting body beneath him seemed to melt away as the vision strengthened. He was more interested in the pale phantom in his mind than in the tangible body beneath him.

CHAPTER

THREE

On the second morning after the ball, Natasha was called in to the office of the second intendant. He was responsible for general discipline.

He regarded her with some hostility. "Petrova, it has been brought to my attention that two nights ago you were to be seen skating on the river. . . ."

Natasha gasped slightly, her gray eyes opening wide. She immediately looked guilty. "Yes, sir."

"Were you aware that in so doing you were breaking the terms of your contract with us?"

"N . . . n . . . no, sir," Natasha stammered. "I mean, I'd forgotten until . . ."

Until the moment he had mentioned it, in fact. The intendant sniffed. He was a monkish-looking man, tall and willowy, with an intense stare. Even in the overheated room he was formally dressed in black frock coat, with a stiffly upright collar.

"You do remember now, I see," he said. "Any activity likely to be physically dangerous is expressly forbidden during the season."

"Yes, sir."

"But you conveniently forgot."

"Oh, no, sir! Not 'conveniently.' I just . . . forgot." She looked up unhappily, and the intendant saw that she was speaking the truth.

"I wouldn't have gone, if I'd thought . . ." Natasha looked wretched. "It shan't happen again, sir."

"It most certainly shall not!" the intendant said sharply. "An extraordinary lapse! The directorate frowns most severely on such indiscretions."

Natasha gazed at him in dismay. Did he mean to punish her?

His next words took her by surprise. "You went, I'm informed, in the company of Prince Verchinin?"

"Yes, sir," Natasha said, blushing. "That is, he was part of the—" She bit back the words, reluctant to betray the others.

"We are quite aware of the identity of your 'chaperon,' Petrova. She has been suitably punished—as you will see if you care to look at the notice on the callboard."

". . . Oh."

The intendant regarded her with increased hostility, distaste even. His voice sharpened. "The prince has expressed an interest in you," he said.

Natasha looked up, frowning slightly. What did he mean?

"The prince is very kind," she said.

"He believes that *as a dancer* you show great promise." The sarcasm in the intendant's voice left no doubt of what he really meant, though Natasha missed it at first. She was merely puzzled to be told that the prince was a balletomane. He had shown no knowledge of dancing.

The intendant stared at her with his peculiar intensity. "He has suggested to Monsieur Khudekov that you are already worthy of a solo appearance in the Imperial Ballet. In Maestro Petipa's new offering, no less."

Natasha looked down at the intendant's persian carpet. All the colors of the East danced giddily beneath her. What could this mean?

"How do you think he came by the idea?" the intendant asked.

Natasha shook her head, bewildered. She had a fair appraisal of her talent and felt that she was not yet ready for "better things."

The intendant now regarded her with open hostility. A warm glow began to stain her cheeks. "The prince, of course, is no judge of the dance," the intendant said. "He is more at home on horseback. But it is puzzling that he should undertake to use his influence on your behalf, don't you think? He has never done as much for any other dancer."

Natasha sat, without words to answer him.

"Tell me, as an artiste, do you think yourself quite ready for the Imperial Ballet?" the intendant asked.

Natasha hesitated. Honesty compelled her to say, "Not as a soloist, sir."

"But you think that you are ready for the corps?"

". . . Yes, m'sieur. I think I'm ready for that."

"Why, may I inquire?"

"Well, twice this season I've been given preferment in the Opera Ballet. Yesterday I received a notice in the *Imperial Gazette*."

The intendant walked to the window. He clasped his hands behind his back. "Well, yes," he said, "it's true that you've been singularly honored. But this is no way to further your ambitions, Petrova. You have created a very serious and difficult situation for us."

"*I* have, sir?"

"Yes, indeed." The intendant looked uncomfortable. "The prince wields a considerable influence in certain circles. He is an old and valued friend of the Grand Duke Nicholas. If he has been *persuaded* to interfere in matters of theatre policy it could make things extremely awkward for the directorate. What do you think would happen to the integrity of our program if each great nobleman decided to interest himself in the career of a junior lady of the ballet?" He regarded her questioningly. Natasha remained silent, still utterly bewildered.

"A dancer must prove herself by her own worth if she

wishes to rise in the ranks," the intendant said. He stopped at the sight of her bewildered face. Tears shone in her wide eyes.

He said more gently, "I can appreciate ambition, Petrova, even when the talent that backs it is still at the fledgling stage. But you must be more careful of the means by which you try to attain success."

Natasha dashed the tears from her eyes. Then her back arched, and her small pointed chin showed stubborn. "Excuse me, sir, but I must protest. You are accusing me of something of which I'm innocent. I really know nothing of this. The prince has shown great kindness, but I can't imagine why he's chosen to speak for me in this way. I've never asked him to. I don't think I need him to champion me. In all modesty, I'm aware of my talent. I have every hope for my future. I have faith in the directorate. I know they'll deal fairly with my career. . . ."

The intendant contemplated her for a few moments, slightly taken aback by her outburst. ". . . Tell me, how did you become acquainted with the prince?" he asked.

"He came backstage on a number of occasions. He . . . he sought me out, I suppose. I hadn't really noticed. He sent me flowers. He gave me a very beautiful cameo brooch yesterday —a figure of Taglioni—as a tribute to my . . . to my dancing . . . in *Romeo*." Her voice trailed away as she recognized the ugly implication behind her words, not from what she had said, but from the look in the intendant's searching gaze.

Was she as artless as she appeared? he wondered. Or was she already an accomplished young actress? She seemed intelligent, but unworldly. He administered another shock.

"Yes, yes," he said, "I understand. Some men regard the ballet as a superior sort of brothel."

Natasha sat up straight. "Sir, the prince has never suggested that I . . . I have not . . ." She stopped, confused and distressed.

No, perhaps not yet, he thought regretfully. But you will one day, and very soon. Such beauty as yours exists to be exploited, in our world certainly.

He walked to the back of her chair and patted her shoulder gently. He could see that his words had genuinely disturbed her. "No, no, my dear," he said. "I understand. You are new to this world. I often think our training is too narrow. A young woman should be taught the rudiments of self-preservation. It is a wonder that you young people grow up as sensible and good as you do, since you are given no real clue as to the true nature of the theatre world."

He stood in silence by her side for a moment. Then he reached a decision. "When you see the prince again, you may tell him that we are considering you for advancement. You need not be specific. . . . But you yourself must realize that such a promotion will only come from your own merit."

Natasha nodded, relieved that the interview was coming to an end.

"You will be fined fifty kopecks for your 'forgetfulness.'"

Fifty kopecks! That meant that she could not buy the hat she had set her heart on. Either that or go supperless for a week. She rose and curtsied, fighting back the tears.

"You may go, Petrova. And remember—no more dangerous pastimes. Choose your company with more care. A woman's reputation, you know, is often best made by the company she avoids, not the company she keeps."

All through class Natasha kept remembering the intendant's remarks. She was swamped with misery, while the world about her was happy and carefree. The winter sun shining through the tall windows of the rehearsal hall enlivened the room, making an airy froth of the dancers' tarlatans. All the people around her looked radiant. Only Natasha felt excluded from the general happiness.

She took her place at the *barre* and began the slow workout, standing in second position, feet quite wide apart, trunk very erect. She tried to concentrate, taking a deep breath.

They were beginning the *pliés*. Bend slowly . . . Not too low . . . Rise to first . . . With trunk inclined, make a clean bend sideways . . .

What an extraordinary thing, she thought. What on earth has possessed the prince? Why should he interfere?

Now ankle work . . . First position . . . *Battement* in second, at *demi-hauteur*, trunk immobile . . . *Pointe* raised . . . *Pointe* lowered . . . *Pointe* in second . . . The other leg.

She had thought of the prince as a kindly man, benevolent. A bit, well, absurd. But that wasn't how the intendant saw him. The intendant had been afraid. And a little scared *of her.*

No, that was ridiculous. But, all the same, it was true. The intendant had treated her with kid gloves.

He had thought of the prince as her "protector," her lover. The room darkened.

"*Raccourcis, mesdames et messieurs!*" the ballet-mistress called. Back to the *barre*. First position. Right leg up. *Raccourci* in second, *pointe* taut, close in first. *Pointe* to inside of knee, hip to side. Lift thigh higher . . . higher . . .

It was true! Tamara had deliberately tried to push her into the arms of this monstrous old man. She could see him now through the eyes of the intendant. The mask was stripped from him. He had interested himself in her career because he hoped to . . . to . . .

She felt sick.

"*Dégagés, s'il vous plaît!*" the ballet-mistress called.

She told herself to concentrate. *Concentrate.* What a novice I am, she thought, with growing anger. What an innocent! I've been nothing but a dupe. Nothing but a pawn. Where were my eyes? Tamara has been calmly arranging for the sale of my . . . my *body*, and I've known nothing about it!

She glanced over to where Tamara stood. She seemed to be fashioned out of porcelain, charming in the becoming rehearsal dress, the thin muslin foaming around her calves. She stood in profile at the *barre*, leg in second *à la hauteur*. She moved faultlessly, leaning to the side with one arm behind her back, the other raised *en couronne*. It was hard to believe from her composure that she, too, had been reprimanded and fined—and more heavily, perhaps, than Natasha. But what did a fine matter to Tamara? Nothing. She had her resources.

Natasha felt the blood surge to her face. A faint dizziness came over her, so that she clung to the *barre*. She felt unbearably tired. The light from the long windows seemed to expose her mercilessly. She felt convinced that every eye in the room was upon her. They all knew!

She took a deep breath, trying to still her racing thoughts, but it was impossible to concentrate. Once they had left the *barre* and begun to work in the center of the room, she lost control completely. Her bones seemed made of India rubber. Her thoughts were swallowed up in her newfound knowledge. Her body was burning, yet she was perspiring freely. When they came to the quick and brilliant steps of the *petite batterie* she weakened completely. Until at last . . .

"Mademoiselle!" The tinny notes of the piano accompaniment trickled away and died in the echoing room. Natasha became aware that the class had come to a halt. All around her the dancers stood as though turned to stone, only their eyes alive and curious.

The ballet-mistress eyed her with severity. "Natalia Ivanovna," she was saying. "Mademoiselle Petrova!"

"Yes, madame?"

For two minutes the ballet-mistress upbraided her in her clear mocking French. Where was her mind? Why were her muscles still cold? Were her slippers made of glass? Or lead? Was she cramped? Were her muscles powered by sour milk? Natasha stood before her wretchedly, shrinking with each cascade of icy comment.

They knew. All of them watching her *knew*—knew how she had been used. Perhaps even thought that . . .

At last, released, she was allowed to return to the exercises. When her confused thoughts cleared, she looked again toward Tamara. For a few moments she felt consumed by a vivid hatred, as Tamara stood by the *barre*, examining her face in the long mirror, apparently bored with the interruption to the class. With cool composure, she smoothed her yellow hair.

"My dear child," Tamara said, "you're a perfect goose!"

They stood by the huge mirror that ran along the wall of the deserted classroom—two diminutive figures reflected in the glass, the huge room empty. Tamara was chillingly self-possessed, Natasha nervously tense, the main force of her anger spent. She had deliberately forced Tamara to stay behind after the others had left, and she had gone directly to the point. Words had poured from her.

". . . You don't understand matters at all, do you?" Tamara drawled, when she had finished.

"I understand that I've been humiliated," Natasha said.

Tamara's eyebrows rose. "Humiliated? Because a great man adopts your cause?"

Tamara looked so genuinely astonished that momentarily Natasha's suspicions were confounded. Because the prince's actions were inept was not to say that they were ill-intentioned. She felt suddenly very immature.

No. However natural Tamara made things sound, Natasha's first instinct was right. The old man had not reached his decision by himself, she felt sure of that. Imaginative sympathy was not in the prince's character.

"The intendant was very . . . severe," Natasha said.

Tamara shrugged dismissively. "Nonsense! What does that fussy old hen matter? You've made a most important conquest."

Natasha stared. "Conquest?"

"A most gratifying conquest." Tamara giggled, an unnerving sound to Natasha. "The prince adores you."

"B . . . b . . . but," Natasha stuttered. "I . . . I don't want him to adore me."

Tamara laughed her grating laugh. "Of course you do. If you *think about it*. You're the envy of every girl here."

Natasha clenched her hands together, blushing fiercely.

"You've turned his heart right over, Natasha darling. Last night, at supper, he broke down like a young boy and confessed everything. He really loves you."

"But I don't want him to love me." The thought nauseated her. She could feel the muscles of her stomach contract.

But Tamara continued as though she had not heard. "He's distracted with it. Quite distracted. And you know how it is with men of Verchinin's breed. A hard-bitten man of the world, a *bon vivant*. When they fall, they really tumble."

"I don't want to hear!" Natasha cried. She gestured angrily, pushing the subject away. But Tamara still appeared not to have noticed her distaste.

"My dear, he could be your devoted slave," she said. "You could ask for anything your heart desired."

Natasha stared at the older girl in scornful disbelief. "Would he make me his princess?" she asked caustically.

Tamara looked surprised at the question, taking it seriously. Then she smiled, recognizing the jibe. "Well, most anything your heart desired," she said, giggling again. There was something alarmingly inane in Tamara's laughter.

Natasha gestured impatiently. "Tamara Fyodorovna, please don't take me for a fool!"

Tamara caught her by the arm. "Oh, I don't, my dear. Truly. But it's a fact. Verchinin wants to make you his official mistress. Settle you in a great house with servants, and—"

Natasha cut her short, twisting away from the hand on her arm. "This is impossible! Ridiculously impossible! How can you expect me to believe that I could have captured such a man. Me, a nobody!"

Tamara smiled. "'Captured,' Natasha? Not captured, my sweet. Merely *captivated*—for the moment. But if you'll be advised by me, who knows what might happen?" Tamara touched her arm, smiling. "You're overcome, I know," she said. "It's only natural. It's taken you by surprise. To be desired by so great a man—"

Natasha's head came up. Her dark eyes took fire. "I'm not at all 'overcome,' Tamara Fyodorovna. Just ashamed. I don't want you ever to speak of this again. Ever."

Tamara gaped, her pale eyes bled of color. "Don't speak of it again?"

"Never. It makes me feel . . . dirty."

"But you don't understand, you foolish girl!" Tamara cried, catching at Natasha's arm.

Natasha shook herself loose. "I understand perfectly," she said. "I'm not a fool, Tamara. I've been here long enough to know how such things are . . . managed—the introductions that are arranged. I've seen the girls comparing their 'trophies,' and I don't want any part of that."

Tamara's voice vibrated with contempt, her smile was bitter. "Do you think you have any choice?"

"I've managed so far."

"Only because everyone thinks you're a man-hater!" Tamara said venomously.

Shocked beyond expression, Natasha stared at her blankly. Tamara reached out and clasped her hand. "But I've always defended you, Natasha—"

Natasha twisted away. "I don't want you to defend me! There's nothing to defend. Leave me be!"

But Tamara still clung to her arm. "Oh, you're wrong, Natasha darling. Dreadfully wrong. I can't leave you be. You don't know what you're throwing aside. The prince's desire for you is probably the most fortunate thing that ever happened to you!"

"Fortunate?" Natasha's stomach was tight with loathing.

Tamara went on quietly, "I don't think you've quite got the idea into your head yet, Natasha. It's not as you think. The prince genuinely loves you."

"Loves me!" Natasha cried scornfully. "He wants to own me! To 'sport' me! Every rich man has to have his pet ballet-girl, just as he has to be a member of the Imperial Yacht Club or own an Orlov thoroughbred."

"He means to treat you well, you silly child," Tamara said, beginning to lose her patience. "Just *think*. As his official mistress you could enter society."

Natasha was silenced. She was frantic now to leave. It was

such a sordid business. Tamara was nothing but a bawd. She strained away from the older girl, but Tamara's fingers were clamped upon her flesh.

"You must take my word for it," Tamara said, endeavoring to make everything sound reasonable. "I know his excellency as well as I know any man—you've bewitched him. You can make your fortune if you will be guided by me. Play the game as I advise, and you'll end up the next best thing to being the Princess Verchinin."

Natasha could feel incredulous laughter bubbling up inside her. Was Tamara quite mad?

"I can make it happen for you, Natasha. I'm such a good friend to the prince. And to you. Believe me."

Natasha stood gazing into the room. The laughter died away in her, and she could only feel a rising wave of nausea.

Tamara completely misinterpreted her passivity. "You will be so *powerful*, my dear. So what does it matter if the intendant disapproves of you? In a few months' time, you'll have him groveling at your knees!"

Tamara's reference to the intendant brought Natasha back to reality. She stirred slightly.

"Just let me make all the arrangements, Natasha darling," Tamara said persuasively. "Left to yourself, you'll only make a botch of it. Verchinin's a very rich fish indeed, my sweet. You don't know what you've caught. There's many a woman lost her hook when trying to land him. But you already have him halfway out of the water, and I shall help you pull him in. . . ." She searched Natasha's face, trying to discover the extent of her success.

Tamara added suggestively, "If you could just show the prince that his case is, well, not hopeless . . . that he is agreeable to you. If you could just be *kind* to him."

"Kind to him?"

"Just a word or a smile. To show his excellency that he's not hateful to you—"

Natasha drew a deep breath. She looked sick. She staggered as though she was about to fall. "Tamara, I can't do that," she said, trying to keep her voice steady. "The prince *is* hateful to me!" She stopped, confused. "Well, not hateful, but . . ."

She drew another great breath. "I could never give myself to such a man—not for all the gold in Russia. Not if he *were* to make me the Princess Verchinin!" She tore herself free from Tamara's grasp at last and fled from the room.

Tamara continued to stand by the great mirror, very self-possessed, apparently untouched by Natasha's contempt. She smiled, and smoothed her hair. Natasha was ridiculously young for her years. It was hard to imagine that she had been reared in the world of backstage intrigue. She was a romantic. But she was not a fool. She would come to see her advantage in the end. They all did.

Tamara did not anticipate any difficulties. She'd never encountered any before. Oh, yes, shock and horror to begin with, earnest protestations. But there was something in the atmosphere of backstage life—the heady excitement of working in a real theatre, the sight of other successful girls with their "treasures," the feeling of newly acquired freedom from the rigorous discipline of the ballet school. All contributed to make new girls readily available, and easy to manage.

It was a pity that Verchinin had singled Natasha out so quickly. A pity that the girl herself had attracted attention by being so damned talented. Any girl dazzled by the possibility of being a star wouldn't be so amenable. That was why she had tried to persuade the prince to help her. If only the old goat had gone about things more subtly. She had overplayed her hand there. But all was not yet lost.

Tamara laughed softly to her reflection. How shocked the girl had been. How furious. How splendid, in fact. But, then, they all were at first, until they acquired a sense of reality. The seed was planted. She would soon see what fruit it bore.

She laughed again. She knew what sort of fruit it would bear. Her hands went to her long neck. She could already feel the diamond and sapphire necklace hanging there.

CHAPTER

FOUR

Richard lunged in quarte and Scavronsky parried with a rapier sidevault, thrusting in seconde, making a touch.

Richard, being touched by the thrust, stood by into line. Scavronsky also lined. They turned to their audience, raised their swords, saluted, and then turned to salute each other. Then they put up their swords and left the fencing area.

It had been a poor match. Ordinarily they fenced well together; both were good sportsmen by temperament. They both enjoyed the quick delicate exercise, and both possessed the steady eye and alertness necessary for a good bout. But today Richard had put up a poor showing. His play had been soft and uncertain. He has problems, Scavronsky thought.

They walked from the fencing salon to indifferent applause. Richard apologized for his poor efforts as they entered the changing room. He opened one of the huge burnished-wood lockers.

"There's obviously something troubling you, *mon anglais*," Scavronsky said, as they stripped themselves, ready for the steam bath.

"No. Just not in the mood for it," Richard muttered, his head disappearing into his shirt.

Scavronsky laughed, disbelieving. "Come, old friend. This is our third bout together this week, and each time I have 'beaten you hollow.' Your mind is elsewhere, always."

Richard sighed in answer, and Scavronsky regarded him with interest. They left the changing room and walked into the soaping room. It was tiled, overheated and full of steam.

Both men were naked. Scavronsky was lean and dark, with a great fan of black hair spreading upon his bony chest and from his groin. His baptismal cross gleamed upon his chest. Richard's large body gleamed in the soft white steam, glossily smooth. Stripped, his body had a clean, spare look. He could have stepped from a Greek pedestal. But there was a look of suffering on his face that was far removed from the serenity of a marble hero. His eyes and the corners of his mouth were tense, his forehead deeply furrowed.

"Is it the 'international situation?'" Scavronsky asked, as they took their places on a white marble table. "Is our play at the mercy of those frightful Turks?"

For the past two weeks the British embassy had swarmed with activity, due to the political situation that had blown up because of the Slav rebellion in the Balkans. The rebellion had started the previous summer when a group of Christian peasants had refused to pay the extortionate taxes demanded by their Turkish landlords. The rebellion had been fanned by Russians in the Pan-Slavic movement, who urged that Russia should go to the aid of her Christian neighbors. All of which, if not properly controlled by the tzar, could lead the country into a European war. For days the embassy had been thronged with spies and informers. It had been Richard's duty to investigate their reports.

He now glanced at the count moodily. Scavronsky laughed. "We have no desire for another 'Crimea,' you know," he said.

Richard frowned and looked away. He was saved from answering by the entrance of two strapping masseurs. They were dressed in linen trousers, each a mountain of muscle above. Conversation languished. Richard was sprinkled with water, lathered with a fiber sponge and rubbed violently. Beside him, Scavronsky groaned under the efforts of the other man. Under the deft hands of his masseur, Richard began to relax. His limbs were steeped in a marvelous warmth, the skillful hands skimming over his body were as soft as those of a woman. He wanted to lose himself in this delicious languor.

Sounds faded around him. An image drifted into his mind: a face, ivory white, high-cheeked; a mouth, gentle and sweetly curving; a nose, small and straight; delicate brows above strangely slanting eyes; hair as black as a raincloud. Her body floated like a landscape before his eyes, wreathed in the steam of his own imaginings: proud smooth breasts, rose-tipped; arms firm and white; a strong slender waist; her spine a slim furrow; long elegant legs, straight and lovely; the

white mound of her belly; and below, a smoky fleece . . .
Unconsciously, his body reacted to the stimulation of his
vision. His erotic dream ended with a dowsing of cold water.

He was turned over, stretched out on his stomach, scraped
and washed. Then he was pushed through a door into a cloud
of steam. Not far from him, Scavronsky was furiously beating
his own body with a broom made of twigs, to stimulate the
circulation.

He paused only long enough to ask, "Is it love or debts?"

Richard had also taken up a twig broom. He began to beat
away the memory of the white dimpled body. "It's not
debts," he said.

"Then it must be love."

"Well, yes . . . in a way."

"The countess has finally refused you?"

The blankness of Richard's expression astonished Scavronsky, and then amused him. He laughed, slapping his belly.
Quite clearly, the Countess Kreuger had been forgotten.

"You have a new love?" he asked.

Richard nodded gloomily. "Yes. Except that . . . well,
only on my part. Though I'm doing my damnedest!"

"You have had no success with her?"

Richard gestured angrily, and the count laughed again.

"Truly, *mon anglais,* you have remarkably bad luck with
your women!"

Richard smiled grimly.

"I have remarkably bad luck with *Russian* women certainly."

"They are creatures apart, I agree," Scavronsky said.

Richard nodded.

"You find Russian women too cold, too puritanical?"
Scavronsky asked.

"I can't seem to get near them," Richard said.

The count regarded him curiously. "Who is she, this new
paragon? Do I know her?"

"You've met her," Richard said reluctantly, "seen her, at
least. She's not in society."

Scavronsky's brow puckered in thought. Then his face
cleared. "Ah, *ça alors!* The little dancer! You have become
interested in her?"

"Yes."

"But, my dear friend, such a bad choice!"

"On the contrary," Richard answered gruffly. "I think she

is the most perfect, most fascinating . . ." He slapped at his thigh with the twig broom.

"My dear Richard, there are any number of sweet, sluttish, compliant creatures in the Opera Ballet, but you must have an itch for 'La Puritana.' For that's what· they call her, you know. She is the most unnatural girl, they say."

Richard looked up. "Unnatural?"

"Cold. And quite monstrously pious. Not even Verchinin has penetrated her . . . defenses."

Richard rose abruptly. "I'd rather not discuss it, Kolya. It could lead to a quarrel."

Scavronsky stared. Richard looked so grim that the count was silenced for a moment. *"Mon Dieu!* You are serious."

Richard regarded him wretchedly. "Yes, I am," he said. "Good God, I don't really understand it myself. What I feel is . . . is . . . I can't put my feelings into rational words, Kolya. All I can say is that I've never felt so damned *interested* in my life. She's really hooked me. I'm struggling and wriggling for my life, but I can't get free."

The count regarded him with sympathy. "Oh, my poor man. We must get you off that hook by all means. We can't have you enslaved to such a monster as 'La Puritana.'"

Richard looked even grimmer. "Well, that's just it, Kolya. I don't think I want to get off the hook. One part of me doesn't relish the experience, but another part doesn't want to do without it."

"You intend to go on pursuing her?"

"I've been laying siege to her for the past three weeks," Richard said. "Since the day after that blasted ball, in fact."

"And you've made no progress at all?"

"None. I've got nowhere with her. I've always had a fair success with actresses and such. But she's not like any theatre woman I've ever known." He smiled. "Which may be why I find her so extraordinarily attractive. She's more like the *belle* of some English girls' school—with that marvelous bloom still on her."

"What does she say to you?"

Richard slapped at his reddened thighs. The broom had softened and was rapidly coming to pieces in his hand. "Nothing! She never looks up! I've waited outside that damned stage door every night—along with all the other *beaux*. I send in flowers, chocolates—along with all the other *beaux*. She sends my chocolates and flowers to the infirmary, and sends back my little notes. She apparently never accepts presents."

Scavronsky groaned comically. "Infamous creature! What will happen to us if her example spreads?"

"I sent her the most charming little trinket the other night—it cost me almost a month's allowance. She sent it back without a word. She never speaks to me, just climbs into a carriage with whatever other girls are not engaged that night—even its windows are screened!"

"Ah, I know that carriage well," the count said.

His body shining with sweat, Richard sank onto the marble bench.

"Holy St. Sergius!" the count exclaimed. "The girl *is* unnatural. You must abandon this foolishness, Richard."

Richard glanced at him impatiently, resenting his flippancy. But, for the moment, Scavronsky looked serious. Foreboding even. Then he smiled. "Such women as 'La Puritana' are doubly dangerous, in my opinion. Those who say 'No entry' at the beginning invariably say 'No exit' at the finish. She'll be the devil to get rid of, I assure you."

Richard swore, in English. "For God's sake, Nicolai! Be serious."

"But I am serious. Believe me, my dear friend, I know women. I am a *professional bachelor!*" The count stretched out on a marble bench. "Richard," he said, "I must find some new pastime for you. You must be eased out of this ill-conceived passion. . . ."

Richard frowned with annoyance. "I've already told you that I don't want to be eased out of anything. I shall find my own way to attract the lady's attention." He smiled. "You pride yourself on being a professional bachelor, I pride myself on being a professional diplomat."

Scavronsky clapped a hand to his head in a gesture of comic despair. "I feel a terrible responsibility toward you, for it was I who brought this implacable virgin into your life. And I was then trying to turn your thoughts away from some equally chilly female."

He swung himself off the marble table. "You must let me help you, Richard. As a friend. Either I must wean you away from her, or I must help you into her bed."

Richard raised himself threateningly. *"Kolya . . ."*

Scavronsky laughed, holding up an appeasing hand. "You don't understand the conventions, Richard. I do. You will never get anywhere with her by just hanging around the stage

door. When a ballet-girl refuses to meet a man halfway
there's little he can do, short of abducting her. The imperial
theatres are strange brothels—quite often they are as impene-
trable as the Temple of the Virgins. . . . No, I must help you
to find a way."

CHAPTER
FIVE

A hundred fan-shaped palm trees stood in tubs upon the
gleaming floor of the great ballroom. Around each palm tree
were supper tables seating a dozen people. The tzar was
giving an 'intimate' party, a *bal des palmiers.* The ballroom
blazed with gemlike radiance. Rosettes of light shone from
the candelabra, reflected endlessly in the long gilt mirrors.
Ten huge crystal chandeliers floated like brilliant constella-
tions beneath the richly decorated green and gold ceiling.

Emerging from the anteroom, Richard was faced with a
dazzling perspective of marble inlaid with jasper. Gilt
gleamed on every side. The reflections of the dancers were
repeated in the shining parquet floor. The shifting colors of
the uniforms and liveries, the butterfly hues of the ladies'
gowns, the coruscation of jewels—all mirrored in broken
patterns—gave him the impression of being at the edge of
some huge multicolored wheel as it revolved slowly to the
sound of a waltz.

The air was fragrant with the smell of wood burning in
porcelain stoves, mingled with the incense carried about the
room by footmen. Exotic flowers in tall Chinese vases,
lacquered pots and silver bowls exhaled a heady scent.
Curtains of sapphire and silver brocade shut out the winter
night. And in the center of the room rose the grove of palm
trees—an oasis of cool shadows in the magical shimmer of the
rest.

A footman in a powdered wig led Richard and Scavronsky to a table. Richard was handsome in full evening dress of black superfine with silk revers, with the order of St. Michael slashed across his black satin waistcoat. The count wore the white, gold-braided dolman of the Hussars of the Guard. Scavronsky, who seemed to be related to everybody at the table, did the honors. They took their places on rosewood chairs upholstered in blue velvet.

Richard, who had not yet attended a *bal des palmiers*, waited to see what happened next, wondering idly why Scavronsky had been so insistent upon his attendance. Three weeks had gone by since their conversation in the steam room.

It was over two hours before it became clear. The count answered all Richard's questions with an amused shake of the head and a gloved finger laid to his lips. He was greatly enjoying his little secret. Then it was nine o'clock and all movement suddenly froze among the guests. Conversation dribbled away. The main door was opened.

In the deadly silence, a loud voice cried, "His Imperial Majesty!" The tzar walked through the gilded door and made the rounds of the tables. He stopped at each one long enough to pick up a piece of bread and touch a glass of champagne to his lips, taking a token bite and a token sip so that his guests could say they had eaten and drunk with the emperor.

Richard was shocked at the tzar's appearance at close quarters. The man looked haunted. He was the spectre at his own feast.

The promenade took just over an hour. When they were seated again, Richard saw that they were about to see a performance on the dance floor.

Six footman brought in a structure of richly carved poles of silver inlaid with mother-of-pearl. From these poles were strung great swags of artificial leaves, laurel and acanthus, fashioned in silver tissue. Veils of azure gauze floated between the silver poles. The six footmen took up their positions, standing as immobile as the poles each held.

A pause, and then the orchestra struck up a chord and began to play a simple Mozartian air. The veils of the canopy were twisted aside and looped between the poles. Six young nymphs were revealed. They were dressed in the style of the early eighteenth century, in hoopskirts with rows of ruching and flouncing, white lace sleeves and satin bows. Their hair was drawn away from their faces, simply dressed and lightly powdered. The pale colors of their costumes gave an effect of fleeting delicacy. It seemed they might vanish in the blink of an eye.

With a start, Richard recognized Natasha. Her taffeta costume of robin's-egg blue and pearl pink might have been especially designed to show off her beauty. Her lightly powdered hair was enhanced with silk flowers and strings of pearls.

Scavronsky leaned forward. "You are content?"

Richard could not tear his eyes away from the motionless figure. "Did you arrange this?" he asked.

Scavronsky chuckled. "In my capacity of 'aesthetic advisor' to the Grand Master of Ceremonies!"

The orchestra began to play a medley of childlike tunes, strung together like a garland, Sicilian airs and dances. The girls began to dance together, moving like a knot of fresh flowers, their light dresses lifting as they moved, the ribbons fluttering at their breasts.

Six young men danced into the room, dressed as Neapolitan peasants in brightly-colored shirts and knee-breeches, with stocking caps upon their dark hair. They started with mock surprise at the sight of the young women, then waved greetings, showing a desire to be better acquainted. One young woman—Richard recognized her as Marie Antonova —took a rose from her corsage and held it roguishly on high, as if inquiring whether such a gift was acceptable. A young man signaled yes, and the rose was thrown and neatly caught. One by one, the girls threw their roses to the boys. Four more found their mark.

Natasha's rose skimmed through the air and her young partner leaped for it. But he failed to reach it in time, and the rose fell to the floor and was kicked across the polished boards. It came to rest at Scavronsky's feet.

Smiling, he stooped to pick it up. He examined the bloom for a moment and then handed it to Richard. One eyelid drooped slowly in a knowing wink.

Richard held the silver-tipped flower cupped gently in his hands. It was made of silk, exquisite and fragrant, for it had been drenched in some sweet clean scent. He looked from the rose to the girl. She was intent on the dance, with the same dreamy look on her face that he had seen at their first meeting. She was, he felt, lost to the world. He had eyes for no one else but Natasha. Her dancing seemed to him enchanting, spontaneous and childlike. Her figure looked ethereal. It was as though God had breathed life into a delicate porcelain figure.

A rose garden of melodies floated through the room. The girls tripped across the stage, pursued by the now ardent young men. The girls were the embodiment of feminine provocation, the boys impetuously male. Natasha danced in the air, away from pursuing hands. Her partner capered around her like a young goat, reaching for her, but she stayed always out of his grasp, whirling and leaping, never coming to rest.

Her friends came to her aid, dancing between Natasha and her suitor, impeding his progress. The would-be lover, temporarily defeated, turned aside. Then, seeing his chance, he turned back, his arms outstretched for her again. But, just as he thought she was within his grasp, she vanished with her companions through a parting in the curtain. Polite applause signaled the end of the performance. The male dancers retreated between the garlanded poles, the veils fell around them. To a stately promenade, the footmen walked away.

"Come," Scavronsky said. "It is time to return your trophy." He touched the rose in Richard's hand.

"Did you contrive this, too?" Richard asked, holding up the flower.

"Everything, I contrived everything," the count said, grinning boastfully. ". . . Come."

After leading Richard through a variety of rooms, Scavronsky knocked upon a door of polished mahogany embossed with gold. A manservant opened it, bowing as he recognized the count. He wore the livery of a minor footman.

Scavronsky gave the man his card. "Please give this to Mademoiselle Petrova, with my compliments. Tell her that I am here to offer the congratulations of the chamberlain's office."

The man opened the door wider and bowed them through into what appeared to be a lumber room, then disappeared. The room was of medium size, its harmony smothered beneath a glut of marble and malachite. Richard saw that he was in the back parts of the Winter Palace. It was very ill lit.

A door at the gloomier end opened, admitting a shadowy figure. Richard's heart thudded as Natasha stepped out of the gloom and into the soft radiance of candlelight. She stood there, hesitating, still dressed in the pastel-colored gown. Her

beauty startled him. Her face seemed to shine with a morn-
ing-star radiance, making the candle glow seem yellow and
grubby. The bodice of her dress was cut unusually low,
showing the whole depth of her bosom. Her breasts had the
lustrous gleam of pearl. She stood, head bowed modestly,
unconsciously adopting a relaxed dancer's pose.

Scavronsky took Richard by the arm and led him forward.
"Mademoiselle," the count said, "you are to be congratulated. You were exquisite."

She curtsied slightly, head still bent. She had not looked at
them directly. Richard wondered if she would know him. The
light was very dim and he stood against it.

"Merci, M'sieur le Comte," she said.

"I have brought you a cavalier, Mademoiselle," Scavronsky said. He turned to Richard with a tigerish smile. "Return
to her the rose," he said, in his appalling English.

Natasha looked up then, flashing a startled glance at
Richard, who offered her the rose. She took it reluctantly,
then lowered her eyes again. Yet for a moment he held her
hand in his. He held it as he would a foil or a little
bird—firmly enough to prevent its escaping, yet not so firmly
as to crush it.

His hand shivered at the contact. A strong tremor ran
through his arm. Startled, Natasha looked up at him directly.
Astonishment seemed to break like light in her eyes. Something in his melancholy expression, the haunted look that
made his handsome face seem haggard, took her by surprise.
He felt the shock of her surprise, saw the look of concern in
her eyes. He felt that she was truly seeing him—and not just
some persistent and annoying admirer—for the first time.

Her hand remained clasped in his, she made no move to
withdraw it. The door opened and the young dancer Marie
appeared. Scavronsky went forward to meet her. Richard felt
that this, too, had been carefully arranged.

The count spoke in a low rapid voice with Marie. Natasha
slowly removed her hand, and regarded Richard with less
shyness and more interest. She still held the rose in her hand.
Now she tucked it into her corsage.

"We should like you to accompany us to supper, mademoiselle," Richard said, his voice low and urgent. "Would you
honor us?"

Natasha paused. He thought she was about to refuse, then
she nodded. She appeared to have reached some decision

regarding him. Although she was still reserved, he felt a new warmth in her. It was as though he had truly come to her notice for the first time.

"I'll come with pleasure," she said, adding to his surprise, "I'm as hungry as a wolf!"

The restaurant was crowded. As always, the contrast between the fierce cold of the night and the stuffy heat of the perfumed rooms struck Richard disagreeably. The count's party was met by the manager himself in the white marble vestibule. Natasha clung to the gilded banister and looked about her. It was her first visit to such a smart restaurant.

The gallery bloomed with so many flowers that it gave the illusion of a summer's day. In a curious way she felt that she was entering the *real* world. She had stepped into a tropical grove or some gorgeous fairy-tale scene or onto a stage—her real world. She felt exactly as she felt then—a twinge of fear and a stab of excitement. Beyond the gallery she could see the pink shaded lights of the restaurant and the peacock colors of the ballroom, mirrors reflecting the glow of lamps. She appeared to be looking into a dozen identical rooms.

She grew aware of critical eyes examining her, appraising her. She was the only woman present who was not in full evening dress. Among the flounces, lace-falls, bows, flowers and jewels of the other women, she felt dowdy. Although Marie had offered to loan her one of her own evening gowns, Natasha had refused. Now she regretted it. Her delicate blue silk dress edged with black fringe lacked style. The train was too short for evening wear, the neckline too high. Her hair wanted for ornament.

Richard, as though sensing her thoughts, stopped a girl carrying a tray full of small posies. "Please," he said to Natasha, "take these. *You* need nothing more."

He bought white persian roses. The frail petals shone in her dark hair. She pinned another cluster at her breast. Looking at Richard, she thanked him, her lips parting in her first real smile. She was grateful to him for the gesture and for the compliment. Richard returned her smile, his breath catching in his throat. There was no artificiality in her. Her eyes were clear, marvelously candid.

The manager led them through the crowded foyer, away from the restaurant and ballroom, until they came to a second set of stairs.

Richard touched Scavronsky's sleeve. The count turned

and Richard stopped, frowning. He spoke in English. "Have
you booked a private room?"

"But of course! Would you not prefer to be discreet?"

Richard was aware that Natasha's dark eyes were upon
him, her fine brows drawn together, perplexed. Did she, he
wondered, understand the meaning of the private dining
room? The table laid for two, the suggestive paintings on the
wall, the tinted mirrors and the curtained alcove with its
oriental divan . . . He looked back down the stairs toward
the public rooms bursting with life and glamour.

"I think you've made a mistake, Kolya," he said, again in
English.

The count looked astonished. "A mistake?"

"Yes. I think we shall all be happier downstairs, where we
can dine and dance."

Marie, not understanding the drift of the conversation, but
amused by the comic look of surprise on Scavronsky's face,
giggled. Natasha's frown deepened slightly. She was only
aware of Richard's displeasure.

"But, my dear Richard," the count said irritably, "the
whole point of this evening is that you can find yourself alone
with—"

"The whole point of the evening for *me*, Kolya, is that I've
been properly introduced to Natalia Ivanovna, and now I can
gain her confidence, not seduce her in some vulgar supper
room." He smiled, but said sternly, "You've misunderstood
me, Kolya, and you underestimate the lady. We shall both be
happier downstairs. If I simply wanted what you appear to
think I want, there are women enough below to accommodate me."

The count paused, then laughed. "Shall I ever understand
the English?" he asked. "But if that is how you wish to play
this little game . . ." He shrugged. "What a waste of opportunity. You may never have such a one again."

"I shall," Richard answered, "now that I've broken
through the formalities—for which I thank you, Kolya."

Scavronsky bowed, his face full of comic despair. Then,
catching Marie by the hand, he trod lightly down the stairs,
back into the glittering life of the ballroom. Richard gave his
arm to Natasha. Looking bewildered, she took it. She was
dimly aware that she had been the true center of the
argument, oddly conscious that Richard had saved her from
some embarrassment.

After, as they danced together, she became aware of the

touch of his hands. She could feel his warm fingers, strong and hard, through the thin cotton of his gloves. She looked up at him. His calm eyes gazed down into hers. His lashes, she noticed, were tinged with gold.

While the music played, she was in her natural element, and Richard was an accomplished dancer. He steered her deftly between the circling couples, so that she had the impression at times that they were alone on the dance floor, dipping and swaying languorously.

"You dance as well offstage as on, Natalia Ivanovna," Richard said.

Natasha laughed. "Perhaps because I follow you, m'sieur. All this is new to me."

"New to you?"

"Dancing with a . . . a . . ."

"An *amateur?*"

She blushed. "Oh, you are very expert, I think. You have been well trained."

Richard smiled down at her. "Part of the diplomatic life," he said.

"What I meant was that I've only danced with students at school before," Natasha said, laughing and shuddering together. "It was very different, believe me!"

"Oh. How?"

"It was always so very solemn, so very stiff. We were never allowed to exchange a single word with our partners. If one boy spoke, or if one laughed—*pouf!* Privileges were lost for days, visits were forbidden. It was *grim.*"

"It sounds it."

"Well, it wasn't easy. Ah, the discipline, as unbending as the rules at court."

Later she asked, "How do I call you?"

"I'd be happy if you called me Richard," he said.

"Richard? Is that your *prénom?*"

"Yes."

"You are not called for your father?"

"Oh, yes. One of my names is his." He laughed. "I'm called Richard Andrew Gerald Anthony Nugent Greville."

"So many! . . . So you are called Richard Andreovich?"

Richard laughed again. "No, that's not our custom in England. We have no patronymic."

"But surely that must make for many difficulties?" she said, frowning. "For example, we cannot be formal, for I have known you some time. But we cannot be intimate, since I have not known you long enough."

"Then you must call me Richard Andreovich until we become good friends," he said.

She flushed, then smiled. With a thrill of pleasure he realized that she meant to see him again. She tested the two names together, pronouncing "Richard" in the French way, soft and slurred. To his ears, his name sounded entrancing on her tongue.

They circled the ballroom once more. They had danced every dance so far, unaware of anything but the growing excitement between them, their blood pulsing to the music. Natasha felt giddy and a little breathless. Her senses were heightened by the lights, the warmth, the fragrance of the banks of flowers, the handsome foreigner—so tall, so broad in the shoulder. It seemed that the noise in the room was increasing, though the other dancers were blurred shadows. Everything was gayer, lighter, more brightly colored.

Richard's arms tightened about her in the waltz. They danced on long after the others had dropped away. His hand was on her waist, feeling the lightness of her bones; she was conscious of his gentle strength. Something was happening to her, something beyond the spell cast upon her by the music and the sheer delight she took in movement. A deeper delight stirred in her body.

She looked up into his face, he smiled down at her. His mouth was well shaped, generous, strong without being too hard. She was struck by a crazy impulse to reach up and touch his lips, trace their outline gently with her fingers. She was filled with a heady excitement.

Scavronsky, watching them, had the impression of two beautiful animals in an elaborate courtship ritual. He felt envious of Richard. She has "proffered the cheek," as the French say, he thought. Very soon they will be lovers.

The pulse in Natasha's wrist fluttered beneath Richard's fingers. She felt tremendously disturbed. The words of an old song came into her mind: "Do not touch me, lest I turn to flame . . ."

A week later Natasha came out of the artists' entrance into the bitter wind. Usually she was reluctant to forsake the backstage atmosphere. But tonight she had removed her makeup and dressed with clumsy haste, hurrying with excited anticipation. It was to be her first evening alone with the Englishman, and she had looked forward to it all day. She was wrapped warmly against the weather, swathed in a greatcoat lined with squirrel skin, with a fur scarf high on her chin. Yet while crossing the snow from the stage door to the door of the *kibitka*, the fur at her mouth was frosted by her breath.

Richard waited by the door of the covered sledge. He opened it and handed her inside. For the first time they were completely alone together. Surprisingly, Natasha had no fear. The thick felt hood of the *kibitka* created a pool of darkness inside the sledge, unexpectedly close. The interior smelled of polished leather, strong cologne and clean hay.

They drove in silence over the packed snow, the only sound the jingle of the bells and the soft crunch of hooves. The sledge dipped and swayed like a boat in a calm sea. She buried her velvet boots in the hay on the floor. Richard had spread a feather mattress over their knees, covered by a wolfskin. Even so, she was still chilled.

Involuntarily, she snuggled closer to Richard. She trembled as her arm touched his. With a sudden temor of fear and a wave of excitement, she looked up at him. The frost of his breath created a strange halo around his face. His eyes gleamed in the darkness. Natasha raised her mouth to his. He leaned down, speaking her name softly. Their white breath clouded the air between them. Their lips touched. Each warmed the other into vibrant life. Her lips, at first cold and stiff, softened beneath the ardent pressure of his mouth, drawing every sensation from the touch of his lips.

Then the *kibitka* drew up before a low building hidden in a clump of trees. Natasha, who had not known what to expect, looked out into the starlit night. The landscape looked deserted, a wilderness of black and white.

"Where are we?" she asked.

Richard laughed. "At sea," he said, "among the islands. . . . Wait here." He jumped from the sledge and crunched through the snow. When he banged loudly at the door of the low building, almost at once a sliver of light appeared in a crack in the door. Then the door opened wider, and Richard turned to beckon to her. She climbed from the *kibitka* and walked quickly across the snow. Music came to her as she neared the crack of yellow light, voices and a guitar.

The cold was so intense that Natasha was almost blinded by the tears in her eyes. The stifling heat of the room met her as

she ducked beneath the thick felt curtain at the door. Wiping
her eyes, she saw that she was in a bare whitewashed room.
Half a dozen dark-eyed Tartar waiters bowed in front of her.
A rough wooden table, with places set for two, stood in the
center of the room. The room was lit by flickering candlelight.

One waiter led them to a table, another brought the
samovar, another the champagne, another seated them. A
gypsy group sat at one end of the room, swarthy men and
snaky-haired. They sang in curiously metallic voices, guitars
thrumming an accompaniment. The songs had a dark, bar-
baric ring to them, a tempest of wild melody in the most
perfect harmony. It conjured up an Eastern world, utterly
strange, sounding novel and fresh and yet immortally old.

Natasha, listening to it, felt absolutely intoxicated. The
sound acted upon her like a narcotic. Richard saw that the
music had captured her, had drawn her away from him
temporarily. As always, he felt baffled by this inexhaustible
ability to lose herself in music. At the same time it left him
free to gaze at her openly, feasting his famished eyes.

In the flickering light of the candles, her face shone, her
dark gray eyes were incandescent. She looked like a water
nymph in her dress of moss-green satin with its apron drape of
silvery green tulle. How strange she was. So far removed
from his experience of women—so sweet, simple, direct, so
lacking in coquetry. Yet so indefinably aloof and mysterious.
He felt himself unable to reach her sometimes. She had the
innocence of an animal. If she was cruel to him, it was with an
unconscious cruelty. She was like a sleepwalker, walking into
the wakefulness of life, as though the real world frightened
her. Sometimes she could be so easy and natural—and then,
with baffling unpredictability, there would be a sudden shift
into shyness. She appeared unable or unwilling to bring
herself to the pitch of self-importance that came so naturally
to the women he had known.

The singers sang of a southern countryside, rich with the
grape harvest. Of nights when the great moon dappled the
shadows that fell on young lovers . . .

She was not indifferent to him. In unguarded moments her
face betrayed her—a clear look, lips parted, velvety eyes soft
and caressing. She was without pretense. Tonight, in the
kibitka, her lips had told him all he needed to know. And
yet . . . She was still afraid of him. His foreignness still
disturbed her. Perhaps, even now, she was not yet ready for
an affair? Or, perhaps, she was looking for more than a

pleasant affair? His own feelings baffled him, too. He had
never been so tender of a woman. He wanted more than the
conventional relationship.

The music ended. Natasha became aware of Richard. The
confusion came back into her face as she saw that he was
watching her. She felt overwhelmed by the feeling that welled
up inside her.

But, again in the chilly darkness of the *kibitka*, she grew
less shy as they lay together in the soft warmth. Somehow
their arms entwined clumsily in the swaddling furs.

Richard held her innocent body in his arms, talking to her
without haste, murmuring strange words, a mixture of Russian and French, a little English. To Natasha, it sounded as
strange and meaningless as the whisper of treetops. Again
their lips met, the coldness melting to warmth as their breaths
mingled. Her body, beneath the thick covers, felt marvelously weak as it strained toward him. His arms were under
her furs. His hands, strong yet gentle, cupped the firm globes
of her breasts.

Beneath the stiff bodice, her breasts hardened, her nipples
ached. A strange confusion grew in her. She yearned toward
him, murmuring incoherently. His lips found the delicate spot
at the base of her neck, in the hollow of her shoulder. She
shivered at the unfamiliar sensation. Then his lips were on
hers again, urgent with desire, forceful yet tender. Her skin
was both hot and cold—hot where his hands warmed her flesh
into new life, cold where the chilly air made contact with her
exposed skin.

He drew back, feeling her shivering beneath him. As he
pulled the wraps around them, they were cocooned in furs.
She lay in his arms, the trembling stilled a little. The muffled
sound of the horses' hooves echoed the beating of her own
heart.

The *kibitka* moved on through the darkening forest, along
the gleaming white track.

CHAPTER

SIX

"Are you saying that I have failed, Tamara Fyodorovna?" Verchinin asked. The perfumed old dandy stared at Tamara sternly. An overwhelming desire to pick up her skirts and run ran through her. She had begun to dread her meetings with him. Somehow her plans had gone completely awry.

"Not 'failed,' excellency. She greatly admires you, but . . ."

Tamara hesitated. Verchinin had never looked so aggressive. "She is young, excellency. Very young, and . . . and inexperienced. She doesn't understand the honor you are doing her."

"I'm prepared to be her slave," the old man said. "I, the master of many, and the servant of none but the tzar."

Tamara picked at the buttons that ran down the front of her blue serge walking costume. "She's such a strange creature," she said, choosing her words delicately. "She's like a guest on this earth. I don't think she cares a scrap for the things that others care about."

"She must want something that I can provide?"

"Her mind seems solely on dancing."

The prince struck at the floor with his gold-topped walking cane. He was dressed in a morning coat cut away to show the fanciest of waistcoats. "I can still be influential in that quarter."

Tamara, remembering his bungled attempts with Khudekov, changed the subject. "She's not yet awakened, excellency. Sometimes I think she's a little backward—as a woman. She's not yet aware of herself. If you will only be patient . . ."

The old man slapped his white kid gloves upon his sleeve. "I have been patient. More patient than ever in my life before, Tamara Fyodorovna. But I cannot wait forever. The snatched word and the stolen touch are not my style. I taste the dry bones when I hunger for the baked meats. You must arrange a meeting for us. A private meeting."

Tamara glanced at the prince slyly. She felt unusually scared. The lecherous old goat had turned suddenly into a terrifying old bull. How could she ever have taken him so much for granted? This was a man that others feared. He would be ruthless to anyone he thought had served him ill. She had overreached herself this time. Spoiled, self-indulgent, unjust—he was not a man who knew forgiveness. Nervously, she tucked a stray hair beneath her hat elastic. Her blue silk porkpie hat perched on her chignon, giving her an impudent air—an impudence she was far from feeling. How desperately she wished that she had never undertaken to play the bawd for him. Yet it had seemed such a simple matter. Natasha had struck her as the usual vapid creature— guileless, unsuspicious, uncomplicated, in a state of nature almost. All she had to do was hang a price tag on her, she'd thought. Who would ever have imagined that the girl possessed the spirit she had shown?

Perhaps she'd been too subtle for her own good. It might have been better to let the old fool do his own wooing in his own way—the luxurious clichés of backstage courtship—furs and finery, perfume and jewels. She looked up from fiddling with her straying hair to find the prince glowering at her.

"Well, Tamara Fyodorovna, what do you plan to do on my behalf?"

Tamara smiled emptily. For the first time in her life, she lacked for inspiration.

Order ruled in the dressing room. Costumes were hung just so, the sticks of makeup were lined up on the communal dressing table. The girls went about the business of transforming themselves with silent dedication. But there was no atmosphere. The two dancers faced each other.

"I have no intention of seeing Prince Verchinin," Natasha said positively. "And certainly not in private."

"But, *ma chère*—"

"Unless it is to tell him frankly that he must stop pursuing me," Natasha said, easing her way into a froth of transparent pink muslin.

Tamara's face grew pale. "Natasha! Oh, my God! You can't do that!"

"Why not?"

"Because . . ." Tamara struggled with her own costume, all thumbs. Her long fingernails ripped through a piece of pale green muslin. She swore.

"His attentions are unwelcome to me," Natasha said quietly. Her self-control appalled Tamara.

She sat down, horrified, looking suddenly a great age.

Aware of the drama unfolding at Natasha's table, the other girls had grown even quieter, so quiet that the orchestra could be heard tuning up above stairs. Singers ran through their scales.

The girls stared curiously at Tamara and Natasha. When Tamara spoke, she kept her voice deliberately low.

"Natasha, you don't yet understand. You must understand. You have no choice in the matter."

Natasha stopped buttoning her bodice. "No choice? What do you mean?" Natasha's voice filled with anger. Tamara gestured to her to speak quietly.

"What do you mean?" Natasha asked, as loudly as before, angry, yet at the same time nervous.

Tamara took her hand and drew her out into the corridor, out of hearing of the rest of the inquisitive girls. Both she and Natasha were dressed now, lacking only the headdress and makeup.

"Oh, my dear little goose," Tamara said, when they were more or less alone. "You're a greenhand in this world. So far the prince has played your little game because it's amused him—"

Natasha shook herself free of Tamara's hand. "My little game? What do you mean?"

Tamara's voice was low and urgent, but above all reasonable. "You've led him on, Natasha. Led him to believe that he has hope. You've never said 'Yes,' but you've never said 'No.' But once you tell him *definitely* that you've no intention . . ." Tamara shuddered dramatically. Natasha was both amused and alarmed, amused because Tamara's acting was so overdone, alarmed because she felt trapped. She realized that Tamara had secretly been weakening —if not destroying—her character. Her reputation was in danger.

Tamara's next words filled her with horror. "Don't you realize how insignificant you are?" she asked. "How unimportant? When such a great man takes an interest in you, wishes to protect you, it is *dangerous* to refuse him."

"Dangerous? What do you mean?"

Natasha stared at Tamara. The older girl gestured with impatience. "You've been a dancer at the opera for almost two seasons now, and you still don't understand. How can you be so naïve? I've tried, God knows, to preserve you from the worst. Believe me, if the prince had done his own wooing . . . that harsh, brutal old man!"

Natasha could only stare, bewildered, horrified. She caught her breath, unable to keep the tremor from her voice. "*You* have tried to protect *me?*"

"Yes, I have. Oh, Natasha, are you such a baby still? Don't you realize the harm this man can do if you reject him finally?"

"No. What can he do?"

"He can make sure you never work in the imperial theatres again."

Natasha stood very quietly, stunned into immobility. "But I am under the tzar's protection," she said quietly. "I am an official of His Majesty—"

"Oh, what does that signify?" Tamara cried, her face ugly with contempt. "So we're civil servants—very lowly civil servants—on the lowest rung of the imperial ladder. But he is a member of one of Russia's richest and most powerful families. He's a friend of the Grand Duke Nicholas. The tzar himself depends on the grand duke."

Natasha, who had been about to move away, paused, remembering. The intendant had said, "He is a friend of the Grand Duke Nicholas. He wields a considerable influence in certain circles."

Tamara felt a swelling of triumph as she detected a trembling in Natasha's hands, a look of fear in her glistening eyes. They widened with fear for a moment, then with bright sparkling anger. Natasha asked, a thin note of defiance in her voice, "Do you mean that the only way I can remain a dancer—or advance in my profession—is to become some great man's whore?"

"Well, not his whore," Tamara said.

"His *what*, then?"

"Well, his mistress. There is a difference."

"I can't see it," Natasha said contemptuously. "Both give themselves for money . . . or favors."

"There is a difference."

"Then there must a very shabby line between them."

Tamara bridled, her irritation breaking through her control. She stared at Natasha with hard fierce eyes. "My dear girl, the line between a dancer and a whore is a shabby one, yes, even in such a noble establishment as this. Do you think a dancer can live on a pittance from the tzar? From the occasional royal gift? All the girls here take a protector. They have to. Haven't you seen that for yourself?"

"Yes, of course I have!" Natasha said. "I've just never associated it with me, that's all. I had thought one had a choice in the matter."

Tamara laughed mirthlessly. "A choice! It's a miracle you've escaped thus far." She stared at Natasha with no softening of her expression. Her eyes were accusing. "Are you still a virgin?" she asked crudely.

Natasha flinched. "Yes. Is that so abnormal?"

"In this world, yes. You're extraordinary to have survived for so long."

"I am twenty-one years old," Natasha said softly.

"I was seventeen and a half when I learned my first 'lesson,'" Tamara replied, without evident emotion.

Natasha stood by the door, staring at the floor. All around her the dancers began to make their way to the stage. A page ran past calling the time.

"Well, Natasha Ivanovna, do you understand me now?" Tamara asked.

Natasha nodded, then her head came up sharply. She said disdainfully, "All the same, I'm not for the prince. You must tell him so, since you are our 'go-between.'"

Tamara started, newly alarmed. "You're prepared to risk your career?" she asked, her voice hoarse with incredulity.

"Yes," Natasha replied simply.

"You must be mad!"

"Perhaps I am!" Natasha laughed softly. She looked calm and certain. Tamara regarded her more closely—why had she not noticed it before? There was a quality about Natasha that was quite different from her normal dreaming way. She seemed caught up in some profound mystery of her own. Only a woman in love could be so indifferent to her fate. . . . Surely?

"You *have* a lover!" Tamara said accusingly.

Natasha stopped laughing. She looked serious, peaceful and strong. "Yes," she said quietly. "I am in love."

Relief poured through Tamara's mind. She was reprieved!

The prince had a flesh-and-blood rival. This was a factor over which she had no control. She could make out a new case in her own defense. She could show that she had been as much "La Puritana's" dupe as he had been. Natasha had proved herself utterly deceitful. She had kept this affair hidden from the entire corps.

She must find out who this man was. Let the prince vent his rage on the rival. She knew a dark happiness. She was safe! Deprived of a reward, but safe. And Natasha was ruined. One can never predict a man's forgiveness, but one can always predict the extent of his rage. Especially that of a vain old dandy who still believed himself, at sixty-three, to possess the seductive powers of a man half his age.

After she had been with one of her "old men," Tamara would return home to her young lover, Simya, a waiter. Her ritual was always the same. First she would immerse herself in soothing, lime-scented water, soaking away the memory of flabby flesh, of blotched and wrinkled skin, of goatish embraces. This was followed by a brisk rubbing down with a warm towel, until her flesh glowed and found its own life again. But this was not enough to exorcise her disgust. She needed Simya's clean young body, his smooth-limbed strength, his primitive animal heat. Only then could she feel truly cleansed.

As usual, Simya took her with astonishing passion, tumbling her beneath him, kissing, sucking, licking, biting and scratching, raking her flesh with his nails. A hot struggle of arms and legs, Simya was goaded on by the thought of the man who had covered her that night.

Tamara cried out all the time, a litany of hate for the old fool who had enjoyed her lithe young body. Her words whipped Simya whenever his efforts flagged. They never failed to arouse him. The barrack-room sentiments seemed as natural to him as endearments. The more he responded to her, the more furiously she countered his attacks, shouting encouragement, moaning with pleasure, groaning with pain. As she rolled beneath his hard agile body, he rose and plunged, forcing himself ever deeper into her, filling her, blotting out memory, bringing her to a shuddering, tumultuous climax. . . .

Later, as she relaxed, cushioned on his lean muscular arms, Tamara said sleepily, "'La Puritana' has taken a lover at last." Simya yawned, staring at her stupidly with his wine-colored eyes. "Verchinin?"

She laughed maliciously. "No. An Englishman. He met her weeks ago. She went with him tonight. He's with the embassy. A nobody—the little fool!"

"What will happen?"

Tamara yawned indifferently. "What can happen? She'll enjoy 'love' for a while. Then he'll tire of her and drop her. She'll be no trouble after that. They never are, once they've been disillusioned."

"But what about Verchinin? What will he do?"

"He'll take his revenge on them both, I shouldn't wonder." She laughed, and Simya winced. He hated the grating texture of her laughter, it set his teeth on edge. "She couldn't have played into my hands better," Tamara said unexpectedly. "She's made an enemy of a very powerful man."

Simya looked uneasy. "And you?" he asked.

"Me? What about me?"

"You promised him . . ."

Tamara stretched contentedly in Simya's arms. "Oh, he won't blame me, his friend. I've done my best for him, he knows that. 'La Puritana' is a sly little minx."

Simya still looked uneasy. "I don't know why you have to play your little games," he said.

Tamara looked toward her dressing table, on which stood a silver-gilt jewel box. "I shan't be young forever," she said. "A dancer's life is shorter than most. Mine will be, anyway. I'll never enter the Imperial Company. Unlike . . ." She checked herself, eyeing Simya slyly. "I don't intend dying in the poorhouse."

"But the games you play," Simya said unhappily, "they're so . . . reckless."

"Nonsense! There's no risk at all." She yawned, her hands stroking his smooth dark skin affectionately, calming him.

"But how can she have played into your hands if she's jilted the prince?" Simya asked, trembling like a thoroughbred beneath her hands. Tamara's face was suddenly unnaturally cold and expressionless. The hairs on Simya's neck stirred. She looked alarming, merciless.

"I hate her," she said quietly. "She's not like the others—fawning, weak creatures. She has a spine, belief in herself—her *destiny*." She shook with fury. "Well, she's ruined her chances. The prince might not have been able to get her *into* the Imperial Company—but, by God! he can keep her *out* of it!"

"Tamara," Simya said, "you're jealous of her!"

She turned to him, snuggling deep into his arms, pressing herself against him feverishly. "Again!" she whispered. "No more talk!"

Her body danced beneath his quick drilling flesh. She answered his violence with heaving flanks, ecstatic eyes and sobs of blissful anguish. But this time Simya was dimly aware that the phantom he was meant to drive away was not the obscene body of an elderly lover, but the light dancing figure of a young girl. "La Puritana" must have some extraordinary quality to have aroused this depth of hatred in Tamara.

CHAPTER
SEVEN

Scavronsky stood by a sleigh drawn by two magnificent Orlov horses. The countryside was warmed into life with the sparkle of new snow. The air was cushioned against noise, the voices from the ice hill were softened. For today, at least, winter was benign.

In the distance the ice hill gleamed in the sunlight—twenty feet high and three feet wide, steeply graded. It was erected on a wooden structure, the oblong of ice falling sheer to the ground. Bright figures in painted toboggans slid down the glittering surface with such force that they continued their course for many yards once they had reached level ground.

One sledge came toward him now, light and low, with upturned front. In it sat Richard, with Natasha before him, enclosed in his arms. The sledge came to a halt before Scavronsky, Richard leaning from his seat at a perilous angle to prevent their overturning.

Richard and Natasha looked up at the count, laughing.

Their faces burned in the stinging air. They both wore
shapeless bearskin coats, their feet wrapped in soft skin
boots.

They clambered awkwardly from the toboggan, gasping,
warming their tingling cheeks with their gloves. Natasha tilted
her head against Richard's chest, the bobble of her squirrel-
skin cap tickling his chin. He smoothed it away with a laugh,
and leaned down to kiss the narrow strip of skin above her
fine eyebrows. She raised her lips to his.

Scavronsky shook his head doubtfully, watching them. The
girl was a beauty—and different. She was no light whore.
What he saw in her eyes was true, each gaze was a caress, a
reflection of what he saw in Richard's eyes. He felt a stab of
jealousy. The girl was genuinely in love.

"Did you enjoy your tobogganing?" he asked.

They both nodded enthusiastically.

"Were you afraid, Natalia Ivanovna?"

Natasha shook her head. "Not once! Richard was marvelous. I could have carried a baby on my head!" She gazed up
at Richard with admiration. Richard kissed her again.

"Come," the count said, "we must go."

Richard tied the toboggan to the back of Scavronsky's
sleigh, then lifted Natasha into the fur-lined interior. They
fell clumsily against each other as, with a crack of the whip,
the sleigh lurched forward and then sped, swaying, over the
snow.

Scavronsky let the horses have their head. Behind him, the
lovers fell silent. The count clucked ruminatively at his
horses' ears. He felt strangely troubled. It was a love match.
There was no disguising that. She was as wild with desire for
him as he for her. Though he thought they were not yet
lovers. There was still an odd restraint in their attitude toward
each other. Although they kissed often, it was as though each
kiss was in the nature of an exploration. A foretaste . . . He
had the feeling that Richard was in some way *afraid* of the
pleasure that he knew their bodies could share. He was
reluctant to raid that storehouse of pleasure.

Inexplicable behavior . . . the count knew Richard to be
very experienced with women. Not a "lady's man" as he
himself was, but a lover of women. Yet, for some reason, with
"La Puritana" he was holding himself back. Whoever saw
such delicacy? If he, Scavronsky, had netted such a beauty,
he wouldn't spend his time in savoring the possibilities!

Yet Richard behaved as though he had an eternity in which

to bed the girl. He was *serious*. It had to be admitted, this girl
was different. She might look and talk like an ordinary
ballet-girl at times, but at others she had the look of a saint, a
mystic. . . . There was something of the true aristocrat in her,
too.

He glanced back. Natasha leaned out of the sleigh, watching the silent landscape, her face touched lightly by the winter
sun. She was dreamy-eyed. A princess, the count thought,
descended from Tartar kings. There are women at court who
would give a fortune to have her style.

Scavronsky felt uneasy. This affair seemed to be turning
into something quite out of the ordinary, deep and intense.
Well, he hoped, once the Englishman had bedded the girl, he
would soon tire. A serious relationship between them was
totally out of the question and doomed to failure. Even a
relationship with a woman of good birth would be difficult for
an Englishman in Russia at this time, but with an inferior—
impossible.

Did Richard understand that? He must. Even their own
friendship caused raised eyebrows in certain quarters. The
Britishers in Petersburg were a class apart. Except for their
official duties, they mixed almost entirely with their own kind.

Richard had been a great exception, for he was fluent in
five languages, curious about life outside the narrow diplomatic rut. He had a truly Russian ability to "get out of
himself." His fellow diplomats were like prisoners in their
comfortable cells.

But if he should seriously involve himself with a ballet-girl?
The ballet was such a strange world—a world within a world,
a jeweled box within an iron safe, part temple, part government office, part brothel—the private possession of the tzar.
A serious relationship with such a girl was as unlikely as an
affair with a Romanov princess. Richard should be warned.

Behind him, the lovers laughed softly together. The movement of the sleigh had thrown them once more into each
other's arms. Scavronsky shrugged and smiled. Later. He
would warn Richard later. No doubt matters would change
once she had surrendered—and that could not be far off.

When Natasha walked into the dressing room that night,
Marie Antonova burst into tears. Over the past few weeks
Marie and Natasha had grown quite close. They had taken
rooms together.

She looked at Natasha with fear in her eyes.

Natasha's beauty seemed to have ripened over the past few days. She moved with slow grace to her place at the long communal table. Her eyes looked deep and dark, heavy with remembered happiness. She loosened her hair, letting it cloud about her shoulders, and went through the motions of undressing. She seemed unconscious of the small crowd of dancers, who stared at her with malicious inquiry. One or two had seen her arrive in Scavronsky's sleigh.

Then Marie burst into tears again. Tamara snapped at her, "Be quiet, goose!" and Marie shrank at her voice. She dried her tears and tried to mend the ravages to her makeup. Marie's tears returned Natasha to her present surroundings. She saw that the other dancers were already dressed and waiting. She hurried into her costume. To Marie, she appeared to awaken from some pleasant dream.

These moments of dressing for the performance had always been the keenest pleasure to Natasha, watching the metamorphosis in the mirror as she put on her costume. Tonight she was dancing the leading Hindu maiden in the ballet of *L'Africaine*. There was the hint of a sari in the folds of her bodice; it was made of magenta silk with an embroidered collar of mother-of-pearl. The sleeves were of flesh-colored moire silk with bands of silver braid. Her green skirt was embroidered with peacock's eyes.

The wardrobe mistress came fussing to see if anything needed stitching, complaining loudly that Natasha was far behind the others. It made Natasha nervous. "I don't need you!" she snapped, and the woman went away grumbling. But the moment she had walked through the door, Natasha realized that the waist of her bodice was torn. It was too late to call her back. It would only mean more harsh words.

By the time she had placed the headdress of gold wire and pearls over her hair, all the girls had left. She stood arranging her veil. Looking up, she saw Marie enter furtively, her stiff skirt rustling. Marie's face was pale and drawn, anxiety was etched deep by the flaring light of the gas jets. She burst into tears again. Natasha looked up from outlining her eyes.

"Masha, darling, what is it?"

Marie fell against the dressing table, weeping. The curtain bell rang and a voice in the corridor called places. Five minutes to curtain. "Where have you been?" Marie stuttered. "They are going to report you for being late."

"I'm not late."

Natasha made frantic attempts to finish her makeup.

Marie's own face was a blotchy mess where the mascara had run into the whitening. "They hate you!" Marie cried. "Tamara Fyodorovna hates you! They know who your lover is—they're all talking about it. They're saying terrible things about you!"

Natasha's heart was fluttering inside her breast, but she went on trying to outline her eyes. From above, she heard the opening chords of the music.

"Holy saints, Masha, wipe your eyes," she said. "Powder your nose. We must go!"

"But you don't understand—"

"Let them talk! What do I care?"

Marie stared at her, red-nosed, shiny-eyed. "Natasha, I really love you!" she cried. "You mustn't throw yourself away on such a man—such a nobody!"

"What?" Natasha turned from peering into the mirror. She stared fiercely at Marie.

"Everybody is laughing at you," Marie went on, blushing and stammering, "because you have such an unimportant lover. . . ."

Natasha was caught in a pose of frozen surprise. She was dimly aware that the music was leading up to the tenor's aria, which preceded the ballet.

Marie struggled to find the right words. "You mustn't throw yourself away."

"I haven't."

"You mean that you haven't given yourself to him?" Marie's doll-like face lit up with relief.

"No, I haven't given myself to him. Not in that way . . . yet."

Marie caught her breath. "You are going to?"

"Yes." Natasha looked suddenly fierce, almost savage. She jumped up from the table, dusting away the loose powder.

"Masha, come, we're late. We shall be punished."

"*You* will be punished," Marie echoed.

Natasha stopped at the door, rigid with shock. Then she turned and ran back across the room. She clutched Marie's shoulder, so hard that the girl cried out. "Whatever my life is going to be," Natasha said passionately, "*he* is going to be my first lover."

"You're in *love* with him?"

"We're in love with each other, Masha."

Marie laughed uncertainly. "But it will do you great harm!"

Natasha's gray eyes smoldered. "I don't care! I would rather have Richka than anything on earth. Whatever happens after, I *will* have him, not some old man who'll—"

"But you'll suffer for it!"

"Then I'll suffer for it."

A boy knocked at the door. He looked in, flushed and grinning. "Places. Places, please."

The two girls hurried from the dressing room, and along the corridor leading to the stairs. Marie panted behind, trying to restore her makeup as she ran.

"You've set everybody against you, Natasha," she gasped. "All the girls are against you. Tamara says—"

"Mesdemoiselles!" The ballet-mistress came quickly toward them from her position in the prompt corner, her black skirt rustling. She looked at them with venomous eyes. The other girls were already in position in the second wing. They gaped with delighted malice at Natasha's humiliation.

"You know the rules, mesdemoiselles," the ballet-mistress hissed. "Position to be taken two minutes after the last call."

On stage, the tenor was ending his aria. The ballet that followed celebrated Hindu marriage rites. The girls danced into the limelight, Natasha followed on Oleg's arm. He was dressed in crimson silk and silver lace, a gorgeous headband on his dark curly hair.

"You're going to catch it," he said, with a wink. "You'll have a neck as long as my arm if you don't watch out!"

Natasha hardly heard him, she was barely aware of him. She felt terribly isolated on the vast stage, facing the blue and silver auditorium. She was blind to the tropical beauty of the scene, she could hardly tell stage right from stage left. She was unable to lose herself in the dance. She did everything with precision, but her dancing was mechanical, soulless. She could not even respond to the music, which she loved.

Oleg sensed her despair, it seemed to have paralyzed her spirit. He did his best to set her off to advantage, and she found herself resenting his efforts. His strong hands, firmly at her waist, were gently offensive. For the first time ever, she hated the casual way her partner's hands made free of her body.

This was an adagio, a love duet, the highlight of the ballet. She was in love, she was loved. She should be able to project these feelings into her dancing. Yet she felt so stiff and unnatural, so heavy. It was ironic that at this supreme moment in her life she was unable to breathe the spirit of love into the conventional gestures.

When Oleg came to hold her high in the final lift, she could feel his whole body trembling from the effort of raising her dead weight. She herself vibrated like a tuning fork. When he set her gently down, his face was covered in sweat from the effort of holding her still.

Once again Natasha faced the intendant across his ormolu desk. The ballet-mistress stood by his side, her face sharp with disapproval. She had told her story. The intendant had listened to her, regarding Natasha wearily. He appeared totally uninterested. It was no new story, just one more backstage intrigue.

". . . It is a question of discipline, intendant," the ballet-mistress said. "Petrova has grown very careless recently— never on time for class or performance. Then, too, she has twice broken the rule about outdoor exercise, violent exercise. She has been seen tobogganing at the *English* Yacht Club."

A pale glow stained Natasha's cheeks, as much from anger that she should be spied upon as from shame. Now she was really in trouble! She looked desperately toward the corner where an icon hung high up, an oil lamp burning in front of it. She breathed a silent prayer.

"Such behavior warrants a severe discipline," the ballet-mistress said, "perhaps a short suspension."

The intendant regarded Natasha coldly. "I have no need to ask if this is true, Petrova. I can see only too plainly that it is."

He rose abruptly and came around the desk. He stood looking down at Natasha, and she gazed back in some confusion. The light pouring through the long windows touched her dark hair with a net of light. Her eyes glinted with unshed tears. She waited for sentence to be passed. Not a muscle moved in the intendant's face as he looked at her. He was genuinely puzzled. What was the meaning of this extraordinary insubordination? The girl had always been so serious, so dedicated. She was betraying her talent. He must decide. Yet it was almost in him to pity her. He felt a little jealous of the handsome young foreigner who had stolen her away from her first love—dancing.

His voice rang like crystal as he said, "You will be fined three rubles, Petrova, and are suspended for the next five performances."

Natasha, although she was appalled by the enormity of the fine—it was a third of one week's wage—bowed her head, recognizing the inevitability of the punishment. She supposed it fair. She had broken the rules, and she had been warned.

The intendant dismissed the two women. But, as they reached the door, he called out for Natasha to return. When the door had closed behind the ballet-mistress, he reseated himself. "Sit down, please," he said quietly.

Natasha was startled by his tone. Why had he called her back? Did he mean to add to her punishment, or had he—please God!—changed his mind?

"Thank you, sir," she said, sinking back into the chair.

He looked at her directly and she was amazed at the compassion in his eyes. "My dear Natalia Ivanovna," he said, hesitantly at first. "I implore you—if you value your work here—do be more discreet in your private affairs. You are extremely young and inexperienced. There will be many men who want your . . . acquaintance—rich men, men of great social position, young sometimes, handsome even. But you must consider your reputation carefully. Many men will offer you their 'protection,' but you must examine not only the nature of their protection, but also the strength of it. If you must accept the protection of an admirer—and, sadly, most of our artists do—then choose such protection as will *last* and aid you in your career."

Natasha was completely bemused by this advice. It seemed a direct contrast to their last encounter.

The intendant stammered on, searching for the right words. "My dear Natalia Ivanovna, believe me, I am full of the most profound sympathy for you, for all our young ladies. It is a great wrong that an art subsidized by our beloved emperor should give rise to . . . should be morally suspect. . . ."

He talked on. Natasha listened in perplexed silence, completely baffled by his advice. What did the behavior of the other girls have to do with her? What did their sordid, commercial relationships have in common with her own marvelous feelings for Richard? How could he compare their squalid embraces with the raptures she felt in her lover's arms? Their paid-for kisses with those exchanged for love? What could this dried-up stick of a man remember of the sweet agony of desire?

". . . this young man," the intendant was saying, "the Englishman. You must consider him carefully, my dear. Ask

yourself, what can he give you of *lasting* value? Compared to
that of, say, the sincere affection of such a man as . . ." He
could not bring himself to pronounce the name. ". . . a
genuine lover of our art," he finished lamely.

Verchinin's name hung unspoken in the air. Natasha sat up
very straight, still and wary. The intendant went on, "Such a
man could offer you a future . . ."

Natasha felt cold with shame for the man before her.

"Believe me, I speak for your own good. Your relationship
with the Englishman—however exciting—cannot possibly
last. For one thing, his term of duty here will end, perhaps
quite soon. He could always be recalled. Who will care for
you then?"

He looked at her, and paused. The girl did not seem to be
listening to him. Her face was closed against him.

"Have you understood me?" he asked.

She nodded. "Oh, yes, sir." She was scarcely able to keep
her voice from trembling with distaste. "I've understood you
very well, and I thank you. You have been very kind." She
recognized that in an ugly way he had been trying to be kind.

"I've done no more than my duty," he said.

Natasha nodded again. "Yes, I understand that," she said.
"And you think I have forgotten mine." She laughed, her
voice fluting. "Well, yes, for a time I did. It's true. I've made
mistakes. You were right to discipline me for them. And I
shall try harder in the future." Her brow was delicately
furrowed with the effort to explain. "It's been so strange for
me, you see. Dancing was my whole life before, it absorbed
me completely. For ten years I've lived like a nun in a
convent, a woman in purdah, unaware of any life outside the
walls of the school or the theatre. It's a special kind of
slavery. I was an indulged slave, and happy to be. But . . ."

Her lids shaded her eyes, her lips were touched with the
shadow of a smile. Her face had a soft, enclosed look. "How
can I explain? How can I make you understand? I thought
that I was happy, that dancing was fulfillment enough. But,
now, something more has been released in me, something I
never expected. It's as though I've been harboring a second
soul—imprisoning it inside me—and now it has burst its
bonds, carrying me away with it. I'm loved, I love."

Her face was softly voluptuous, very pale. "How could I
deny such a gift?" she asked simply.

The intendant had been both embarrassed and moved by

her confession. "You must not let your feelings steer you away from your duty," he said.

"Have I only one life to lead?" she asked.

"You have only one duty," he replied. "To obey the rules and to dance to the best of your ability."

"Isn't it possible for love to make me a better dancer?" she asked.

"Yes, love can make you a better artist," the intendant said. "But you must still give thought to your future."

She smiled. "Ah, yes. The future."

"There is a future still, you know," the intendant said, with something of his old asperity. "The present will not last beyond the moment."

"Then I must be happy while I can," she said, with devastating simplicity.

The intendant smiled sadly. "Happiness can be a great luxury, Natalia Ivanovna."

She laughed again. "Then I must indulge myself while I can!" She grew serious. "It is the only luxury I need, m'sieur. I know how things are managed, but I shall manage in my own way."

"If you can," the intendant said.

"I'm not really interested in the things that other girls want," she said. "I want different things."

"And the Englishman can give them to you?"

She laughed again, softly, assuredly. "He has already, sir."

He recognized her expression—a woman remembering her lover's embraces. He sighed, recognizing defeat, and rose abruptly from his desk. "That will be all," he said formally, looking disappointed. He made a short stabbing gesture of dismissal and Natasha rose thankfully, glad to escape from the room. But his words had penetrated her defenses. She recognized the veiled threat behind the kindly "advice." She felt acutely anxious, even alarmed.

CHAPTER

EIGHT

Richard lived in a small apartment in a tall blue granite house near the Summer Garden. Natasha had not yet been there. She climbed the long staircase to his door, after finding his name on the panel listing the tenants. She knocked on his door, breathless with excitement. She had scarcely noticed the long climb.

The door opened and a manservant gazed out at her from the dark hallway. She saw at once that he was not Russian and spoke to him in French. The man regarded her with stolid curiosity and invited her inside. From his expression it was hard to tell whether he considered her a "lady" or not.

She had dressed, with exacting care, in a princess-style promenade dress of gray poplin with cuffs and yokes of ultramarine. The close-fitting line of the dress was smooth over breast and hips, the draped material of the skirt carefully massed at the back and caught up with bright blue bows. She had swept up her dark hair at the sides, leaving it to fall in ringlets at the neck. One hand was buried deep in a fur muff, a furred cloak hung from her shoulders; she had not worn the hood. Her cheeks glowed from the stinging cold and from her inner agitation.

"*Par ici, madame,*" the servant said.

They walked down the gleaming parquet floor of the hall and the man showed her into a small sitting room. It was a dark room, with heavily embossed wallpaper, indefinably foreign to her eyes and yet strangely familiar. There was a red upholstered sofa and twin armchairs, with a grand piano. Pictures of landscapes and hunting scenes hung in large gilt frames. A birch-log fire crackled cheerfully in the fireplace.

What made it unfamiliar to her were the incidentals. There were family portraits and daguerreotypes in heavy silver frames. Here was a hidden side of Richard, his "sporting" side—rows of silver cups stood on the mantelshelf and sideboard, awarded for polo and riding. There were regimental drawings, mementos of his days in India. There were English magazines, sporting and social. The room smelled of tobacco, polish and a light clean scent.

She felt suddenly uneasy. It was the world of a different man than the one she knew, not simply the rich leisured grandness of it, but the foreign grandness of it. How little she truly knew of him. He had been absorbed into her world, and she knew nothing of his.

She found herself staring at one of the portraits, of a beautiful woman dressed in a white ball gown with rosebud trimming, her creamy shoulders rising from a froth of lace. The portrait had been painted in the sixties, her crinoline was fashionably huge. Another portrait that caught her eye was of a man in evening dress, a black tailcoat, black satin waistcoat and snowy linen. He was almost a mirror-image of Richard. At first, until she noticed the old-fashioned cut of his clothes, she had thought it was her Richard.

A sort of despair seized her as she gazed at the portraits, faces from his past, faces of privilege, faces from a distance. The social gulf between herself and Richard was so wide, so impossible to bridge. For a moment she was tempted to turn and run from the room.

Then the door opened, and Richard stood before her, startled to see her standing at his table, examining his personal effects. They stared at each other in silence for a moment. Then he strode toward her and wrapped her in his arms. She stood there, stiff and unresponsive, evading his eyes when he looked down at her.

"What is it?" he asked.

She turned away. "I am so ashamed!" She gasped out the words, catching her breath. He stared at her with deep concern.

"They are all so . . . *dirty*," she said. "They would try to dirty us."

Without exactly being able to identify the cause, Richard felt a terrible emptiness inside him, and then a gnawing dread. "You've been forbidden to see me," he said.

She turned to him. "No. Not exactly. Not directly. I've been warned against seeing you, that's all." She clenched her hands together. He held them tenderly, offering her consolation through his touch. She looked pale, wretched, deeply ashamed. Although they stood so close together, he felt the gap had widened between them. He tried to find the words to reach her, but all sense seemed to have left him.

"It's so unjust!" Natasha cried. "It's not their *business!* I do my work properly, I obey their orders in the theatre. I truly believe in the ballet. I'm not . . . not like the others. Yet they make it seem as if . . . as if I'm . . ."

She turned away from him again, her eyes filled with pain and longing. She could not conceal the chaos within her. "I know you, Richka," she said, forgetting how alien he had seemed to her only moments before. The strength and vigor of his presence dispelled such doubts. "You wouldn't harm me, I know that. . . ."

His hand enfolded hers, now grasping her fingers roughly. She winced with pain. He caught her against him. Fiercely, she put her arms around him. The tears still glimmered beneath her eyelids, but they did not fall. She touched his face, as though memorizing every line and contour—the feel of his skin, the crisply curling hair, the stiff bristle of his fair moustache. Her eyes, her touch, gave him the impression that she was saying farewell. She looked to be drawing him, the very essence of him, into her memory.

But she was not saying good-bye. "We've got to be together!" she cried. "To be apart would be such a waste!" She clung to him. "I shall take no notice of them. We must go where our instincts lead us. Why should we give each other up?" Her fingers twisted into his. "They shan't separate us!"

Richard kissed her then. Their bodies swayed together, two promised bodies moving together with the inevitability of waves that must break on each other. Natasha drooped against him. His arms went about her and she leaned into his embrace, whispering, "I love you so much."

"And I love you." His voice was unnaturally low. He felt stifled by the weight of his emotion.

He pressed his lips to hers again, her lips parting softly beneath his. The familiar shock of pleasure ran through his body. He caught up her hands, kissing them fervently. He wanted her. God, how he wanted her! Longing was a continual pain in him. He had contained his soul in patience for just this moment, and now she was offering herself to him. But she was surrendering to him out of her own pain and humiliation, and he had not wanted that. It was not how he had imagined things.

"What is it, Richka?"

He sighed, struggling for words. She stared into his face, as though she would read his mind. "You mustn't be afraid for me," she said, divining his thoughts more clearly than he did himself. "It's what I want, truly want. . . ."

She pressed her body urgently against him. There was nothing but the touch of her lips beneath his and the feel of her body trembling against him. He held all the girls of paradise in his arms.

"Natasha, my dearest Natashenka . . ."

Shocked, humbled, grateful, tormented—and then inescapably caught up in her reckless mood—his arms tightened about her. Lifting her, he strode across the room to lay her gently upon the red velvet sofa. She lay there, calmly beautiful, eyes closed, at once receptive and mysterious.

Strength moved through his blood. His hands went to the collar of her gown, unbuttoning it quickly, almost tearing the buttons from the cloth in his haste. Raising herself, Natasha helped him to ease the skin-fitting bodice from her body.

As he uncovered her, Richard had the impression that his eyes were forming her—the proud smooth breasts of ivory, tipped with rose; her firm white arms, gracefully curved; a smooth straight belly and strong slender waist; her legs like two white columns, their dancer's strength softened by the gentle flickering of the lamp.

Freed of her clothes, she lay beside him, panting slightly, with glistening lips and half-closed eyes. Smoky hair darkened the tops of her thighs.

Their bodies came together. She relaxed, pale and yielding, without fear, apparently, but still with a trace of shyness. He kissed her throat and she began to tremble violently. His fingers, strong and skillful, skimmed over her flesh. His mouth sought hers, his arms cradled her.

She felt curiously protected within the shelter of his arms and yet strangely vulnerable, feeling fragile and helpless against his lean hard bulk. She was not unused to the near naked male body; backstage it had always been taken casually. Neither was she unused to a man's hands on her limbs. But on stage or in the rehearsal room, the body was no more than a divine machine; in the intensity of the dance the maleness of her partners had been forgotten. But Richard's nakedness was without disguise; he was as naked as the first man. The lamplight gilded his body, spilling over his wide shoulders and narrow hips, brightening the golden hairs on his long sinewy legs, revealing the thickening shaft of his manhood.

His nakedness aroused in her mixed feelings of sensuality and fear. The length of his body against hers made her experience her own more intensely. There seemed to be a thousand secret places on her body whose existence she had never suspected. A breeze seemed to pass over her skin, and her flesh sprang spontaneously to life, stirring into self-perception. She clenched her legs together against the spasms that shook her. Her hips rose, as though seeking a consummation in the air. Her whole body rippled with pleasure.

Richard cupped each breast in his hands, bending over to kiss the silken skin that swelled at his touch. She shivered. His lips found the rosy tips of her nipples. Currents of sheer ecstasy charged through her mind and body continually. Mind and body. It was impossible to distinguish one from the other. They were both and neither.

She stretched like a cat as Richard's hands passed down her body, over the curve of her raised hips, slipping between her thighs. Her body straightened as his fingers touched the soft lips. His muscles tightened, hers were stretched. Then her body weakened and slackened.

"Don't be afraid," he whispered.

She shook her head, beyond words, caught up in the mystery of the moment. Her entire happiness appeared to depend upon the hand that seemed to be gently dividing the two halves of her being. She grew warm and moist, spreading herself to his hand.

He poised himself above her, holding her helplessly wide beneath him, aiming his taut body between her thighs. Of its own volition, her body rose to meet his. Her legs encircled him, drawing him down and in. . . .

Pain shattered her pleasure. Pain that seemed to break her body. She was engulfed with terror, suffocated by it. The odd thought that she had been physically damaged, that she would never dance again, flashed into her mind.

Was any pleasure worth purchasing with such agony? His swollen flesh inside her was monstrous, enormous, terrifying, unnatural. Her whole being felt invaded. She struggled beneath him, trying to make him feel her pain.

He sensed her anguish. His face, looking down, was

shattered with pity for her. For a time his striking loins were idle. He appeared to withdraw a little. The pain became less, almost bearable.

She relaxed, or tried to, resisting him less. His hands were at her breasts, stroking her nipples. Pleasure, which had vanished, returned a little, still mingled with pain. Then pleasure grew more noticeable, becoming intense. She was sinking into blackness, then swimming upward into soft clear light. A swirling softness. The pain had changed in some subtle way. . . .

Her flesh shook and quivered beneath his skillful hands. The pain dissolved into warm dark joy—a pure and faultless joy. She gave herself over to it. Her body began to move in time with his, drawing him deeper and closer, feeling his flesh as part of her.

They made love throughout the long winter afternoon, until the yellow fog of light at the window had faded to blackness and the lamp glowed like a beacon in the gloom. Natasha felt an exquisite languor overwhelm her. She lay savoring the tender ache that still lingered in her loins.

Beyond their mutual longing, their need for each other, beyond the suffering that he had inflicted on her at first, they both felt the sensation of a strange new emotion rise in them, a height of joy that neither of them would ever forget, or possibly ever experience again with such power and clarity. "They shan't separate us," Natasha murmured as she drifted into sleep, her head pressed into the fold of his arm.

CHAPTER

NINE

There was an unpleasant duty to be faced, Tamara told herself. She could avoid it no longer. The game was over. The light-hearted intrigue had turned into a bad dream. There were problems to be owned up to—they could be put aside no longer.

She had told herself that the prince could not possibly blame her, but she remained unconvinced by her own arguments. When it came to the moment, Verchinin would react like a wounded beast; wounded in that most delicate of places—his vanity.

She burned with resentment against men, particularly against rich and powerful men, the "old men." As often as one tried to use them, they turned the tables. One was no more than an exotic flower in their buttonhole, a showpiece to be flaunted on their arms, but in reality of less value to them than the medals on their chests.

As her carriage drew up outside Cubat's Restaurant, Tamara nerved herself to meet the prince. Unless she managed this very cleverly, it could mean complete humiliation. She had a distinct impression of a curtain falling forever as she walked through the door into the brilliantly lighted vestibule. She had chosen to break the news to him in such a public place in the hope that an audience would help him keep his temper within bounds. Faint hope, she thought, as she passed up the stairs between the lines of flunkeys. She regretted her decision. The prince was too sure of his place in the world to care about the proprieties. She should have asked for a private room. If he was to unleash that fearsome temper on her in public, all Petersburg would be laughing at her.

She tried to remain calm. He must not guess at the fear that swelled inside her. She held herself very erect, breathing slowly and deeply, returning the contemptuous stares of the flunkeys with an impassive gaze.

She looked beautiful, she knew that, and she looked right. She had taken great pains with her appearance, dressing herself as though for some role, striving to look elegant but not ostentatious. Tonight was not the best time to remind the prince that she had made a fortune from such men as he. Her dinner dress of green satin and mauve ribbed silk had ruffles at neck and hem. The neckline was deep and square, showing the white depth of her bosom, but otherwise the gown was modesty itself. The color set off her flaxen hair—hair that looked almost powdered. Her sole piece of jewelry was the plain gold chain that carried her baptismal cross. The cross was tucked between her breasts. Her throat was slashed with a velvet neck band of deep purple. She had made no errors with her appearance.

The prince was waiting for her at the top of the stairs. With one look at his face she knew the worst had happened. His face was beef-red with temper. His hands shook.

Without a word of greeting, he grabbed her by the arm and pulled her into the ballroom. Her flesh was pinched between his fingers, but she was too afraid to cry out.

"Look!" the prince ordered.

At first she was unable to see, the light in the ballroom was so dazzling. The room was crowded, the dancers turning gaily before her.

Then she saw them. They were at the very center of the room, although they could have been on some distant planet. Both of them were lost to the world, conscious only of the insistent beat of the music and their own rhythm as they turned and dipped in the waltz. The Englishman was taller than any man present, fine and handsome in immaculate evening black, his fair hair brushed back from his forehead, gleaming like a burnished helmet. Natasha was in a pale rose satin gown trimmed with silk ribbon, rose pleated tulle and lace. She wore a rose in her hair, a silver-tipped rose of silk.

Tamara's thoughts were scattered. She vaguely recognized the dress as belonging to Marie Antonova. Both of them looked transformed. The girl had never looked so beautiful—

starlike, radiant. Their faces were withdrawn and dreamy. Unaccountably, beyond the panic that consumed her mind, Tamara felt a swift burning spasm of jealousy. They were so intimate, so remote, so locked into each other.

The prince moved impatiently at her side. She forced herself to turn to him, dreading to see the expression in his eyes. When she did so, she was amazed at what she saw there. His eyes were not blazing with anger as they had been. Now they were without a spark of life or feeling. She shrank from him as his hand tightened around her wrist again.

"Come!" He led her to a table in the restaurant. Waiters came running, aware that the prince was in a temper, anxious to accommodate him.

Verchinin insisted on a table well away from the ballroom. He sat on his gilt chair, as still as a corpse, staring blindly at Tamara across the silver and crystal. "Well?" he asked, as she remained silent, paralytic with dread. He waved a waiter away. "Well, Tamara Fyodorovna, I'm waiting. Explain yourself." He gestured arrogantly toward the ballroom. "Tell me about *them.*"

It had been easier than she imagined once she got under way. The expected storm had not broken over her. Rather, he had remained cold, almost indifferent.

When she had finished, he looked up, snapping his fingers for the waiter. "Bring my carriage."

The waiter hurried away.

"Come with me," Verchinin ordered Tamara.

He took her to the Dom Restaurant. She had not dared to refuse, though the Dom was forbidden territory to any self-respecting woman. It was a cheap dive, the haunt of chorus girls and gypsies. No gentleman would ever expect a state dancer to accompany him there. Ordinarily no dancer would have gone with him.

But Tamara was still too terrified to refuse the prince. His cold grimness, his air of freezing implacability, deprived her of will. She was dimly aware that he meant to revenge himself upon *her* in some way. She was to be humiliated in order that his self-esteem might be restored. Well, if this was the only way to manage it, so be it. Let him heap humiliation on her if that would be an end to the matter.

So she had gone along with him. Coming out of the arctic night, they plunged into an immense and overheated room. Tropical plants spread among the guests. small jungle patches among the tables. Fountains splashed into basins. A Hungarian orchestra played on a raised platform. Tamara regarded them with interest, despite her fear that deadened all sensation. All the performers were women, very pretty and very young. They were dressed in frogged waistcoats, white skirts and soft leather boots of scarlet and yellow. They played a medley of gypsy songs.

The head waiter hurried up to the prince, greeting him obsequiously. "Such a long time, excellency, since you last honored us. . . ."

The prince refused a table in the restaurant, instead he demanded a private room. The waiter bowed low, eyeing Tamara with veiled insolence. Tamara scarcely noticed as she gazed about her with stupefaction. Gypsy dancers in vivid shawls, gold glittering at ears and throat, sat among the customers, as exotic as the greenery. Their strident laughter filled the air.

The private room was furnished with a dining table, Louis Quinze chairs, a velvet sofa and a piano draped with a fringed shawl. Four Tartar waiters converged on them, fawning over the prince.

Verchinin put his top hat on the table and ordered iced champagne. When the waiter had withdrawn the cork, Verchinin threw it into the hat. The waiters grinned. It was going to be that kind of night. The prince intended getting drunk. Tamara relaxed a little. The prince was going to drink himself into a stupor, that was how he would cope with his anger.

Disappointment seemed to give his appetite an edge. He munched his way through fresh caviar, liver *au madère*, sterlets, chicken Kiev . . . washing it down with bumpers of champagne. By the end of the meal three corks were in the hat.

Over dessert, he called for a group of singers with their balalaikas. Russian songs gave way to gypsy choruses, and girls with the dark faces of wild creatures slipped into the room. Verchinin knew them all. Tamara, who had recovered something of her usual nerve, examined them with interest. They were not ordinary whores. Their jewels were huge, their diamonds glittered with an authentic light.

Behind the girls came three musicians, dressed in red silk tunics. Next came the soloist, a large women with moist black eyes. She placed a glass of champagne on an upturned plate and advanced upon Tamara, breaking into a drinking song. Her small mouth was as dark as wet cherries.

"Empty the glass," Verchinin ordered.

He was already drunk, waistcoat unbottoned, tie adrift, his eyes were unnaturally bright, cruelly bright.

Tamara drank, and drank again, as song followed song. The corks were thrown into the hat. Foolishly, she had scarcely touched the food set down before her. Now the wine went directly to her head. The singers' harsh voices brought easy tears to her eyes. Sadness, alternating with wild gaiety, engulfed her. Her moods changed with each song.

"Never mind," the prince murmured drunkenly. "Never mind . . ."

Tamara was reassured. He appeared to be taking things well, with true Russian stoicism. Bottle after bottle of champagne—for singers and guests—followed one another onto the table. The top hat was a quarter full.

Tamara was drunk. Drunk with relief, light-headed with it. Poetically intoxicated. Drunk, drunk, drunk! The singers were her friends. She would never leave them. Poor Verchinin was no monster to be feared, but a poor brute to be pitied. Oh, how she pitied him! The gaudy finery of the gypsies fascinated her. That diamond must be worth three hundred rubles, surely?

She beat time with her hands on the table and no longer heard what was being said. Then, suddenly, she was alone with the prince. . . . She could not understand why she was lying naked on a sofa, her blond disheveled hair flying about her face, wet strands in her mouth. The ceiling spun dizzily above her, the crystal on the table danced, every light showed an unsteady ring of radiance.

Then she became aware of the fleshy body of the gypsy singer, as naked as she, wearing nothing but her jewels. Two enormous paps swung above her head, dark skin and mulberry-colored nipples. Her own body gleamed by comparison —firm, young, outlined in fairness. The tiny rosebuds of her breasts a delicate contrast to the dark pulpy nipples of the other woman.

She tried to focus her eyes. Tamara wrinkled her nose with disgust. The woman's body reeked of a dozen interblended stenches. The feel of the body, too, was nauseating, soft and obese, and full of folds. Soft arms held her fast—they were surprisingly strong, or else she was unnaturally weakened by drink.

She became aware of another presence. Male hands, thick and white, speckled with age, slid along the satin skin of her inner thigh. They reached the fork of her legs, probing brutally at the opening of her body. Then Verchinin reared slightly, bringing his body to the level of her eyes.

Tamara stared dully at the vast belly, the tangle of wiry gray hair, the flabbily swelling length of his member, the shaft veined with purple . . . she lay there, helpless, in the suffocating embrace of the singer. Verchinin straddled her, directing his shaft toward her mouth. His hands clutched at her hair, pulling at it savagely. Her mouth opened in a silent scream. Then his immense body blotted out the light.

His great warm beard brushed her parted thighs, his mouth chewed gently at her outer lips, his tongue plying busily. . . .

She lay beneath him, smothered by his sweating belly, choked with his engorged flesh, fighting back her nausea— bestially placid, accepting all. This was to be her punishment. The price she had to pay to regain his favor.

Later she found herself, dressed, wrapped in furs, in complete darkness in a snowy landscape. She was alone in a sleigh. Her ordeal was over. As far as she could remember she had pleased the old man.

She felt uneasy still, and strangely dissatisfied. His lust had been temporarily dealt with, but would that be the end of it? She shivered, remembering his eyes—cool and aloof, touched with mockery. Surely he would not let things rest? He would want to revenge himself more adequately.

She prayed to God that he would want nothing more from *her*.

CHAPTER
TEN

The tyranny of winter was over, the grip of ice and snow loosened. The dull gray blanket of cloud was at last stripped back from the sky, revealing a clear deep blue. Along the boulevards the trees burst into leaf overnight, a pale immature green. St. Petersburg was full of the scent of lilac and the smell of the awakened sea. Spring was a cascade once it began. Everything came in a rush. The sunny streets were bright with people. Winter garments—furs and padded jerkins—were cast aside.

The ballet season was almost over. Natasha looked forward to a brief respite from the theatre. Since her interview with the intendant she had conformed to the rules, never putting a step wrong, on or off the stage. But there was an atmosphere.

She bought two new gowns, using money she could ill afford, but eager to please her lover, wanting him to be proud of her. She looked beautiful and elegant in them, as though she had stepped from the fashion pages, yet she had dressed herself with less money than a fashionable beauty spent on her coiffure.

It was typical of Richard that he should at once realize her sacrifice and try to set things right. It led to their first disagreement.

One day as they walked among the fine oak trees of the park, Richard said to her, "Darling, I want to do something for you."

From his tone she half guessed what was to follow, yet she still felt shocked when he said that he wished to make her an allowance.

"Why?" she asked.

78

"Because I know that your salary is not enough," he replied. "I can't ask you to spend money you can't afford just so that I might not be socially embarrassed."

He gestured at her new dress. It was of silk, the color of wild honey, with looped up draperies fringed with bronze trimming. She wore it with a bonnet of yellow silk and a light yellow shawl. "I don't know what that creation cost you, darling," Richard said, "but I hate to think of the meals you've gone without in order to buy it."

"I needed the gown," she murmured, toying with the handle of her green watered-silk parasol. "Please don't let's speak of it."

They wandered along the verdant paths. From beyond a clump of trees came the sound of a military band. The air resounded with music and laughter. The promenade was crowded with elegant strollers. Richard, himself, was fashionably at ease in a light tweed suit with braided edges. He wore a black bowler hat and carried a cane.

"I must speak of it," he said. "The fact is that I want you to be beautifully dressed, and I don't want you to go supperless. After all, sweetheart, it's *my* vanity that you'll be gratifying! I want us to live a social life together, and I don't want you to feel dowdy or uncomfortable among better-dressed women just because you're too proud to accept an allowance—"

"Well, I can understand your concern," Natasha said. "And I don't want you to be ashamed of me."

"I could never be ashamed of you," Richard protested. "I'm proud of you. You perform miracles on a pittance. But I don't want you to have to make needless sacrifices."

Natasha laughed gently, her fingers stroking his arm. "I shan't," she said. "But I can't accept an allowance."

"But why not?"

"Because . . ." She looked away, downcast. "Because it will make me . . . like them," she said. "And I don't want that."

She looked up into his face, her cheeks flushed, her eyes shining with unshed tears. "Let me go on performing the miracles, Richard. They won't be too hard to manage, I promise you. I'm not a great lady, or a *grande cocotte*. I shan't be expected to live beyond my means. I don't want people to think you 'keep' me. I want them to know there's no price attached to me."

He began to protest again, but she cut him short. "The tzar is coming to the opera three more times before the season ends. So I shall be given three commemorative gifts. They don't mean anything to me, I can easily turn them into money, and I know a very reasonable little dressmaker—"

"But, Natasha, I *want* to give you things!"

She stopped, and buried her face against his chest. "Oh, Richka! Richka, my darling. You've already blessed me with so many gifts!" She touched his lips with the tips of her fingers. "Please, darling. Don't speak of it again. I can manage, and you *will* be proud of me."

Deprived of helping her in this way, Richard compensated by swamping her with gifts—a pair of gold earrings with gold filigree cords, a pair of crystal drop-earrings, a gold ring set with diamonds and rubies, a jeweled comb, lace fans, silk fans, lockets, cameos, a pearl necklace, three bracelets.

She responded to each present by making him a small gift in return. Although each of his gifts had made him dig deeper into his private funds, he knew that her own gifts were equally impoverishing for her. The knowledge baffled him, humbled him, and yet made him feel proud of her.

They went about the city together. It never occurred to Richard to be secretive. Afterward, he thought that love must have dulled his political sense in some way. He had no thought of danger—either to him or to her.

They would roam for hours through streets alive with color, or would wander along the embankment of the wide flowing Neva. They were mesmerized by the beauty of the city, dazed by their feelings for each other. Days drifted by.

On the days when they were both completely free, they would hire a carriage and drive out to Peterhof or Orienbaum to picnic in the woods by the sea, in the salt-rimmed air.

They would wander by the surf's edge on bright days, with the swift-dipping birds and sea-spray in the wind, the white waves breaking. They could see sails across the Gulf of Finland. Gulls, sandhills, shadow and sun. The sea was waiting, ceaselessly breaking.

They walked, arms linked, through the woods. Richard began to teach Natasha to speak English, and she to teach him peasant songs, primitive, sentimental, highly melodious songs. She had a soft sweet voice of great purity.

She never ceased to surprise him. Although not "educated," her head was filled with poetry and folklore. She

could quote whole passages of Shakespeare and Pushkin.
Richard loved to listen to her reciting. He loved the sensuous
beauty of the language, its haunting sadness.

The days grew longer, spreading into the "white nights" of
St. Petersburg—the nights when crowds flocked to watch the
sun set in the Gulf of Finland and rise almost at once again in
the east—long, endless days. . . .

Or endless nights, the nights spent in his bed. Their
lovemaking was as exhilarating as dancing to Natasha. An
adagio, sensual and harmonious, the line of her body joined
with his, forming a whole. Both of them moving to the same
marvelous inner music, music that bore them up, in harmony
with Time. Their hands, exploring each other's body, untied
the knots of day. They were in touch with the gods. . . .

Only one thing marred Natasha's happiness—her life at the
theatre. She seemed to live in total isolation there.

Two incidents, in particular, distressed her. The first
seemed an omen. It occurred during a performance. The
dance itself had been exhilarating, a small but perfect pas de
deux in which she was partnered by Oleg. Her body had
responded completely to the music, she felt it within her, she
pulsed to the beat, each movement flowing, one into the
other. She was borne up by the sound that rose from the
orchestra pit. She had reacted effortlessly to the slightest
pressure of Oleg's hands as he supported her in a series of
dazzling pirouettes until she came slowly and smoothly to
rest, like a top that had exhausted its momentum.

Then, to her horror, when she had returned to the wings,
she had found blood on her costume—streaks of red at the
waist, drops scattered like scarlet tears on the billowing
muslin of her yellow skirt. The bodice of her costume was
heavily spangled—the glittering gold discs had cut into Oleg's
hands, drawing blood.

She had crossed herself, making the sign against the "eye."
The other dancers, seeing the blood, had crossed themselves
as devoutly. It was an omen. The atmosphere backstage
seemed suddenly heavy, the darkened wings charged with
foreboding. It was hours before Natasha could shake off the
feeling of impending sorrow.

The second episode came three days later. She was deprived of her solo in the ballet of the skaters in *Le Prophète*.
At the last minute it was snatched away from her. No reason

was given. A brief notice appeared on the callboard. Her attempts to discover why she had been replaced were ignored. The doors of the intendant's office were closed to her.

Natasha was upset. But, more than that, she was apprehensive. She seemed threatened by some terrible menace. There was a tenseness about her backstage life that left her feeling stirred and restless, yet exhausted.

The night she should have danced, she stood in the background, unable to watch her replacement dance alone on the front of the great stage. The scene of the frozen lake was brilliant, light exposed every corner mercilessly. Natasha's eyes misted with tears, though she felt anger more than sorrow. The dancer, through her tears, seemed insubstantial, almost disembodied. Natasha followed all her movements in her mind, rather than seeing them in reality.

To a spinning tune, the dancer glided about the stage, simulating the movements of a skater. Swooping, gliding, fast and fleet, turning rapidly on her partner's arm. The dance was mostly on point, the steps quite hard technically, little quick jumps from one foot to the other, beating steps, a ceaseless spinning motion.

It was an agony to have to stand still, holding a pose in the background while her supplanter went through the movements so carefully, so painstakingly rehearsed.

Natasha was aware of the motionless group of dancers around her. Did she imagine it, or where they more interested in watching her distress than in watching the restlessly turning soloist? She blinked the tears from her eyes furiously, her head coming up defiantly.

She could see Tamara standing just before her, rigidly staring into the auditorium, dangerously feline, sinister in the stage lights. She was dressed like Natasha in a deep blue ballet skirt edged with white fur, a gold belt circling her slim waist. Tamara, alone of all the rest, appeared totally unmoved by Natasha's fall from favor.

If only there were shadows to hide in, but the light spread into every corner. She stood out like a cardboard silhouette, each feature revealed, her only cover the deep gauze hood of her Flemish headdress. Thank God that Richard was not in the audience tonight. He would wonder at her sudden replacement. She had been so proud of the new solo, so eager and excited. It was a blessing after all that he had been forced to attend some boring reception. If she could only keep herself out of range of the opera glasses she could perhaps pretend that she had been unable to dance that night—some slight injury. . . .

The dance ended to scattered applause. Her agony was over.

That night, as she stretched languorously on Richard's bed, pale and brooding, she considered the possibility of telling him the truth. Could it be that the directorate were showing their displeasure in their relationship by denying her the new role? She could think of no other reason; her behavior at the theatre had been impeccable. But even as she opened her mouth to tell him, he reached down and kissed her gently. His hands, moving over her shoulders to her breasts, scattered her thoughts. Affected by his strength, his virility, the firm globes of her breasts cupped in his hands, the nipples stiffening quickly beneath his skillful touch, she was silenced.

Afterward, he felt that she had been in a strange mood that not even their lovemaking had been able to disperse. He had the feeling that she had been about to confide in him. The room was still and silent, save for her restless stirring at his side.

What had she been about to say? Nothing, or she would have said it after. It couldn't have been important. She had been upset, poor darling. It was a dammed shame that she had been unable to dance that night. It had meant so much to her. He had really not understood her explanation—one of those boring muscular ailments dancers were so prone to.

"I cannot see you," Natasha said a few days later. "I must keep the Fast."

She smiled at his bewilderment. "I must keep the Paschal Fast, Richka. Through Passion Week." She clung to him. "My dear, you've made me forget. I've ignored the Great Fast for almost the whole of Lent, but I must make myself ready for the Festival." She looked at him with curiosity. "Don't you have to prepare yourself for the Great Feast?" she asked.

"Yes. But not as rigorously as you do," Richard said, feeling strangely uneasy.

"Yes, it's hard for a Russian," Natasha said, smiling. "It's no light business."

Richard's feeling of uneasiness grew. During the past few weeks he felt that he had grown to know Natasha, had begun to think that their differences were fewer than the things they had in common. But here—with religion—the common ground between them might come to an end. He knew how religion intruded upon every aspect of life to the devout Russian.

Now he felt a sudden qualm at her need to attend the Easter Feast, to make confession. Could it drive some sort of wedge between them? He gazed at her blindly. He could almost smell the waves of incense rising between them

Seeing his uneasiness, and to some extent understanding it, Natasha raised her lips to his and kissed him tenderly.

"I shan't take the veil, darling," she said, laughing. "But I *have* to take part. It's different for you Westerners. You can worship God alone. We Russians need others to share our joy."

It was true, he knew from past experience. Being gathered together in the church was the greatest state of blessedness to a Russian.

Her next words took him by surprise.

"Why don't you join me in the Feast?"

"Go to your church, do you mean?"

"Yes. . . . Well, not inside. I like best to stand outside the church, to watch the priests when they come to search for the vanished Christ." She laughed softly. "Often I think He will appear to us there—really come among us again—rather than show Himself in the church. . . ." She gazed at him, completely carried away by her feelings. "*You* don't need to be prepared," she said. "But I would like to share it with you."

The thought of their sharing this experience together caused Richard the most intense personal joy. "Yes, I'll go with you, darling," he said, "willingly."

She threw herself into his arms. "Oh, I'm so glad! So glad!" Her face was radiant. "You'll never regret it, Richka!" She laughed. "It might even convert you. For when you've tasted something so sweet as our Holy Russian Church, you'll never accept the bitter again. . . ."

The service began two hours before midnight on Easter Saturday. Richard, who had shared Natasha's fast for the whole of Passion Week, felt rather light-headed as he took his place beside her outside the church.

They stood in the darkness, in the midst of a dense crowd. In the church, a choir sang in a minor key, low and subdued. The atmosphere was one of tense expectancy.

Then, just before midnight, the priests marched in procession around the outside of the church, searching for the vanished Christ, hesitating to believe in His Resurrection, like the apostles. They stopped before the church door, which had been closed to them, to symbolize the stopped mouth of the tomb.

Richard felt Natasha stiffen at his side. Then, as though by magic, hundreds of candles flared in the darkness. The banners and icons carried by priests glowed in the light. The doors of the church were thrown open and, in a burst of gold and candlelight, to the triumphantly swelling voices of the choir, the priests entered the church to chant the Easter hymns. Then the doors closed again behind them, to be flung open upon the stroke of midnight. A priest appeared on the threshold, proclaiming loudly and distinctly, "Christ is risen!"

The whole congregation roared in reply, "He is risen indeed!" The atmosphere was full of a joyous solemnity. The stone had been rolled away from the tomb and the faithful were experiencing the Resurrection once again. Even Richard felt something of this—it explained something of Natasha to him. He felt drunk with emotion. How far removed it was from the cold devotions of his own people. He was seduced by the beauty of the ritual, moved by an almost unbearable longing.

The bells of St. Petersburg rang out above the city. All around him people were greeting each other with the three-fold kiss, accompanied by the cry "Christ is risen!" "He is risen indeed!" None could refuse this sign of Christian love.

Richard looked down at Natasha, shaken by her rapt expression as she exchanged greetings with those around her. He was deeply moved by the realization that, in some mysterious way, this ceremony had brought them closer together. Her involvement in it was something that he could never know for himself, yet he felt something of her emotion. He had been able to enter into the companionship she felt with others.

Natasha turned to him with a radiant smile. He took her arm as they edged their way through the still ecstatic crowd. "Everything is forgiven!" she said, clutching his arm.

Richard felt both bewildered and relieved by this remark. She was closer to him than before—in some mysterious way she had been liberated.

Afterward, he talked it over with the count.

Scavronsky laughed at his bewilderment. "My dear Englishman! She is not a cold-blooded *Anglican*, but a true believer in our sweet Russian Church. She is an ordinary sinful creature. Even the worst of us can be touched by the Divine—through the sacraments, of course!"

"Do you mean that *taking part* is more important than anything else?"

"Exactly."

"But why did she need to confess?"

Scavronsky laughed again, but observed Richard keenly. "How else could she have been restored to the fold? We must all confess to our *common* sins—and yours, *cher ami,* is a common sin—if we are to be restored to the fold." He grew very serious. "It is very important for us Russians to belong to the fold, you know. A Russian who is not an Orthodox is unthinkable. To say Orthodox is to say Russian. We cannot visualize life without the ceremonies of the Church. Your little dancer would be very unhappy without the consolations of the Church."

His words seemed to Richard to be more in the nature of a warning than an explanation.

CHAPTER
ELEVEN

Richard was never sure at which point he became aware that they were being watched. It was a gradual realization that broke gently into the dream of his days.

At first he thought that he was imagining it. It was little more than a sensation of eyes fixed upon him continuously; odd glimpses of the same head lowered too quickly when he turned around. But once he was alerted and began to single out the "shadows," he soon learned that it was real enough.

There were, in fact, two men. One was tall and slender, with pale features. The other was short and stocky. But both were shadowy sorts of men, neither shabby nor smart in appearance, with nothing about either of them that would make one remember them. This, no doubt, qualified them for the job, Richard thought. But why were they being followed? And by whom?

He soon realized that their attendants only pursued them when he was with Natasha. Alone, he went unobserved. So they were following *her*.

St. Petersburg detectives were an easy joke in the British embassy. "One can always recognize a plainclothesman here," it was said, "because their plainclothes are so *uniform*. Pea-green overcoats and galoshes in all weathers, old chap."

Well, neither of these men wore such a uniform. They wore stout cloth suits with steel buttons. They looked like domestic servants. But they were unmistakably detectives.

Fear gripped him—not for himself, but for Natasha. Reality broke in on him. He had, by his relationship with Natasha, somehow compromised her with the authorities. It was only too obvious. Moving in the enclosed, secure, neutral world of the diplomatic service, it was fatally easy to forget temporarily that Russia was a police state. He had exposed Natasha to danger of some kind.

Lord Loftus offered Richard a cigar. They were sitting together in the ambassador's study. It was a splendid room; not even the heavy, ugly, modern furniture could entirely destroy its marvelous harmony.

Richard realized that Lord Loftus was trying to put him at his ease, but it only increased his disquiet. The dull, cold, froglike eyes of Queen Victoria regarded him with animosity from her portrait on the wall. The same kind of disapproval showed in the ambassador's eyes, though he did his best to keep the conversation on a man-to-man—even a friend-to-friend—basis.

Richard inhaled deeply, drawing the aromatic smoke down into his lungs, trying to relax. ". . . These men were set to spy on us," he said. "Not me, individually, but on the two of us. There's no doubt of that in my mind."

"But my dear Richard, what else can you expect? These are very trying times. Very. You understand the situation here as well as any man. The horse is running away with the rider. There are some very black storm clouds massing on the horizon. Everybody—but everybody, my dear fellow—is suspect."

Richard sat up stiffly. "I can't see how my relationship with Miss Petrova is affected by the political situation, sir. We've been quite open about it. . . ."

"You would appear to have been remarkably indiscreet, actually," the ambassador said mildly.

"That apart, what have she and I to do with the Turks butchering a mob of Bulgarian peasants?"

The ambassador looked away, partly to hide his annoyance, partly to hide his embarrassment. "Aren't you being rather naïve, old chap?" he asked, frowning.

"No," Richard answered. "As I've said before, our relationship is completely open."

The ambassador did not reply directly. He blew a perfect smoke spiral from his cigar. "It's a damnably critical situation," he said finally. "We're on the brink of war, man. The first officers of the Russian army have arrived in Dalmatia, on Austrian territory. The Russian government has started to supply the rebels with money and provisions. And arms. Without this help the insurrection against the Turks would have collapsed long ago. Officially, Russia is seeking peace with Turkey. Unofficially, she's inciting war. The situation couldn't be worse. But you know all this as well as I do."

"Yes," Richard said, as stubbornly as before. "And, I repeat, it has nothing to do with my relationship with Miss Petrova."

"But you must see, Richard, that in one sense Great Britain is already at war with Russia over the Turkish problem. It's only a matter of signing declarations. In many respects the embassy staff can be seen as enemies. Your . . . friend . . . is seen to be consorting with the enemy."

Richard sat puffing slowly on his cigar.

"So you must see," the ambassador went on when he made no reply, "you must appreciate that not only is your liaison creating a difficulty for you—and, therefore, the embassy—it is, perhaps, making life difficult for . . . ah . . . Miss Petrova."

Richard extinguished his cigar. It had suddenly lost its flavor. "Love, sir, is not a crime against the state," he said morosely.

"It may well be in some circumstances," the ambassador replied sharply. "There are enough instances in history."

"I had not thought us so important," Richard said.

"Neither, I'm sure, did any of the others," Lord Loftus

replied. He, too, appeared to have lost his taste for his Regalia. Putting the cigar away, he went on, "Quite simply, it's not politic for you to know this woman at this time. And don't you think that you should consider the possible risks and consequences to her? Isn't that important?"

Richard glowered into the empty fireplace, recognizing the hopeless truth in the ambassador's words, wondering at the narcotic power of love that it could so much have dulled his political sense. He should have been—no, he had been—aware of the dangers. He had deliberately buried his anxieties, blinding himself to the reality. He smiled grimly. For the past few weeks he had thought that he was smiling at the world. Actually, he had disdained it.

The ambassador pressed his point. "Despite her profession, I should think she is a simple girl at heart—tied to Russia completely, I'm sure, by birth, kinship, nature . . . Moreover, she's dependant upon her loyalty to the state for her position, her loyalty to the tzar certainly. The ballet is, after all, a minor branch of the civil service in this country. Her whole life is lived under the tzar's protection. The authorities here know how to repay disloyalty, or what they consider disloyalty. Would you subject her to that?"

He regarded Richard shrewdly. Richard looked up from his contemplation of the carpet, hollow-eyed, the fine bones of his face standing out in sharp relief.

"Is there any real danger?" he asked.

"There's every danger. Believe me, my dear fellow, your relationship has no future. For both your sakes, I should end it now."

Richard stared dolefully before him, his mind consumed by dread. The depth of his anguish took him by surprise. He was terribly, appallingly, aware of his need for Natasha, of the inescapability of his love for her. He was powerless to move in the matter, but he must. Decisions must be reached. They must separate—at least for a time. She must, at any rate, be told.

Could he voluntarily cut himself off from her now? . . . Could he cut off his own right arm? How radically his love for her had changed him. He didn't need Lord Loftus to tell him that he'd been remiss in his duty, lacking in political foresight. He had lost all taste for career matters, for society. Was it only ten short weeks ago that he'd been seeking to impress himself on Glaphira Kreuger, losing sleep for "love"? What a pitiful business that had been, heartless and artificial beside the lavish bounty of his love for Natasha, love that replenished him even as it exhausted him.

How boring, flat and conventional his life had been before meeting Natasha. How suspicious he had been of the unconventional, and how changed he was. Life had moved into a new dimension.

He sat before the ambassador, gloomily. Uncertainty gripped him. He tried to listen to Lord Loftus, but he could not follow the sense of the words. His lordship's attempts to advise and reassure him only served to increase his pain.

"Richard, there is something you should know," Scavronsky said, as they drove in his brightly painted phaeton along the Prospekt.

"Oh?"

"Yes. But please don't repeat what I tell you."

Richard said that he wouldn't, half knowing what he was about to be told.

"A few days ago I played cards with General Trepov," Scavronsky said. "He was very interested in you."

Richard was startled. Trepov was the chief of the gendarmerie. So far they had never met.

Scavronsky flashed a sharp inquiring glance at Richard. "He was very curious about your relationship with the ballet-girl. What's she called? 'La Puritana.' Though I suppose that epithet no longer applies to her now?" He flashed another inquiring look at Richard. ". . . It still continues?"

Richard nodded.

"Well, the general was very interested. He asked endless questions about you both."

The skin on Richard's scalp tightened. "What sort of questions?"

"Oh, the sort of questions such men ask, I suppose. Nothing that gave me any clue as to what he was after. 'How long have you known her?' 'How often did you meet?' That sort of thing."

Richard knew with a sickening certainty that Trepov had a pretty exact idea of how often he and Natasha met.

"Anyway, he certainly seemed to disapprove of your choice," Scavronsky said, turning smartly into Winter Palace Square. Military music sounded from far off, above the rumble of traffic—fifes and drums, a warlike march. It underlined Richard's feelings of increasing apprehension.

"Perhaps I'm wrong," the count said, negotiating a turn, "but I fancy the police may make difficulties for her, may be making them now."

Richard's heart palpitated gently. "She hasn't said," he muttered.

"Well, maybe I'm supposing too much, *mon cher*, but I think you should drop your little dancer, perhaps. For the time being, at least. For her sake as much as yours."

"Why?" Richard asked, his mouth dry. "Because of the political situation?"

Scavronsky jerked on the reins in surprise. The hooves of the horses skittered on the cobbles as they pulled to one side. Having brought them into line, the count turned to stare at Richard owlishly. "The political situation? Is that it, do you think? Do they suspect she is passing information to your embassy through you?" He frowned. ". . . No, it can't be that. I can think of other girls who might be suspected. They sleep with half the guard's corps. But not 'La Puritana.' She appears to sleep only with you. In fact, she seems quite tediously devoted to you, one never sees her in the usual places. If one thinks about it, that might be the reason for Trepov's interest in you."

Richard stared in amazement. "Trepov wants Natasha for himself?"

Scavronsky laughed. "Hardly, my dear Richard. The general loves only pain. . . . No, no, my dear friend. I think that you've thwarted some important man, between the two of you. A very important man. With a *long reach*. Word has descended from above. You are to be 'officially' separated, to make the way clear for the long-armed man."

They were in Senate Square, riding past the statue of Peter the Great, the bronze tzar, dressed in his Roman finery, forcing his mount to rear, on a rock, hurling defiance at the waters of the Neva, at the whole Russian nation.

Richard felt a terrible rage against the bronze figure. It seemed to personify the iron curb of Russian autocracy. So it had been officially decided that he and Natasha were to be separated. For a moment he felt defeated at the thought of fighting against such awful power. Then rage burned in him again. He would—he *must*—find some way to keep Natasha.

CHAPTER

TWELVE

There were a number of tables in the room, and four clerks to a table. They sat, tired and ill-tempered, their pens moving lethargically across piles of parchment. A pungent blue smoke from their innumerable cigarettes floated to the grimy windows.

A grandly dressed gendarme stood at the door, colossally intimidating. People passed him with an obsequious bow. The room was filled with a deafening clamor, the plaintive whining of the petitioners drowned by the shouting of the officials.

Natasha looked about her, feeling dazed. The letter commanding her attendance at the gendarmerie shook in her nervous fingers. What did it mean? Why had General Trepov sent for her?

A group of gendarmes hauled a man toward a door, brushing past her. The man's face was blank with terror. Natasha instinctively cowered away from him.

"Yes, miss?" A resplendent gendarme barred her way. Hastily, Natasha produced the letter and showed it to him.

"I have been asked to call. . . ."

The gendarme glowered at the paper, then straightened up, saluting. The letter had been signed by General Trepov personally. It was couched politely—the lady was clearly important. His attitude toward her changed completely. He cleared a way through the press of shabbily dressed people, opened a door and showed her into another office.

This office was much quieter than the reception hall. It was almost elegant in its gray institutional way, smelling strongly of beeswax-polish and disinfectant. The policeman knocked upon another door and handed Natasha over to another gendarme. He, in turn, passed her to another, and Natasha was passed through a series of rooms, each grander than the last, until she arrived at Trepov's office.

Her state of anxiety had grown with each succeeding transfer, each room had grown more awe-inspiring. She was totally intimidated by the size and splendor of the general's office. His desk stood at what seemed to be the end of a corridor of dark red carpet. By the time she stood before it, her legs trembled so fiercely that her skirt rippled like a sheet of water.

"Please sit down." The general's voice was low, courteous, unexpectedly gentle. Natasha sank gratefully into a French armchair of buttoned blue velvet.

She forced herself to look at the general. Fear clouded her vision. The general smiled at her, filling her with further confusion. He was a handsome man, with a yellow moustache and glittering blue eyes, a dandy in his immaculate green uniform. There was no sign in him of the brutal arrogance for which he was notorious.

Involuntarily, Natasha returned his smile. Her own felt unnaturally tight. Feeling slightly less nervous, she fixed her eyes on his face, respectfully attentive. After the tzar, this was, perhaps, the most powerful man in St. Petersburg.

Trepov continued to smile at her. His smiles came easily to him.

"Miss Petrova, you must be wondering why you have been invited here today—and I must apologize for any fears that you might have entertained. You must, on no account, regard yourself as being *under suspicion*. . . ."

Under suspicion? Fear mingled with increased bewilderment in Natasha's mind. What did he mean? She was still too intimidated to ask for an explanation.

". . . Though, of course," Trepov continued, "your recent behavior cannot be ignored. Your actions lack a certain . . . how shall I put it? . . . a certain 'propriety'?"

Natasha felt herself flushing. She knew at once to what he referred. Richard. At the same time her astonishment increased. What could her relationship with Richard Greville have to do with the chief of gendarmes?

Trepov regarded her glowing face with fixed attention. At the same time he looked mysteriously amused. "Miss Petrova, you are not a child. Did you suppose that your affair could remain a secret from the servants of the tzar? Not that you have ordered your affair with discretion—there has been more than a touch of showy display in your relationship with the Englishman."

From dusky red, Natasha's face was now blanched white. "I cannot see that I had anything to hide, excellency," she said, her voice little above a whisper.

The general's eyebrows rose quizzically. He twirled his yellow moustache, then leaned toward her. From where she sat across the desk, Natasha could smell the overpowering sweetness of his pomade, his perfumed body. There was something almost sinister in his fastidious cleanliness. His smell sickened her slightly.

He, in turn, was examining her closely. He seemed pleased with what he saw, though there was no hint of sexual interest in his gaze. He regarded her, rather, as though she was some beautiful specimen of butterfly. Natasha felt as if she had been stuck upon some giant pin.

She had taken some care with her appearance, thinking that it might matter. She had borrowed a brown walking costume from Marie, far grander than anything she owned. The skirt was of brown georgette trimmed with flounces of velvet, the jacket was brown silk that was also trimmed with velvet. Small gold buttons ran from neckline to waist, the skirt was looped up gracefully, and around her throat she wore a white tie of Brussels lace. On her head she wore a small black hat, bound around the brim with black silk. She looked, she knew, discreetly fashionable, but above all, respectable.

From the look on Trepov's face, she knew that he was evaluating her clothes. He was the sort of man, she felt, who could tell to a kopeck the price of her lace. She wondered if he guessed that she wore borrowed finery.

"Your relationship with this gentleman has aroused considerable displeasure at all levels," Trepov said, pressing his fingers together primly. "You have managed to alienate your fellow artists, your friends, admirers, superiors and . . ." he paused before saying emphatically, "certain members of the court."

He paused again, watching her face intently. "It is not, of course, simply that the gentleman is so far above you in station, but have you ever stopped to think of the *political* implications of your relationship?"

Natasha answered nervously that she had not. Nor did she now.

"Then I shall explain them to you. . . ." Trepov began to drum gently on the surface of his desk. Natasha found herself watching the tapping fingers; the drumming entered her mind, rhythmically underlining his words.

". . . Can you wonder that your relationship is found to be shocking?" Trepov asked, at the end of his explanation. "The man is English."

Natasha sat bemused. His clarification of the situation had passed over her head. What had the inevitability of war with Turkey to do with Richard and herself? Even if Great Britain sided with the Turks? They had never discussed politics. Only Trepov's suggestion that the British embassy itself was a possible link between her country's enemies had shaken her. For the first time she found herself wondering what Richard's duties were exactly, but the rest meant nothing to her.

"Well, Miss Petrova?" The general sat back, smiling at her in his meaningless way.

"I have done nothing to shame my country, excellency." Her voice sounded weak and unconvincing even to herself. "Unless falling in love with Richard Greville is an unpatriotic act."

Trepov sat up straight; the shadow of a frown crossed his face. "One does not expect a member of the ballet to take an interest in political matters," he said condescendingly, "but you must have been aware of these *side issues?*"

Natasha shook her head, feeling suddenly foolish. "No, sir."

Trepov's smile was tinged with disbelief. "Incredible," he murmured.

"But it's true!" Natasha protested, adding, "I've almost ceased to think of Richard as a . . . a foreigner."

"And now that you have been enlightened, do you still see nothing wrong with the relationship?"

Natasha hesitated, feeling more bewildered than ever. During Trepov's explanation she had seen Richard through new eyes. She had a glimmering of how others saw them both together, enabling her to understand something of the nature of their hostility. But then pictures of herself and Richard came into her mind, strong and clear. How intensely they had lived in these past few weeks, the world well lost. She supposed they had been thoughtless, reckless, extravagant, giving no thought for the future, caught up in the marvelous moment.

Trepov felt a stab of something approaching an emotion in his unromantic breast, seeing the slow droop of her eyelids, weighted with sweet secret memories. He leaned forward, and noticed that she shrank away from him slightly. It was a gesture he was accustomed to seeing, and it was a sight that always gave him pleasure—the twitch of fear, the turning away—it filled him with a magnificent surge of power.

But he knew how to curb that power when it was necessary. Choosing his next words carefully, when he spoke, his voice was honeyed, coaxing, seductive even. "Listen, Natalia Petrova. Listen to me carefully. It should be possible for us to understand each other. You are a woman of intelligence, and I—believe me—have your best interests at heart. . . ."

Natasha looked at the general, fascinated—the shallow blue eyes, the yellow moustache bristling above the delicate, well-shaped lips, the dead white hands. Was it true that this perfumed dandy had once almost whipped a prisoner to death?

She shivered slightly, and saw the gleam of pleasure in his eyes, an almost voluptuous look. In his way, the general was a sensualist.

"You must be aware of your duties to the state," Trepov went on, in his soft enticing voice. "We are all servants of the tzar, but you are a specially favored servant, an imperial *danseuse*. One day you will be a *soliste* of the Grand Ballet. I have heard as much said by your superiors. . . ."

Natasha stared at him. Was it true? And, whether it was true or not, where was he trying to lead her?

"Whatever your feelings for this man," Trepov said, "you must consider not only your future, but the future of your country." The white hands gestured expressively. Natasha felt mesmerized by them. His words dropped like a slow poison into her mind—". . . future of the country." Had he brought her to the gendarmerie to officially end her affair, to forbid her meeting Richard again?

Apparently not. He came to the point. "We shall not prohibit this liaison—for the moment, Natalia Ivanovna," he said. "You may continue to meet the Englishman."

Natasha caught her breath.

"But, in return, we shall require you to honor our confidence in you," Trepov said.

"Excellency?"

"Indeed, yes." His eyes held hers as he said with slow

deliberation, "You have a patriotic duty to use your relationship with this Englishman."

So that was it. They meant her to spy on Richard.

Trepov's manner underwent an astonishing change. Natasha had a chilling glimpse of the man of blood beneath the suave exterior.

"I see that you have understood me perfectly," he said.

Natasha nodded. "You mean to make use of me." She shrank back against the padded back of the chair.

"Exactly," Trepov said. "Your lover is a man who is *possibly* engaged in activities hostile to the interests of your country. The British embassy is a hotbed of intrigue, and Richard Greville may be at the very center of it."

"I don't believe that," Natasha whispered. Her hand went involuntarily to her mouth. The color ebbed from her face. Her body seemed to have grown unbearably heavy. "Mr. Greville is a man of honor."

"No doubt," Trepov said. "But he is an honorable *Englishman*. And you, Natalia Ivanovna, are a servant of the All-Russian Emperor."

Natasha trembled with an intense inner trembling. There was a silence, broken only by her breathing. Trepov regarded her with bright interested eyes, interested in the phenonomen of her fear, her confusion.

"What do you want of me?" Natasha asked. "How do you mean to use me?"

The girl was calmer now, he saw. She appeared to have regained her self-control remarkably quickly. He approved of that. Moreover, she seemed to understand the situation. Natasha listened with growing revulsion as Trepov outlined his plans for her.

". . . We are aware that Richard Greville, in the course of his duties, has interviewed many undesirable people at the embassy—common informers, double-dealers, trimmers, men of that ilk, and women, too."

Trepov smiled. His light words had struck Natasha like a lash—as intended. "All this activity has, so far, been reasonably open, but we have reason to believe that Greville is in contact with an altogether different level of scum. These he meets secretly. It's important that we learn something of these meetings. . . ."

He paused. Natasha managed to sit upright in her chair, her hands clutching the arms desperately, staring with mesmerized horror at the bland face before her. There was no movement in her, except for the rhythmic rise and fall of her breast.

". . . We may ask you to feed him information," Trepov said, "a snatch of intelligence dropped artlessly into the *conversations amoureuses.*"

Natasha forced herself to turn away. She wanted to cry out, to scream. She was filled with a conflict of emotions—fear, sorrow, an aching longing, a burning anger, disgust. These feelings swept through her mind incessantly, each pushing out the other violently, driving her thoughts in every direction. Her body felt chilled, and at the same time consumed by a terrible fire. Could it possibly be true? Was Richard an enemy of Russia? Her Richard, the Richard who had revealed so much of her own country to her? Aspects of Russia that she had never suspected? How could it be true? Richard took so much pleasure in her country. He loved Russia. He was Russian himself in so many ways. He had the Russian qualities, the broad nature of her people.

No, it couldn't possibly be true. Men like Trepov saw enemies in every corner. Images of Richard flooded her mind: Richard reciting Lermontov, explaining her own literature to her; Richard walking in the forest—he knew the creatures of the woods and fields as well as any peasant; his love of her language, the customs, the ordinary people. No, he couldn't be an enemy of her country.

Trepov was speaking again, reminding her of her duty, pointing out that their relationship could be seen as an act of disloyalty.

She shuddered, thinking of the labyrinth of rooms between herself and the outside world, remembering the look of stony terror on the face of the prisoner being dragged to . . . to where? The rooms below. She had heard tales of the rooms below.

The general was asking if she was willing to help them. She heard his voice dimly, as from a terrifying distance. She could make no reply. Her tongue felt too large for her mouth. She could only sit, staring rigidly before her.

Trepov smiled, taking her silence for consent, an indication of submission.

A few days later Natasha learned that she was to dance the leading role in the ballet in *Faust*, in a special performance.

The offer shook her out of her trancelike state. Clearly it was an inducement. They were telling her that she could be reinstated to official favor. It was an easy matter . . . if she was to provide them with the information they thought she could procure for them.

She was caught between loyalty to her own people, and loyalty toward her own feelings. Thank God she had not yet been challenged. It had been impossible to meet Richard for the past few days. He had gone on diplomatic business to Austria.

The days of rehearsal passed like a slow-moving dream. She performed her dances with unfailing precision, but mechanically. She felt incapable of thinking clearly on any matter. She felt injured in some way.

On the night of the performance she arrived at the Maryinsky more than an hour before the curtain rose, hoping that the atmosphere backstage would soak into her mind, ease her, revive her. She changed into her practice clothes and went through a class by herself at the back of the stage. Then she warmed up by herself, holding onto a chair for support as she did her *pliés* and *battements*.

Her new partner, Sergei Fomitch, came over to help her during her practice *pirouettes*. He was a thin, highly strung man, looking like a marvelous cat as he yawned and stretched himself into relaxation. He was a leading dancer with the ballet, loaned to the opera on this occasion, cool and distant. To Natasha, in her heightened state of nervousness, he appeared especially hostile. She missed Oleg's warmth and strength.

After the warm-up, Natasha washed and changed.

The dressing room had filled up, the other girls chattering and giggling together. The air was filled with their secret confidences, their malicious sallies, their brittle laughter.

Natasha scarcely noticed. She still felt stiff and cold. Only when she saw herself in the mirror, clothed in the brilliantly beaded bodice and tutu, did she begin to emerge from the dull apathy that held her bound. She felt that she was looking at a changed being—one who had no connection with the world beyond the great theatre curtain, the sordid outside world of lies and intrigue, blackmail and treachery.

Waiting in the wings, she turned her head to catch Tamara regarding her with spiteful amusement tinged with anger.

Natasha's body quivered with shock. Tamara believed she had submitted to the prince! Or why else would she have been restored to favor?

Then the truth broke in on her at last. By accepting the role, she had tacitly accepted their bribe, had conveyed her willingness to be used, her willingness to betray Richard. She burned with humiliation. Her instinct was to turn and flee. Only the dancers pressing around her, brilliant as tropical birds, kept her in her place.

Sergei led her onto the stage, and they took up position. Her music sounded, lilting and sweet. She went through the motions, but her body seemed to have been taken over by another soul. Was this Natasha Petrova dancing? Rising, falling, spinning? She had the impression of being outside herself, watching the other body as it moved nimbly to the sparkling tune, turning in the *pirouettes,* arms held open, one up, one down, the head tilted back. Arms together, *en couronne*, rising *en pointe*. Finishing with a *diagonale* of tripping steps, hands held at waist level before her, fingertips touching, and finally . . . coming to rest.

Who was this woman, this painted doll, head held high? This exotic-looking beauty with the tight-fixed smile, the brilliant eyes? Were those tears that glittered on her made-up face?

CHAPTER

THIRTEEN

Richard walked beside Natasha, feeling acutely miserable, so caught up in his own wretchedness that he failed to notice how cast down she herself was. They had driven out to the lake of Duderhof, near the imperial village of Krasnoe Selo. And now they wandered through the woods of silver birch and ash. Sunlight cut through the slim trunks in flat blades of light. In the distance, the waves of the lake glittered like a razor's edge.

Slowly, hesitating at every sentence, he had explained the situation to her, giving her the ambassador's version, but passing on Scavronsky's warning. When he had finished, she said nothing for a few minutes. She was, in fact, debating how much to tell him of her own version.

Her continuing silence disturbed him. He wondered how much she had understood. She walked with him, appearing to be unconscious of her surroundings, though she looked about her continually.

They had shared so many happy days here, beside the placid lake. Memories flashed into her mind, of Richard swimming from shore to shore, his naked body gleaming athletically in the clear water, of herself sitting in a dinghy, cool and sedate, of Richard rowing her into the middle of the lake, their sitting together hour after contented hour, patiently waiting for the fish to bite, then returning to the shore with their catch of perch, grilling it over a birch-twig fire. One day he had caught a one-and-a-half-pounder. He had been like a boy in his excitement over it. . . .

She could also remember their picnics together, setting off in a cart, laden with provisions and a samovar, wandering by the shore, gazing into its crystal depths, Richard, with binoculars, pointing out the wildlife of the lake and shore, Richard starting the charcoal under the samover, blowing on the flame, using a Russian boot as a bellows, in the traditional manner. And on the journey home they were spread comfortably on the sweet-scented hay that filled the cart.

Despite the heat of the day, the familiar sights seemed flat and chill. That remembered happiness was far off. The thread of happiness had snapped.

For a few cruel moments all hope was gone. She could think of nothing. It was as though she had passed into some cold dark tunnel. Then hope revived in her. It was like awakening from sleep, though Richard's voice was at first like a distant sound from across the lake.

". . . It's for you to decide, Natasha," he was saying. "You have to decide whether our happiness together is worth the risk. It's simple enough for me to say that we should enjoy to the full the little time we have together. For me, even the smallest, briefest moment is as vital as . . . my next breath. But it's not I who shall suffer if we go on seeing each other. The most they can demand of me is that I leave the country—though, God knows, that would be an agony, being separated from you. But it is you who could really suffer. And I've no right to ask you to make a sacrifice of yourself. . . ."

Natasha shaded her eyes against the slanting sunlight. The sun cut through the trees like a knife. "I think I could bear anything except the pain of being separated from you," she said.

He took her hand in his and held it to his lips, unable to speak. She smiled sadly. "How strange, Richka. I thought the only thing I ever truly loved was dancing. I thought no mere *man* would ever touch me, but now I know that I have no choice. If I have to decide between the ballet and you, I shall surrender the ballet. If I have to choose between my country and you—"

Richard looked at her, startled. Her hand went to her mouth. She had meant to say "career" and not "country". . . .

Then, abruptly, the words falling from her lips in hurried flurries, in an agitation of mind, she told him first of Verchinin, and then of the general and his proposal.

When it was told, they were both silent. There was no sound but the ripple of the lake water breaking on the shore. Natasha's smile grew tight and brave. Richard felt overwhelmed by the power of his emotions. He shook inwardly with jealous rage at the thought of Verchinin, and the account of her interview with Trepov filled him with cold dread, and a consuming sense of guilt that he should have exposed her to such a trial. He struggled to remain clearheaded.

He cradled her hand within his own. "Oh, my dearest," he said. "I've put you in the gravest danger. I can't accept your sacrifice. And it would be a sacrifice. They would destroy you. To go on seeing you would not be the act of a man of honor, let alone the act of a man in love. It would be the worst kind of selfishness. I must think of your future—"

She began to protest, but he silenced her with a kiss. They clung to each other, her head resting against his chest, his heart hammering in her ear.

His hands cupped her shining hair, almost reverently. "I've put you in danger, my dear soul Natashenka. And, God forgive me, I still don't want to put an end to—"

She raised her lips to his again, with a low moan of pain. "Don't speak of it," she whispered.

"I have to speak of it, " Richard said, drawing away from her, forcing himself from her side.

They had come to a small clearing. Between the trees stretched a carpet of wild anemones, delicate, white, six-pointed stars.

Natasha turned to Richard. "You are all my happiness," she said solemnly. Her huge pure eyes seemed to absorb him. "I never imagined that I could know such happiness. I would rather suffer as the result of loving you than not love you." Her foot crushed the edge of the flowery carpet. She drew back, hating to bruise the slender-stemmed flowers.

"If loving you is some sort of treason, then I'm a traitress," she said. "I can't live happily without you, Richka, I know that. It's also selfish in a way, but I would be unworthy of my feelings if I were to ignore them." She looked up into his face earnestly. "I'm not afraid, and you must not be afraid for me. I don't even ask you to think of me. I can stand alone, if need be. I've done so in the past, and I can do so in the future."

She had gathered up her courage and stood before him with eyes aglow. Her face was flushed. She had never looked so beautiful to him. Her spirit revived him. He felt humbled by her. How changed she was. It was impossible to remember her as the shy, remote, insensible girl he had first met at the ice ball. Love—which for him seemed hard, full of strange terrors and jealousy, which made him feel weak and even a little disordered—appeared to bring her nothing but strength and selflessness.

Her face was filled with a curious kind of peace. Even now, when she must be feeling the same currents of fear and despair that ran through him, her face was irradiated by a shining serenity, a sort of inner certainty. At the same time she had never looked so passionately, so vitally alive. Not for the first time since he had met her, Richard experienced an odd, unsettling sense of his own imperfection. He was faced with an almost unanswerable problem. They could be certain now that their relationship would bring increasing hardship. But could they be certain that their happiness together could outweigh their miseries? The love they felt for each other would make demands on them that he was not sure they could meet.

He felt that he was moving into a world in which he was a stranger. Too often in the past weeks he had taken their happiness for granted. Now he knew that their happiness together carried its own price.

One part of him said that it would be best to let go now, cause pain at this moment, but save Natasha from much worse to come. At least they should call a halt to their affair temporarily, until the political situation was less explosive.

But the lover in him, the part of him that could not bear the thought of separation from her, argued that he was exaggerating the risks. Surely he could devise some way of dealing with the situation? They should grasp at what they could, while they could.

What was the answer?

Natasha touched his arm gently. "Make love to me, Richka," she murmured. "I need you. I need you terribly."

They sank down into the long springing grass at the edge of the white spread of wood anemones. Desperation gave a sweet aching intensity to their lovemaking. She pressed herself into his arms as though seeking succor from his lean hard body, his arms a shield against the terrible fears that beset her.

The sun, striking through the pink silk of her parasol, dappled their bodies. Richard laid his tweed jacket aside, her shawl was spread beneath them. Soon her hair was loosed, her white lace collar was open, her light-boned bodice unhooked, the layers of white starched petticoats abandoned. Then she lay in Richard's arms, as naked and free as a wood nymph. He, too, was soon stripped. Their warm smooth bodies came together amid the heap of discarded clothing, buried deep amid the spring grass. The grass smelled warm and sweet, the mild fragrance of the wood anemones reached them, the creamy scent of wild orchids.

They came together with a violent urgency. For a moment her cheek was crushed against his breast and his heart hammered in her ear. Then he raised himself, her head was thrown back, resting on his arm. The brilliant white branches of the trees flashed in the sunlight, blinding her.

Then his body shadowed hers, his lips were on hers, bruising her mouth with the force of his passion. The whole length of his body covered hers, shuddering. He was murmuring distractedly in her ear, but she could not distinguish the words. She moaned gently. His lips moved over her face, gently nuzzling her ears, passing to the nape of her neck so that she cried aloud.

Her body moved to his touch. She had experienced nothing like this before. It was an attack of madness—ecstasy and total surrender. She was aware of him as both a separate body and as a part of herself.

With eyes closed, she was still alive to every individual part of his body—the strong chord of muscle between neck and shoulder, the bulging energy of his shoulders, the long hard line of his forearm, the power of his wrists. Each finger traced its fiery patterns on her flesh, her own fingers ran lightly over the straining muscles of his back, the tight drum of his waist, the ridge of muscle down his spine. She could feel the jutting bones of his hips, his thighs thrusting against the soft skin of her own. Her back arched to meet him in an upward tilt. Her legs were clasped around him like a belt, tightly, tighter, drawing him close and in. She could feel his manhood, perfectly sheathed in her own flesh, pulsing within her.

When she opened her eyes, she could see his chest gleaming with sweat, like an athlete rubbed in oil. Sweat beaded the rough gold hair of his chest.

They reached their climax together, in a long shuddering spasm. It seemed the total liquidation of their bodies. . . . In the silence that followed, Natasha was keenly aware of the woodland around her. In the warm haze of sunlight, a squirrel ran across a branch; a flight of swans rose against the black firs; she heard the grating call of a jay.

Then all again was green peace. She lay with her head pillowed on Richard's chest, her fingers entwined in the damp tangle of hair.

Gazing at the blue sky between the slender shafts of the birch trees, the answer came to Richard. There was only one thing that he could do. It was unbearable to contemplate any other.

In the innermost part of his being, he felt a new kind of happiness and, at the same time, a keen sense of despair. He knew that he was tasting the real sweetness of love. Making love was only the surface of it. He was shattered by the force of his feelings. So far, in love, he had swum in shallow waters; now he felt a fierce and dangerous undertow.

Beyond everything, he needed Natasha. He felt diminished by even the thought of her absence. He could not imagine his future without her. They were bound together, tied by the knot that suddenly binds two quite separate existences.

"We must marry," he said.

Natasha sat up, gasping. Her sun-and-shadow-patterned body was stiff and erect, her face frozen with disbelief. ". . . Marry?"

"Yes."

"You would marry me?"

Richard reached for her, drawing her into his arms. She shivered slightly as his hands touched her sun-caught skin. "I will marry you, Natasha! By God, I will!"

He turned her toward him, grasping her arm, ringing her wrists with his lean brown fingers. "I need you, Natasha. I know that now. We must let our lives run together from now on. If I lost you, my dear soul, I know that I would lose some blessing—some immense blessing. It would be lost forever."

Then she was in his arms again. He was making love to her again, both brutal and tender, his kisses too fierce and yet so gentle. His strength both frightened and exalted her. She had the impression that their bodies were being absorbed into each other. Her breasts burned from the pressure of his chest, her nipples ached from his milking kisses.

Beyond that, she felt that their bodies were dissolving in a great shimmer of light and warmth. Everything was joy, glory and love—warm bright joy and upward-surging love.

CHAPTER

FOURTEEN

The vicar of the English church in St. Petersburg was an old man, rheumy-eyed and snowy-haired. His slightest movement caused him to grimace with pain.

Richard watched him compassionately, moved by the old man's arthritic hands and disfigured fingers.

Mr. Cutforth, on the other hand, regarded Richard with something close to hostility. "You have not discussed this matter with the embassy?" he asked.

"No, sir. I thought it best to find out the position from you before I approached the ambassador."

"Well, I certainly could not move in the matter until I have authority," The vicar said, tetchily. "It is all rather unorthodox."

He looked up, reminded. "The young woman is of the Orthodox religion?"

"Yes, sir. She is."

Cutforth nodded. "Most irregular," he said. "She would have to receive a dispensation from her church, and permission from the secular authorities. But you must understand all that yourself."

Richard was silent. In the circumstances it was impossible to seek permission from the authorities. Hopeless. Trepov, if not Verchinin, would see to that.

"We'd hoped to avoid all that," Richard said, "and just be married quietly."

The vicar gestured impatiently, the gesture making him grimace. "That would be out of the question, Mr. Greville. Quite impossible." He frowned. "The young woman is prepared to flout the authorities and renounce her faith?" he asked.

"Yes, sir. She is."

Cutforth's frown deepened. "Has she considered this *seriously?*" he asked. "Have you, come to that, considered this seriously?"

"Yes, vicar. We both have. Very seriously."

"No clergyman could proceed in such a matter unless he was convinced of a sincere desire to convert to our church."

"Miss Petrova is prepared to leave her church," Richard said again.

"But is her intention based upon conviction?"

Richard kept a tight rein on his temper. "I have already said that it is, sir."

"My conscience would forbid me to accept such a renunciation unless I was fully convinced of the purity of her conviction," the vicar said maddeningly. He shrugged, causing a fresh ripple of pain to cross his face. "But I doubt if I could undertake this matter in any case. In the present political climate, it is hardly to be supposed that the authorities will grant your request. The English Church does not claim diplomatic immunity, you know."

"I had thought that we might be married in the embassy itself," Richard said firmly. "That would be on English ground."

The vicar looked scandalized. "Out of the question, Mr. Greville! I am surprised at you, sir. You must know that such a procedure would be most irregular. It would be tantamount to giving political asylum to the young woman. The Russians would regard it as a most offensive procedure."

He regarded Richard balefully. "Have you truly considered the religious differences between you?"

Richard paused, then answered honestly, "No, sir. At least not as carefully as *you* might wish."

"Indeed," the vicar said, astonished.

Richard shrugged apologetically. "Religion, for me, has always been a matter of moral conduct rather than a form of outward observance, sir," he explained. "I have always judged people by their actions rather than by their beliefs."

"And does the young lady share your lack of *prejudice?*" The vicar's tone was waspish.

"Miss Petrova is very devout, vicar. The fact that she is prepared to marry out of her faith, as well as lose her nationality is—to me—the greatest proof of her love. It is my good fortune that I am not being asked to make such a sacrifice—though I would," he added firmly.

The vicar digested this statement. It disagreed with him. "This is not the best time to pursue such a line," he said, "though I respect your candor."

Richard bowed.

Cutforth's eyes were fixed on him as he asked, "Why do you need to be married in such haste, may I ask? If it is not a delicate question."

Richard took a deep breath, but spoke steadily enough. "There would be some opposition to Miss Petrova marrying me, sir. She has attracted the attention of an important nobleman—his unwelcome attention. Once it becomes publicly known that we wish to marry, he may—we feel sure he *will*—put obstacles in our way. That is why it would be more convenient to be married in the embassy, on neutral ground. With the minimum of fuss."

Would nothing move the old brute? Richard thought. The vicar clucked with disapproval and seemed to blame Richard for the situation.

"You must see my position, Mr. Greville," he said, lips pursed. "The Anglican Church is only just tolerated in Russia. We are only a small community here. We have no power. Before I could draw a member of the Orthodox faith into our church, I would *have* to seek permission, certainly from her church, and possibly from the state."

He regarded Richard with sharp distaste. "Particularly since you say the young lady is a member of the *ballet,* there would be insuperable problems. The young woman is a servant of the tzar. Moreover, she is not in your social sphere. There would be the question of identity papers for a beginning. . . ." The vicar said nothing more for a moment. His expression said everything. He was saving his church from pollution and Richard from social suicide. He suffered another rheumatic attack.

The silence grew until it was a palpable thing.

"I understand, vicar, " Richard said bitterly. "It is not possible to conduct a marriage service simply at the bequest of the two people concerned. "

"Mr. Greville, you must know the situation as well as I do! Better. It is a question of political etiquette. If her government should not desire this lady's marriage to a foreigner . . ."

The old man sucked in his breath sharply, whether in pain or disapproval it was hard to tell—perhaps both. "It would make matters very awkward for our church, at such a time. But you understand all this as well as I do."

"Yes, I do, vicar," Richard said. "But I had hoped that my desire to be married would not be regarded as fuel for politicking—naïve of me, I know."

"Very." The vicar settled back in his chair, seeking a more comfortable position. "You could, of course, marry outside Russia. Sweden would be a convenient place. Or Austria. Though your marriage would have no validity here in Russia, and you would be *persona non grata.*"

"It would be impossible," Richard said. "She would not be granted an exit visa."

The vicar regarded him with open mouth. "They would deny her an exit visa?" he asked. "You're sure of that?"

"Yes."

The vicar swallowed noisily. "You appear to have involved yourself with a most unusual young woman," he said. "And created a most delicate diplomatic situation for yourself. Have you discussed matters with Lord Loftus?"

"Not directly," Richard replied. "I had hoped to settle matters with the Church first."

For a few moments neither man spoke.

"I shall, of course, respect your confidence," Cutforth said.

"I had expected no less," Richard replied. A silence settled upon them again. The interview appeared to be at an end.

"Is there nobody in Russia who might marry us?" Richard asked.

"Do you mean another Church of England clergyman?"

"Not necessarily, vicar. I mean a man of some other denomination—where no political obstacles exist."

The vicar looked shocked; his eyes watered. "You would renounce your church?" he asked.

"If necessary."

"Well, it is not for me to suggest such a thing to you, sir!"

Richard stared at him obstinately. "But would it be possible?"

"I could not advise you, Mr. Greville." The vicar rose, getting to his feet with difficulty. "I'm not able to help you, Mr. Greville. I cannot undertake to marry you without the express permission of the ambassador— and he will require a similar authority from the Russians."

Richard, too, had risen to his feet. He held out his hand, aware that he had bitterly scandalized the old man. "I see. . . . Well, thank you for your time, sir."

He shook the old man's crippled hand, and left the room.

"Marry her!" Scavronsky said, astonished. "*Ça alors!* You want to marry her? Richard, dear friend, have you considered the matter carefully?"

"Yes," Richard replied wearily. ". . . Very carefully."

"But, *mon cher!*"

Richard cut the count's protestations short with a gesture. "It's no use, Kolya. I know all the objections—nationality, religion, social inequality. . . ." He shrugged irritably. "None of it matters, Kolya. With every day that passes I realize more deeply how much I love her, and how much I want our lives to run together."

"But *marriage!*"

"Yes, marriage."

"It is a bad move," Scavronsky said, with a bemused look on his face. "Well, few people choose the person they fall in love with, I suppose. One may say, 'I have a preference' or 'I could love somebody like that,' but in the end one is selected rather than selecting."

"Yes," Richard said. "I had no choice in the matter.

Though even if somebody had said to me at the start that I was making a bad choice, I would still have made it. The only thing is that I know—without the shadow of a doubt—that I have made the best, the only choice. She is the most extraordinary girl . . ." He fell silent.

"What a curious thing love is," Scavronsky murmured.

Richard said quickly, "Do you think that you could do me a great service, Kolya?"

"Of course. If I can."

Richard made his request, searching for words. "Your estates in Finland are far enough away from Petersburg—and the religious climate is, I should imagine, much easier. You are the sole master there. If we were to travel to Mustamakki, wouldn't it be possible for a clergyman there—a Lutheran—to perform the marriage service? If we could perform a quiet ceremony at your estate. Once the thing is accomplished, you see, there'll be no difficulty, I'm sure." He stopped, seeing the count's astonished expression.

"You're not serious!" Scavronsky cried.

"Yes, I am. Deadly serious. Once we are a married couple, the embassy will be forced to protect us."

The count regarded him with cold amusement. "Do you think we could get away with such a thing?" he asked, and laughed.

"You don't think we could?"

"My dear man, my priest at Mustamakki is a virulant Protestant-hater. Holy St. Serge! he even disapproves of the Greek Orthodoxy! If the pot-bellied cretin were to learn that I had invited a Lutheran parson to officiate at such a marriage—lured one of his flock to a new pasture . . ." He whistled. "No, my dear Richard, I couldn't command his silence. He would go at once to the police, and we should all spend some time in provincial exile. The girl, perhaps, in Siberia . . ."

He stared at Richard dolefully, making a swift chopping motion across his throat. "Believe me, my dear friend, I'd help you in this if I could, even though I completely disapprove of your plans."

Richard swore, pounding his hand upon the table. "My God! Is there nobody in this damnable country whom I can find to marry us?"

"None, I think, Richard," the count replied gravely. "All religious bodies are subordinate to the will of the tzar."

"Then I shall seek the tzar's permission," Richard said.

"Do you think you would receive it?"

"Don't you?"

The count looked doubtful. "*Mon cher,* the tzar is guided by the procurator-general of the Most Holy Synod. I know the procurator-general. He is the most rabid Pan-Slavist. He loathes the heathen Turk—and all their *allies.*"

"But the tzar himself? Good God, Kolya! *He* should sympathize with what I'm going through. His own relationship with the Princess Catherine, his desire to regulate their liaison, tie the nuptial bond, all that . . ."

The count smiled. "There is one major difference between your case and his," he said.

"Yes, he's the lord of all he surveys," Richard answered vehemently.

The count looked grave. "That apart, he and his mistress are *both* of the One True Faith. In his primitive way, the tzar is a pious man."

Richard sat hunched in thought, deeply miserable. "Then I must find another way," he said.

"But if you change your church, we shall both be exiles," Natasha protested.

"My dearest, if you're prepared to sacrifice your religious life, why shouldn't I be asked to do the same?" Richard asked. "And it's the only way we can get a clergyman to take a chance."

"It seems a wicked thing that either of us should be asked to renounce our faith," Natasha said.

Richard kissed her. "We still worship the same God," he said, explaining that the Mennonite Church was a Protestant sect, and that the Mennonite pastor was sympathetic to their cause—provided that Richard gave him written proof that he had renounced the Anglican Church and asked for permission to enter theirs.

At first Natasha had appeared to be consoled by the news. Once again he had been humbled, thinking of the extent of her sacrifice. Asking her to give up her church was almost like asking her to give up the Russian part of herself. His sacrifice had seemed trivial by comparison.

But she still had her doubts. "This is all wrong," she said. "I feel it here." She touched her breast and shivered.

Richard regarded her with concern. She looked ill. Her

skin was sallow, unnaturally dark beneath her eyes. Her cheeks were hollowed out.

"Our love is hopeless," she said.

Richard caught her by the shoulders. "Don't say that!"

"But it's true!" she cried.

Richard stared at her in anguished disbelief. "You don't want us to marry. Is that it?" he asked.

The pain in her eyes knifed him to the heart. "Oh, I do! You know that I do," she wept. "But it's all wrong. If you desert your church, it will cut you off from your people. Then we shall both be . . ." She stopped, unable to frame the words.

"But you do want to marry me still?"

"Oh, yes, Richka! Yes! But you mustn't leave your church."

She cried out as he grabbed her roughly by the arms, catching her to him. "I thank God it's too late to go back!" he cried.

"Too late? What do you mean?!

"I've already done it, I've already renounced my church," he said.

"What?"

"I've already been to see old Cutforth. I've said a final farewell to him, taken the Bible in my hands, uttered the words of renunciation. I have it in writing. It is *done*." With which, he put the paper in Natasha's hands. It was written in English and meant nothing to her. "Our troubles are over," he said, as she stared at the writing incomprehensibly. "At least some of them are."

But their troubles took an unexpected course. The Mennonite pastor had learned that he could not perform the ceremony without first notifying his superiors in Switzerland. He had sent a telegram to the consistory advising them of the forthcoming marriage. He held it out to Richard. It was written in German. "Will you be so kind as to send it for me?"

Richard had agreed. In company with Natasha he had hurried to the post office, only to be told that the telegram could not be sent. There was a national crisis. Only telegrams of national importance could be sent. Did they think their marriage was of state importance?

Richard had protested strongly, but Natasha had appealed

to the postal clerk, and the clerk had relented a little. He would send it as soon as he could, he said. They were forced to leave, not knowing if the telegram would be sent.

The pastor handed Richard the reply. The message was in German: "Permission expressly refused."

Richard gazed at the sheet of flimsy paper, unable at first to appreciate the printed words.

"You said that the reply would be just a mere formality," he said, his voice gruff with anger and disappointment.

The pastor's round face was overlaid with sorrow. He shrugged his fat shoulders apologetically. "I am powerless, Herr Greville. I cannot marry you. I cannot solemnize such a marriage without proper permission. It would not be legally binding. . . ."

He rambled on, deeply upset, abjectly apologetic, but Richard had ceased to listen. He was looking at the telegram in his hand. On one corner was the covering mark of the postal department. The date of receipt was scribbled on it.

It had been held in the post office—or somewhere—for the last two days.

"When did you receive this telegram?" he asked, wondering if the pastor had tried to reach him earlier.

"Three hours ago," the pastor said. "I sent for you at once."

Richard's thoughts were a maelstrom. The receipt mark sharpened his own fears. The telegram had been in the hands of the secret police—that much was evident. Or why the delay?

"Permission expressly refused."

The wording itself meant little, unless the interceptors knew what permission had been sought.

What of the outgoing telegram? The one that he and Natasha had sent? That, too, must have gone through the censor.

God damn his unthinking stupidity! In his rash haste he had jumped in with both feet.

But what else could he have done? He could not have managed to send it through the diplomatic channels without arousing suspicion at the embassy.

Too late now. The authorities were fully alerted. He was caught between paralyzing despair and urgent desperation. What the devil was he to do?

What would the authorities do?

CHAPTER

FIFTEEN

Richard sat opposite the smuggler—a man whose character was as shadowy as his calling. Richard knew him as "Grigory."

He suspected that he was a Ukrainian. The man was whip-thin and dark, blazing-eyed. He had been recommended by one of Richard's contacts, one of the dozens of "politicals" whom he had met in secret during the past few weeks.

"Can you do it?" he asked. "Can you get us into Germany?"

Grigory nodded. "It'll be hard," he said. "Especially for a woman. Your friend would have to put herself into our hands without a murmur."

Richard frowned. "She'll do that. If I trust you, she will."

Grigory looked slightly ruffled. "It won't be practicable for you to travel together," he said.

Richard looked up sharply. "Not travel together?"

"You have a valid passport," Grigory pointed out, "and diplomatic immunity. There's nothing to stop you from leaving the country in the normal way."

Richard's face hardened. "Nevertheless, I don't feel I can leave her to manage alone."

Grigory shrugged, his shoulders reaching his ears. "If she's got guts enough to defy the authorities in the first place—"

"I'm not questioning her courage," Richard said. "She's got pluck enough for two. No, it's not that . . . I simply couldn't allow her to travel alone."

Grigory scowled. "You don't trust us?"

"I wouldn't be here if I didn't trust you."

115

Light broke in Grigory's dark eyes. "Ah," he said, "it's your own courage that's in question! You don't want to take the easy way while she takes the hard."

Richard flushed. "If you like. I won't ask the lady to take a risk I'm not ready to share."

"Even if it makes the job easier for us?"

"I think it will be as easy to procure a false passport for me as for her," Richard said. "And one more passenger can't be all that hard to cope with. I'm a resourceful enough man." There was a note of finality in his voice. Grigory recognized it. He was not a man to argue with certainty.

"If you understand the extra risks," he said, with another shrug.

"I do. And you can depend on me to play my part."

Grigory smiled, his mouth crooked. "Aye, as you said, you're a resourceful man."

But, all the same, he thought, you're going to stand out like a monk in a brothel!

He looked at the chiseled features, the fine hands, the smooth athletic elegance of Richard's body. Could this fellow ever be mistaken for anything else but an Englishman?

How the devil was he going to turn this *milord* into a *mujik?*

But Richard made a very passable peasant in his woven caftan, broad belt, red cotton shirt and baggy breeches. His legs were wrapped in puttees, his shoes were of bark. He had darkened his skin with walnut oil.

Natasha, too, looked at ease, dressed in the Sabbath clothes of a young peasant girl, homemade and traditional. She wore a brightly colored frock over an embroidered shirt, covered by a linen coat. A square of yellow cloth hid her hair. She, too, will pass, Grigory thought. Unless they're questioned too hard.

Both Richard and Natasha listened as he gave them instructions. They had changed in a "safe" house. Now they were to slip out of a back entrance into a dark alleyway, after a labyrinthine walk through the corridors of a dozen buildings. Grigory appeared to know every escape route in the capital.

Once free of St. Petersburg, they traveled by coach to an outlying village. There a carter met them, to take them on to Pskov, where they would catch the train to Vilna. At Vilna they would be entrusted to another man, a "reliable man."

Jogging along in the swaying cart, lying on the dried and dusty hay, they were both reminded of their earlier journeys, made under the early summer moon, when the hay was freshly cut and sweetly scented. They said little, each under the spell of their memories; each awed by the step they were taking. Natasha felt that she had cast herself on some broad strong river, there was little she could do but be drawn along by the current under the wide northern sky. She murmured sleepily at Richard's side.

What a change has taken place in me, Richard thought. How swiftly his love had grown, and how strongly. Who would have thought five short months ago that he would be chancing everything to make this sweet dear soul his wife—this tiny feminine creature wrapped in her peasant's coat? Was *she* afraid? Wavering even now? She lay in his arms as though overwhelmed by an immense weariness.

Did he himself regret his action? . . . No. But why this vague, uneasy, gnawing sensation? Why this inexplicable sadness?

Natasha trembled against him as though she was cold. She snuggled against him. Then she raised her face to his and their lips met in a lingering kiss. He gazed down into her face. Her eyes were closed, she moved indolently in his arms, her trembling ceased.

Richard's heart swelled inside him. He was wrung with a sudden rush of emotion, a deep sense of gratitude. Natasha was not regretful or afraid, only apprehensive. She would go with him wherever he wanted, without so much as a backward glance.

At Vilna they were handed over to another guide. The "reliable man," who was Jewish, was clad in a long black coat that was green with age. Two traditional sidelocks hung from his ears, shining black corkscrews of hair.

Richard's immediate reaction was of anxious suspicion. This man, with his outlandish appearance, would surely only succeed in drawing attention to Natasha and himself? Every poor Jew was at the mercy of the police. Yet when they climbed aboard the train, he saw the point of using "Moise." The third-class carriage teemed with poor Jewish travelers. They filled the air with an unceasing din, the children shouting and crying, their worn-out mothers remonstrating with them, men and women trying to converse above the uproar.

There was a burst of music from one end of the compartment—loud, hoarse music, the music of the oriental bazaar. Moise grinned, and signaled to Richard to take a place behind a family group. Richard noticed that there were other peasants like himself and Natasha scattered among the Jewish passengers, sitting in isolation like themselves.

There was little danger that they would be drawn into conversation. It was impossible to make oneself heard above the guttural clamor. They could already be in some strange land, instead of traveling through the flat weariness of Lithuania. Richard passed the time in trying to follow the Yiddish dialogues around him.

At his side, Natasha, too, took a keen interest in everything around her. Listening to the unknown tongue seemed to reveal to her the extent to which she had committed herself. She was filled with an intense excitement, feeling that she had already made her escape.

The carriage was hot and grimy, poorly ventilated, smelling of stale food, dried fish and onions. The air was thick with the pungent smoke of strong tobacco. After a while, Natasha grew sleepy. She leaned her head on Richard's shoulder. The noise washed about her.

The first part of their journey was uneventful. They reached Vilovishi at midnight. The border was now quite close. Moise nodded from his corner and rose. Richard tapped Natasha's arm. She awoke at once, peering about her excitedly. She looked for all the world, Richard thought, like some young peasant woman who was traveling by train for the first time in her life, visiting country cousins.

They left the train, descending into the moistly warm night air. The freshness of the air revived them both. Richard's arm was numb from supporting Natasha's weight; it tingled with new life as the blood flowed. He picked up their small satchel and followed Moise when he motioned them to follow him.

They walked over to a large wagon, which did service as a stagecoach. It was a high affair; men and women clambered up the spokes of the wheels, jostling each other for places. Richard made to lift Natasha into the interior, but she waved him back. Still in character, she climbed aboard as the other women had done. Richard swung himself up behind her.

Five bare boards had been laid across the cart, as seats. Shyly, smiling politely, the Jews ceased from their rough pushing to make room for Richard and Natasha.

For a moment Richard felt uneasy again, thinking that the Jews had penetrated their disguise. If such simple people could recognize them so plainly, what chance did they stand against professional eyes?

Natasha, divining his thoughts, touched his arm gently. Smiling, she pointed out—without a word being spoken— that they were the only Gentiles in the wagon. Richard relaxed. To the long-suffering Jews, even the meanest Russian peasant must be treated with respect. He smiled at Natasha and she smiled bravely back.

The coachman hoisted himself onto the coachbox; he wore a lined overcoat, soiled and muddy. He cracked his long whip over the backs of his huge but half-starved horses, and—with a massive heave—the cart was on its way.

It was a slow journey over a poor road. The moon rose through lowering clouds, making the landscape more mysterious than before. They passed through large and unkempt villages, tumble-down collections of sagging thatch and broken walls.

Such a contrast to the quiet order of England, Richard thought. What would Natasha make of England, with its sweet shape of cottages and gardens, its cosy villages, lovingly decorated? Would she grow to love it as he did? Or hate it for the differences from what she had left behind?

At last, late into the night, the cart trundled to a stop before the door of a meanly lighted inn. Moise rose from his seat behind the coachman and climbed down, beckoning to them to follow.

They clambered from the cart, stiff and sore. The air had turned damp and chilly, with only a hint of light in the eastern sky. More than anything else, this change of light convinced Natasha that they were free of St. Petersburg. They were hundreds of miles away from the long "white nights."

A plump, slatternly-looking woman came puffing up to meet them. Moise exchanged a few words with her in Yiddish, coins passed from his hand to hers. She nodded, with a brief glance at Natasha and Richard.

Again Moise beckoned them forward. He seemed reluctant to speak Russian, but by now Richard could follow something of what they said. Their language was a mixture of High German, Slavonic and what he took to be Hebrew.

Before they entered the inn, the woman turned to them,

speaking with difficulty in Russian. Richard spoke to her in German and her face tightened.

"Speak Russian!" she hissed, with a nod at the window.

There was an outburst of drunken violence from within. Men swore loudly and unmistakably in Russian. It was the first time that Natasha had heard her language spoken by strangers all day.

"Soldiers," the woman muttered, drawing her shawl around her. She was very nervous, seeming almost reluctant to admit them. She showed no animosity toward Natasha and Richard, but the lined face beneath the unbecoming wig showed definite alarm.

Moise led them away from the inn front, one arm around the fat landlady. He spoke quietly but persuasively, calming her. They walked around the corner of the building, and Richard and Natasha followed the other two through the back entrance, low under the eaves.

The landlady opened a door and they slipped into the stinking warmth of the inn, the air heavy with the fumes of vodka and the sour smell of rye beer. They walked along a narrow passage—past the room where the drunken soldiers laughed, shouted and sang—to a solid-looking door. The landlady opened it and almost pushed them into a small dark room. Then she followed them in, closing the door behind her.

The room was crowded with furniture—table, chairs, cupboards, kitchen utensils and a pile of mattresses. There was a large bulbous stove, cold now. The bed, with its antimacassarlike trimmings, was a little island of neatness in the general confusion.

Now the landlady allowed herself to speak German, a language in which she felt more at ease. "You must go straight to bed," she explained. "It's too late to get you over the bridge tonight. The last train went two hours back, and our usual men aren't on duty. Tomorrow, well, tomorrow might be hard. There's something in the air—I don't know what. I can't get a word of sense out of that scum in there—" She gestured toward the carousing soldiers. "They're not the usual border guards. They've brought in a lot of new lads."

She patted the lumpy-looking bed. "You're best off in here," she said. "You mustn't show yourselves. Stay in here. You can't lock the door, but if folk come in they'll leave when they see the bed's not empty. I'll wake you in the morning."

"I should like to eat," Natasha said, suddenly aware that she was famished. Richard, too, said that he was hungry.

The landlady regarded them with surprise and admiration. "Well," she said, "you're a rare pair. Usually folk in your situation don't have much appetite. . . . I'll bring you a bite."

She, in fact, brought a fairly substantial meal, with many apologies for its simplicity—pickled cucumbers and tomatoes, a bowl of richly steaming cabbage soup, a dish of mushrooms, boiled chicken and hunks of black bread. Natasha and Richard settled themselves at the table and made short work of the meal.

Despite their danger and their anxiety, both felt elated by the situation. They were so close to freedom. Tomorrow they would cross the border. In a few days they would be married. It would cause a scandal. They would be punished. Ostracized, at least. But they would be beyond reach of Verchinin, Trepov, the tzar. They retired for what remained of the night—to *hide in the bed*, as the Jewish landlady put it.

They sank into the prickly mattress stuffed with horsehair, their bodies falling against each other clumsily. They drew back from each other. The strangeness of their surroundings, the discomfort of the bed, seemed to define their bodies in some new way. They were aware of an awkwardness between them, a reserve, almost a shyness. They could have been sharing a bed for the first time.

To Richard, Natasha's body had never looked so delicate, so warmly white, so soft, so fresh, so pure. He had the feeling of this being their bridal night.

She had insisted on removing all her clothes for fear of fleas, though the room appeared to be scrupulously clean. She lay with one arm across her breasts and the leg nearest him drawn modestly across her other thigh. Both lay in the bed as stiffly as effigies, not touching. This strangely unsettling shyness between them vanished at a sound from the passage, the drunken laughter of a man and the coarse whispering of a young woman. The doorknob rattled, the door half opened.

"Who's there?" Richard called in Russian, gruffly.

The man cursed and the woman giggled. After more intense whispering, they retreated along the passage. There was a silence, broken only by the regular thumping of the woman's body against the wall and the strenuous breathing of the man as he took his pleasure standing. There was the rhythmic slap of a rough hand on soft flesh. Like all Russian peasants, the soldier believed that beating was an indispensable part of the sexual act. The girl whimpered and sniggered together, apparently finding the experience painful but stimulating.

At the opening of the door, Natasha had almost jumped into Richard's arms. He could feel her heart fluttering against his breast. His arms closed about her. The strange restraint that had been between them vanished. Now, as they listened to the frenzied coupling beyond the wall, their bodies came together, their flesh kindling as they touched.

Richard took Natasha with a fierce hunger. His wildness frightened her. The musk of his body, male and pungent, his hands on her body hard and grasping. She cried out, but the sound was muffled against the hard shell of his chest.

He raised himself, bent his head and kissed her, again smothering her cries, the hard line of his lips on hers, her body trembling uncontrollably beneath him. There was nothing but the sensation of his lips on hers as they opened to the insistent pressure of his warm tongue. His tongue filled her mouth. Her body undulated helplessly beneath him, rising and falling, opening spontaneously. "Take me, take me," she heard herself begging

He took her then, his shaft fantastically engorged, his arms locked about her, and they sank into the well of the bed. She was frightened and yet elated by the force of his passion, experiencing a wild thrill, a complete abandonment to his overwhelming strength. At the same time she felt shattered by a feeling of intense pity for him. The brutality of his movements was part of his hunger for her, the need that drove him so ferociously to possess her. It was as though he sought to possess her utterly, forcing himself deeper and deeper into her so that their bodies fused, as though by possessing her body he could grasp her spirit.

For a few wild moments she had the impression that their bodies *had* blended together, melting and solidifying into one. Pain, humiliation, elation and pleasure were the same thing. Spasm after spasm shook her body as it rose to meet his.

After, they lay together, exhausted. The room had grown unbearably hot, their bodies gleamed with sweat and darkened the sheets and pillows.

Richard's head lay on her breasts, her tortured breasts. He

stared at her as though he would find the meaning behind each feature. "God, how I love you," he murmured.

Her hand stroked his damp hair, cupping his head. Moisture glistened in the hollow of his shoulders. "I know . . . I know. . . ."

The passageway was quiet now, the "lovers" gone.

How strange, Natasha thought. They and we were both indulging in the same act. She shuddered, remembering the coarse endearments of the man, the inane sniggering of the girl. The same action, and yet . . . one so crude and lascivious, the other a consummation.

She turned to Richard at the touch of his hands. He murmured in her ear. When he kissed her neck, her skin grew rosy with pleasure. How totally her body responded to him. Would it always be the same? How long could they live on this high plateau of sexual bliss?

His lovemaking was so completely different the second time that she could have been making love with a different man. He was gentle with her, deftly stroking her tenderly aching body back to life. He gathered her into his arms, kissing the flesh he had bruised earlier, pleading, she felt, for her forgiveness, her understanding.

In the strange room, so close to danger, a new thread of intimacy was strung between them. The knot that bound them was drawn tighter. This time she had no need to struggle against him, but returned kiss for kiss, opening her body to him placidly. Suddenly she knew beyond all doubt that she wanted above all things to bear his child. She experienced an ache in her loins that was beyond all sexuality. She yearned for him to enter her, to plant his seed, to ripen her womb.

In a few days' time they would be man and wife. But would they ever be more truly man and wife than they were at that moment? She lay awake long after Richard had fallen asleep, thinking of the future with a mixture of fear and excited anticipation.

It was a strange night. Several people shuffled into the room during the next hour, whispered together and left when they saw the bed was occupied. Beyond the far wall, the riotous drinking went on without diminution. Through the squealing and laughter of the women, and the bawling and bellowing of the men, Natasha heard fragments of melancholy Jewish songs. The woman who sang sounded vulnerably young, almost childlike. Her voice wavered and broke roughly, moving Natasha unbearably. The songs were quick with the pain of longing.

Natasha raised a hand to her face to find that her cheeks were wet with tears. Finally, she slept.

In bright daylight the room looked repulsively shoddy. When Natasha awoke, through the window she could see a small courtyard, piled high with refuse. A high wall surrounded it. There was no exit that she could see.

Richard's limbs were wrapped like a cat's cradle around her. He woke as she stirred. He kissed her. "In an hour we'll be free," he said.

No sound came from beyond the bedroom wall. There was the curiously oppressive silence of an abandoned public place. They dressed, and waited for above an hour, until the sun flooded the room. They lay quietly together on the bed, almost without speaking.

Then, from beyond the wall of the courtyard, they heard the sound of a distant trumpet and the tread of marching feet. There were shouted commands, the shrill neighing of horses.

"What is it?" she asked, shivering. "What's happening?"

Richard frowned. "I don't know," he said. "Sounds like a full squadron—cavalry, by the sound of it." His arms tightened around her. "Courage," he whispered. "I don't think the tzar's sent them to look for us!"

The landlady came quickly into the room, motes of dust dancing in the sunlight as her skirt swept the floor. She looked alarmed. "You'll have to go back," she said. "There's half the tzar's army out there."

Natasha and Richard had jumped from the bed as the landlady entered. "What's happening?" Richard asked.

"We don't know," the landlady answered. "You're to come with me."

They followed her from the room. Although their danger seemed to have increased, Natasha began to breathe more easily once they were out of the narrow confines of the bedroom. For the past half-hour, it had begun to take on the appearance of a cell.

Trying to remain calm, measuring her steps to Richard's, she followed the landlady up a flight of rickety steps to an upper room. There, standing at an angle to the window, they found Moise. He beckoned them to join him.

They peered through the dusty glass. "The Alexandrovsky

regiment," Moise muttered, nodding at the scene beyond the window.

The road in front of the inn was packed with marching soldiers. A mob of urchins ran along beside them. Trumpeters sat astride gray horses. An officer held the regimental standard, flanked by two fellow officers. The colonel came next, alone, on a superb chestnut. Then came the squadron, raising an ankle-deep layer of dust. The men were sunburned and weary, their uniforms dirty.

They drew up in a line in the square. The regimental priest had donned his vestments, the sleeveless chasuble and tall cylindrical headdress. A field altar had been erected. The standard bearer ranged himself beside it.

Orders rang out. "Dismount!" "Caps off!"

A few men were assembled to form a choir, and the prayers began. The priest spoke in a hurried voice, but the voices of the choir swelled out, the sound soaring into the clear air.

"What do you think this means?" Richard asked Moise.

"Who knows?" Moise answered. "Some whim of the tzar's?"

Richard frowned. "This looks like more than ordinary maneuvers. These men have marched a hell of a long way."

"There's a rumor that the soldiers are massing along the whole of the frontier," Moise said.

Natasha, watching Richard, saw his frown deepen. "How does this affect us?" he asked Moise.

The smuggler shrugged again. He nodded beyond the square, to where a narrow bridge crossed a deep gorge. "That's your only way out," he said. "The only way out for sixty miles each way. Sixty miles without a decent road. Normally, we can bribe a regular soldier—usually there's only a small unit here—but we can't move while this mob's around. And they're staying for some time. They've requisitioned a score of houses."

"Can't you take us through further down the line?" Natasha asked.

Moise was emphatic. "No."

"Why not?"

"Because I don't know the way," Moise said. "It's not my territory. As I said, there are no roads, there's nothing for miles." He nodded at the village. "This is my patch. I know who I can trust here . . . and who I can't."

"So there's nothing you can do?" Natasha asked despondently.

"Nothing. Nothing you can do, either."

"You sound too damned sure of that," Richard said.

Moise stared at Richard stolidly. He gestured toward the soldiers massed in the square. "I am," he said. "I made inquiries round about. I've heard a rumor. These lot are not the only ones on the frontier. Somebody said that there's forty thousand men between Tilsit and Kamanets."

Christ, Richard thought, what infernal timing! This sounds like war. The army has been put on a war-footing.

He turned to Moise. "If you can find somebody to take us across, I'll treble the price."

"Save your money, friend," Moise said with a shrug. "Sit tight. You'll find nobody to take you if you treble the price ten times over. I tell you, something's up. The army has the border sealed off. The only way you'll get across is in a shroud."

Richard stared out toward the west, at the bridge with its guard post at either end. A sentry box stood on his side, striped with the imperial colors. He concentrated all his pent-up hatred on the box, and on the soldiers in their shabby uniforms. Beyond the bridge, a broad white road disappeared in a haze of dust on the horizon.

"To me, that line between the earth and sky is nothing but a horizon," Richard brooded. "To Natasha it must seem a prison wall."

There was no way, at present, of spiriting her away beyond that prison wall.

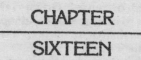

CHAPTER

SIXTEEN

They returned to St. Petersburg to find the capital in a state of patriotic fervor. The Pan-Slavic tri-color, red, white and blue, fluttered from many of the buildings. The station itself was packed with soldiers in uniform. They had to fight their way out of the echoing station, pushing their way between the crowds that had assembled to wave away the soldiers.

Coming out of the strange limbo of their own journey, back to normality, Richard now knew the reason for the troop movements at the frontier.

"It is war, I think," he said to Natasha.

She walked over to a group of women. Pretending to be a young peasant girl fresh from the provinces, she questioned them. Returning to Richard, she said grimly, "War!" and continued to elbow her way through the jostling crowd.

Richard followed her, his heart pumping. Russia had declared war on Turkey. Had Great Britain been drawn into it? He murmured a brief prayer that they had not. It would mean recall.

In the street, Natasha turned to him, grasping his arm. "It's not us!" she said breathlessly. "We're not in it yet. Serbia and Montenegro have declared war on Turkey. These are volunteers that are going to join them."

"Only volunteers?"

"Yes."

Richard relaxed a little. It was not yet official.

They made their way to the "safe" house by the complicated route they had been shown, hoping they would be received since they were not expected back.

"I thought you might not get through," Grigory said, when

127

they arrived. "That's why I stayed on. I kept your clothes, too. Just in case. All hell's broke loose here."

As Richard changed back into his own clothes, stripping the peasant rags away, Grigory told him of how the Bulgarian insurgents had risen and killed the local Turkish population, and of how the Turks had retaliated with grim ferocity. "The Turks were terrified, of course," Grigory said. "Only imagine it! An insurrection so close to Constantinople. Whoever won would control the main road to Europe. It would threaten the very existence of the Ottoman Empire."

"So the Turks have panicked," Richard said. "It's to be expected, I suppose."

"Damn right!" Grigory said. "They've armed the local Moslem population, the *Bashi-bazouks*."

"The *Bashi-bazouks?*"

"Voluntary Moslem troops," Grigory explained. "They don't fight for pay, just for loot. Anyway, it's those bastards who've put down the revolt. Slashing their way through sixty villages, killing everybody in sight. It's been a massacre." He spat. "So Serbia and Montenegro have declared war on the Turks. After all, they're next on the list after Bulgaria."

"When did they declare war?" Richard asked.

"Three days back."

If I'd been at the embassy, I could have saved myself an uncomfortable journey, Richard thought. Aloud, he said in disgust, "What hope do the Serbs have—even against the Turks?"

"Oh, they have hope," Grigory said. "They hope to draw the tzar into the war." He laughed. "Englishman, you don't know what it's been like here in these past few days. Madness. The Pan-Slavic Committee has been busy, I can tell you. They've inflamed the public."

Richard's transformation was almost complete. The peasant had vanished and a young man-about-town stood in his place, elegant in narrow brown trousers, a white Marseilles waistcoat and cream-colored shirt. He put the finishing touches to his yellow and khaki striped tie and shrugged his wide shoulders into a light duster coat.

"It's unbelievable," Grigory said. "The sentiment is all to the Slav cause. They practically force folk to hand over their kopecks on every street corner. Even the tzarevich is at it. He's come out and said that men should volunteer. He's fitted out a complete detachment of Don Cossacks."

"Has the tzar lost control entirely?" Richard asked.

Grigory laughed, with a sly look for Natasha, who had re-entered the living room. She was dressed in a gown of light blue chiffon strewn with silvery flowers. She looked like a water sprite, a *Russalka*, luring men to drown themselves in the depths of rivers.

Richard saw something of the same thought in Grigory's admiring eyes.

"The tzar neglects everything in his passion for the princess," Grigory said, still looking at Natasha. His voice rose. "Have we Russians gone mad? We're Russians, not Slavs! And Turks are Moslems. Can we expect them to act like Christians?"

On the point of spitting, he checked himself. "Besides," he asked, "what hope have we of chasing them out of Europe? We should leave them well alone."

"Men are always anxious to 'beat the drum,'" Natasha said, at Richard's side. She had slipped her hand into his; it felt unnaturally cold.

Dear God, Richard thought. All this has happened in three short days. Natasha and I have been living in a vacuum for the past few days. How did we not hear of this?

At the corner of Natasha's street they parted, embracing casually, as though they had been for no more than a walk in the park. But there was tension in Natasha's body, and she clung to him in a lingering way. They had returned to reality.

"I shall have been missed," she said, shivering.

He held her hand against his chest. "You've only to remember what to say, darling. You've been with me. All the time. At my apartment. My man will have kept the visitors at bay. He knows what to say."

"But will they believe me?"

"Why should they not? It's not unknown for lovers to stay together for days on end. And, if you feed Trepov the tidbits we've decided on, he'll be content."

He kissed her again, with greater force. She seemed to gather strength from his embrace. With a brave little smile, she turned and ran up the steps to her apartment house.

CHAPTER

SEVENTEEN

It felt strange to be back in class in the great, sun-filled room, with the familiar smells, the familiar sounds, the women in their romantic tarlatans, the men elegant in their cotton tunics. Years of her life were in that room.

Natasha stood alone among the kissing, gossiping women, the laughter and shrieks—a still small figure among the friendly commotion. Only Oleg came to kiss her hand. He smiled down into her eyes, his own glinting mischievously.

"I heard a rumor that you'd *eloped*," he said.

Natasha felt the blood drain from her face. She staggered slightly, and would have fallen but for Oleg holding on to her. "Who told you that?" she whispered.

Oleg's grin grew wider, but his velvety eyes regarded her acutely. "It was only a joke," he said. "We were all wondering where you've been hiding yourself."

The room came back into focus. Natasha withdrew her hand and sought for the support of the *barre*, still trembling faintly.

"Natasha, what is it?" Oleg asked. "You look as though I'd hit you in the ribs."

Natasha managed to smile at him. "It's nothing . . . nothing." She was calmer now.

She was saved from further embarrassment by the arrival of the ballet-mistress. She clapped her hands and the chattering ceased immediately. The dancers took up their positions. Then the pianist plunged into the music for the exercises, the banal melodies tinkling into the air.

Gradually, under the influence of the lesson, the steadying

comfort of tradition, Natasha recovered her composure. She relaxed. It felt so good to be dancing again, feeling her muscles warm to the challenge and regain elasticity, becoming supple. She was able to empty her mind of everything but the sequence of steps. The simplicity of this world had never struck her before. If only life could be so well ordered, with no need to lie. Oleg's innocent joke had been like a blow over the heart, and she had been fined for missing two classes. Her excuse, too, had not been accepted, she felt sure. . . . In *profile*, fifth position. *Dégagér* in second. Lift the leg *à la demi-hauteur*. Bend working leg, bring foot behind ankle of supporting leg. Tighten, tighten, place *pointe* in second. Foot brought back . . . slowly, slower. She felt her body blossoming under the old familiar spell. . . .

"Natalia-Ivanovna_"

She turned, not at first hearing the voice, her concentration still totally on her movements.

"You are wanted in the intendant's office," the voice said. The ballet-mistress pointed toward the door. A uniformed messenger stood there. "You are to go with this man, as you are. Here, take this shawl."

The ballet-mistress thrust a woolen shawl over her shoulders. Natasha, glowing from the exercises, left the room. Curious stares followed her. It was almost unheard of for a practice to be interrupted. Once again, Natasha Petrova must be steeped in trouble.

She followed the messenger up the marble stairs, her fears growing with every step. Her story had not been believed! She should have gotten a letter from her doctor. The man stopped outside the intendant's office. He tapped on the door, then stepped aside to let her enter. The door closed behind her.

"Come forward."

She stepped further into the room, and stopped, her heart contracting. The intendant was not in the room. In his place, sitting at his desk, was the dapper figure of General Trepov.

Today he was dressed in civilian clothes, a smartly-cut black frock coat, gray and black striped trousers and spats, a perfectly knotted striped tie around his stiff collar. His lightly gloved hands played with the horn top of a heavy can.

"Sit down, Miss Petrova."

Natasha sat down quickly, her legs in danger of giving way. She fought to control the panic that rose in her. She saw, from

Trepov's smile, that he perceived her struggle to compose herself. It amused him. She knew, too, that she must look guilty. She fought to clear the expression from her face.

The fine muslin of her tarlatan quivered like the wings of a thousand butterflies. She laid a hand on her knee to control her trembling, summoning all her power to command her body.

Trepov treated her with exaggerated courtesy. "You have been absent from St. Petersburg," he said.

"No." From somewhere she found the strength to tell him that she had spent three days in Richard's apartment, in Richard's bed. From his smile, she felt that she was disbelieved.

"So that is why you escaped the vigilance of our agents," he said.

Relief poured through her. So they had not been tracked to the border—unless the general was playing with her. Under his glittering gaze, his perpetual smile, a terrible sense of impotence overwhelmed her. He *was* playing with her. It had been madness to go. How could they escape the attentions of the secret police?

Trepov asked bluntly, "I hope you have been of service to us, *in Richard Greville's bed?*"

Terror paralyzed her. She could not speak, the words lay like pebbles in her throat. She could neither swallow nor breathe properly.

"Well, my dear?"

Her silence alone must surely betray her? Yet when she spoke, he would see that she was acting a part.

"You seem reluctant to tell me, Natalia Ivanovna." The lines on Trepov's face hardened perceptibly, but he still displayed unnerving courtesy. "I rely on your good sense to withhold nothing from us."

She found her voice. To her astonishment, it sounded natural. ". . . I don't wish to injure one who has been kind to me," she said. Trepov looked up, pleased as a cat. "Then you *are* in possession of information?"

She nodded, swaying slightly, grasping the arms of her chair for support. She suffered a moment of what seemed like stage fright—the lines she had memorized deserted her temporarily. Then, speaking hurriedly, she told the general the story that Richard had concocted. It had been cleverly devised to reveal nothing that Trepov could not possibly have learned from other sources; it was only designed to show that she had made an effort.

When she had come to the end of her recital, Trepov said, "The emperor is happy in such servants." She bowed her head, not daring to raise her eyes to his. From the tone of his voice it was impossible to know if he was pleased.

"You must stop at nothing that your duty dictates," he went on, laying a hand on her shoulder. "The tzar counts on you in this hour of danger, as he counts on us all."

His hand on her shoulder grew heavier. She could feel her muscles contracting beneath his touch, she was powerless to stop them. "The honor of our country is at stake," he said. "But we shall know how to guard it." He stood for a moment in silence, wrapping her in a thick cloud of sweet cologne.

He has told her nothing of the least importance, he thought irritably. He's not to be caught that way—still, the girl might yet be useful.

He dismissed her. Bobbing a quick curtsey, she escaped from the room. She returned to the rehearsal, to the speculative glances of the dancers, and to the hard bright stare of Tamara Krupenskaya.

Oleg noticed the thin film of sweat upon her face and the dazed way she stared about the room. She looked at him as though he had risen from the dead to accuse her. Thank God I've never been in love, he thought, if this is how wretched it makes one. He could only guess at the cause of her distress. The Englishman.

At about the same time that Natasha was being interviewed by Trepov, Richard sat in the ambassador's office. He had been called from his desk.

He had gone expecting the worst. But if Lord Loftus knew about his mad journey, he gave no sign of it. He spoke only about the political situation. He spoke in a rambling, wide-ranging manner, finding his own way to the heart of the matter. Finally, he looked across his desk at Richard, pulling at his heavy moustache. It was the first time he had looked directly at Richard since the start of the interview. He was coming to the point.

"Of course, this war can't possibly last. Don't give it three months myself. Nevertheless . . ." He cleared his throat. "Nevertheless, we must have a reliable man there."

He pushed a crisp-looking parchment across the table.

"I'm afraid that it has to be you, Richard. Quite frankly, there is no other man of your caliber here."

Richard stared at the parchment. It bore the foreign office crest.

"You wish me to go to the front, my lord?"

The ambassador's moustache underwent some vigorous tugging. "You've been *ordered* to the front, my dear chap." He tapped the papers. "Those are direct orders from Her Majesty's government. Elliot, in Constantinople, has orders to send one of his embassy staff to investigate the Turkish massacre and keep his eye on the war from that end. This embassy must be equally well informed, from the Russian viewpoint. You're the best man here."

"But . . ." Richard paused, aware of the futility of trying to escape the mission. What possible reason could he give that would be acceptable to the ambassador? It was his duty to go. But, oh, God! the thought of leaving Natasha . . . at such a time.

Natasha regarded him with troubled eyes. "They are sending you away," she said.

"It's unavoidable, I'm afraid. They have nobody else to send."

Natasha raised an eyebrow, looking dubious. Since her interview with Trepov a change had taken place in her. A wariness and something of her old remoteness had returned to her.

Richard explained. "The whole situation seems to have taken everyone by surprise. The Russians are sending observers to the front. We need to see the war from that side, too. I'm the only one that's properly qualified to go, and we must have first-hand information."

She sighed. "Ah, yes, of course." She sounded almost abstracted. Then, suddenly, she sobbed and moved away from him, dashing the tears from her eyes. He checked himself from moving after her and stood watching her, darker suspicions aroused.

"Natasha, darling, has something happened?" he asked.

She tried to lie, but her eyes betrayed her.

"Tell me the truth," he said sharply.

Her voice, when it came, was muffled. "I saw Trepov again. He came to the theatre."

"When?"

"Yesterday."

"And you weren't going to tell me?"

She made a tiny guesture of despair.

"You should have told me," Richard said. "Did he come for a report?"

She shivered. ". . . Yes."

"And you told him what we had arranged."

"Yes, what I could remember."

She shivered again, and this time he went to her, holding her gently by the wrists. Was it his imagination, or had she lost weight? Her bones felt fragile through the thin stuff of her blouse.

"Did he believe your story?" he asked.

She shrugged wearily. "I don't know. He gives nothing away."

Richard held her close, kissing her hair. "My poor darling. Was he *grateful* for your information?"

"He was without emotion. He frightens me."

She turned to him suddenly, pressing herself to him. "Oh, God, Richka! What do we have to do with this? What crime have we committed?"

He took her face between his hands, kissing her tear-stained eyes. "The crime you've committed, my dear sweet soul, is to be the most lovable woman on earth. The wrong you've done is to make me love you so much that without you there is no world to enjoy."

She pressed herself more deeply into the shelter of his arms. "Ah, yes," she murmured, "for me, too. I'm a Russian no more. I have no country now. Their 'politics' mean nothing to me. England, Russia, Turkey, what do they have to do with you and me?"

He grasped her by the shoulders tightly, catching her roughly against him, laughing softly. Then he held her very close, growing serious again. "My dearest," he said, "when you are Mrs. Richard Greville we can forget about their 'politics,' perhaps. You'll have lost a country to gain a whole new world. But for the moment . . ."

His arms were tight around her. "There's going to be a war, Natasha. It's inevitable, I'm afraid. We're caught in the middle." The full realization of their coming separation flooded into them both.

"My darling Natasha, I thought I was being tender to you, yet I was nothing but a selfish brute. You've asked nothing

from me, you've given me everything—and my carelessness
has brought you nothing but trouble." His voice was heavy
with misery.

She pressed her hand to his mouth. "We're neither of us to
blame, Richka. Not for what we feel for each other. It is
them. They make things dirty." She smiled up into his face.
"But I'm strong enough to stand up for what I want. I can
bear anything but our complete separation. We theatre
people are quite hard, you know. It's not all soft lights and
bouquets. You've only to think of yourself, take care of
yourself where you're . . . going. I'll be here when you come
back. Only promise me—"

"Anything!"

She clung to him. "We shall be married, Richka?"

He swept her back into his arms. "I swear it. Once things
return to normal, when I'm back from Serbia, I'll petition the
tzar."

She sighed, quivering in his arms. "Ah, dearest, when you
come back . . ." She looked up, suddenly alarmed. "Will you
be in danger?" she asked.

He laughed. "Very little. I'm only going there as an
observer, sweetheart, not a participant." Though that might
come later, he brooded, if the situation worsens. War seemed
very close.

She reached up to touch his face, her hands straying like a
blind woman's over his features—the strong line of his chin,
the full-lipped mouth, the fine straight nose.

He was reminded of the first time that she had come to his
rooms. Then as now it was as though she was storing every
detail of his face in her memory. Her hands cupped his head,
drawing him down to her. He kissed her tenderly. Her face,
with its closed eyes, had a lost—almost childlike—
appearance.

"Will this be the last time?" she asked, opening her eyes.
Even when they were open they had a curiously blind look.

He nodded. "It can't be put off beyond tomorrow," he
said.

Her hands grasped at his shoulders, her body was hard up
against him, her breasts warm against his chest. Desire stirred
in her, sharpened by the thought of separation. He buried his
face in her hair, taking in the sweet clean scent of her, the feel
of her silken hair, her faintly perfumed flesh.

How strange, he thought, we've never had much need to

talk. We've laughed and touched, kissed and caressed, but
rarely talked. Language was the least necessary thing. We've
talked more in these past few minutes than ever before. And
now there was no time left for all the things he wanted to say
to her, for all the comfort and assurance he wanted to give to
her. God damn the Turks and the Russians—and the British,
come to that. God damn political greed and struggles for
power!

They were together on the sofa—the sofa on which he had
first taken her, initiating her into the raptures of fulfilled
desire. Now he ran his fingers through her soft dark hair, so
that it fell about her shoulders as he loved to see it.

They shed their clothes between gentle kisses. He wore
only a robe and pajamas—she had come to him in the early
morning. Her loose French blouse and underskirt were soon
removed—a froth of white lace and pale blue *faille*. It was
their last day together. For how long?

What did that matter? A week was as endless as a year.
Already Natasha could feel the long hours of boredom as she
waited for him to return.

At first they lay gently together, his head in the hollow of
her shoulder, her fingers locked in his thick fair hair. Then his
head moved slowly downward, his lips grazing her skin,
leaving the usual trail of aroused desire behind. His lips
explored her body, finding no part of it negligible. It was as
though he wanted to leave his mark upon every part of her
body, like an animal tracing its boundaries. She shivered with
pleasure, her breasts ached, delicious pain radiating from her
nipples. When he kissed the hollow between hip and waist she
squirmed in ecstasy. His lips found all the secret sensitive
place on her body, her clean-limbed, shapely body. Until he
had seen her naked, he had not realized what a marvelous
machine her body was, so perfectly designed for the work it
did—her small neat head, the swanlike neck, the firm strong
back, the long slender columns of her legs.

His fingers stroked her legs, reaching higher, to the silken
tender flesh that led to the triangle of hair. His head came up,
following his questing fingers, until his tongue found the
fold. . . .

Natasha writhed and moaned, her hands drawing his face
into the dark hollow of her loins. When he reached up, raising
himself above her, looking down at her in silence and
humility, she reached up to take him by the arms and draw

him down to her. She was ready, her sex pulsating. He entered her gently, her legs clasped him, her inner folds fastening around his rigid shaft with a warm velvety embrace.

It was a madness, a paroxysm. Only the next few hours were certain, not a moment should be wasted. They pleasured each other with an aching honeyed tenderness. Natasha sobbed with rapture, her face stained with tears even as Richard kissed her tears away. Their mouths were salty with tears in their last hours together. The memory of those hours would haunt their minds for the coming weeks.

Dawn found them exhausted, Natasha dry-eyed and wakeful and Richard sleeping in her arms.

She shivered as a dewy chill seeped through the open window, listening to the stirring city, unwilling to move, to ease the heavy body from her arms. A train whistle blew mournfully, speaking of departure, of distance. She felt completely alone, even with his beloved body in her arms.

She would have nothing in the weeks ahead, not even the ballet until the season opened. Not that she wanted that. She had lost all interest in dancing—all ambition had paled beside the intense excitement of these past few weeks.

She was afraid, not simply of the empty weeks ahead, but of the change their separation might bring. Would their relationship alter? Would he see her differently on his return? His going was more than a wound to her, it was a tearing apart. He would have the demands and excitements of his profession. Men could lose themselves in the intoxication of battles. She would have nothing but the suspense of waiting.

A clock chimed. Once away from her, would his passion cool? The last chime died away. Gently, she shook him awake. "Time to go . . ."

They took a long and lingering farewell of each other, their tired bodies renewing themselves in the cool dawn.

CHAPTER

EIGHTEEN

There was a loud knock on the door, demanding answer. Marie, who shared Natasha's rooms, went to open the door. Her mouth fell open and she gaped like a stranded fish at the two uniformed giants who stood outside. The gendarmerie. They stepped aside as an officer appeared between them. He was well groomed, almost dainty in his appearance. Marie's pretty mouth snapped shut. She had recognized the insignia of a general on his shoulders.

"Good morning," the general said pleasantly. "I wish to speak with Natalia Petrova."

Marie had enough presence of mind left to bob a curtsey. She stood aside to let him enter the room. Babbling, she "prayed" the general to wait while she fetched Natalia from the bedroom.

In the bedroom, her babble grew hysterical. "A general! Of gendarmes! It must be *him!*"

General Trepov in *their* rooms, the chief of gendarmes, the second most powerful man in Petersburg. "Why has he come?" she asked.

Natasha was trembling, too. Marie's quick eyes noticed it. Natasha covered her fear quickly, but the moment had been unmistakable. Marie crossed herself.

Both girls walked back into the living room. Trepov smiled with implacable courtesy, bowing as Natasha curtsied. He eyed Marie with an interrogative eyebrow raised. "Miss Antonova? Marie Antonova?"

Marie blushed, looking ridiculously guilty. Trepov knew her name! For a moment panic blinded her. Then her thoughts cleared. Naturally, he would know her name. The porter kept a list of all the tenants—he informed the police of every new arrival. She was in the police register. She had nothing to fear. . . .

But had Natasha? She glanced at her slyly. Natasha stood before the police chief with no more expression in her face than a block of wood. For a moment Marie wondered, in her silly romantic way, if the general was interested in Natasha emotionally. What a triumph for her if he was.

But she saw from the look on Trepov's face and the hidden fear in Natasha's eyes that this was not so. Besides, what suitor would come courting accompanied by two guards? This was a police matter. She felt another spasm of fear. After all, she shared these rooms with Natasha—and if she'd offended the authorities in some way, might it not involve her?

"I should like to speak with Miss Petrova *in private*," Trepov said.

Marie excused herself quickly, and Trepov watched her with pitiless amusement as she hurried from the room, almost tripping over the hem of her dress in her haste to quit his company.

He looked around the room with interest. It was without luxuries of any kind, a dull room, papered in yellow with a floral design. It was crowded with furniture of forty years before, green plants brightened the darker corners and faded paintings hung in tarnished gold frames. Yet the room was touched with grace, evidence of a female hand in the old pieces of bric-a-brac. Plainly the Englishman had not kept his mistress in much style—which brought him to business. He turned to Natasha.

For the second time in her meetings with him, the veneer cracked, showing a glimpse of the real Trepov, the beast beneath the dandified exterior. It was easy enough, she thought, to imagine this man whipping a student near to death.

"Natalia Petrova," he said, "we have reason to believe that you are in secret communication with Richard Greville—have been, in fact, since his departure two months ago."

Natasha remained completely motionless, trying not to betray herself by a gesture, little realizing that her very stillness, her lack of expression, betrayed her.

"You have received letters from him through the diplomatic post, what is called 'the bag.'" It was not a question, but a flat statement of fact.

Natasha stared at him, benumbed, deprived of all feeling, all thought. It was true. Richard's letters had been brought to her by a young Englishman from the embassy, a personal friend. What fools they were to have thought the letters could have been passed to her unnoticed. How could one put one's trust in anybody? The porters in the building were beholden to the police, certainly the doormen at the Maryinsky were in their pay.

"They were conveyed to you by one of Richard Greville's associates at the embassy," Trepov said. That, too, was a flat statement. So they had been watching her at the theatre. Slater had delivered the letters at the stage door, accompanied by the conventional box of chocolates or a bouquet. He had been greatly taken with his role of romantic intermediary.

Trepov waited for her to speak. When she did not reply, he asked, "Do you deny this?"

She shook her head, and the action seemed to clear her mind, triggering off a spark of anger. "No, excellency. Why should I deny it? I have done nothing wrong."

"Indeed?"

"No, sir. His letters contain nothing of interest to . . . to the state."

Trepov's blue eyes gleamed. He talked to her as though she was no more than a naughty child. Yet there was something chilling in his glance. "But why did he write to you in such a secret way?"

"Secret? I had not thought of it as 'secret,' simply convenient—as, I'm sure, did he. Even the most *patriotic* Russian could not say our general post was very efficient."

Trepov's smile grew steely. "He thought you would receive the letters more *directly?*" he asked.

Natasha almost said yes, but managed to bite back the reckless word. She flushed.

"He thought I would receive them more speedily," she said. "The letters were brought by special courier. Your excellency must know how long it would take an ordinary letter to reach me from the Balkans."

He nodded, as though in perfect agreement with her. "Exactly my point, Natalia Ivanovna. Diplomatic letters evade censorship. That is one of the reasons why they arrive more *speedily*. That is why they are illegal. Did you not realize that you were breaking the law in receiving the letters?"

Once again words deserted her momentaily. Then she said, with an attempt at a conciliatory smile, "Excellency, I am a woman in love. I could only think that the letters would reach me faster."

Trepov was unmoved by her appeal. "It is an offense for a private citizen to indulge in such a correspondence," he said.

"But why?" Natasha asked, looking bewildered. "The letters are harmless."

Trepov sat down and crossed his legs. Natasha could see herself reflected in the gleaming leather of his high boots.

"I have only your words for that, Natalia Ivanovna."

Natasha concentrated on her own reflection, trying to stop herself from swaying. "You may read them, if you disbelieve me," she said reluctantly.

"You still have them?" Trepov asked.

Natasha could feel nervous laughter fluttering in her throat. What an extraordinary question! Did he think she would burn them as incriminating evidence? What minds they had. "But of course I've kept them, excellency. They are *love* letters."

"Ah," the general said with a nasty smile, "no doubt tied up with a ribbon and laid up in lavender. Show them to me."

This is madness, Natasha thought, as she left the living room and entered the bedroom. Did he really think that Richard would write to her of politics? Secret letters! Did he think they were in code?

She found Marie standing against the wall, behind the door, trembling uncontrollably. It was obvious that she had been listening. Her expression was a mixture of fear and loathing. She crossed herself superstitiously, making the gesture against the evil eye. Then she collapsed in a tremulous heap before the icon in a corner of the room. She prayed in a frantic gabble, too frightened for easy tears.

Grimly, Natasha opened her trunk. She reached in, separating the layers of underlinen, until her hands closed on the letters. She smiled. Trepov was correct—the letters were tied with a silk ribbon and they did smell faintly of lavender.

She handed the small packet of three letters to him when she returned to the room. Trepov untied the ribbon and she watched him as he read through the letters. When he reached the end of the second letter, his face betrayed his irritation. He looked disappointed. What had he expected to find? Natasha wondered.

When he looked up his face showed nothing beyond a polite contempt for the contents of the letters. "Your lover has quite a poetical streak," he said. "And he is to be congratulated on his command of our language."

Natasha said nothing. Inwardly, she smoldered with rage and humiliation. She wanted to tear the strong white hands from the papers they held. How *clean* his hands are, she thought frantically. Yet his touch dirties everything.

The thought of him leering at Richard's tender expressions of love caused her pain, a feeling of degradation, almost of shame. She felt as though he had actually molested her body, as though he was pawing at her naked body as his eyes ran over the lines she had committed to memory.

> . . . *At night I murmur your name before I fall asleep. A magic incantation, my darling. If I go to sleep with your name on my lips and your image in my mind, it must mean that I shall dream of you. And I do dream of you—continually. You haunt my nights. I think of all the variations of your name, all the sweet pet-names, repeating them endlessly. I think of you, my darling, my femmka, so small in my arms, your soul so large. So dear to me, so dear. Oh, how I bless the sweet Russian tongue. I think of you so tenderly. Your name is a lullaby, a cradle-song. If I can't sleep in your arms, I sleep in the nest woven of your names: Natalia, Natasha, Natashenka, Natasheshka . . ."*

There was no mention of the war, no mention of conditions in Serbia. The letters were one long hymn of thanksgiving for their love.

Trepov looked up from reading the third letter to say wearily, "Lovers are rarely amusing about their condition." Then he folded the papers.

He paused for a moment. Natasha reached forward to take back the letters. His shallow eyes brightened with malice. With a smile, he held them just out of her reach. Then he opened his uniform and placed the letters in an inside pocket. "These, Natalia Petrova, are the property of the state."

Natasha opened her mouth in astonishment.

"They are evidence against you," Trepov said.

She gasped. Trepov watched her with interest, taking an acute pleasure in her wild anguished glance. Then she turned her head away, like a child trying to hide its tears, determined not to show its fear.

"How are they evidence?" she asked, turning. There was a hint of defiance in her voice.

"You have broken the law," he replied. "*You* do not have diplomatic immunity." He rose from the chair, staring at her with heavy-lidded eyes, lazily delighting in the suffering that he inflicted. Why had he come? she wondered wildly. Only to force her to hand over the letters? What had he hoped to gain from reading them? Did he really imagine that they would contain information about the conditions on the battlefield, even between the lines? It was all so preposterous. Who was she, who was Richard even, that they should have come to the attention of the chief of gendarmes, the tzar's right-hand man?

It crossed her mind that the general had no more motive in visiting her than merely to indulge his own cruelty. It was no more than his idea of a morning's entertainment. Plainly he enjoyed inflicting suffering and watching its effect.

Despite her numbing terror, she found herself fascinated by his eyes. They looked curiously soft, almost closed, as if he wanted to shut out everything but the sight of her suffering. His face was suffused with an almost inhuman sensuality.

But there was a point to his visit, beyond his pleasure in victimizing her. He placed his fingers together delicately. "You must face up to your position, Natalia Ivanovna. You have placed yourself in considerable danger. You are putting your career—if not your freedom—in jeopardy, the career that is natural to you, and that I know you love . . ."

Loved, Natasha thought. The theatre is a prison to me now, the regime of the ballet as confining as that of a convent. Yet it was a safe world, and one in which she was pampered and sheltered. She was surely spoiled for any other. Without Richard . . .

Her hands began to tremble. She thrust them behind her. She had to force herself to remember that Richard would return, that he would offer her his protection, his name.

Trepov, as though reading her mind, shattered her uncertain composure with his next words. "Even if Greville returns to St. Petersburg, it is more than likely that he will not return to you. A man in his position, with responsibilities, a duty to his country, his class . . ." He looked amused. "There is, you know, a remarkably beautiful and brilliant lady at court who is most put out that Richard Greville has neglected her for the past few months. She is, I'm told, quite determined to have him back. . . ."

But Natasha had ceased to listen to him. Her attention had stuck at "if he returns."

Again Trepov seemed to read her thoughts. "In view of what we know of his 'unofficial' activities, it is always possible that our government shall request his removal—if we allow him back in, that is."

Natasha was breathless with shock. Trepov regarded her slyly. "Of course," he went on, "if we thought that his presence here was in our best interests . . ."

Natasha waited for him to enlighten her, half knowing what he was going to suggest. She felt sick and cold.

"He could, perhaps, give us information that we should find instructive," Trepov said. "From the Russian lines one is only able to obtain certain intelligence. . . ." He tapped the letters in his pocket. "I had hoped to deduce some information from these letters—however trifling. But, clearly, he does not wish to depress you with news of the war." His eyes were mere slits in the white smugness of his face.

"But if he is allowed back, and if he still shows an interest in you, he may tell you things that he will not tell others. That is, if he is so *inspired.*" He opened his eyes to their normal width, and said, "On condition that you agree to prompt his memory, Natalia Ivanovna, we *may* allow Richard Greville to stay on in St. Petersburg."

Natasha stood motionless before him. As before, she endeavored not to betray her feelings. As before, she failed. The general's smile told her so. He now looked positively good-humored.

"Do you understand me, Natalia Ivanovna?" he asked, when she still remained silent.

She nodded slightly, looking crushed.

Trepov went on more kindly. "If I speak to you thus, it is in the hope that you will help us to lighten the punishment that your actions have deserved. It is possible that you are genuinely unaware of the nature of your crime, and are willing to atone for it, so far as it is in your power."

His words passed through her mind without taking root there. They were meaningless, she only recognized the threat they held. She felt weak and resourceless, stunned by the developments, despairing and alone. Inhumanity and injustice were the order of the day. How could she explain or justify her love to men like Trepov? Richard must return. He *must*.

But what would she do when he returned? She must betray him if she were to see him again. If she was to betray him, how could she keep him? Yet he must return if he was to take her away.

No, she thought suddenly, her courage rising. The future is not always fixed. They would find a way. She would face the future when it stared her in the face. The important thing was that Richard should return.

As it happened, she was not to be tested. The letters that Trepov had put away in his pocket were the last she was to receive from Serbia.

CHAPTER

NINETEEN

Serbia was a primitive spot, wild and beautiful, but very primitive.

Mr. Stillman, the correspondent of the *London Times,* had attached himself to Richard. He had taken a fancy to him. Mr. Stillman, an American, was a man who had no great liking for Englishmen, usually.

Although Richard found his company largely irksome, the man was a brimming stream of information—if one reversed almost every opinion he held. Richard's dispatches (written on the same expensive vellum that carried his tender messages to Natasha) were largely inspired by Stillman. He would listen to the heavily biased remarks of the correspondent, winnow the chaff of prejudice from the wheat of objectivity, and sit down in the sultry heat of the summer evening to compose his reports.

It was all very depressing stuff. The Serbian soldiers were badly led, supplies were inadequate, roads largely impassable. Serbian arms were inferior to those of their Turkish enemies. The Serbs had no cavalry. They were indifferent horsemen. They could not consolidate their positions. The peasants had no heart for the fight—it was not their war, it was their masters' war.

While the Montenegrin tribesmen cut magnificent figures in their long white coats and jeweled belts, the Serbian peasants wore inadequate brown serge. They looked bewildered by the fighting. They had a disconcerting habit of running away.

Five thousand Russian volunteers did their best for them, but stories were soon circulating that many of them were being shot in the back while trying to lead their Serbian troops forward.

Army headquarters swarmed with Russians in the brilliant plumage of the Imperial Guards. The battlefield bloomed with white tents and pavilions. They sprang up like the booths of a traveling fair. The scene was a strange mixture of squalor and splendor. Grand dukes and high-ranking officers marched through the white dust, past the rotting carcasses of dead animals, while servants in Asiatic dress made them comfortable. They had large retinues of cooks, valets, aides and English grooms leading high-stepping horses. Coachmen sat atop staff carriages, with peacock feathers in their hats.

The Russian officers watched the engagements from a railed platform, one half of which was covered with an awning under which a table was laid with white damask and spread with the choicest food and wine. It reminded Richard of some ducal luncheon on the grouse moors of England.

"They were just the same in the Crimea," Stillman told him. "Damned offensive, eh? Watching men get blown to kingdom come while one stands gnawing on a chicken bone and sipping champagne rosé."

"Personally, I find all battlefields strange places," Richard said. "It's hard to imagine that hearts beat faster in these commonplace landscapes."

Between writing dispatches, in the loneliness of his room in a local inn, Richard penned his lines to Natasha, wondering if they would reach her. He had received one letter from her five weeks before, but nothing since.

Two months had drifted by. It was now July. The weather had grown hotter and drier with each passing day. The landscape, like the international situation, was tinder-dry.

The expected recall to St. Petersburg did not come. If he had not heard from Natasha by the week's end, he would write to young Slater at the embassy.

"We'll see some action today," Stillman said as they rode out to the Serbian position on the hills above the deep green River Morava. Richard had not, so far, been so close to the front.

It was a lowering, oppressive day. The sun filtered through dark sagging clouds. Richard was already sweating.

They ran into heavy shelling from the Turkish lines almost as soon as they breasted the hill and came in sight of the battle.

The Serbian artillery opened fire as the Turkish columns advanced. Dotchtourov, Chief of Staff to the Russian Commander, gave the order, and the gaudily clad Montenegrins began to push back the Turkish left. Dotchtourov then ordered a small detachment of Serbian peasants to attack the enemy center. Battling through a sudden shower of tepid rain, the leading troops succeeded in seizing a slight eminence that could give the Serbs a valuable advantage.

But the Turks were strong in cannon. Discharge after discharge of grapeshot was fired from their iron mouths, ploughing wide lanes of death through the brown-jacketed Serbs, until the first lines were almost annihilated.

The Serbs fell back as a horde of half-savage Circassians and the dreaded *Bashi-bazouks* came charging down on the survivors. The chilling cries of *"Allah! Allah!"* sowed panic among the remaining Serbian troops. Nearby, Richard saw two Serbians of the reserve each shoot off a finger of his left hand in order to escape being sent back into the fighting. Others collapsed on the ground, shivering and wailing in terror. Still others simply turned around and bolted.

"Dotchtourov will now send in the reserve, to go to the rescue," Stillman said. "That is, if he can make the men move."

He pointed up to a hillock away to their left. "We'd get a better view from up there," he said.

It took them almost ten minutes of hard riding to reach the hillock, by which time the battle had degenerated into a wild confusion. There were scores of small bands of troops locked in bloody hand-to-hand combat—with, here and there, gallant but futile cavalry charges by the Don Cossacks. With fanatical bravery, they charged into the Turkish ranks, hacking a way through them to reach the first lines of cannon. There, they began to saber the gunners.

But the Turks had not yet used up their reserve. The fire from a second line of infantry halted the Cossack horsemen. Moments later, a fresh barrage of Circassians was launched against them. They were driven back in disorder.

Then a body of *Bashi-bazouks* emerged from the tangle of conflict and, with a fanaticism that equaled that of the Cossacks, fought its way through the Russian lines.

Seen from above, it was a chaos of stabbing, clubbing, shouting, cursing, screaming men. Knots of two or three soldiers clung to each other on the ground, in their death agonies. Above them, there was a surging mass of heads and the butt ends of rifles rising and falling as mounted men swept their swords down upon the exposed heads beneath. Colors flying, the horses charged, rolling over, mutilating further the mutilated men beneath them, burying them in horseflesh. Everywhere Richard looked he saw frantic faces, streaming blood. It was a mad scene, an open charnel house, with over all the thin terrifying scream of the Turks, *"Allah! Allah! Allah!"*

"Look, by God!" Stillman cried, pointing back toward the Serbian position. Line after line of the Serbian reserve had broken in disorder. They were running with great speed, firing off their guns and cheering loudly. But they were running in the wrong direction! They were streaming away from the battle.

"Why don't the Russians drive them back?" Richard asked.

Stillman shrugged. "Nothing will stop 'em now," he said contemptuously. "Hardly worth wasting powder and shot on. The day's lost for the Russians."

He turned away, and suddenly stiffened.

"By Christ, Greville! We'd best move sharpish if we're not to be cut off!"

From an inlet between the hills, a body of Turkish reserves —fresh and vigorous—were rushing to attack the fleeing Serbs upon their right flank. Already they had reached the outer columns of the Serbs. The churned-up soil was stained with the blood of men and horses. Here and there the ground was broken by the dark tangled heaps of corpses several feet high. Others were scattered in pairs, or singly, crumpled where they had been shot or struck down.

"Come on, man! We've dispatches to send," Stillman

shouted, goading his horse into action. Richard lowered his head and followed, charging down the hill and across the lines of the advancing Turks. Crouching low over his mount, he rode a zigzag course, at times swerving to avoid wrecked guns and timbers, at others jumping his gray over the heaps of dead and wounded.

He was halfway across the bloodstained plain, urging his charger forward at racing speed, when he came within range. At once muskets began to flash, bullets sang past his ears with a melancholy whine. One jerked the hat from his head.

He pressed on, spurring madly, until suddenly the horse lurched. Sensing rather than feeling that the animal had been shot, but not knowing where or how badly, Richard made to throw himself from the saddle.

He was a moment too late. Shot through the heart, the horse fell heavily, jerking in one direction but dropping in another, bringing Richard down with one leg beneath the blood-soaked belly.

Excruciating pain shot through his ankle. He knew that it had been broken by the stirrup iron, caught between the weight of the horse and the sharp edge of a stone slab.

For a few moments he lay perfectly still, waves of nausea pounding through his head. Sounds came to him faintly. He listened to the confused shouting. It grew faint again as the waves of pain shook him. His entire body trembled from the effort as he tried to free himself. Had his ankle not been broken, he would have succeeded in dragging himself from the dead weight of the horse's carcass. But his pulling on it resulted in such agony that he fainted.

When he returned to consciousness, the Turkish fusillade aimed at him had ceased, and he could hear only distant sporadic fighting.

He tried to ease his way out from beneath the dead horse. But with each twisting movement, stabs of pain streaked up to his heart, causing him to break out in a sweat. At length he was forced to resign himself to the fact that, without help, he must remain the prisoner of his dead mount.

He had no need to wonder who had won the day. The Turks were unquestionably the victors. But he was no longer concerned by it. All that concerned him was the dead weight that lay upon his leg, and the succeeding tides of pain and nausea that engulfed him. He was already in the grip of fever. The sweat on his body chilled as night fell. His chances of survival were slender on that primitive battlefield. There were no rules of war; he had learned that in his weeks of observation. It was just possible that the Turks would send out stretcher bearers, but there was no sign of them by nightfall. It was more probable that the human vultures would find him, and kill him for the money in his pocket.

Richard lay there, alternating between lucidity and feverish fantasies. There seemed every likelihood that he might just die of slow starvation.

The moon rose, a great yellow disc, serenely gilding the grim shapes of the deserted fields. Richard raised his head. He had caught the sound of voices. He could not distinguish the language, but he could tell from the tone of their voices what they intended. In his money-belt he had over fifty sovereigns. They would finish him off for fifty dinars!

Squirming over, he pulled his pistol from the upper holster on the dead mare. As he moved, the voices stopped. They had seen that he was alive. His heart thumping madly, Richard turned over. Above him loomed two tall figures, made grotesquely bulky by the clothes they had stolen from the dead men.

Raising his pistol carefully, Richard leveled it at the nearest man, offering up a prayer that the powder had not become damp.

He pulled the trigger. There was a flash, and a loud report that shattered inside his head. The man at whom he had aimed gasped. He sagged at the knees and fell heavily. With a furious curse, the second man flung himself at Richard. Richard brought the pistol up again. . . .

Before he could pull the trigger, there was a blinding flash in his eyes, followed by a dull retort. Somebody else—for whatever reason—had come to his rescue. The man fell on him in a slow spiraling descent, trapping him further. A heavy weapons case fell from the man's shoulder bag, followed by a rattle of stolen sabers. They cascaded around Richard's head.

The case caught him a glancing blow, striking his forehead. A series of bright flashes sparkled behind his eyes. The moon was haloed in a light that rippled and spread like rings of water. Then darkness came.

Consciousness returned as he was roughly shaken. He cried out at the pain that shot through his body. A voice spoke to him gruffly in a strange tongue.

He had no idea where he was. He could remember nothing.

His body felt cold and clammy. To his astonishment, he realized that he had been stripped naked. The dead horse had been heaved from his leg.

Men crowded around him. Between them they hauled him to his feet, supporting him. They ran their hands over his limbs to see where else he might be wounded. He gasped with pain, not remembering the injured ankle. A flask was thrust into his mouth, spirit poured down his throat, the fire of it making him choke. His ankle throbbed. Slowly, rhythmically, agonizingly, the blood began to flow in his deadened leg.

The men spoke again, conferring with each other. One felt at Richard's ankle. Richard winced, the breath hissing from his lungs. Then another man— a giant, seemingly—lifted him up, tossing him over his shoulder like a sack. Richard passed into cold sweating blackness again as the man set off across the field.

When he came to, he was on the edge of the battlefield, by a peasant's cart. He was lifted into it. Other men lay there, like bundles of fetid washing. None of them moved.

Two of the bearlike figures who had rescued him clambered onto the wagon, and they set off. The journey seemed without end. He was traversing the full nine circles of hell. Every jolt of the unwieldy vehicle caused the wounded men to groan with pain. Richard passed in and out of the void, in and out of torment.

He revived slightly as the wheels rattled over cobblestones. The journey came to an end in the pale light of lanterns. Once the cart had creaked to a halt, the wounded men were taken out.

Richard was carried into a barn, a dim cavern of a place. A man appeared, large, coarse-faced, swarthy, with a hooked nose. He wore a red fez. The man barked orders in a hoarse, guttural voice. Other men came into view, carrying basins of hot water and a supply of coarse bandages. They bound up the wounds of Richard and the men, then carried them into another room which was large and bare, with a vaulted ceiling. Pallets of straw were against a whitewashed wall. Richard was laid upon one of them.

He lay there, looking at the other men in their dirty tattered uniforms. He himself had been given a pair of brown breeches and a shabby shirt. Who were these men? he wondered. Where were they? Who was he? Why was he there? He felt anxious, but tired, overwhelmingly tired. Sleep poured over him in a great swirling cloud.

He awoke in the late afternoon, as the warm sun sifted through a small barred window set high up on one wall. The room, large though it was, looked like a cell. Richard could remember nothing. His hands and feet felt as though they belonged to another being.

He closed his eyes and sleep claimed him again. Even the people in his dreams lacked identity. He walked through long nameless streets searching for a remembered face. He sat, very high, in the interior of a mysterious building. Far below, on a vast bare stage, a small figure clad in a gleaming bodice and pink tutu turned effortlessly on long slender legs. Behind her stood a forest of birch trees, with trunks as white as dried bones. Then he was with her on the stage. He flew across the stage to her, she shyly and conscientiously executing the extraordinary steps he devised. They were deep into the painted forest, dancing toward a rustic church. Brilliant sunshine flashed from its golden dome.

He awoke to find the sun, in fact, glaring into his eyes. This was a new day's sun, bright and strong. Then a shadow fell between Richard and the blinding glare. He had been aroused by the swarthy giant. He now wore some sort of oriental robe. A ring glittered in the lobe of his left ear. He knelt by Richard's side, speaking to him, trying several Eastern European languages before settling on a guttural, heavily accented French.

"You wore no uniform," he said. "Who are you?"

The words seemed familiar to Richard, yet he could make no sense of them. French seemed as incomprehensible to him as the other languages. He could barely think in English before the waves of pain washed out thought completely. He murmured a few words, but something seemed to have happened to his articulation, the words came out as a meaningless slur.

"You are not a soldier of Russia?" the voice asked.

No reply. He recognized the words "soldat" and "Russie." The rest meant nothing to him. A few Russian words drifted into his mind, and drifted out again. It doesn't matter, he thought. I don't understand . . .

"Who are you?"

Again the words escaped him. He frowned with the effort of trying to make sense of them.

The swarthy man nodded at a huge Circassian. The Circassian picked Richard up and carried him from the room, to where a cart stood in the sunshine.

"You will be taken to Adrianople," the swarthy giant said. "You will be interrogated there."

Adrianople? Wasn't that in Greece somewhere? No, in Turkey, near the Greek border. For a moment he remembered clearly. Then his mind fogged up again.

He was to be interrogated? What did the man mean?

CHAPTER

TWENTY

In September the season opened as usual with a performance of Glinka's *A Life for the Tzar*. As always, it was an ostentatious occasion. The audience sparkled and glittered more theatrically than the stage, a riot of precious stones, silks and velvets, rare furs and flowers, lit by the enormous chandeliers. Lorgnettes and opera glasses raked the house from every angle. St. Petersburg was on show.

Natasha, from the stage, gazed with a slight feeling of dizziness at the swelling tiers of balconies, the gilded fronts glimmering in the stage lights. She felt oppressed by the splendor of the scene before her; the whole weight of the massive building seemed to press down on her spirit. The tiers of boxes looked like the ramparts of some fantastic castle.

The tzar, as always, sat to the front front of the imperial *loge*, as rigid as a metal icon, a gaunt figure in the plain white uniform of the knight guards, with the blue ribbon of the Russian order of St. Andrew. He appeared to have lost his taste for military ornament since visiting the battlefront. He was surrounded by the grand dukes in their brilliant uniforms, their chests heavy with medals, ribbons and orders. St. Petersburg was still affected by war fever.

Natasha strained her eyes, trying to distinguish figures in the semidarkness of the auditorium. She looked toward the

British diplomatic box. She could distinctly see the figures of the ambassador and his wife, but those behind were obscure.

For a moment the outline of a tall straight figure made her catch her breath. Then the man leaned into the light and she could sense rather than see that it was not Richard. There was something different in his stance, and his hair had a reddish gleam.

With a stifled groan she concentrated on the stage action, though she was weary with boredom. She felt like a stone as she stood waiting for the dance to begin. She hated her costume—the brightly colored *sarafan*, the stiff blue diadem ornamented with glass trinkets that pressed down on her brow. She felt that it summed up her condition. She had no more control over her fate than the Polishwoman that she protrayed. In the old days they had called the serfs "souls." The tzar had owned these souls. Well, she was still the tzar's property—he owned her as he owned the building. The spirit that had always lifted her on stage had flown.

Oh, God! Richard . . . Where are you? Why have you gone so completely from my life? She shivered, remembering the long gray days since parting, the long gray days ahead perhaps.

"Wake up!" Oleg hissed in her ear. Dashing in embroidered jerkin, blue breeches and red top boots, he stood with one foot behind the other, waiting for the beat. Natasha took up the same position in reverse.

The orchestra sounded the opening chords of the mazurka. At the right bar, Oleg glanced down at Natasha with a triumphal air. He tapped with one foot and bounded springily from the floor, lifting her with him. He whirled her around, and they flew across the stage to stop short on their heels with a flourish. Oleg stood in second, stamped with both feet, whirled rapidly around, left foot clapped against right. In a daze, Natasha followed him by instinct, abandoning herself to him. One moment she spun around, first on his right arm then on his left, skirt whirling around her thighs.

He fell to one knee, twirling her around him. Then he was up in one bound and they were galloping across the stage again, dashing forward with such vehemence that she thought they would be carried into the wings, but they stopped again, at full tilt, feet clapping together, herself spinning round and round.

The mazurka ended. She sank into a curtsey, flushed with

exertion, totally exhilarated, only to spend the rest of the act staring out into the darkness. Her gaze was drawn toward the British box, willing the loved familiar figure to appear.

Winter came. The first snows gripped the city in late October. By November it was packed hard, with the grip of iron. The world seemed full of despair. Two-thirds of the Russian volunteers had been killed. People said that it was impossible to fight an "unofficial" war, and it was wrong to speak of emancipating the Slavs. Instead, the fight should be for the acquisition of Old Serbia and Bosnia. They should be taken from the Turks. New Serbia must be forgotten and activity must be concentrated on Bulgaria. Bulgaria was more important then New Serbia for the future of Slavdom.

Russia was moving inevitably toward real war with Turkey. On November 12, 1876, the tzar gave the final order for the mobilization of six army corps.

For five months Natasha had known utter desolation. After the armistice in August she had gone to Count Scavronsky's apartment day after day, to ask if he had news of Richard. The count was her only means of contact with the embassy.

"Richard is missing. They presume he is dead," he had told her directly, believing that one should never tell bad news slowly.

She had stood before him, every sense deadened with shock. He waited for her to cry out, to weep, to faint. But she had simply continued to stand before him, her body unnaturally tight. Even at that moment he had to admire the control she had over her body. Other women would have been as limp as rag dolls.

"Do you understand?" he asked.

"Yes," she answered, calmly enough. Hope refused to die in her. "They don't say he's dead for sure."

The count offered her a drink. She took it with a nod of thanks, but barely sipped it.

"But he may not be alive," the count said gently. "You must prepare yourself for that."

"No, I won't do that," she answered fiercely. "He's alive. I must believe that."

"When did you last hear from him?" Scavronsky asked.

"A month ago. At the beginning of July."

She had received no letters from Serbia beyond the first three that Trepov had taken from her. Every word was still

etched on her memory. At night she would repeat them over
and over in her mind, like a prayer. She had learned them like
poems. His letters were lost to her, held in police files. She
was officially suspect, her patriotism in question.

"I'm sorry that I can't give you greater comfort, Natasha
Ivanovna," Scavronsky said. "But, really, I know no more
than you do. You must accept the possibility that he is dead."

She shook her head, stubbornly refusing. She must cling to
the hope that he would return to her, how, or on what terms,
was unimportant. If only he was alive!

She knew that if he was alive, he must be wounded. If he
was wounded, he would be repatriated to England. But from
England would he not surely manage to reach her? To send a
message?

Scavronsky was disturbed by Natasha—by her persistence,
her desperation, above all, by her appearance. She had lost a
great deal of her spirit along with her flesh. She was as white
as tallow, her eyes huge and brilliant, almost feverish.

There was something so pathetic, so shy and helpless in
her, that it went directly to his heart. At the same time he
found himself experiencing a strong desire for her. She
looked more virginal than ever.

How long would it be before she realized that the affair was
over? he wondered. For whatever reason, it looked as though
Richard Greville was lost to her. Even if he was alive, it
looked to be unlikely that he would be returning to St.
Petersburg in the foreseeable future. How soon would she
realize that it was the fate of women like her to be passed
around? That was the way of their world. He was filled with a
deep sense of shame. Although he made no move to touch
her, he felt that he had betrayed Richard.

The whole business was a mystery. He could learn nothing
of Richard's disappearance. The embassy staff was totally
uncommunicative on the matter. It was maddening. If Richard was alive, then he must be in the hands of the Turks. If he
was in the hands of the Turks, why had he not been
repatriated? The English were the allies of the Turks.

He must be dead. The girl must accept that fact and start to
live her own life again. And now that she was broken in . . .

Damn the girl! She was not innocent, or sexually untried,
so why did she have this power to make him feel contemptible
for wanting her? It was not just the matter of taking advantage of an absent friend, there was something in the girl
herself. She looked so damned inviolable.

He wished that she would not come to his house. But how to turn her away . . . with delicacy? One thing was certain. If Greville remained missing, and if she continued to visit him, he could not see how he was going to keep his hands off her.

In the end, her calls became irritating. The count directed his manservant to turn her away from the door. The message conveyed was always the same: No news.

In desperation, Natasha went to the embassy. Plucking up her courage, she approached the great door. A Russian porter showed her into a small reception room.

The elegant and languid Slater—the man who had brought Richard's letters to her—interviewed her. He treated her with gentle concern, recognizing her grief, but he had no news for her, either. The embassy knew no more than Count Scavronsky. Richard had last been seen on the battlefield at Nishbazar. His horse had been shot from under him, according to the *Times'* correspondent. He was missing, presumed dead.

CHAPTER
TWENTY-ONE

Verchinin came back into her life. With his rival out of the way—if not removed forever—the prince resumed his attentions. Night after night he waited for her at the stage door. Time brought no variation to the ceremony. The same words were spoken, the same compliments passed. She was haunted by his leering smile. The touch of his lips on her fingers brought a flood of bile into her throat. Tamara, fearing to be further involved, her caution overriding her greed, stayed in the background. She interfered only to the extent of dropping ceaseless hints.

For a week or two the old roué appeared to be genuinely
anxious to please Natasha. He moved like a cat on hot plates
whenever he was near her. His huge body was laced into his
stays until it seemed that his chest must burst like the frog in
the fable. Natasha began to dread the moment when she must
step out of the stage door to find him waiting, his eyes
beaming.

She had no art to disguise the misery she felt in his
company. She moved like a wax figure between whichever
girls were free that evening, desperately wishing that she
could find a new protector—in name only. She would answer
the prince coldly, with half-concealed irritation, at the same
time trying to ease herself away from him with as much
diplomacy as she could muster. It was hard to hide her
feelings, much easier to feign a female "sickness."

"Your excellency is too kind . . . does me too much honor.
Forgive me, but I'm very tired tonight . . . I am not well."

"At least allow me the pleasure of driving you home,
Natasha Ivanovna."

"We have engaged a carriage, excellency."

She found the answer for a week or so. The prince was
terrified of "female ailments." He had a primitive fear of
them. But menstrual blood can't flow indefinitely. On the
eighth night his eyes no longer beamed. They were cold,
steely and devouring.

"Natasha Ivanovna, I must insist. My carriage is at your
service."

"Your highness . . ."

"You will honor me by using it tonight."

There was no opposing him. Natasha was using Marie as
her shield that night. She turned to appeal to her, to back up
whatever excuses would float to her mind. But Marie had
fled. Natasha was alone with the prince. She knew that she
could no longer evade the issue. To walk away from the
prince in such a public place would mean his open enmity.
She was aware of the curious glances of the men still standing
about the stage door. The snow whirled about her.

It was all so embarrassing, so incomprehensible. Why did
he continue to pursue her? Why was he so ridiculously
devoted? Marie had said that he was trying to be "her
friend." But the promise of that friendship filled her with
foreboding. She felt it as more of a menace. She must find
some way of talking to him. She would appeal to him. In

private. The prince had already beckoned the doorman. An attendant shouted for a carriage. The carriage came at once. Everything waited on the word of this one man.

Lanterns swung around in the windy darkness, steam rose from the horses' flanks. Without another word of protest, Natasha allowed him to lead her through the crowd and into his carriage. By the time they reached it, she was dusted with snow.

For the first few minutes alone, she busied herself with shaking off the snow. His assault took her completely by surprise. He literally threw himself upon her. His hands were everywhere at once. Anger surged in her. She fought him off with all her strength. It was both terrifying and farcical.

"Natasha, my darling," he moaned. "I'm in agony. Only be kind to me. Be kind, and you may have what you want of me. Command me. In all my life I've never met your like. You're a woman above her sex. . . ." He gabbled on, incoherent with lust. Natasha protested at every move, twisting and turning to escape his hands. He had never looked so imbecilic and senile, yet she was amazed at the strength of his grip.

"I think of you all the time, Natasha. You are an enchantress, a charmer—"

"Prince, I beg you . . ."

"Night and day," he moaned. "At all hours, in all places." His hands were at her breasts, trying to open her coat. "I think only of you, Natashenka. For all these months . . ."

"Your excellency—"

"Don't call me that, Natasha. Speak to me as an equal."

"Your *excellency*."

"I want you, Natasha . . ." His hands were beneath her furs, snatching at her breasts. Natasha threw herself aside. He would have fallen, had his hands not twisted in her furs.

"But *why?*" Natasha asked, exasperated. "Why do you want me?"

"Because you're unlike any woman I've ever known."

"Excellency, that's not true. There are a dozen women you could have, a score . . ." Flatter him, a voice inside her cautioned. You must manage him tactfully. All the time she fought down the distress that threatened to make her vomit onto the dressed-leather seat. "A man like yourself, highness, can have his pick of women. A man so great, so splendid, so generous and well favored . . ."

It was no good. He still pressed in on her, forcing her back against the cushions. "None are so adorable as you, my little pigeon," he murmured fatuously. "I don't know what's happened to me. Ever since I first saw you, I've been a different man. Touching another woman's face now means no more to me than touching my own. All my feeling for other women has vanished. When I can touch your hands, your arms, your waist—" He suited the action to the words. Natasha squirmed beneath him. His huge body had penned her into a corner. She could feel his warm sticky hands through the cloth of her bodice.

"Prince, please! Please don't, your excellency—"

"Natasha, I need you. An old man needs you, my darling. I love you. . . ."

She fought to evade the persecuting hands, managing to slide from beneath him, edging along the seat toward the door. She was filled with a deep terror of him, mingled with revulsion, and a strangely unaccountable feeling of compassion. She had some glimmering of his feelings, hateful though she found them. If only she could find the right words, or a tactful way to deal with him.

At last he said querulously, "Natasha Ivanovna, don't you realize that I am trying to honor you?"

"Honor me?"

"Yes, my dear. You don't appreciate my intentions. . . ."

"Oh, but I do, excellency. Really, I do. But, you see, I *cannot*—"

"*Cannot?*"

"Yes. I mean, no—"

"I am sincere, Natasha. Do you doubt my sincerity? Is that it?"

To her horror, he lost his balance as the carriage turned a sharp corner. He fell clumsily to his knees. The carriage dipped. She herself was forced to cling to a leather strap. Verchinin remained on his knees, subsiding against her legs, his fingers scrabbling at her skirt, holding a fold of it against his face. She turned away, unable to look at him, looking instead into the black square of window, at the swirling snowflakes. But even here she could see his reflection—a gross old man, his face as scarlet as the ribbon on his chest.

He pressed his face into her skirt, pressing hard against the taut length of her thigh, leaving a trail of spittle on the green velvet of her dress. He was babbling into the bunched material. "I'll do anything. Anything. Name your terms. Only let me have you. . . ."

"Your excellency," she whispered. "Please! Do get up!"

It took all her strength to thrust him away. He fell heavily against the seat, then lay for a moment, breathing loudly, trying to regain his wind, with no thought for his dignity. He lunged again. Panic triumphed in Natasha. She thought that she might be sick. She reached for the door and managed to open it. The carriage swayed dangerously. The snow-covered street rose up to meet her, then fell away as the carriage righted itself. She was able to reach up and tap on the ceiling.

"What are you doing? What are you doing?" Verchinin cried, vainly trying to hold her back, thinking she might jump.

She struggled free, and the coach came to a long sliding halt, just long enough for Natasha to throw herself into the snow, praying it would be a new drift. But the snow was hard and slippery where she landed. She sprawled in a flurry of skirts. Her foot twisted awkwardly to one side.

The coachman, looking down, cried out, and made a move to clamber down, impeded by his greatcoat and cloak.

Natasha could see a narrow passage between two houses. She hobbled toward it, her right foot twisting over painfully. She expected to hear the coachman crunching through the snow behind her, but nobody followed her. Dimly, she heard a voice cry out, "Drive on!"

Only when she was safely lost among the looming houses did she slow her pace. She became aware of an intense pain flaming through her ankle. By the time she had found her way through the narrow, unlit, treacherously glassy streets to a cab rank, her ankle had swollen. It pressed against her laced boots. She managed to remove the boot while riding in a rented carriage through the streets, and she raised her foot to the seat opposite. She knew she must keep it raised.

She managed to hobble into her house, trying to keep her foot clear of the snow. She woke the doorkeeper and persuaded his wife to provide hot water, with which she made a poultice as hot as she could bear it. The pain was relieved somewhat. The doorkeeper's wife had found some tincture of arnica to add to the poultice.

But the long journey through the snow had worked some damage. Support and rest were what she needed most, the doctor said when he called the next day. She had badly sprained the ankle. He bandaged the joint firmly with a strapping plaster to take the strain off the damaged ligament while it healed.

"It will be some time before you can stand on this foot," he said. "And then you may find difficulty in using it for some time."

Marie, who had returned late the previous night, stood by Natasha's bed, her eyes bulging. She had been amazed to find Natasha at home.

"I must send a note to the theatre at once," Natasha said. "Will you take it for me, Masha?"

"Yes, of course." Marie twittered with nervousness. "But what on earth will you say?"

"I shall say I fell in the snow, which is the truth."

"Yes, but—"

"Just take the note in for me, be a darling," Natasha pleaded wearily. She had not the strength to listen to Marie's homily—the text according to Krupenskaya.

"You're a fool, Natasha," Marie said, flouncing out of the room.

Yes, no doubt I am, Natasha thought. I certainly handled the situation badly. I don't need her goggle-eyes to tell me that.

She felt a faint, ever-present chill of fear, not knowing what might happen. Though she took some comfort in the knowledge that she was assuredly free of Verchinin's loathsome advances. He'd surely trouble her no more. She shivered, remembering the feel of his hands on her breasts. Then she shivered more, thinking about the revenge he would most certainly seek. She suffered torments of anxiety, wondering what form his revenge would take, knowing that he would seek to injure her in some way.

She received a formal note from the theatre saying that she was temporarily suspended. She was to call at the theatre on the 19th of November. Seven days before, the tzar had mobilized the troops.

Natasha limped past the withered old concierge and up the marble stairs to the anteroom of the second intendant's office. The intendant's secretary, staring with intense disapproval, waved her to a cane-seated chair. It was hard and uncomfortable. After almost an hour's waiting, it grew intolerable.

Thirty more long minutes passed. Natasha's nerves felt strained to the limit. Six times the bell had rung on the secretary's desk. Each time she had been braced to enter the inner room, only to be ignored when the secretary returned to his desk. Once she had dared to ask how much longer she must wait. The secretary, a young man with a large head and an imposing manner, replied curtly that she must wait for the arrival of "His Excellency." Natasha asked, with sudden foreboding, who this "excellency" was, but at that moment the bell rang again and the lordly young man had disappeared into the intendant's office. When he returned this time, she was ushered into the room.

To her astonishment she saw that there were three other men in company with the intendant. They were lined up in a formidable-looking row behind him. She recognized two of the men vaguely, she had seen them at the theatre. General Zubov and Count Viasemsky. Both were fierce balletomanes, but she had not known that they were members of the directorate. She knew at once that this was a disciplinary committee.

The third man was heavily jowled, with a flushed veined face. He, too, wore a uniform, but she could not recognize it. The other men deferred to him, though he made no contribution to the conversation. All three men appeared to find his silence unnerving. Natasha, already deeply apprehensive, found him terrifying.

The four men regarded her with varying degrees of repugnance. The intendant looked shocked, his face pallid. There was something furtive and ashamed in his expression. When he spoke to her, his voice was soft, almost apologetic.

"You may be seated, Petrova."

Natasha limped to a chair set before the desk, placed in obvious isolation. The light from a milk-white globe shone into her eyes. She shielded them with her hands, turning in her chair slightly, which brought her to face the unknown man. He met her gaze with an imperious stare. She shifted in her seat again, feeling exposed and vulnerable, pathetically small. The desk was high and the chair set low. This was to be an interrogation.

"Your injury still pains you?" the intendant asked. His voice showed no apparent sympathy, only a formal interest.

"I still have some pain, your high nobility."

The intendant held up a paper, which she saw was her letter.

"You do not state how you came by your injury," he said.

Natasha felt the color rush into her face. She clenched her hands together until the knuckles showed white. "I fell from a carriage when I alighted from it, sir," she said. "It was a stupid mis . . . miscalculation."

"Indeed."

The long wait and the sight of so many people in the intendant's office had unbalanced her. Since receiving the news of her suspension she had almost cheated herself into the belief that her alarm was foolish, though she could think of no legitimate reason for it. But now, when she looked at the formidable figure of the unknown man, it was as though the hand of an accuser already touched her shoulder. Grim, stern and unbending, the man watched her with a searching gaze that stifled hope and held her chained to her seat. Verchinin has been at work here, she thought. This man is a crony of his.

She waited for the intendant to question her further. But instead, he pulled a large volume toward him and opened it at a marked page. He began to read from it. To Natasha's astonishment, it was a catalogue of her offenses against discipline, starting from her visit to the ice rink and ending with a series of complaints from the ballet-mistress regarding her manner during class.

"You know our rules," the intendant said severely. "You are a privileged citizen, but with those privileges goes great responsibility. Our public is demanding. They demand the highest behavior, both in and out of the theatre. The ballet is a cult, the theatre is its temple. An artist must not deviate the slightest from the established rules. For the past few months you have been an increasingly disruptive element, as witness this list of complaints." His voice was dry and formal. He glanced at her severely, but at the same time with something of shame in his face. "There are four times as many complaints against your name than against any other artist in this book. And now you tell us that you have injured yourself by falling out of a carriage!"

General Zubov leaned forward to ask, "Were you drunk, Petrova?"

Natasha looked up, startled into indignation. "No, I was not, excellency."

"Then it is an obvious case of carelessness," the general said, maddeningly dismissive.

The intendant paused. The expression on all four faces before her clearly stated that her story was not to be believed. But the intendant made no further reference to her accident. Instead he said, "There is also the question of your moral behavior." His voice sounded hollow and unnatural as he went on, "Your relationship with the Englishman, Richard Greville."

Natasha's head came up. To all four men she looked suddenly dangerous, stunningly beautiful, challenging. The fur around her neck contrasted darkly with the exquisite whiteness of her skin.

The intendant's accusations had held her tongue-tied, for she had recognized some truth in them. She *had* been slipshod in her work, dramatically and technically. Her performances since the beginning of the season had lacked spirit and conviction. But now, at the mention of Richard, the feeling of impotence left her. She remembered the true reason for her suspension. To question her moral behavior on the grounds of her relationship with Richard was the purest hypocrisy. She would not be here had she given in to Verchinin's loathsome embraces. She faced her examiners with new courage, leaning back against her chair defiantly. She reproached herself for cutting so sorry a figure earlier. She prepared to defend herself. She could answer any of *these* accusations with an open conscience.

But she was given no opportunity to speak.

"A report has been handed to us from the gendarmerie, Petrova," the intendant said, picking up a parchment. "It appears that you were repeatedly warned of the inadvisability of your relationship with Richard Greville. Yet you persisted in ignoring the advice of your superiors. Your behavior, while not being criminal—" General Zubov objected strongly at this, "—can only be viewed as unpatriotic in view of the present crisis," the intendant concluded, with an apologetic smile for the general. He turned to Natasha, speaking with greater severity than before. "Your position as a servant of the tzar requires your complete loyalty toward our master." He took a deep breath and then said, "You are a great sorrow to us, Petrova. Your attitude leaves us with no alternative than to dismiss you from the Imperial Opera Ballet. You are dismissed under article three, which, as you may know, applies to cases of disgraceful behavior, fortunately rare in our institution. This decision has been taken at the highest level. There is no appeal."

The intendant rose. She was dismissed. But Natasha could not rise from her chair. She was helpless with shock. She had clasped her hands together. Now she forced them apart and clutched at the arms of her chair, using them as a lever to raise herself to her feet. When she finally stood, she trembled from the effort.

Seconds had elapsed while she strove to disentangle the

words of protest that raveled in her mind. "Sir," she said, her voice muffled. "I must protest—"

"Your protests are futile," the unknown man said, leaning forward. His voice was low and harsh. "You have already been told, there is to be no appeal against this decision."

The intendant had rung for the haughty secretary. The young man took her by the arm and led her out.

CHAPTER
TWENTY-TWO

Who were they? Who were these men who tormented him? Starving and humiliating him, leaving him naked in the cold and darkness of a filthy cell? Who were they who made him stand for hours of interrogation, or forced him to squat on the low stool until he felt that his back must break and the pain hammered like a clenched fist at the wall of his abdomen? Who were these bastards who deprived him of sleep and denied him the basic daily facilities? Who were these animals?

Oh, God! what did they want from him? Their questions were beyond him. But still they went on. The interrogations always appeared to follow the same pattern. He would be blindfolded, taken up the steps—he knew there were twelve of them by now—and he would find himself in the slow welcoming warmth of the interrogation room. That warmth would soon grow into intolerable pain as the blood began to flow in his frozen body. His whole body sang with pain, the sensations so intense that the stool he sat on would rock beneath him.

Then they removed the blindfold. Light seared his eyes. At first he would be able to see nothing, for the light blazed directly into his eyes. He shouted at the pain, cursing. The transition from utter blackness to this terrible light was like being slashed across the eyeballs with a knife. He could not evade the light. The lamp was set too near. Its heat scorched his cheek. The rays enclosed his entire head.

Now the heat as well as the light became his enemy. His whole body was alive with agony, sweating, his heart thumping against his knees.

Then the questions would begin. The voice from beyond the lamp spoke a thick, slow, guttural French. Richard could not remember a word of French. He had no clue as to what his questioner wanted. Sometimes he could discern a pattern among the words, but after hours of sitting on the stool, fatigue and stress blurred any hope of remembering the meaning of one word in ten.

He could see nothing of the man who questioned him. He was an obscure outline beyond the violent light. The voice was calm, even precise, prosaic, relentless. The thought that terrified Richard most was that he could never find the answers to the questions they asked. His tormentors were after something that he was unable to give them. They would torment him indefinitely to no purpose.

Then he would be returned to the paralyzing cold of the cell. The cold enwrapped him like a tight imprisoning tunic. His nails tingled, small squares of torment in the swollen flesh of his finger ends, the flesh itself bruised and gray. He ached with a fierce continual pain. How long had he been there? Who was he?

His legs swelled from the enforced periods of standing and squatting. Lack of sleep drained his system to the limit. He lost all power of feeling.

They would start the questions from the beginning, whenever he was taken upstairs. He learned to recognize the opening words without ever being able to make sense of them.

"Nom?" "Rang?" "Régiment?"

He grew to hate the slow insistent voice more intensely than the pain. Its harshness cut into his mind like the steel tip of a whip. Standing at attention, sitting immobile. Standing, sitting, standing, sitting. He was interrogated for hours at a stretch, the brightly glowing lamp only inches from his face. His senses reeled with overpowering heat, intense cold, searing light, total darkness. Soon he would go mad. He must go mad. What mind could endure it?

His, apparently. Miraculously, the torment ceased.

One day he announced to the blurred image behind the merciless light: *"Je suis anglais. Je m'appelle* Richard Greville." The words dropped into the sudden silence with the same clarity that the full realization came into his mind. "I am English. My name is Richard Greville."

He felt strangely euphoric, like a man sighting land after a long and stormy voyage. He felt that he had been on some vast journey to an unknown shore. He was taken from the room, washed and wrapped in a blanket. Hard warm hands massaged him through the cloth, carefully and steadily. Warm milk was poured gently into his mouth. He felt drowsy, blissful. The face of a woman teased at his memory.

Then sleep. Sleep in a soft warm bed. Oh, sweet Christ, the luxury! To sink into the measureless warmth of uninterrupted sleep, and into another kind of forgetfulness.

Fazil Pasha came into Richard's room. Richard, as always, smoldered with anger at the sight of his late tormentor. This was the man whom he had known all these weeks as the blurred image behind the light—a tall, whip-taut man, lean in the face, with heavy-lidded eyes over a curved nose. It was a face that never failed to make him incoherent with rage, remembering the long days of torment at his hands. One day, when he had recovered his strength, he would make the Turk pay for his cruelty.

Richard still spent the greater part of his days in a light delirium. Almost a week had passed since his return to normality. But on this morning, Fazil Pasha's grim face was wreathed in smiles. Since learning of Richard's true nationality, he had treated him with exaggerated courtesy.

"You are to be returned to your people," he said. "I have orders to send you to your ambassador in Constantinople."

Richard stared at him blankly. Over the past few days the gaps in his memory had been filled in, but he was still painfully aware of a deficiency. "I'm not to go back to St. Petersburg?" Richard asked, fighting to keep his voice temperate.

"I don't know," the Turk replied. "Your country, too, may be at war with the Bear before that can happen. You are, in any case, still too weak to travel far."

With no small thanks to you, Richard thought. Sometimes it seemed that his memory had been teased out of him with hot wires. "When do I leave?" he asked.

"Within the next few days. I shall take you to Constantinople." He regarded Richard morosely. "I have wasted many weeks on you, Greville Pasha. One cannot ransom an ally."

Richard remained silent. So the brute had scented a profit to be made out of him, once his identity had been established. He had endured long hours of agony so that this monster might profit from it.

The Turk sighed. "You have been a great and sad disappointment to me. When you were first brought to me, I thought from the fineness of your hands alone that you were some great *milord*—Russian, Serbian, Montenegrin, no matter. Now, after all these weeks of effort, I find that you are no more than an English official—a neutral, and no great lord—my endeavors have all been in vain. At first I thought you were a spy, and my own government would reward me handsomely for your capture. Or your people would reward me for your return. But no! You were an accredited observer of the war. Of no value to my country or its enemies. A sad disappointment to me!"

He looked at Richard craftily. "You will not feel ill will toward me for the way you have been interrogated? You realize, I'm sure, that it was my duty."

Richard nodded. Something unclean seemed to have crawled under his skin.

"I have treated you with honor since I learned that you are not an enemy of my country," Fazil Pasha said. "And I am very out of pocket over your presence here."

Richard looked at him in astonishment. Good God! he thought. Does the brute expect me to pay him for his hospitality? He clenched his fingers together, forcing himself to remember that he was still enjoying the Turk's "hospitality." Fazil Pasha must still hope to profit from him, otherwise he would have had him strangled days ago.

"You will be rewarded when I am returned to my people," he said evenly.

Fazil Pasha sent Richard on to Constantinople in style. Or with as much style as he could command. For over two weeks Richard was jogged about on the back of a mule cart, resting on a thickly tufted smyrna carpet over piles of straw. He was hemmed in by a company of riders.

They arrived in the capital on a black December morning, when the seven hills of the city were covered in a thin film of hoar frost. The cart creaked over the treacherous cobbles.

Richard huddled in the cart, swaddled in blankets. The fever had returned. In his moments of lucidity he wondered whether he had ever received proper treatment for his injuries. Or had he simply survived through virtue of his own willpower and natural stamina? As they entered Constantinople he was blind to the remarkable skyline of domes and minarets gleaming palely in the frosty air.

They began to descend a steep hill, the hooves of the mules slipping on the thin ice. Suddenly, from a side street, a horseman dashed in front of the cart. The mules half-reared, terrified. The muleteer tried to back them as they slipped about in panic on the frozen cobbles, trying to back the cart side-on, to act as a brake.

Richard, his faculties dulled, was vaguely aware of the carter's attempt to keep balance as the mules' hooves clattered frantically. A man ran out to grab at the harness of the nearest mule, but it reared away from him in added terror. The wheels edged onto a curbstone. The cart began to tip over. There was a grinding crunch as the cart wheel came up against the stone, and then a great sliding of wheels.

Richard, half roused to his own danger, struggled to free himself of the constraining blankets. The cart was already at a crazy angle; he was slipping toward the edge. Entangled in thick fabric, he sought to jump clear, but the ground was coming up to meet him fast, and his feet were still wrapped in the twisted blankets. The carpet, too, had become entangled around him. He fell heavily, sliding over the blue ice, the blankets billowing around him. Wood splintered around him, straw rained over him.

He landed with his weak leg twisted under him, his head at a sinister angle, having struck a stone post. Blood seeped from a cut beneath his fair hair. For a moment he could feel the blood pulsing madly through his veins, a tingling agony in his limbs, then darkness.

CHAPTER
TWENTY-THREE

The new year dawned, 1877. A faint gray light struggled through the brooding clouds. The days began to lengthen.

Natasha dragged her life through these dark days. By the beginning of February she was convinced that Richard was dead. The cold dread inside her was more intense than the grip of ice and snow in the streets that she wandered so aimlessly. Events in the outside world passed her by.

Her life before Richard had been regulated by the progress of the opera season and the cycle of religious festivals. Now they passed almost without acknowledgment. Christmas, the Blessing of the Waters, the opening of the Pre-Lenten Season, the Shrovetide Fair, the closing of the theatre for the first week of Lent. She knew that palaces and restaurants blazed with light and color, but it was a pageant in which she no longer had any part. Feast days and fast days were all alike to her.

Around her was a ceaseless flow of Pan-Slavic talk. Patriotic feelings still ran high. Ladies in the churches that she visited fluttered about lighting candles in the cause of Russia's holy mission.

Natasha found little comfort in the churches that she visited, though she continued to go. Her prayers evaporated in the smoke of the candles, her mind was numbed. She would find her gaze floating vacantly over the mass of faces. For the first time in her life she resented the air of abandonment in the faces of the faithful—those who still had hope. Although her mind told her that Richard was dead, some part of her still refused to accept it. She went on praying, even when prayer seemed futile. She kissed the icons and repeated the lists of saints whose names must be invoked. Only the music, the heavenly purity of the voices, comforted her. She needed the sound of human voices, if they could be called such.

She was so terribly alone. Weeks ago she had left the apartment she had shared with Marie. As soon as she had been dismissed, Tamara had whisked Marie away before she could be contaminated by Natasha's disgrace. The rent had been too high for one person to pay. Natasha had to continually remind herself that she no longer had a regular income of sixty rubles a month.

She had taken a room on Vassili Ostrov Island, the student city. The room was only ten rubles a month. It had no separate entrance. Among other inconveniences she had to pass through her landlady's parlor to reach her own room. It was small and austerely furnished, with a narrow bed, a table, a chair, a handbasin and a pail. She hung her rapidly diminishing wardrobe in a small alcove. Each week some item was sold to pay for essentials, though she gave up each article grudgingly. She allowed her more summery gowns to go first, in a belief that by next summer she would be able to afford new clothes. Her luck *must* change. Once she had her papers her luck *would* change. She clung to the gifts that Richard had given her until poverty threatened her squarely and she awoke one morning to find that she had barely a ruble left. Then, one by one, the cherished pieces of jewelry found their way onto the pawnshop shelves. Yet, even here, she was optimistic. She would not sell them outright; one day she would reclaim them.

The room was none too clean when she moved in. She spent her first days in scrubbing it out, to her landlady's amusement. "In the spring, I'll clean the apartment," she had said. The landlady, Mrs. Gritzenko, was a plump woman, superstitious and talkative, who spent most of her day kneeling before the icon. She provided a simple but sufficient luncheon for a few extra kopecks. For supper there was a little bread and meat, and Natasha was supplied with enough water to make tea.

At first life was no great hardship. Natasha knew how to live economically. She had saved two hundred rubles from her last year's salary, even after buying her pretty summer clothes. Mostly, she just felt cut off from any acceptable reality.

Once her foot healed she began to practice again, using the

table as a *barre*. Despite her disgrace and the feeling of being cast out, she had not given up hope of dancing in the future. She still felt that she had a goal to reach, though it appeared distant and obscure.

Training consumed her days, the donkey work of training, the fight to improve herself. One part of her mind told her that training was as futile as praying, but the only alternative was to give in to total despair. Besides, it was in her blood, and one day—surely—she would be taken back into the fold. They would not waste her talents.

Despite depression, despite the days when her body refused to work for her, she went on with the drudgery of training. It was her one escape. One day she would find her luck again, she must be ready for it. She must find work. But what hope had she of doing that in St. Petersburg? The theatres that employed dancers were a state monopoly. Only a few private theatres existed, and they were unable to provide permanent employment. Besides, they were owned by aristocrats, dependent upon the ministry of the court.

The edict forbade her from working in any state theatre. Tamara had been poisonously accurate when she had said that Verchinin could make sure she would never work in the Imperial Theatres.

But the prince's terrible influence could not extend to every major theatre in Russia, surely? Natasha began to think of leaving St. Petersburg.

At the beginning of March—on the day of the Forty Martyrs—she applied for a permit to travel. It was as though the arrival of the larks from the southlands awoke her from some long hibernation. She was in a brave and reckless mood, risking trouble, taking chances.

"There's no point in hankering after what's gone," she told herself firmly. "And Richard is gone. I have to stop moping, pretending, dreaming. I'm on my own now. I've got to help myself."

No one else would, except her parents, perhaps. She decided to go to Ekaterinburg, where her mother was appearing in a highly improper French melodrama. Natasha's mother specialized in playing gaudy females *à la Française*. She knew everybody worth knowing in her sphere. She would help her to find work in some provincial company. Nobody allowed talent to rot. She was blessed, she must cling to that fact.

She was not beaten. If she wept, it was only for the loss of love. She must not allow them to wear her down with false remorse. She regretted nothing of those months with Richard. She was guilty of no greater crime than loving "not wisely but too well."

So, Ekaterinburg it would be, a thousand miles away, beyond the Ural Mountains. Surely there would be some company in that vast waste who would use her? All she needed, surely, was the permission to travel?

She opened her door one morning to find Oleg Mikhailovich sitting in her landlady's untidy parlor, charming the old lady away from her devotions. He had brought Natasha a small, bird-shaped loaf to celebrate the return of the larks.

She was touched by his gesture, and overwhelmingly delighted to see him. But when he began to speak of the Maryinsky she cut him short. "I don't want to hear."

He was full of bemused admiration for her—at her attitude, her determination, her strength. She looked magnificent, he thought. Pleasure at seeing him gave her an unaccustomed color. He noticed, too, that despite the poverty of her surroundings she was hanging on to her self-respect, if only by keeping her body trim and clean. Her blouse was fresh, her dark hair a soft and shining mass. She was battling with poverty as though it was an enemy to be routed.

He had expected to find her downcast and disheartened, but she seemed to be coping remarkably. She was even cheerful, though he realized that might be an act put on for his benefit. Still, he was amazed, and said so.

She laughed. "I've been through my dark night," she said. "It lasted a whole winter. But I *won't* be defeated."

She told him of her plan to visit her mother and seek work in the provinces. "I've applied for a travel permit," she said.

"When?"

"Two weeks ago."

Oleg pulled a face.

"And I came to offer you help!"

She watched him warily, her face closing with sudden suspicion.

Oleg laughed, flashing an embarrassed glance at Mrs. Gritzenko, busy at the samovar. "Oh, I'm not here to make a proposition, Natasha. I think of you as a *sister!* And I'm not the pimp of the Maryinsky, either!"

"Then what?" she asked curiously.

"I've been asked to give dancing lessons to the children of a merchant called Piltz," Oleg said.

Mrs. Gritzenko looked impressed. Piltz was a famous businessman in the city, a millionaire at least.

"What sort of dancing?" Natasha asked.

"Oh, polkas and gallops, that kind of thing. Nothing classical, thank God!" Oleg paused, looking suddenly shy. ". . . But I've had to turn it down."

"Oh? Why?"

"Too busy," Oleg said, with a diffident smile.

"Too busy doing what?"

Oleg grew more self-conscious than ever, looking almost guilty. "The truth is," he said in a rush, "I'm being transferred to the Bolshoi theatre in Moscow. For one ballet."

Natasha's eyes opened wide. "You are? To the Bolshoi?"

"Yes. They're doing a new ballet. Julius Reisinger, the German choreographer, has asked for me."

"In a new ballet?"

"Yes. It's called *Swan Lake*. The music's by a man called Tchaikovsky. He's a teacher at the Moscow Conservatory."

He looked away unhappily, unable to watch the unbearable sadness that came into Natasha's face. "He had a concerto performed a couple of years ago—for piano—" Oleg said, feeling a need to run down his achievement. "It was a terrible failure. The music for the ballet's not very usual, either, I'm told."

Natasha, aware that her melancholy was spoiling the pleasure he took in his good fortune, stepped forward and kissed Oleg's cheek. "Congratulations, Oleg. I'm really pleased for you."

"Really?"

"Really and truly."

Oleg's face shone with happiness. "Thanks. I'm pretty pleased myself." He looked at her uncertainly. "So you'll take the job if I can get it for you?"

Natasha still felt slightly envious. It clouded her judgment. A role in a new ballet! The luck of it! Reisinger wasn't Petipa, and the Bolshoi wasn't the Maryinsky—but still—to be singled out. Not that Oleg didn't deserve it, he did! He was an outstanding dancer. They had been so good together. If she had still been at the Opera, Reisinger might have asked for her . . .

"Oleg," she said. "You're an angel. Thanks for thinking of me. I'm very grateful. . . ."

"But?"

Unaccountably, she found herself refusing the offer. Afterward, she could only suppose that it had been a mixture of jealousy and false pride that had made her act so. "I prefer to try to get work in the theatre," she said.

Oleg's handsome face looked gloomy. "But, Natasha, you're banned from working in the theatre. If you don't get some sort of teaching post, God knows where you'll end up! I've been worried sick about you."

She squeezed his arm, trying to project more confidence than she felt. "Don't worry about me. My mother and father both work in the theatre, you know. They'll be able to arrange something for me."

Overcome with a feeling of ingratitude, she leaned forward and kissed him lightly on the cheek again. "I'll be all right, I promise. Mama's a mistress of guile and trickery. How else could she have survived in such a jungle? Not on talent, I assure you! She'll find something."

"But will you be allowed to travel? It's halfway across Russia!"

"Oh, I'm sure I will. Why should they refuse me? They've done enough harm."

Oleg looked doubtful still. "Well," he said. "If you don't hear anything, please contact me at this address in Moscow." He scribbled out an address on his usual card. "I can perhaps persuade Mrs. Piltz to hang on for a bit."

He looked at her shyly. "I don't suppose you'd like to come to see the ballet? I can get you in, and as for the train fare . . ."

Again she felt overwhelmed by a sense of ingratitude. The thought of being a member of the audience brought tears to her eyes.

Oleg saw her feelings reflected in her face. He pressed her arm. "I know . . . I know," he said. "If it would cause you pain . . ."

"Oh, Oleg," she said. "I'll come if I can—just for you. But if mama can get me work, I might be too far away."

"I understand. Anyway, there's a ticket for you should you want it."

When he had left, she felt more isolated then ever. He had brought a sense of the world she lost. Oh, to be spoiled again,

to be petted and admired. Not to have to think of money, the
weekly bills, the rent. Theatre life had been the only natural
life for her.

All the same, Oleg was a friend. She felt comforted by that.
She was in Oleg's thoughts, too, as he went back to the
theatre. Natasha Petrova had courage, and by God she'd
need it! She was too honest, that was her trouble. Honesty
anywhere was a liability, but in the theatre it was fatal! The
situation was too silly for words. She was born to be a dancer,
born for the stage. What a waste. He smiled, remembering
the proud way she had refused his offer to help. What spirit!
Good luck to her. . . .

On Palm Sunday people moved through the streets of St.
Petersburg carrying bunches of silver-gray catkins. All the
balloon sellers were out; enormous multicolored balloons
swung lazily on their strings in the spring sunshine. Urchins
ran among the crowds, blowing tin trumpets and swinging
hand rattles. The fine weather brought out the social merry-
go-round. Calashes and landaus paraded along the Prospekt
and the great *Morskaya*. The air was alive with a continuous
murmur.

Everything stirred with the approach of spring, but Natasha felt deader than ever. For five weeks now she had
waited to hear about her travel permit. She relapsed into a
deep depression. She went out only when Holy Week began
and the streets were relatively deserted, the bells silenced.
Otherwise, she remained mostly in her room.

Mrs. Gritzenko had come to life after her winter sleep. The
rooms were cleaned, "for the Lord." A glazier came to
remove the double frames from the windows. Daylight invaded the rooms. Mrs. Gritzenko polished everything she
could get her hands on, the doorknobs shone, the floors
reeked of wax. The curtains were taken down and washed,
the carpets taken out and beaten. The icon was bowered in
willow branches with their silvery buds.

Mrs. Gritzenko set Natasha to coloring the eggshells for the
Easter Feast. She greased them with a scrap of bacon fat until
they shone like jewels. Natasha's hands shook with exhaustion from the Fast—which had not been entirely voluntary
this year.

A year ago Richard had bought her a tiny enameled egg,
the blue of a della Robbia sky, surrounded with a clasp of
white topaz and diamonds. It nestled among the folds of her

last good dress, a polonaise dress of deep violet silk with self-color piping and trimming. That, and a tea gown of delicate blue muslin were all that she had left of her beautiful summer wardrobe, though she still had two of the better pieces of jewelry that he had given her.

Natasha longed to receive the permit to travel, to escape from Easter in St. Petersburg with its now unbearable reminders. The outside world intruded upon her at last. She was amazed to realize how much she had pushed away from her. She had been living in a winter dream, a snow princess with a splinter of ice in her heart, deadening thought and feeling, deadening pain.

Mrs. Gritzenko and her elderly sister insisted that Natasha accompany them to midnight mass. Amongst the compact crowd, Natasha felt completely alone, numbed with the weight of her memories. A year ago she had stood outside another church with Richard. Then she had been able to forget him, caught up in the mystery of the moment, in the exaltation that she felt. Now he seemed more substantial to her than the faded ladies at her side. The faces that gleamed in the light of hundreds of candles were as meaningless to her as the waves of the sea. Why were they so joyful? What reason had they to be happy?

Only the distant singing flowing out through the church doors tore at her deepest feelings.

Oh, Richka! *Richard, Richard, Richard* . . . she longed to escape from the crowd, but she was hemmed in on all sides, trapped between a thousand flickering flames. It was an eternity before the procession—a scintillating river of gold and silver—emerged to seek the Risen Christ. It was another age before the bells gave out the signal for rejoicing.

She felt the touch of dry lips as Mrs. Gritzenko gave her the triple kiss. Natasha kissed the withered cheek and opened her arms mechanically.

"Christ is risen!"

"He is risen indeed!"

The words thundered in her ears. *Richard is dead, Richard is dead*, echoed in her mind.

CHAPTER
TWENTY-FOUR

On April 21, 1877, the tzar declared war on Turkey. Two weeks later, Natasha received the necessary permit from the internal security office—she was free to leave. She pawned her one good winter coat and took the train to Ekaterinburg, a three-day journey.

Her mother was not pleased to see her. Olga Petrova was well suited to playing gaudy females in cheap melodramas. She carried her acting into real life. She was a small woman with blazing blue eyes, ringed with kohl, a tiny crimson mouth and a florid complexion beneath the layers of face powder. Her hair had been every color over the years; it was now flame red. She was as tough as a grenadier's boot.

She regarded Natasha with a mixture of despair, disgust and distaste, and came to the point immediately. "You've been a fool! A fool! You had a chance in a thousand. No, a million! And you've thrown it away—career, security, the lot. What did they teach you in that damned school?"

"To dance," Natasha said bitterly.

"To dance!" her mother echoed scornfully, dabbing at her mouth with a scrap of soiled lace.

"You should have sent me to a school for whores," Natasha said, "or kept me at your side." She looked at the cheap jewelry littering her mother's dressing table, and at the glittering locket on her mother's breast. It did not, she knew, contain a portrait of her father.

"My God!" her mother screeched. "Listen to the silly little bitch! Haven't you learned yet that admirers are an actress's one form of insurance? What do you think happens to most women in the theatre when they become too old to draw an audience? They're thrown aside to rot."

Her mother looked up from painting her eyebrows to regard Natasha with a look of almost naked hatred. "It's up to every woman to get what she can, while she can," she said. "And you could have landed a prince!" Her hand shook, ruining the line of her eyebrow. She wiped it off and began again. "I myself never managed to collar more than a baron—and a *parvenu* at that! And, Lord knows, I was your equal when I was your age."

Natasha shuddered inwardly, looking at her mother. Olga Petrova wore a ball gown trimmed with tinsel, spangles, paste and jet, stridently colored in magenta and royal blue, and of a baffling cut. Her every rounded line was made by the dressmaker, none by nature. In her heavy stage makeup she looked unspeakably coarse.

Is that what I shall become? Natasha thought. She glanced away unhappily. Her mother's dressing room was as unclean and untidy as she had always remembered, a sad contrast to the immaculate orderliness of the Maryinsky. Her stage clothes hung from a line strung between two walls, her outdoor wear was thrown over a chairback. A *cuirasse* bodice lay on the floor among a pile of frilly underwear, all of it cheap, none of it well laundered.

Her mother found Natasha's appearance equally unsatisfactory. Her jacket bodice of blue and white striped silk and her unflounced gray skirt were too modest by her mother's standards. Her cream straw hat with blue and white ribbons was too simple. Her mother could take no pride in her, she was not dressed like a fashionable dancer from the capital.

"I was doomed to the provinces," her mother said, with maudlin self-pity. "But you . . ." Her voice sharpened accusingly. "I shifted heaven and earth to get you accepted by the Imperial School."

It was not true, but Natasha made no effort to deny it. Gerdt, the *danseur*, had performed that miracle. Oh, if only she could contact Gerdt, he would make things right for her again. But he was still touring abroad.

"You had the most wonderful opportunity," her mother said. "The Prince Verchinin! You must have been the envy of every girl in the corps."

"I don't think so," Natasha said, without irony. "I was only one of a long line."

"But you could have held him!" her mother cried. "If you'd only *tried*. You could have made all our lives easier."

Natasha's eyes opened wide. She gasped, as though her mother had struck her in the stomach.

"Your poor father," her mother continued, unnoticing. "Do you think I enjoy being separated from him half the year? He touring Siberia and me stuck here in the Urals? Didn't you ever think of him?"

Still shocked, Natasha remained silent.

"Do you think he can go on working forever?" her mother asked. "Oh, granted, he's still supple enough, muscular as a serpent, without a pucker of fat on him. But he's forty-seven years old! He's on the slippery slope—from here on it's downhill all the way. You could have helped him. They say everything Verchinin touches turns to gold—"

"Or dross," Natasha said, finding her voice.

"You could have made a fortune with no effort at all," her mother persisted. "A man of that age can't be too demanding."

Natasha sat down, quivering with anger. But her mother continued mercilessly.

"Luxury is the only way of keeping out of trouble, my dear. To be so rich that nothing—nothing—can ever let the ugly fear of want put an end to one's enjoyment of life! You've let a golden opportunity slip through your hands. . . . No, you've not let it slip. You've deliberately thrown it away! Like a spoiled unthinking child. You must be mad. Mad!"

Natasha felt sick. *"Matushka,"* she said gently, hesitantly. "I was in love. Am in love," she corrected herself.

"As though that excuses you!" her mother cried, fastening a comb of paste brilliants into her red hair. "Do you think I don't love your father? Of course I do! I have the habit of love. That's why I have to take care of his future, and you had such a superb opportunity. You could have taken care of us all, secured your father's retirement and taken me off this damned tenth-rate treadmill."

In other circumstances she would have resorted to tears, but with Natasha she just continued to storm and rage, pouring scorn on her "sensitivity," her "fine, too fine, feelings," her "fastidiousness," her "love."

"Don't talk to me about your love," she fumed. "Such love is like madness. There should be a cure for it!"

At last she ran out of breath and insults. Natasha rose from her chair, feeling sick and exhausted. "You won't help me?" she asked.

Her mother turned on her furiously. "Not, 'won't' child! I *can't*, you stupid girl. What can I do? I can hardly keep body and soul from tearing apart. I have the devil's own job to find work myself. The manager here is a goat. If you think Verchinin is disgusting, you should meet Sokolov. The demands he makes . . ."

She groaned theatrically, patting her cheeks with a soiled powderpuff.

"I have to think of your father—on the scrap heap at sixty, and not a kopeck in his pocket."

Natasha walked stiffly to the door as an elderly page walked through the corridor shouting, "Places!"

Her mother looked up from powdering to ask, "What will you do?"

Natasha's shoulders sagged wearily. "I shall go to see father in Tobolsk. It's not too far from here."

Olga threw up her hands in mock despair. She really is as bad an actress off stage as she is on, Natasha thought.

"Good grief!" Olga screeched. "The girl *is* crazy! Do you think your father will welcome you then? Another mouth to feed? He thought he was well rid of you!" Her voice rose uncontrollably. "You were set up for life—a good career and a state pension at the end of it. Do you think he'll sympathize with you for throwing it all away?"

"He might be able to find me a place in the troupe," Natasha said stubbornly. "They use dancers don't they? I, at least, am properly trained."

"Exactly," her mother shouted, losing her temper completely. "Do you think he'll let you waste your training? Throw away your talent and your beauty on a flea-bitten harlequinade?"

She began to laugh in her cheap theatrical way, then her laughter turned to tears of helpless rage. Her tears caused the kohl to run, blackening the skin around her eyes. Furiously, she wiped the smears away with a rouge-caked rag. She creamed her face briskly and began to reapply the eye shadow as the call came for her to take her place on stage.

Natasha left the room quietly.

Sadly, Natasha noticed the signs of age in her father's body—the suggestion of a paunch, the hint of loose flesh on his once superbly muscular chest. Time had thinned out his arms and legs. He sat in his dressing room in the dingy theatre, surrounded by the pathetic props, wigs and garishly tinseled costumes of the harlequinade. He himself was dressed in the lozenged tights of the Harlequin, worn and tarnished and much repaired.

He stared at his daughter broodingly. She had inherited his fascinatingly slanted eyes and high cheekbones, though his eyes were now bleared with alcohol. Looking into them she had the impression of gazing into a cracked and clouded mirror.

"It's impossible, my girl," he said sadly. "Business has never been so bad. The house is never more than half full. It may well be that we shall have to turn off some of the other acts. Though we can't get rid of any of our girls. They're our most valuable asset."

Their girls were three young women of doll-like placidity, their veined cheeks plastered with rouge, their eyes glazed with vodka. Remembering their mean furs and cheap jewelry, Natasha could well imagine their value. Her father's face said clearly enough that a young woman who had turned away a diamond-studded prince would certainly stick at a provincial moneybags. Women like his Columbine and Pierrette were essential to the survival of the troupe.

Her father turned to his brother. "It's no time to be taking on extra hands, is it, Rodya?"

"It isn't," Rodya said gloomily. "It would only cause trouble among the players."

Rodya was dressed in the long white robe of the Pierrot, looking like a dirty ghost in the dimly lit room. His expression was half hidden by a mask, but Natasha could guess at it well enough.

"Besides," her father said unhappily. "*We'd* have to apply for a work permit for you. You've no idea the trouble we have with permits. And if the big theatres won't take a chance on you, what hope have we?"

Natasha looked around the shabby dressing room despairingly. She had used almost the last of her money to reach her father in the dreary little town of Tobolsk in the wastes of western Siberia.

"It's a long way from St. Petersburg, papa," she said. "I doubt if the restriction extends this far. Don't they send 'difficult' people to Siberia?"

Her father took her hands in his, patting them comfortingly, as he had done when she was a child.

"You don't understand, darling," he said. "This part of the world's not what it was. The theatre's dying here, has been ever since they built the railroad. People just whisk in and out." He turned to his brother, on whom he had always relied. "What do you think she should do, Rodya?" he asked.

Rodya looked up from removing his moustache papers. He brushed his glossy black hair reflectively.

Natasha knew the answer before he spoke. She could read it in the look he exchanged with her father. There was a hard knot of aching in her breast.

"You should go back to Petersburg, dearie," Rodya said. "Make your peace."

"With whom?" she asked bitterly. "The directorate?"

Both men shifted uneasily. Really, her uncle thought, who would ever have thought that Olga and Ivan—as easy as cats in that department—would ever have produced such a monster of purity?

"With the prince," he said firmly.

Natasha's father avoided her eyes.

"Ah, yes. Of course," Natasha said.

"All your trouble stems from your . . . well, from your attitude," Rodya said, managing to imply—in much the same way that her mother had done—from her *willful* attitude. He went on, "If you could convince him that you're suitably—well, *sorry*—he might forgive you, don't you think? Take you on again . . ."

"He has nothing to forgive me for," Natasha said. "*I* have done nothing wrong."

Rodya lost his temper. "You're very young, dearie. Very foolish. You didn't understand the honor that he was doing you."

Natasha smiled sadly. "Yes, that's what he said."

Her father looked wretched. He dabbed at his face with a makeup stick. The silence that fell lay on all three like a heavy blanket. The room was very still, hot and stuffy.

Natasha clutched at the brooch holding the lace ruffles at her neck together. She found difficulty in breathing, she longed for clean air. For the first time that she could remember, she felt truly oppressed by the tawdriness of the backstage scene, the smell of size and greasepaint, dirt and cockroaches, the dusty spangles on her father's tights, the

worn and patched material. She felt that she was seeing it
clearly for the first time.

At the same time her heart twisted with pity for her father,
condemned to live out the rest of his theatrical life in this
gaudy squalor, and then be "thrown on the scrap heap" as her
mother had said. Could she find it in her to blame him for his
weakness? Harlequin in the pantomime sometimes played the
pander. Had he grown into the part?

"Well, Natashenka, my dear," her father asked, brushing
out his silky moustache, "what will you do?"

Natasha gestured uncertainly.

"It would be sensible to do as your uncle suggests," her
father said. "Go back to Petersburg. Make your peace. Only
think of your position, pigeon. You were a member of the
civil service, a part of the great big glamorous world. What
will you be without the tzar's protection? Nothing. Out in
limbo."

Natasha sighed. A current of pure horror charged through
her mind and body. There was no help to be found here. She
shivered though the room was unbearably hot. She was truly
alone.

Madame Kalitin sat opposite Natasha on a velvet-uphol-
stered sofa. She was a large woman, encased in black silk,
ribbons, fringes, trimming, even her lace was black. Everything about her was oversize—her face, her bosom, her drop
earrings, her pearls.

She examined Natasha with damp black eyes above prominent cheekbones. From beyond the room came the sound of
an orchestra playing a Viennese gallop. There was the muted
roar of voices, occasional boisterous cries, snatches of wild
song. The Golden Cockerel Restaurant was filling up.

Madame Kalitin was the director of the chorus. She was the
fifth director that Natasha had seen that week, but the only
woman. All the men had rejected her after a brief interview
—if she had got that far. Something in her manner, an
uneasiness, an air of superiority, convinced them that she was
"difficult" even when they had not been told her story.

But Madame Kalitin had been sympathetic from the first.
They had been closeted together in the overdraped dressing
room for over half an hour.

Madame Kalitin appeared to be genuinely moved by
Natasha's story. She had been describing her long slow
journey back to St. Petersburg, and the depressing encoun-

ters with theatre managers en route. At the end of two months, she felt the authorities had branded her with a large "U" for "unreliable" on her forehead, for that was the word most managers used when they condescended to see her.

Throughout her story, Madame Kalitin had expressed disapproval with a whole range of deprecatory noises. She dabbed at her eyes with a black lace handkerchief. But she clearly did not believe Natasha's story entirely.

Now she asked, "But why did they really turn you off at the Maryinsky, dear. Between four eyes, you can trust me."

Natasha had told her—as she had told the theatre managers —that she had been dismissed for disobedience. She had concocted some story about turning her ankle at the ice rink. She imagined that the official reason for her dismissal would be suitably vague, if the directorate were approached for a testimonial.

"Was it over a man?" Madame Kalitin asked sentimentally. Her monumental bosom heaved.

Natasha hesitated for a moment. She realized that Madame Kalitin's sentimentality was only superficial; deep down she was as hard as the men who had interviewed her. In fact, madame's "heart" was unlikely to be in proportion to her girth. Could she be frank with her? Or should she concoct some cheap version of the truth? She hated to talk about her relationship with Richard. But she needed work—and soon. She was almost at the end of her resources.

"Tell me the truth," Madame Kalitin said again, her curiosity really aroused. "Did you get into trouble over a man?"

Unaccountably, and against her better judgment, Natasha found herself spilling out the details of her disastrous affair. After a few words, she felt the stirring of real warmth in the woman opposite. Madame was genuinely touched by her story.

When Natasha came to a whispering halt, Madame Kalitin rose—in all her vastness—stepped forward, and clasped Natasha in her huge embrace. "My faith!" she said, sniffing. "What a child you are! No more idea of how to take care of yourself than a carrot!" She shook with indignation, going through her whole repertoire of disapproving noises. "Whatever did they teach you at that school?"

Natasha, her head held tightly against the shelf of the massive bosom, suddenly gave way to her grief. She sank against the older woman. Dimly, she realized that Madame

Kalitin was not a woman to judge her. Simply to talk about Richard brought her face to face with reality. She had pushed so much of it away in the past months. There had been moments when the emptiness of her future had driven her to such depths of terror that she had feared for her reason. A yearning for sympathy, a sense of tremendous weakness, overcame her.

Madame stroked her hair, as though she was no more than the child she had called her, waiting for the storm of tears to blow itself out. The girl was as innocent as an animal, she thought, but without claws to defend herself. She had no eyes for her own interests. What she needed was good management. She was undeniably a beauty, with her high cheekbones and slanting mysterious eyes. Her peridot-green dress —cheap though it was—revealed the superb line of her body—a dancer's body, lithe and supple—the true line of her figure, too. No whalebone there. The girl had style. She'd dressed herself with a ten ruble note and had change to spare, yet she still managed to look like "quality."

But was she right for the Golden Cockerel? Most of their clients preferred more buxom stuff, a good handful of flesh— and easy, too. This girl had nothing of the cocotte about her. The Englishman looked to have been her one experience. Gently, she began to question Natasha about her other admirers at the theater.

It was like watching a flower curl up its petals, Madame Kalitin thought. There was clearly some mystery here. She was intrigued, and she had a genuine urge to help. The girl had been reared to dance, what other career was open to her? Natasha had already told her about her failure to procure new papers for herself. She was legally barred from taking other work. Her papers described her as a dancer, and a dancer was what she was. That's what came of being involved in politics.

Could the girl still be troublesome? For her own part, Madame Kalitin disliked politics or anything that disturbed the easy ripple of her life. But, surely, the child had been no more than headstrong? There was no real harm in her.

"If I gave you a place here, I'd have to clear it with the authorities," she said. "Of course, it won't be all that difficult, if you've told me *everything.*" She winked. "I have some influence. Our girls are very popular in certain circles." She looked serious. "But you do understand that I'll be taking a chance with you?"

"Because I'm 'unreliable?' " Natasha asked.

"Good grief, no! Because your appearance is against you, not your reputation. This place thrives on lost reputations."

"Oh," Natasha murmured.

"On the other hand," madame said, seeing Natasha's shoulders droop, "there is something about you that might appeal." She laughed at the realization of what it was. "Among my lot you'll pass for a virgin!"

Natasha flushed, and Madame Kalitin pressed the point. "You'll have to understand how we arrange things here," she said, becoming practical. "We pay two rubles a night, but you can earn up to five times that amount if you take somebody's fancy. The tips are princely. All you have to do mostly is sit about, dressing up the place, when you're not on stage, though you must dance with any man who asks you. No refusals. But I'll take care of you, don't worry. Usually I choose the partners for you. I know most men's tastes."

She regarded Natasha with kindly amusement. "You don't have to go with anybody you don't want to, if they ask you for a 'special favor.' The men understand that, so we never have any trouble."

She laughed at the look of relief on Natasha's face. "You won't have any trouble with the dancing, either. We don't have the waltz here—too much like licensed cuddling. The men prefer to dance the old Russian dances. So it's really all walking about in three-eight time." She laughed again. "Our clients are the safest in Petersburg. After three bottles of savory vodka they're not fit to collect any dues. They have to be poured into their carriages. They come here to be taken out of themselves. They'll spend just to listen to good gypsy songs and dance like bears." She looked at Natasha solemnly. "The rule of this house is that a man must wait for a girl to finish her work here before they can 'come to terms' with her."

Natasha nodded, overcome with a feeling of degradation. Then she shrugged. None of it really mattered. She was already a social leper. She had no option but to take the work, if it was being offered to her. The Golden Cockerel was little more than a licensed brothel, however much Madame Kalitin tried to disguise it. She would simply be exchanging a tolerated "house" for a more disorderly one. She had no option. To work in a shop or a factory required new papers. It would take her months to receive them—if she ever did. She

lived in a present so precarious that it seemed foolish even to
think of tomorrow.

"So I'll arrange for you to come here," Madame Kalitin
said.

When Natasha rose from the chair, she staggered slightly.
She had not eaten for two and a half days, but did not realize
how weak she was.

CHAPTER
TWENTY-FIVE

Richard sat beside a pool in the green shade of a broad-leafed
fig tree, in the gently decayed garden of the British embassy
in Constantinople. For the past few months he had fought his
way out of the darkness of fever. Now, in the pale April
sunshine, he learned something of what was going on in the
world.

When Elliot, the ambassador, had finished telling him of
the developments in the war between Russia and Turkey,
Richard said, "So what is to happen to me?"

"You're to take a ship to Venice as soon as you're fit,"
Elliot said. "Then proceed overland to London."

Richard protested. "But I must go back to St. Petersburg!"

"St. Petersburg? Good God, man, whatever for? Loftus
and his men will be out of there bag and baggage if Disraeli
does come to the decision to declare war. The British women
have already left."

"All the same, I want to go back," Richard insisted.

"All in good time," the ambassador said, humoring him.
"What you must do is rest, old chap. You've been damned
sick, young Greville. You'll be no earthly good in Russia. You
need time to fully recuperate."

Richard stared into the distance moodily. He realized that
he was as yet in no condition to make the long journey back to

St. Petersburg, but the thought of Natasha burned in his mind at all times.

Why had she not replied to his letters? He had written off to her within hours of regaining full consciousness. The letters should have reached her, even though they had been sent by a tortuous route—first the embassy in Petersburg and then to Scavronsky. Surely he could trust the count?

He opened his mouth to protest again.

"No argument, young fellow," the ambassador said. "Those are official instructions."

"But, sir, couldn't you help me—"

The ambassador cut him short. "There's nothing for you in St. Petersburg," he said. "The tzar and half his court are at some godforsaken place in Bulgaria."

Richard felt a moment of hope. Scavronsky must be with the tzar's party. That was why he had not yet heard.

"You're ordered home," Elliot said. "You've done your duty, man. I personally shall see you off in two weeks time—for Venice. You'll be given no visa for Russia."

Richard bowed to the inevitable. He would make his way to London as quickly as he could. Once there, he would petition every member of the House of Lords if need be. He must be allowed to return to his post in St. Petersburg.

CHAPTER
TWENTY-SIX

As the first notes of a banal waltz tune sounded, Natasha danced into the light, a flashing figure in silver and mauve. She appeared to gust across the stage, a leaf at the mercy of a light breeze. The fast swinging rhythm kept her leaping and twirling incessantly on the tips of her toes. Round and round, to and fro, she turned with pale drifting arms until—as the tune drew to a close—she sank into a deep curtsey. One more phrase, and she ran across the stage to leap into the wings, appearing to fly up and away from the applause that broke in on the music that followed her exit.

Later, she re-entered the restaurant to join an admirer. He was left sitting alone at his table, impatiently waiting for her return. But Natasha had dawdled, as usual, over her change of costume. She paused by a mirror to check her appearance once again. She wore a dinner dress of electric blue satin and gray ribbed silk, with blue bows and accordian pleats at the hem. She hated the dress, but it had been chosen for her by Madame Kalitin, "who knew best." The white lace ruffles at the low square neck were her own work. She had sewn them there to counteract the deliberate lewdness of the original dress, which had barely concealed her nipples.

It was not the only thing for which she had had to fight madame's taste. There was her makeup, for example. Madame's original idea had been for her to wear very heavy rouge and underline her slanting eyes with kohl. She had resisted all the way, and madame had eventually given in. "Well, perhaps you're right," she'd said. "You'd look like a nun who's taken to the streets."

During the past two weeks at the Golden Cockerel, Natasha had found that her untarnished appearance was her best protection. Men found it hard to make advances to an unpainted woman. All the same, it was wearisome work, and she must look for something less arduous. Reluctantly, she made her way into the immense and overheated restaurant, with its penetrating odors of spiced food and warm flesh.

She walked to where her admirer waited for her at a white table. She arrived in time to see him being led away, politely but firmly, by three waiters. They were either taking him to the men's washroom to bring him back to his senses, or else they were showing him to his carriage. To his carriage, Natasha thought with relief. He was far too drunk to be sobered up easily. His knees buckled beneath him, his pink face was glazed into insensibility. She might be spared one fawning idiot for the night, at least. If her luck held out, she would be left alone for the rest of the evening. The tables were all occupied, every customer had his "charmer."

Dimitri, the head waiter, came to her side. "Madame Kalitin wants you to go to her in the red damask room," he said.

Natasha regarded him warily. The red damask room was one of the private rooms leading off the main ballroom, through a glazed bay. So far, she had not been asked to retire to such a room.

She had learned within hours of Madame Kalitin's deception. Customers were not always asked to wait until the girls had finished work before calling on their extra services—a favored few could be accommodated within the building. Natasha had learned, too, that only the stars of the show could do as they pleased. The rest were chosen by madame at her client's request. She did—as she had said—have a remarkable gift for matching every taste.

Up to tonight, Natasha had—apparently—not been to anybody's taste. The men appeared to prefer the fleshier girls of the chorus, who seemed gentle and good-natured. Up to now, she had thought madame was genuinely seeking to protect her from the worst of the men's advances.

But perhaps she had just been saving her for someone special? A new face would have a certain cachet, even if the body did not come up to their voluptuous standards.

Natasha paused on the stairs, frowning. She looked back over the gilded banisters at the lively crowded room below, crimson and gold beneath the shimmering lights of the huge chandeliers. It appeared suddenly warm and agreeable to her, though fifteen minutes before she had dreaded entering the room.

Her hands were trembling. She pressed them together, then began to smooth out the wrinkles in her long blue gloves. What should she do? She was owed almost one week's money by the management. If she turned about now and refused to do as madame asked—whatever it might be—she would be out of work and almost penniless again. It would be next to impossible to force them to pay her what they owed.

What was it her mother used to say? "To pass comfortably through this life one needs a hard heart, a supple back and a good digestion." Oh, *matushka!* Natasha thought. If only I had your hard heart and supple back!

But perhaps she was being too suspicious? Be over-suspicious and you'll find what you suspect. Nothing seemed quite real to her. Even the memories that had sustained her for almost a year eluded her now. Those wonderful months with Richard were like something that had happened to another woman, a story she had read and been moved by, but one that had never involved her, the person she was now.

She entered the red damask room slowly and reluctantly, little expecting to find madame there at all. But Madame

Kalitin, resplendent in purple satin, rustled forward to take her by the hand. Natasha saw that there were three girls from the gypsy chorus already in the room, plus three musicians in their red tunics. Relief welled up inside her, blotting out her suspicions.

A large, red-faced man with huge silky moustaches sat at the table. The remains of a feast littered the cloth. Behind him stood a grand piano draped with a shawl.

Natasha saw herself reflected from a dozen painted mirrors around the room. On one wall a high-complexioned nymph— an expanse of billowing flesh—was being ravished by a leering satyr. It looked erotic but unlikely.

Madame Kalitin introduced the gentleman with gracious formality. Natasha saw that Count Fenster was an old and valued friend. Then madame advanced on Natasha with a glass of champagne on an upturned plate. To Natasha's bewilderment, she broke out into a drinking song. Her voice was a fine ringing contralto. As she sang, she offered the glass to Natasha.

Natasha, at madame's insistence, drank the champagne at one draught. The count swallowed an enormous bumper of wine and the chorus shouted with delight.

Madame Kalitin also polished off a glass of champagne when she had come to the end of her song. She offered a second glass to Natasha, who drank it less quickly this time. The count, bursting with satisfaction, consumed another bumper. His moustache was askew, his small eyes bright. But he made no move toward Natasha, beyond kissing her hands clumsily. Glass followed glass. The chorus sang song after song, harsh, melancholic songs, their voices as wild and dark as their appearance.

Tears filled Natasha's eyes, remembering the gypsies at her first rendezvous with Richard. Sadness overwhelmed her, and at the same time she felt dizzy with relief. Nothing was really expected of her. She was there merely to help fill the room.

"The count has a mania for singing," Madame Kalitin had whispered to her as she drank her first glass of champagne. "Don't worry about him."

The strange thing was that the more she listened to the gypsies, the more she wanted to drink. She felt that some wonderful revelation was about to be unfolded. The plaintive music was soul-melting. She shivered. She could barely hold the glass in her hand. The music opened in her such intimate feelings, such tender thoughts. She was living out her sorrows to the melancholy strains.

Somehow, in the mood created by the music, it seemed quite natural that she should receive kisses from Madame Kalitin and the three singers. They were sisters. Even the garlic-laden kisses of the musicians were not objectionable. They were her comrades, summoning up these marvelous sounds.

She was aroused from her dreaming by the feel of hands on her shoulders. Somebody stood behind her. Lips brushed the nape of her neck, the bristles of a silky moustache tickled her. She turned, startled, still dazed from the music, the heady power of the wine. She was alone with the count. The others had faded away like ghosts at cockcrow

Fenster smiled at her blearily, far from sober, yet not drunk.

Natasha struggled to clear her mind. But she was caught in a confusion as fine and clinging as a cobweb. The count was trying to turn her toward him, but bungling it badly. His face kept plunging toward her, his wet red mouth seeking hers. His face was damp, it shone with sweat.

Natasha laughed tipsily, despite a spasm of fear. The ends of the count's moustache were wet with wine. She could smell it on him. She tried to slip away from him, twisting from under his hold on her shoulders. But he clung to her like a great white leech.

"Aren't you warm?" he kept asking. "Lie down, do lie down. Loosen something."

She struggled again, feebly. She had the impression of moving through some soft and gluey liquid. All her movements were so slow, she was overcome with a feeling of intense weariness. She felt dizzy. The room whirled about her with majestic slowness. What was happening to her? Was she drunk?

Dimly, she knew that she must go on struggling. A face teased at the edges of her memory, a name tormented her—though face and name slipped tantalizingly away before she could fully grasp them.

Rough hands at her bosom roused her. A button sprang open, the cloth was torn. The hand was on her breast, squeezing it crudely, pinching and twisting her nipple between thick fingers. She shrank away from the count, who had succeeded in turning her to face him. One hand held her firmly, the other tormented her nipple, chafing her breast. Somehow the whole front of her dress had come apart, both her breasts were freed.

The hand left her breast and grabbed at her own right hand, plunging it downward. Shock rocked Natasha as her hand encountered the count's hard swollen shaft, jutting aggressively from a bush of grizzled hair. His trousers gaped open obscenely.

Crying out, Natasha reared back. She struck out at the inanely lustful face in front of her without thinking. With a muffled curse, the count released her, the blood rising in his face. His right hand swung up and forward, catching her on the cheek. Her head snapped back, and lights flashed before her eyes.

The blow seemed miraculously to clear her head. She stood for a moment, frightened, mortified, chilled. She saw that her dress was torn and there were bruises on her white skin.

The count, too, seemed to have been frozen into immobility. His breath wheezed as he leaned against the draped piano, fighting for command over himself. The wave of panic over, Natasha felt remarkably cool-headed. She saw that her bag was on the table, her long gloves and lace shawl, too. Calmly, she stepped forward and picked them up.

Then, without looking at the count, who was bent almost double by the piano, she walked from the room, clutching the torn remnants of her bodice over her exposed breasts, throwing the filmy shawl around her shoulders, clutching it tightly.

Madame Kalitin came toward her as she reached the bottom of the stairs. But with a furious look, Natasha pushed past her, making for the main door. Madame Kalitin turned quickly and, with surprising speed for a woman of her size, ran up the stairs to the outraged client.

Once she had gained the open air, reaction set in. Natasha began to tremble violently, her whole body shaking. Tears poured down her cheeks. She brushed them away angrily. Rage burned in her.

At the same time she felt a curious sense of relief. It had happened, as she had always secretly believed it would happen. Now it was over. She was free of it, free of cheap music, drunken fools and coarse embraces.

Tomorrow she would return her tawdry dress and claim her wages. Tomorrow, too, she would apply for an exit visa. The Imperial Theatres might bar her from working in Russia, but surely they would not stand in the way of her trying her luck elsewhere? She would throw herself on their mercy, appeal directly to the tzar, if that was possible.

At the corner of the street she found a droshky waiting, its driver nodding over the reins. She reached in her bag for the fare, then took the carriage to her safe, *clean* little room at Mrs. Gritzenko's. Gradually, the fresh morning air and the steady clip-clop of hooves calmed her.

CHAPTER
TWENTY-SEVEN

Venice lay basking under a gentle sun, exhausted at the end of an early summer day. Richard sat at the open window of his hotel room, overlooking the Rialto. The bells of the city had just chimed the hour, the streets below were alive with the hum of voices and the echo of footsteps.

He had visited Venice in his youth, but the unique pageantry of the city was as new and wonderful to him now as when he had first seen it. The square outside his window was like some vast baroque drawing room, where people of all nationalities congregated. Its enchantment never faded, a rich movement of life filled it day and night. He never grew tired of watching the people.

One day he would bring Natasha to share in the beauty of this fabulous place. She would love the colorful parade, the marvelously clear light, the beautiful tints of sea and sky.

The breeze that blew through his curtains was fresh, blowing into his room from a perfumed garden, tinged with the salt smell of the sea. His room was large and comfortable. He was almost seduced to stay a day or two longer. Venice was a haven, since no news of conflict reached him unless he sought it out.

But he must leave tomorrow. He had already delayed too

long, waiting for a letter that had not arrived. Impatient to receive news, he had written to Scavronsky from Constantinople, saying that he would be at Venice on such a date, could the count send word of Natasha. He had waited now for three days, but there had been no reply.

Tomorrow he must leave. There would be no news. He must expect none. The thought of Natasha haunted him. He must return to her, cut through the red tape and go back to Russia. He had already written to half a dozen influential people back home.

What a change there's been in me, he thought. I was always so damned *English*, too careful, too remote, living my life according to the book, considering the implications of every action. How distasteful it is to be always considering the cost, balancing one's feelings against what is suitable.

Well, one touch of passion had put an end to that. He had cast himself upon a strange sea. God alone knew where the journey would take him, but they would be together, of that he was determined. In the meantime, he must pack.

There was a knock at the door. Richard, turning, called out, "Enter!"

The door opened, and Richard sprang to his feet. "Kolya!"

The count, dapper in his braided coat and light check trousers, stood just inside the doorway, posing. He advanced with outstretched hands. *"Mon vieux!* Thank God! I thought I might be too late. Your letter reached me in Carlsbad."

"Kolya," Richard said, grasping his hands. "How good to see you."

"And you, old friend."

"I was waiting to hear from you."

"I decided to deliver my news in person. It's not easy to make contact with your embassy these days." The count looked about the room. "Have you been here long?"

"Four days. A century!"

"The devil!" Scavronsky exclaimed. "I came with all speed. Your letter took eight days to reach me at Carlsbad. The rail system at home is in chaos. I think all the engineers must be in Bulgaria with the tzar."

"You decided against going?"

"Mon Dieu! I won't be caught up in that madness," the count said. "I've no desire to die by inches in some Bulgarian swamp. Only flies and fools are attracted by the horrors of war."

"The news is bad from there?"

"What can you expect? The Imperial High Command is the last word in inefficiency. The generals are refighting the Crimean disaster, and the tzar has no real stomach for the war. Less than myself!" He regarded Richard slyly.

Richard laughed. "You're an extraordinary man, Kolya."

Scavronsky joined in his laughter. "I flatter myself that I'm a patriot, Richard. But a *sane* one. I can see no moral usefulness in such a war. . . ." He clasped Richard by the hand again, wringing it in his pleasure. "But you, my dear friend. We had given you up!"

"*We?*" Richard asked, unable to hold back any longer. "You've seen Natasha?"

The count was unable to meet his eyes. "No, I haven't. Not for some time. . . . I meant our friends."

"You haven't seen her?" Richard's disappointment was so keen that Scavronsky could almost feel it. Richard's face—so pale and furrowed beneath the light tan—disturbed the count. The man had aged unnaturally in the past nine months.

"*Diable!*" he said, smiling to hide his discomforture. "Look, I have much to tell you. But I am hungry. I came here directly from the train. We shall lunch, and talk afterward—"

"But I must know—"

"Later. Come, let's go to luncheon. I have much to tell you—a hundred things! I am a young boy again at the sight of you."

"But Natasha—"

The count took Richard's arm. "It's a long story, Richard," he said seriously.

In fact, Scavronsky was having difficulty in knowing how to approach the subject. He felt, suddenly, that his own part in it (or, rather, his negligence) must arouse the Englishman's contempt. He almost regretted his impulsive decision to travel to Venice. He felt that he had betrayed his friend by the extent of his own inaction.

Only as they sat at the table, with the champagne foaming in the long Venetian glasses, did he broach the subject. And then only at Richard's urging.

Slowly and hesitantly, he told Richard of Natasha's dismissal from the Opera Ballet, of her attempt to learn of Richard's fate, and of her eventual disappearance. Richard listened with growing anguish, and with growing contempt. When Scavronsky came to the end of his story, an embarrassing silence lay between the two men.

The food lay untasted on Richard's plate. A terrible
stillness had settled on him. When he had first seen Scavronsky, it had seemed a rare day of fortune—the next best thing
to meeting Natasha in these magical surroundings. Now all
was desolation.

When the cloth had been removed, they carried their cigars
and liqueurs to a little bower of palms in the ballroom.

"Richard," Scavronsky pleaded. "What could I do? If I
had interested myself in her—when both of us thought you
dead—what else would she have thought but that I intended
to profit by her loss?" Which consideration, he thought, *had*
been present in my mind.

He was appalled by the look of suffering on Richard's face.
"Besides," he went on, "I was not aware of her dismissal until
it was too late. She has left Petersburg. No one knows where
she has gone." He stretched out a hand. "Richard, you are
my friend, my brother. If I had *known*, I would have done
everything in my power to help her. But she did not ask for
my help, and I—God forgive me—was blind to her need."

The note of sympathy in his voice was so genuine, his
sincerity so unmistakable, that Richard's anger softened
against him. "But you are willing to help me now?"

"But of course! Whatever I can do. You may depend upon
it!"

"Could you trace Natasha for me?"

"I can try."

"It shouldn't be too hard, surely?" Richard asked, frowning. "She will be dancing in a theatre somewhere."

"In none that I know of," Scavronsky said. "At least, I
never came across her. She could, of course, be working in a
café."

Richard cursed, remembering the night cafés of St. Petersburg—the gaudy, overheated restaurants, the private rooms,
the whores in their garish finery. Was she reduced to that?
His hand trembled, pity combined with anger at himself. He
should never have left St. Petersburg without her.

The count was totally disconcerted by the situation. The
"love creed" was a thing he had always despised. It had no
reality for him. If he had ever felt anything for a woman, he
had made damned sure that he forgot it in another woman's
bed—or in a dozen beds if the case had been unduly hard.

But mockery died in the face of Richard's anguish. He was
astonished by such passion. He felt like the witness at some
mystery. He could only believe that long separation had kept

Richard's love alive. Had he stayed in Russia, he would have been cured by this time. Separation fosters such complaints. And pity for the girl was a factor. The count stared moodily at the fire of his cigar. "She must be found," Richard said. "And I must go to her."

The count puffed slowly at his cigar. "That may be difficult," he said. "You, too, have incurred the anger of powerful men. They could make sure that you never return to Russia again."

"That may be so," Richard said. "But I should still go."

Scavronsky looked up, astonished. "You would enter illegally?"

"Yes. It's not hard." Richard frowned, remembering Vilkovishi. "Well, it's not impossible."

To Scavronsky's mounting dismay, Richard told him of their attempt to leave Russia. The count felt increasingly angry. Was the man determined on his own ruin? But the pain written on Richard's face turned his anger to pity.

"Richard, you can't blame yourself," he said. "You've done all you can. . . ."

"But I do blame myself," Richard answered. "I left her without protection."

"Oh, come now. You were called away to do your duty."

"But I left her unprotected. I should have known. I saw the way that things were going. I'm responsible for the harm that's befallen her, however unwittingly. Christ, Kolya! I feel that something has been torn from my soul. I'm guilty. I must set things right."

"You still intend to marry her?"

"More than ever. There's not a better woman breathing, her sincerity, that openness of soul. It is the soul of her that I love. Oh, I know it's hard for you to understand it. You cared nothing for her—you saw nothing of her qualities. . . ."

Richard jumped up excitedly. He began to walk to and fro, attracting the attention of the other diners. "We were children! Children!" he said. Memories from that world of love and happiness rose up in his mind. Love and tenderness swelled his heart, stronger than ever. He turned to the count, who was now displaying an intense interest in the relighting of his cigar. "She taught me how to love," Richard said. "Quite simply, she showed me how to love. That's why I can't part with her. I can no more part with her than with life itself."

"You will ruin yourself for her sake," Scavronsky said.

"She has ruined herself for my sake," Richard answered.

Scavronsky experienced more trouble with his cigar.

"You said that you will help," Richard said.

"As I will, dear friend. Have I not proved my friendship for you? I am here. But I shall not raise my hat to your marriage. You wish to marry in spite of yourself. It will be disastrous, *mon cher*. You cannot escape your world. . . ."

Richard stopped by the count's chair in his restless pacing. "Kolya, you still don't understand. Natasha is everything to me. Everything. Every hour since I've been conscious has been an hour of pain for me. My life has stood still. The only way that I can move is *toward* her. I rely on you to work for me until I can reach St. Petersburg. But reach St. Petersburg I will—with or without official approval, British or Russian."

Anger, contempt and a cold determination showed in his blue eyes, a look, Scavronsky thought, almost of fanaticism. He had the air of a man who has planned everything and whose plan must be put into execution at whatever cost.

CHAPTER
TWENTY-EIGHT

Three months after she had left the Golden Cockerel, Natasha was almost destitute. She possessed only a rough cloth winter coat trimmed with rabbit fur, her last remnant from the previous winter. Already, in late September, the nights had turned cold. It cut into her half-starved body.

"I must go to see Oleg," she decided.

She hesitated to write to him, largely because she feared the letter would be intercepted, but also because she dreaded his not replying.

Since his appearance in *Swan Lake* he had not been near her. She imagined the new life he would be leading as a favored artist—the smart new clothes, the expensive presents, the giddy social life. Natasha, being honest, felt the purest envy of him, to be so spoiled, so sheltered, to be taken to exciting places and bought pretty things. The life was so natural to a dancer.

She went out into the autumn night, walking slowly through the streets, weary in body and wearier in soul.

As she neared the colossal building, she saw that the audience was leaving. Carriages stood before the imposing doors, lit by the milky globes of lamps. Policemen shouted orders in hoarse voices, coachmen swore as they dragged at the reins. Lines of carriages rattled away from the brilliantly lit palace of pleasure. Women, wrapped in furs, crowded upon the steps.

Natasha had forgotten how imposing the Maryinsky was, how glorious. She slipped into the shadows beside the artists' entrance.

The singers and dancers began to leave the theater in small groups. If she were to meet Tamara Krupenskaya, what would she do? She caught the eye of one or two dancers before they looked resolutely away. Marie, startled into spontaneity, began to approach her before she was drawn aside by the hand of a friend. They entered a closed carriage together.

Tamara walked out into the blazing light, her arm around the shoulders of a young girl. The girl looked up into her face, laughing, fascinated. Natasha shrank back into the shadows, but her movement appeared to draw Tamara's attention. For a few long seconds she stared hard into Natasha's face, pale and wasted in the flickering lights of the lamps, haggard with cold and fatigue.

Tamara was wrapped in a soft gray fur, her hands buried in a muff. Her face, within the hood, was bright with malice. With a toss of her head and a low aside to the girl at her side, she swept forward to enter her carriage, helped in by a military-looking man in a huge cape and fur cap. The girl, with a last curious look at Natasha, followed the others into the carriage.

A moment later, a handful of kopecks were thrown from the interior of the carriage. They rang at Natasha's feet. She looked up to see Tamara's face regarding her with calm vindictiveness. She started forward with upraised arms—half infuriated, half supplicating—but Tamara gave a curt command and the brougham rolled quickly away.

Natasha left the coins on the pavement and walked, blinded with rage, to the corner of the street. She screwed up her eyes against the cold. Shining crystals danced before her eyes.

She stopped, then turned around and ran to where the coins lay. Stooping, she gathered them up into her hands. Tamara owed her this money, at least.

A few minutes later, Oleg came through the door, fortunately alone. He stopped, with a stifled exclamation, at the sight of Natasha. "My God! You look terrible!" he cried.

"Thank God you're here," Natasha whispered. "I was beginning to think you might still be in Moscow."

"I go back on Wednesday."

She stumbled into his arms, falling heavily against him. Her strength left her. Oleg called for help, and a porter came running. Between them, they bundled her into a hansom cab. The driver, his blue eyes sparkling, asked, "Where to?" and Oleg gave him the name of a small café nearby.

Natasha lay back on the seat, half fainting with relief. Her face was tinged with blue. Hastily, Oleg muffled her up to the neck in a bearskin. During the journey, neither spoke. There was no sound but the grating of wheels on the cobbles.

Natasha sat back in her chair and looked at Oleg gratefully. She had munched her way rapturously through five courses of a simple meal. Her hunger had lasted for almost three weeks. She explained all that had taken place since their last meeting, ending with her departure from the Golden Cockerel.

"You never went back?" Oleg asked.

"Only to collect my wages," she said, flushing.

"And did you get them?"

"Oh, yes. I would have sat in Madame Kalitin's office all day otherwise." She looked up, frowning. "I'd have starved weeks ago if I hadn't. Do you know, Oleg, I earned more in two weeks at the Golden Cockerel than I earned in two months at the Maryinsky!"

Oleg smiled, with some sadness, thinking of the fortune she *could* have earned at the Maryinsky.

". . . So I've reached the end," Natasha said. "I've hardly any money left. I've hardly any strength. I shall have to quit my room by the end of the week."

"Quit your room?"

"Yes. I can't pay Mrs. Gritzenko, and I can't live off her. God knows, she's as poor as Lady Poverty herself."

"Is there nobody who can help you?" Oleg asked.

She shook her head. "I've written to everybody. I even applied for an exit visa."

"And?"

"It was refused. No appeal." She shook her head angrily. "I even petitioned the tzar, my 'protector.'"

"And nothing happened?"

"Not a thing. I've looked for other kinds of work, too. But my papers are still not in order. I've applied over and over again, but I never receive an answer. I've no talent beyond dancing," she ended dully.

Oleg was appalled by her appearance. Her limbs looked stiff, she moved clumsily. Her bones showed through her flesh, the flesh itself was sallow and blotchy. Her eyes burned hugely in her wasted face, they were rimmed with red. Her dark hair had lost its sheen.

"But how have you been living?" he asked.

She showed him her hands. They were marked with the scars of tiny needle pricks. "Mrs. Gritzenko takes in sewing," Natasha explained. "I've been helping her with corset-making. It's a terrible job, so complicated and time-consuming. One only gets two and a half rubles for three days' work—three days' constant work, twelve hours a day." She smiled wanly. "I won't get better at it, that's for sure."

She stared beyond him to where a cracked and spotted mirror hung upon the wall. "I've only three alternatives left," she said. "Find work, commit suicide, or go to Madame Kalitin and beg to be taken back, though I doubt if she'd have me after what I said. And, anyway, the men prefer acres of flesh. I'd have to be fattened up."

She took a deep draught of wine. "Of course, I could always go to the prince. Beg his forgiveness." Her mouth twisted. "That is, if he should still want me." She gazed at her reflection. Her appearance seemed to terrify her.

Oleg swore. "God damn them, Natasha! You mustn't go to Verchinin. If you do, everything will have been in vain."

"Not entirely in vain," Natasha said, smiling dolefully. "It's taught me a great deal." She laughed hollowly. "The worst thing about experience is that it can only be learned after the event!"

"All the same," Oleg muttered, "don't give in now."

"But how am I to find work?" Natasha asked. "I've spent hours at police headquarters. I've pleaded for the right papers. I've written six letters to the ministry, but all they say is that the matter is 'pending,' whatever that means. They lose my letters in their files, I'm sure."

She shrugged wearily. "Until I get an official permit, no law-abiding person is going to employ me." Bitterness made her voice ugly. "I've resigned myself to the fact that the way *up* is barred to me, but neither can I go *down*, apparently. . . ."

Oleg whistled between his teeth, looking sick with disgust. He glanced at her curiously, stealthily. He found it impossible to recognize the dark dreamer of a year before, though she was still elusive. She was such an odd creature, maddening, so impractical—for a ballet-dancer. She was a strange orchid amid the self-seeking balletic narcissi, the victim of her own emotions.

What a pity she hadn't come into the theatre this season. This season Krupenskaya had a new protegée. She was turning the new girl to great advantage, passing her around as though copulation was going out of fashion. This year, 'La Puritana' would have been safe to indulge her passion for the Englishman.

He had to help her. She had touched the depths. It would be on his conscience forever if he refused her. But what kind of embarrassment would he be exposing himself to if he helped her? None, if he passed her on.

Natasha was saying, ". . . I've been trying to find work in a factory. There are some places where one can get in without papers. But it's a hard time for business. Besides, employers don't seem to know what to make of me. I'm so *threadbare*. They think I'm bankrupt gentry, I think—too genteel. So I won't be much use to them." She smiled. "If only they knew how strong my body is . . . or was. It's been trained for hardship, nothing but dancing and more dancing."

"Exactly," Oleg said sharply. "Your body's been highly trained, all those years of energy, constancy, self-discipline. You've devoted half your life to perfecting that body."

He snorted with disgust. "Such a waste!" he said. "It's like throwing away a Stradivarius because nobody in the house knows how to play it!"

"But I have to find work," Natasha insisted. "Or what's left? Plain prostitution?"

Oleg frowned. "An overcrowded profession in Petersburg," he said unexpectedly. "Over five percent of the population are on the game. *Officially.*" He grinned. "Anyway, you'd make a poor whore—you haven't the 'turn out' for it."

Natasha flushed.

"You don't want to try for factory work, either," Oleg went on. "It's almost impossible to get work. For every woman employed there are twelve waiting to take up her job when she fails. And the failure rate's appalling. Most women work through bouts of illness. You'd never be able to stand it, Natasha. Strong as you are, it would grind down your soul—the filthy dormitories, the rotten food, standing barefoot in water and mess all day. Most of the women suffer from chest infections." He smiled. "No, I can't see you sorting thread or hemp."

Natasha stared, amazed that Oleg should know so much about such things. What could he possibly know about the life of such women, cocooned as he was in the artificial life of the theater?

As though reading her mind, he said, grinning, "Strange talk coming from me, eh? Well, I'm not just a fine pair of legs, you know." Then, before she could question him further, he took her breath away with his next words. "What we should do is marry you off!"

"What?" She half rose from the table. He waved her back into her seat, refilling her wine glass.

"A fictitious marriage," he said. "A marriage of convenience, that would automatically give you a passport. That is, if we married you off to the right man."

She began to protest strongly, but he continued, laughing. "It's nothing like that, Natasha! No cattle market. That's for the *bourgeoisie*. Quite the opposite, in fact. We'll find you an enlightened man. He'll marry you just to give you a passport. A passport to independence. You could leave the country and soon find work in a foreign theatre. Abroad, Gerdt would help you. . . ."

He stopped, becoming aware of the expression of total astonishment on her face.

"Don't worry, Natasha darling. Such an arrangement would exclude any *matrimonial nonsense*. You could part company as soon as the ceremony's over."

Natasha stared at him, more bewildered than shocked. "But who would do such a thing?" she asked. "And why?"

Oleg grinned, his handsome face alight with mischief. "Oh, there are good men about," he said. "It's only a question of finding one. There are men, you know, who genuinely want to give women independence, and this is one way of doing it. Once a girl is married, she can break away from her family. That sort of thing."

Natasha was silent, tingling, scandalized.

Oleg smiled gently at her outrage. "You've never heard of a fictitious marriage?" he asked.

She shook her head, dumbly.

"They're all the rage among a certain set," Oleg said airily. "Among girls who want emancipation. There are men who want to help women establish themselves financially and intellectually. Sex has nothing to do with such relationships."

Natasha stared at him with ever deepening amazement. His eyes were like coals, his face flushed with amusement, half mocking, half earnest.

This side of him was so totally unexpected, so totally *unsuspected*. Oleg Mikhailovich was in touch with young radical women. Emancipated women. *Amazons*. The nihilists!

Oleg laughed softly at the confusion in her face. "Not all of us in the ballet are untouched by the world, you know. Some of us have embraced a life *outside* the theatre."

"But . . . isn't it dangerous?"

Oleg laughed. "To embrace life?"

"To know such people."

Oleg laughed again, but not so lightly. "Isn't it dangerous to know anybody? Didn't you find it dangerous to know 'respectable' people?"

Natasha sat up, tearing at the fingers of her gloves. "All the same, I couldn't . . . I couldn't be involved with . . . with radicals." She regarded him solemnly. "You were joking about the . . . the fake marriage?"

"No," he answered, perfectly serious now. "It could be managed."

"But I couldn't accept it! Marriage is a sacrament." Her fingers toyed with the glass. She had picked a hole in the finger of one glove.

Oleg asked, "How did you think I could help?"

"You said you might be able to find me work with a family . . . a teaching post."

Oleg scowled. "What respectable family would accept you, Natasha? Where would you find a reference?"

"But you said that you knew of a family . . ."

"Oh, yes. I asked them about it. It would never have worked. The first thing they asked for was a recommendation from the theatre. Are you likely to get one, do you think?"

"I could ask."

"Yes, you could ask."

"Oh, God!" Natasha sat back in her chair.

Oleg leaned forward, taking her hands in his. "Natasha," he said, his voice low and persuasive. "You can't really expect help from that quarter. Haven't they already proved it? You'll only get help from people who truly sympathize with you. My friends. They won't use you, or compromise you. They're very careful of people like you. They know what it is to be vulnerable."

Natasha stirred uneasily.

"We're not all callow students and rebellious children," Oleg said. "We number quite a lot of respectable people among us—people of influence. It's time you had a voice raised in your defense. We might find somebody to do that for you. In the meantime, you have to live."

He suddenly slapped his hand against his forehead. "Of course! The very woman! If she's still around."

"Who?"

"I can't give you her name. She's the most extraordinary woman I know." He flashed a grin. "Even more extraordinary than you. Yes, she must know somebody who can employ you."

"As a dancer?"

Another grin. "Well, not as a cocotte! Cocottes are not at all the thing among her set." He took a leaf of paper from a pocketbook and began to scribble on it with a thin gold pencil.

Natasha found herself evaluating the cost of the pencil. Suddenly she noticed the rings on his lean fingers, the diamond scarf pin, the cuff links. Oleg, too, had his admirers, she realized. She wondered about them. What a puzzling man he was. Yet he had always seemed so simple, so open.

Oleg, looking up, caught her looking at his jewelry. He winked, and gave her the scrap of paper on which he had written an address.

"Meet me there tomorrow night," he said. "About seven o'clock."

Her hands closed nervously around the paper. He gently unfolded her fingers, took the paper and put it in her bag.

"Be there, Natasha. She can help. And she won't put a price on her help. She detests corruption."

He tapped the paper lying crumpled in her open bag. "You will be there?" he asked.

After a moment's hesitation, she nodded.

CHAPTER
TWENTY-NINE

Oleg's woman friend was tiny, much smaller than Natasha. She looked like an overgrown schoolgirl. But Natasha saw at once that for all her girlishness, the woman was extraordinary —as Oleg had said. She radiated energy and purposefulness.

She was striking rather than beautiful, with a round face, very pale against her black dress with its modest white collar. Her eyes were gray and stubborn beneath a broad white forehead.

Oleg introduced her as "Rosa." "A 'Rosa' by any other name," he joked.

Rosa spoke to Natasha directly, with a vague hostility in her voice. "Oleg Mikhailovich has told me about you— everything he thinks I need to know, at least. Secrecy comes naturally to us. I must say you're not quite in our line, but . . ." She smiled, her smile small and faint. Her face gave little away. Natasha felt that no unnecessary word would ever pass her lips.

"It will be best if you leave the country," Rosa said. "We'll have to smuggle you out. Oleg says you don't want to acquire a passport in the usual fashion with us."

Natasha flushed. "I just want to be allowed to work," she said.

"Ah, my dear, millions do." It was said with a flash of bitterness.

"When do you think she can leave?" Oleg asked.

Rosa shrugged. "I don't know yet. Not for six weeks, at least. Not until the trial ends."

She turned in time to catch an expression of alarm flit across Natasha's face. Natasha had heard of the trial of the 193—radical students imprisoned by the government. She felt a sudden compulsion to run from the room at this reminder of what company she kept. Only total despair and a strange sort of hope that this extraordinary girl could whisk her magically abroad kept her where she stood.

Rosa frowned, as though she, too, was reminded of something, something unpleasant, in her case.

"You can find your sort of work easily in Europe?" she asked. The way she pronounced the word "work" left Natasha in no doubt of how greatly she despised it

"Yes, she can," Oleg said enthusiastically. "Well paid, too. And I'm sure that Natasha will prove grateful."

"Yes, I will," Natasha said, understanding him to mean that she would make some contribution to their funds.

But Rosa still looked distrustful. "You could have gained a passport by volunteering to work for the Pan-Slavists," she said. "They'd have sent you to Bulgaria as a nurse, or something like that."

"No, they wouldn't," Natasha said. "I tried that."

Oleg looked startled. "You didn't say!"

"Didn't I? . . . I forgot. It was only one of many rejections."

"They wouldn't take you on?" Rosa asked.

"They said they only wanted experienced women, and thousands had come forward. . . ."

Rosa snorted, though she gave Natasha a look of grudging admiration. Oleg looked impressed.

"I think they suspected my motives," Natasha said. "I had none of the right answers to their questions, and they already had a considerable file on me. I seem to have acquired a complete dossier."

Rosa regarded her with more sympathy.

"I should have rehearsed my role more carefully," Natasha said, smiling.

The mention of rehearsal jogged Oleg's memory. "My God!" he said, looking at the clock on the otherwise bare mantelshelf. "I must go. I have a train to catch."

"You're going away?" Natasha asked.

"To Moscow—I told you—for what I hope is going to be the last flight of those bloody swans!" He pulled a wry face.

"Isn't it a success?" Natasha asked.

"It's a disaster!" Oleg cried. "Impossible music, and Reisinger is a man with two left feet. The sooner he goes back to Leipzig, the better. And as for Karpakova! She's a *bitch-assoluta*. She keeps making Tchaikovsky write new music. You never know from week to week what's in and what's out. Then most of the——"

He stopped at an exclamation from Rosa, who had shown increasing impatience with the theatrical gossip. "Moscow!" she said. "She must go with you to Moscow. We can find her a place there."

"But I have a place here," Natasha said. "With Mrs. Gritzenko."

"You can't afford to pay her," Oleg said.

"Besides, we shall need you under our wing," Rosa said. "And Petersburg is too risky for us at the moment. Most of our people are on the move."

"But where will she stay?" Oleg asked.

Rosa gestured irritably. "A friend of mine will put her up," she said. "It needn't concern you, Oleg. The less you know, the better. You know that." She spoke quite sharply. Oleg looked intimidated, and Natasha saw that he was full of a deep respect for the young woman. A look, almost of adoration, came into his face. Is he in love with her? Natasha wondered.

She felt sorry for him, if he was. Rosa had made no secret of her contempt for love. It obviously rated as highly as dancing in her catalogue of useless activities.

"Where shall I take her?" Oleg asked.

"To the Bolshoi, where else. Get her a gangway seat. We'll pick her up from there."

CHAPTER

THIRTY

The auditorium hummed about her like a gigantic beehive filled with exotic bees. All around her fashionable Moscow glittered and gossiped. Taking her seat on the aisle, she was recognized as being a dancer; traditionally dancers were allowed to take unoccupied seats on the aisle. Her plainly draped gown of beige velveteen, too, set her aside from the other women in their ruinously extravagant gowns. Her dress had been given to her by Rosa. She had changed at the station, leaving her small leather bag at the luggage office. God knew where Rosa had found the dress. It had not been passed on from any talented modiste.

Alongside the lavishly dressed women and gorgeously uniformed men, in the purple splendor of the Bolshoi Theatre, Natasha felt like a moth in a jewel box. She was relieved when the lights were lowered and the crimson curtain rose.

At the sound of the music and the faint smell of backstage that wafted over the footlights, pain stirred in her, an anguish that dilated the heart. For a moment she thought that she might actually faint, the pain was so intense.

She saw little of the first act, and what she saw appeared to be taking place behind a mist. At the end of the act she knew nothing beyond the fact that a bored young prince had seen a flight of swans and had decided to go hunting at midnight. There had been little dancing, a lot of tedious mime, and some very glib stage effects.

But her mind had cleared by the time the curtain rose for the second time. She had almost forgotten her reason for being there after a few minutes. The scene was a lakeside.

There was a ruined chapel and a small forest silvered by moonlight—*Giselle* country. The scene had the romantic look of forty years before.

This act was almost all dancing from the first arrival of the swan-maidens. Led by their queen, they glided onto the stage. In the background, their enchanter swooped, a vampire-figure in batlike velvet sleeves. The corps de ballet were ethereal in transparent white muslin, their filmy skirts dappled by moonlight.

The prince entered, in tan-colored suede, with hose of hunting green. Appealingly, the swan-queen begged him not to loose his arrows against them. She explained that they were enchanted humans, only allowed at midnight to resume their natural form for a brief span of time.

The prince had fallen in love with the queen. He made to embrace her. She herself was attracted to him and repelled, coming to his arms only to fly away when the evil enchanter came between them. The prince threatened to shoot the old man, but the queen ran to prevent him. His arrows were powerless against the enchanter's magic.

Her agitated steps imitated those of a bird, with preening movements of the arms, feet beating together like the quivering of wings, each tremor of her feet like the fluttering of a score of tiny feathers. She and the prince had a fine adagio pas de deux, the music rising from the pit with irresistible melancholy.

Otherwise, the music was the most extraordinary mishmash, the mood created by the composer suddenly broken by the intrusion of other works, banal pieces by Minkus and Pugni.

Tchaikovsky's contribution struck Natasha as being totally original. It had a haunting quality, excessively emotional, filled with an aching pain. It spoke to her far beyond the action on the stage. It was unlike anything she had ever heard in a ballet, but difficult for a dancer.

The choreography, too, was unlike anything created by Petipa. Instead of the virtuosity she knew from the Maryinsky, the Moscow dancers concentrated on emotion. Not that technique was entirely missing. Karpakova's partner was very good, visible only when the role called for it. His holds and lifts looked effortless. Karpakova floated at his fingertips, turning, drifting, raised on high and set down again with the feather-light delicacy of great strength. She rose like a bird about to take to the skies, her feet beating together like fluttering wings. Then she stopped to pose on one point, arm curved, to end in the prince's arms, her own arms closing like wings about her body, enclosed, sheltered, gazing up into his eyes.

An image of Richard superimposed itself on Natasha's vision. She was enclosed in his arms, his arms like wings about her. Tears misted her eyes. Then the critic took over in Natasha. Karpakova was somehow wrong. She was always the ballerina, eternally posing. There should have been more of the bird in her nature, and more of the stricken human, too. Natasha performed the role in her mind. One should be constantly reminded of the enchanted queen trapped in the guise of the swan, she thought. The dancing should be more broadly spaced, the arabesques should flow. One felt nothing of the romantic agony of impossible love, for Natasha knew that the ballet would end in death, it was implicit in its beginning. The music itself spoke of unfulfillable longings, of inevitable tragedy.

The prince's attendant, Oleg, entered, dressed splendidly in a canary-yellow doublet and bronze-colored hose, with a cape of emerald green. He leaped high into the air with springing steps, rejoicing in his strength, in the height he reached. He saw the girls, swans or maidens, and turned to call his companions.

Natasha could not tell whether he acted well or badly. She was amazed that she had not recognized him earlier. It had been Oleg, she realized, who had drawn the prince's attention to the flight of birds in the first act. But everything seemed so remote, the figures on stage were dwarfed by its dimensions.

The swans had reappeared, drifting like gossamer between the trees. She was more deeply moved by the sight of the corps de ballet than by anything that had gone before, though they were only the usual line of girls in white, glimmering in the fake moonlight. Yet they were what the ballet meant to Natasha—an abstract idealization of the human form. They had nothing to do with base reality, their only reason for being lay in the sorcery of their movements. She was unbearably touched by their mysterious beauty as they formed and reformed, in ever-changing patterns. She knew that the costumes and scenery were second-rate and the dancing undistinguished. She knew the effort behind each step, the physical agony behind each pose. She understood everything technically, it had no mystery for her, yet their movements still retained a magic, marvelous and inexplicable.

The second act curtain fell to indifferent applause. Yet the stage was filled with magnificent bouquets. Natasha's anger smoldered inside her. Had her career not been interrupted, she could have danced a better Odette than the affected little woman making her *révérence*. She could have made more emotional sense of the role, made the music more danceable.

By the middle of the third act she knew that she could not endure much more. She longed to be taken from the theatre, but there was no sign of her contact.

Odile's entrance was brilliant, danced by a younger dancer than Karpakova. It ended with a scintillating series of traveling pirouettes with legs turned elegantly outward. Her pas de deux with the prince was a dazzling contrast to the second act adagio in the moonlight. Odile's movements were a mockery of the swan's winged lyricism. Odile—as black as Odette was white—was filled with arrogant vanity. The steps were full of tricks to match the taunting jubilant music. The choreography was all acrobatic lifts and catches, countless pirouettes, incredible runs on point across the stage, reckless dives into the prince's arms, and amazingly lovely poses. The Odile was infinitely superior to the Odette.

Natasha closed her eyes, unable to watch further, consumed by a sick jealousy. Her pulse raced madly, her head throbbed to the rich, too rich, music. It pounded in her temples.

"Natalia Petrova?"

She opened her eyes, looking up. A young man stood by her side, tall and broad, with a stern though youthful face. He was elegantly though quietly dressed in black evening wear, with a white waistcoat. Natasha was surprised by his appearance. There was nothing in his dress, his gestures, or his mild voice to suggest that he was anything other than a young man-about-town.

"Yes," she said. "I am Natalia Petrova."

The young man smiled. There was little warmth in it. "I am a friend of Rosa," he said. "Shall we go? Before the crush starts?"

Without thinking, Natasha said, "There's another act."

He looked surprised, even a little shocked. "Do you want to stay?"

"No. No, of course not." She blushed in confusion.

"Thank God for that!" he said. "The evening's interminable."

Natasha rose. Her legs began to tremble. His words had reminded her that he was a young nihilist, with no patience for frivolities.

They left the auditorium as the music mocked the prince who was now swearing eternal fidelity to the false love, and as Odile revealed her true nature, disappearing with her evil genius in a cloud of sulfurous smoke.

Turning at the door, Natasha saw her last Russian ballet. The prince rushed from the ballroom, followed by his faithful Oleg, dashing in cream, gold and brown.

To Natasha's amazement, the young man insisted upon their walking through the icy streets. "Cabmen have convenient memories," he explained, "usually unlocked by the meanest bribe."

His casual acceptance of the situation shocked Natasha. It brought home to her the knowledge that she was entering an illegal world.

"It's close by the Kitrov market," the young man said, ". . . not too far."

It meant nothing to Natasha. She trudged on forlornly through the mud and slush. A keen north wind nipped her ears and cast hail into her eyes. She drew her shawl closer and walked with lowered head. At first she wanted to turn about and run back to the theatre. She would beg Oleg to loan her the money to return to Petersburg. She longed for her little room and the warmth of its poor stove. But after a few minutes of walking she was totally lost, completely dependent upon her guide. The young man walked with tremendous strides. She was hard put to keep up with him, but it kept her warmer. There was not the shadow of another human being on the street.

Her mind was in a turmoil, busy with the extraordinary events that had led her this far. If anybody had told her, even a few months ago, that one day she would knowingly consort with "illegals" . . .

She stumbled after the man, touching his sleeve. She would ask him to take her back to the theatre. There was still time to catch Oleg . . . Her hand fell away from his sleeve. What was the use? What choice had she? She was herself half an illegal. She was apparently unemployable. Who had cast her out from security? For what reason? She was alone and friend-less. She must take what help was given her. Once she was free of Russia . . . A hand touched her shoulder. She was startled out of the numbness of her misery.

"We're here," the young man said.

They were in a narrow street. The houses were low, mean buildings with flaked and rotting walls. At the end of the street a river gleamed icily. Everything was blanketed in mist. Taking her by the arm, the young man drew her toward the warm yellow light of a window. He opened a door and propelled her through it gently.

They were in some sort of café, a low dark room, foul with the smell of kvass and vodka, blue with the fumes of bad tobacco. The thick smoke dimmed the light of an oil lamp standing on the counter. Faces floated in the half-light. In a corner a drunkard had collapsed upon a hard bench. He still clasped his bottle of vodka to him. In another corner, two men quarreled in low intense tones. A disheveled-looking woman, with a bleeding nose and a crazed expression, drifted past.

Then Natasha saw an icon, lit by a night-light, hung upon three little silver chains. She bowed, crossing herself, some-how calmed by the sight of the sacred image.

The young man guided her to the counter. He introduced her to Sergei Sergeivich. She scarcely heard, in her over-wrought state.

"Pleasure to meet you, miss."

The man's voice was pleasant. Slowly, out of a dark mist, his face revealed itself. It was a strong dark face, pensive, but with smiling eyes and a gentle expression.

"What will you drink?" Sergei was asking. "Tea with lemon, or tea with a 'towel?'"

"With a towel."

"You'd better have a brandy, too. I see the 'General' here has made you walk. Come along through here, miss. We'll be more private-like." He led her through a curtained alcove into another part of the bar. The thick cloth blanketed the sounds from the other room.

Sergei gave her a glass of sweet Armenian brandy and a glass of strong tea from the samovar. With the heat of the stove and the tinted tea, warmth began to seep back into Natasha's body. Perspiration beaded her forehead. He passed her a surprisingly clean napkin and smiled encouragingly. Natasha sponged her face and neck. The tea revived her a

little, but she still felt remote from her surroundings. She felt
vaguely that she should not be there.

Sergei gave her another brandy and another glass of tea.
Once again he passed her the towel. Observing her curiously,
his eyes smiled warmly. "The General here's told me all
about you. You've had a bad time."

Natasha answered vaguely, dabbing at her face.
". . . Yes."

Sergei leaned forward to take the damp towel from her
fingers. "We're not what you're used to, I know," he said.
"But you need have no fear of us." His voice was touched
with an infinite compassion, his brown eyes lit with a soft
glow.

"I know," Natasha said. "I do . . . I do trust you."

Beyond the curtain, the two men in the corner suddenly
started yelling, roused to a fury by the raw vodka they had
consumed. Natasha started up in terror, but the General held
her arm firmly but gently, calming her.

Sergei walked from behind the counter and disappeared
behind Natasha. She was amazed at his giant stature. His fists
looked as heavy as stones. The voices beyond the curtain
grew shrill, and then were suddenly choked off.

Natasha felt sick. She should not have come. Trembling
violently, she rose to go—but go where? At once the room
spun dizzily around her. Lights coiled and sparkled before her
eyes. The dusty wooden floor rose up to meet her.

When she recovered consciousness, it was to find that
Sergei and the young man had lain her down on a thick rug.
Her dress had been loosened at throat and waist, her face was
stippled with water and a phial was held beneath her nose. It
had a sharp pungent smell. She coughed, and tried to sit up.

More clearly then, she saw Sergei watching her. His face
seemed to recede into a mist behind him. At his shoulder
stood a large comfortable figure, an elderly woman, her face
as red and wrinkled as an apple.

"Granny," Natasha murmured faintly, and the woman
smiled.

"That's right," Sergei said, also smiling. "She's my son's
granny."

"Here, drink this," the old woman said.

She placed a glass of colored liquid to Natasha's lips. It had
the same pungent flavor of the phial. Natasha sputtered at the
taste, but drank it submissively. Then she lay back exhausted.

"How long is it since you last ate?" Sergei asked.

Natasha shook her head to clear it, unable to remember.

"On the train, for a fact," the General said. "Before that, God knows."

Sergei turned to the old woman. "Granny . . ." The woman came forward again, this time holding in her hands a bowl of richly steaming cabbage soup and a hunk of good rye bread. She pushed the bowl at Natasha stolidly.

"Eat," the young man ordered.

The smell invaded Natasha's mind. Her mouth filled with saliva. She reached for the bowl. Sergei, the old woman and the General watched her eat. After, she protested strongly that she must pay for the meal, even as she recognized that her protest was absurd. She took the one thing she had of any worth, a small enamel brooch that she had been unable to sell because it was so trifling. She offered it to Sergei.

"For the lady," Natasha murmured.

Sergei shook his head and the old woman backed away, clucking like an outraged hen. Overwhelmed, Natasha began to weep. The tears that she had kept back through all the long months of bitterness and loneliness ran down her cheeks.

Silently, Sergei handed her a napkin. Natasha wiped her face. "I must go," she said.

"Where?" Sergei asked gently.

"Why?" asked the young man.

A movement from Sergei silenced him.

"Home," Natasha said. ". . . I mean *back,* to St. Petersburg."

"It's a fair way," Sergei said.

Natasha was silent.

"You don't want to stay with us?" Sergei asked.

Natasha half nodded, and then shook her head—like a confused child.

"You don't trust us, is that it?" Sergei asked.

Tears gleamed again in Natasha's eyes.

"I don't blame you," Sergei said. "After what you've been through, you shouldn't trust anybody."

"But this is foolishness!" the young man said sternly.

"Hush!" the old lady said. "Can't you see the poor thing's fair frightened?"

"She has no need to fear us," the General said.

Natasha frowned, trying to concentrate. She felt exhausted.

"Are you still frightened of us?" Sergei asked.

Natasha's eyelids fluttered. Sergei reached out to steady her. For a moment it looked as though she might keel over again. "I can't let you help me," she said at last.

"Because you think we're on the wrong side of the law?" Sergei asked quietly.

She nodded, unable to look either man in the face.

The General looked sterner than ever, but his voice was calm and reasonable as he said, "But, Natalia Ivanovna, you yourself are illegal. Don't you yet understand that? *They* have made you illegal—with a stroke of the pen. You are a suspicious character."

"But I'll never be able to clear myself, if . . ." Natasha's voice died away, her fine hands stroked her dark hair distractedly.

"You'll starve first," the General said. A gesture from Sergei silenced him. Natasha could see that the innkeeper had considerable influence over the young man. At first she had thought him so assured, but now he looked like any other student.

"I could find work," Natasha whispered. "If I could get to Odessa. They say it's not too difficult there. One can live without a permit, or even without identity papers."

"As you can here," Sergei said. "If you know how to handle yourself."

She stared at him solemnly. Again he was struck by her childlike nature, the innocence that still showed beneath the marks of suffering.

"I can use you here," Sergei said. "And no harm will come to you. I'll give you my word on that holy picture there."

He nodded toward the icon.

"Besides," the General insisted, "it will only be for a few weeks. We can get you a new passport—a new name—and you'll be out of the country. We have friends in Switzerland. They'll help you to find work in a European theatre."

Natasha listened in confusion. She felt that she had lost sight of herself. Since being dismissed, she had been like an empty bottle in a swiftly flowing river, waiting for the flood to submerge her. Her life was no longer hers to command. The influences around her made it impossible for her to go in any direction but in the way she was directed. Yet she still struggled against the inevitable.

Sergei gazed at her ruminatively. "We're not trying to

recruit you, lass," he said. "We only want to help you. You've been abominably treated, you've had a raw deal. The authorities have acted like the spiteful fools they are."

"And you must realize," the General said intently, "you must realize that your life is already ruined. If you stay, you're without any further hope of advancement or success. God knows what will happen to you without our help."

The heat of the room, the brandy, the unaccustomed richness of the food, produced a powerful effect upon Natasha. To be in the company of sympathetic souls, for the first time in so many months . . . She found she wanted to talk, wanted to confide in somebody, not to make a confession, but simply to talk to another human soul. She felt strangely at ease with the strong-faced, calm-eyed Sergei.

She began to tell them of her life since her dismissal. The whole story spilled out of her. The men listened to her in total silence, the old lady exclaimed from time to time, shocked and disapproving.

When she had finished, Sergei surprised her by saying, "I'm well acquainted with your prince."

Natasha looked up, astonished. "You are?"

"Aye, that I am. If I took off my shirt, I could show you where he's set his mark on me."

"Set his mark?"

"Aye. Twenty years ago I was his serf. Before the tzar *freed* us." Sergei's smile was bitter. "Your prince had me whipped often enough when he owned me. And for what? A word spoken out of turn, that's all."

The smile vanished from his face, the bitterness remained. "The scars have healed, but not the memory," he said. "I'm not a true-born Russian, born to taste the lash and the knout. No, I have Armenian blood in my veins, and we Armenians have long memories . . . and wait our day."

"God will repay their injustice," the old granny said, crossing herself devoutly.

Sergei and the General exchanged telling glances, then Sergei turned to Natasha. "I can understand pride," he said. "I've suffered enough for mine. But rest easy, little miss. You'll be repaid. At the moment we haven't the rights of a dog—less if the dog is some great lady's pet, but—"

In their corner, the two men began quarreling again. Sergei left the bar and went to deal with them. Their voices dropped away to a grumbling murmur. Natasha noticed that Sergei himself had not raised his voice. Order was restored with the minimum of fuss.

When Sergei returned he could see that her uneasiness had been reawakened by the outbreak.

"So you want to work?" he asked.

"Yes."

"Come and look at this, then," Sergei said.

Natasha took the massive hand that was offered to her. It swallowed up her own protectively. Then Sergei led her over to a corner of the room, where a small circular platform was curtained off with a long piece of shabby velvet. He pulled the material aside.

At the side of the platform stood a mechanical piano, a "cylindichord." It was a handsome example of the cabinet-maker's craft, richly inlaid with colorful fruitwoods of contrasting tones, and embellished with ivory, brass and mother-of-pearl.

"It's French," Sergei said proudly. "I bought it in a sale, for a song."

He opened the lid. On the underside was a numbered program of the airs that it contained. It played five waltzes, a polka, a mazurka and a gypsy dance. Sergei set it in motion and, with a flourish, the instrument began to play. Natasha was surprised at its volume and rich tone. When she closed her eyes it was almost possible to imagine that some ghostly fingers strummed the keys. The sound enchanted her, so pure and simple. Tears sprang to her eyes and washed away the proudly smiling face of Sergei.

"Would you like to dance to it?" he asked unexpectedly.

"Now, do you mean?"

"Aye."

"But . . ."

"Let's say in payment for the reckoning."

Natasha nodded. She removed the clumsy felt boots from her feet, then stepped onto the stage, feeling extraordinarily light and free.

The two drunks had come to the curtained alcove at the sound of the music. They watched her with drunken bewilderment. The General, too, was watching her with careful regard. Self-consciously, she adopted the *position de départ*, facing forward. She closed her eyes, trying to feel the music, trying to forget where she was. The first piece came to an end and a sweet, soft, lyrical waltz began.

Natasha began to dance . . . clumsily at first, her feet refusing to obey her. Then, as she warmed to the silvery tune, her movements became looser, more pliant. Gracefully, she adopted the poses of the ballet to the cruder variations of the waltz. Only the close-fitting line of her borrowed dress impeded her, the accordian pleating at the hem hid her delicately arched feet.

To Sergei, the old granny and the astonished customers, she seemed like some exquisite vision, a creature from a higher world. Only the General, though he was uninterested in the ballet, realized how limited her performance was. A year away from the theatre had wreaked havoc on her technique.

It was not dancing, he knew, just invention. The girl looked to be dreaming her steps. Her dance was an unfolding of herself. She was unburdening her suffering in a way that mere words could never have conveyed. Despite himself, he was moved.

When the waltz ended and the polka began, Natasha went on dancing. Her eyes were open now, her face unclouded. Her body moved at the bidding of the music, leaping and twisting to the lively tune.

The waltz that followed was slow and languorous. Natasha's whole personality changed with its rhythms. She drooped and pined with yearning melancholy. She posed, hovering on her toes, her arms held above her head *en couronne*.

After, she danced another waltz, romantic and dreamy. Then her body appeared to change shape to the brisk melody of a mazurka. She was quick and bright, sparkling and vivacious, then slipped smoothly into the slumbrous drifting of a waltz, dipping and turning, wheeling with undulating arms, turning slowly with arms drifting, circling the stage with wide sweeping gestures, rising on tiptoe, sinking into a deep curtsey.

She was transformed. She had slipped into another world, a world of gaiety and glamour. Her hardships were forgotten. But, at last, the music came to an end, the last notes fading into the air like spray from a fountain. Natasha stood in the classical pose of a dancer taking a curtain call, making a deep *révérence*.

She emerged from an ecstasy, glancing around her timidly, only gradually becoming aware again of the drab, ill-furnished room. The light died in her face. The drunken customers and the old granny stared at her wordlessly. Even the crazy woman, who had crept up to the curtain to watch, stopped her whispering. Nobody applauded; they were too deeply moved for that.

Sergei, too, was moved. But he was also watching the expression on his customers' faces. They had been too engrossed to quarrel. Now he clapped his great hands together, splintering the silence, as Natasha stepped down from the platform. The others followed him. The spell was broken.

Natasha sat down at the counter. Once again she was the shy, awkward, deeply wretched girl who had been brought to the café. Sergei took her slim hand in his great paw. It looked white and bloodless, almost transparent in his rough hand. The misery in her eyes pierced him.

"Wouldn't you like to dance here every night—while you stay?" he asked.

"Dance? For an audience, do you mean?" She gazed at him uncertainly, almost mistrustfully.

Sergei smiled his sweet, disarming smile. "Aye. To pay for your keep, like. I reckon I could bring in a few more customers if I was to put you in a pretty frock and let you dance. Folk'll think I've captured a spirit."

Natasha still looked doubtful. Sergei misinterpreted her silence. "I'll pay you," he said. "Not much, it's true. But it will give you something. You'll have the room above, of course, as arranged. And food. Then, if the customers come, as I think they will, I'll raise the pay."

Natasha stood irresolute.

"It will be a 'limited engagement,'" the General said, with his stern smile.

Her hand still lay clasped in Sergei's. He pressed it gently, encouragingly. She looked up and saw the calm clear look in his brown eyes, his easy smile.

"You'll come to no harm, lass," he said. "Granny here'll look after you." Tears pricked at her eyes. Words rose in a lump to her throat, it was impossible to speak.

"I know you don't want to be obligated," Sergei said. "So will you do it?"

Natasha turned to the General. He laughed. "Do it," he said. "If you're to audition for the Paris Opera, you'll need the experience!"

The hard knot in her throat dissolved in laughter. She felt

suddenly almost hysterical, light-headed from the heat of the room, the waves of friendship flowing from the people around her, the exhilaration of dancing for the first time in months. She wanted to climb back onto the platform and show them how she could *really* dance. Her dark mood was banished, her old strength returned.

"Well, lass? Will you?"

"But won't *they* know that I'm here? I mean, a trained dancer in . . . in this area?"

Sergei laughed. "God kiss you, miss! Who's to know? *I'm* not on anybody's list. There's not a policeman hereabouts would report you. It's because they close their eyes to what goes on in this street that they remain on the job. Otherwise, they'd have been rotting underground for a long time. They're here to guarantee order, not to denounce those who've disturbed it at some other time."

"It's true," the General said. "That's why I brought you here. You couldn't find a safer place than Sergei's café. And it's only for a few weeks—until you leave the country."

"Well, miss?"

She nodded, her head shaking loosely. Then she fell, half fainting, against the counter. Sergei caught her in his powerful arms, and lowered her with surprising gentleness into an armchair. The old granny came forward with a reviving dram.

And so Natasha began to dance nightly at the Eye café, dressed exquisitely in a Venetian masquerade costume that Sergei bought cheaply from a tailoress in Karetnaya Street. It had been made for a lady of the court, but she had decided against the colors, a rose satin with a cream and blue damask underskirt, and white silk and lace at neck and sleeves. It had passed from hand to hand since the first rejection of it, the lace was torn and the satin discolored, but newly washed it still looked pretty in the lights. In her hair she wore the silk rose that Richard had returned to her so long ago, the last reminder of him.

After a few days, the news began to spread. Sergei had installed a good-looking dancer in the Eye. It was a rare and unexpected thing to happen. He had found her starving in a night shelter, it was said; she had fallen on evil times.

Sergei gave out that she had been a dancing instructress in a small-town academy who had been disgraced by a pupil's brother, a young limb of the provincial nobility.

Intrigued by this story, new customers came to leer and
stayed to be charmed by the bewitching young beauty. They
were tantalized by her, she was a mystery, for she always
wore a domino and disappeared the moment the performance
ended, concealing herself in one of the back rooms that lay
behind the restaurant, in a maze of passageways.

CHAPTER
THIRTY-ONE

Richard returned to St. Petersburg to find the embassy in a
state of siege and diplomatic hysteria. He was plunged into it
at once. A week slipped by in which he and the other staff
lived like prisoners within the embassy, cut off from any
private contact with Russians, forbidden to go about the
capital except in groups. Feeling against the British was
almost as virulent as feeling against the Turks.

Yet in the middle of the second week, disobeying orders,
Richard made his way secretly to Count Scavronsky's apartment. The count received him with guarded warmth.

"So you have managed your return," he said.

"I told you I would," Richard replied grimly, "though it
took some doing. I've moved heaven and earth, Westminster
and Mayfair, to get back here!"

"Then I wish I had better news for you," Scavronsky said
unhappily.

"You have not learned where I can find Natasha?"

"Alas, no. I've come up against a solid wall of silence," the
count said. "The trouble is that the few friends she had at the
Maryinsky don't trust me. If they know anything, I am not
the man for them to tell it to. . . ."

"But you have looked for her?"

"Assuredly, *mon vieux*. Did I not give you my word? I,

personally, have investigated every night café and theatre in Petersburg and Moscow. And beyond. She was briefly employed here at a place called the Golden Cockerel, but she was dismissed for 'incompetence'—"

"What?"

"Presumably in *that* department," the count said, smiling scornfully, "she still clings to her standards. Anyway, that was some months ago. Madame Kalitin—her employer, a charming hell-hag—would certainly know if any similar establishment employed her."

He stared at Richard gloomily. "There's no point in pursuing that line, I'm sure. She must have found some menial sort of work though, since she's not applied at any of the *registered* employment offices. Though, even here, I've drawn a blank. My men have scoured the night shelters of Moscow and Petersburg. We've searched every common lodging house and factory dormitory. She can't be in either place."

Richard swore. "I can't bear to think of her in that appalling world," he said. "I'm haunted by the thought of it." He stared at the count wretchedly. "How can she survive in such a jungle?"

"Poverty is everywhere, *mon cher,*" Scavronsky said. "One survives if the will is strong enough."

Richard shuddered. "But will she want to? What has she to live for? She has lost everything."

The count was silent. Then he shrugged. "Not everything, Richard. She has a grievance. One nurses a grievance. It is amazing how much purpose it can give you."

Richard gestured impatiently. "She was so defenseless," he said. "Her one offense lay in being desirable."

"Perhaps she has developed claws," Scavronsky said. He laid a gloved hand on Richard's arm. "You mustn't give up hope, old friend. There are many ways she could have taken. You must ask yourself what you know of her. Was she a coward?"

"No. She had courage enough," Richard said. "But it was the courage of love. She was sustained by the thought that I would return and carry her away." His hand shook as he lit a cigar. "Well, I have returned, and I must find her. I've brought her so much sorrow, and I love her more deeply with every day that passes." He looked at the count, his blue eyes brooding. "Can you believe that love can grow without sustenance?"

"Yes," Scavronsky answered seriously. "One's soul can feed upon its own misery."

"I would never have believed myself capable of such . . . passion." Richard's handsome face was filled with dazzled wonderment. "These past few months have been dead to me. Not because I've missed what has been happening in the great world—God knows, I've never been more involved—but because I've been without Natasha. I would never have believed that I could know such suffering, feel such anguish."

Scavronsky looked away, unable to face the agony in his friend's eyes.

"I'm in a maze," Richard said. "I'm terrified that I might have reached a dead end. I've tried to reach her through every channel that's open to me—proper and improper. But I'm checked at every turn. The trouble is that—just now—I can't move around freely. If only the political situation was easier."

The two men fell silent.

"Help me, Kolya," Richard pleaded, his voice muffled.

"Have you tried her friends in the theatre?" Scavronsky asked. "They might talk to you more comfortably than with me."

"I've talked to the 'little doll,'" Richard said. "Marie Antonova—the girl who used to share rooms with Natasha. She was just too afraid to speak to me. And she is the only one who would know, I'm sure. She was the closest to Natasha. It's hopeless."

He sank back into his chair wearily. Then he looked up, his eyes flashing. "I should challenge the blackguard," he said.

Scavronsky regarded him in astonishment. "Verchinin? An old man? That would simply result in being transferred to some other post—in disgrace."

"I meant Trepov," Richard said coldly. "He was behind it all, I'm sure. Verchinin might have sought to punish her—out of wounded vanity—but it was Trepov who took matters further. He would have real pleasure in tormenting her." His hands clenched and unclenched. "If only I could find some way of getting at the dandified brute . . ."

Scavronsky laid a restraining hand on Richard's arm. "It would only have the same result, my hot-headed friend. Besides, since the attempt on his life, the general's barely stepped out of his house. He has the tzar's full protection, night and day. And attacking Trepov at such a time will hardly help Natasha Ivanovna."

Richard was silenced. It was true. And it would serve no purpose to be banished from St. Petersburg. It had been a hard enough struggle to regain admittance.

The message was terse, hastily scrawled in a large uneducated hand. "Meet me at the Balalaika, Friday night. Have news of N.P. I shall make myself known to you. A friend."

Richard carried the letter in his breast pocket as he sat in the tawdry splendor of the night café, at a table alone. It was quite late and he had begun to think that his correspondent would not appear. For the past two hours he had run the gauntlet of the dancing partners—large, overpainted women of a mechanical flirtatiousness. He had stared at them grimly, sending them scuttling away. One, seeing his expression, had crossed herself and spat, making the sign against the eye.

He had gone to the café barely able to control his excitement. Now misery overcame him. Was it possible that he—loving Natasha as he did—had reduced her to this? This sordid world with its whorish entertainers and unbreathable air?

Oh, Christ, he breathed. Natasha, my love. How could she exist in this world and not be crushed by it?

He raged inwardly against Verchinin and Trepov, against all who had conspired against her. He poured the last of his wine into his glass, and decided to leave. Either his unknown well-wisher had lost heart, or the letter had been a hoax. Slowly, he drained his glass and made his way to the men's washroom.

As Richard entered a voice addressed him, in German. Richard recognized the man immediately. A dancer, Natasha's partner—Oleg something . . . Mikhailovich?

Oleg smiled, darkly handsome in his black evening wear with a white piqué waistcoat and white bow tie. "It is best that we speak in German," he said. "The attendant has not this language."

Richard glanced at the attendant sitting by his little table. The man glanced at Richard and Oleg curiously, storing their faces in his mind.

"It was you who wrote to me?" Richard asked.

"Yes. A friend dropped the letter in your box. I thought it best not to come to your house. I thought here would be better. Neither of us are known here, I think."

Richard stared at the dancer, admiring his prudence. Then he asked eagerly, "You have news of Natasha?"

Oleg nodded, suddenly serious. "Yes. I know where she is. When I heard that you were back in Petersburg and making inquiries, I decided to contact you."

"You can take me to her?" Richard was almost breathless with excitement, his whole bearing had changed.

Oleg shook his head, to Richard's consternation. "No, I can't take you to her. But I can bring her to you—if you can prove to me that she will be safe."

"Safe?"

Oleg's smile was tinged with sadness. "You are dangerous to know, Herr Greville. At the moment, Natasha is secure. Soon she will be more secure."

"How? What do you mean?"

"She is soon to leave Russia. It is all arranged."

Richard caught his breath. "She's leaving? She has a visa?"

"Yes. It is all arranged for next week. She is going to friends of ours in Zurich."

"But I must see her! She must be told that I am here, that I have been looking for her!"

"You have returned to marry her?"

"Good God, man! Yes! It's been my only thought for months."

"Then I shall tell her," Oleg said, smiling broadly now. "I had to find out first, do you see. She has suffered so much, and I had to make sure that your intentions weren't just to amuse yourself again."

"My thoughts were never that!" Richard said angrily. Then he stepped forward and grasped Oleg by the arm. "But we must meet. Can you arrange it?"

"Yes. I can arrange it. I will bring her to you. Leave it to me."

CHAPTER
THIRTY-TWO

As promised, Oleg brought Natasha and Richard together again. Or, rather, the General did. He arranged for them to meet in a "safe house" in St. Petersburg. Each was brought by a circuitous route, in a closed carriage with the blinds drawn.

Natasha, who had been told twenty-four hours earlier of Richard's return, had not yet absorbed the fact. The knowledge that he was alive and well and had come back for her had cast a spell upon her. Her heart raced with anticipation, but her mind was numbed. Only when the hansom stood before the tall granite house where her lover waited for her, did she come to life. The blood coursed in her veins, bringing a flush to her cheeks and a brilliance to her eyes.

She felt an immense surge of excitement and a sudden fear. Her thoughts swung wildly between joy and anxiety. It could not be happening. It *was* happening, but it would not end happily. He would find her too changed.

She wanted so much to look the same for him, wanted to obliterate the time that had separated them, so that they could be as they had been. But she knew that she was changed. And he, too, would be different. . . .

She climbed the stairs, unaware of how beautiful she looked in her simple dress of pale blue wool, its drapery bunched low on the hips. She had thrown back the fur-trimmed hood of her dark green velvet jacket.

The General let her into the apartment, leaving her at the door. The hallway was dimly lit, and Natasha was almost blind to her surroundings, though they seemed unexpectedly rich. The house belonged to a sympathizer, she supposed.

The door to a small sitting room stood open. She walked through it, seeing nothing of the room. She saw only Richard.

He had been pacing up and down the narrow room, but had turned and stopped at her entrance. For a moment he stood, staring at her with a wild blue gaze. They were both held irresolute by the force of their feelings, drained of movement. Then he was across the room to her, his arms locked about her.

He held her, one hand at her head, pressing her against him hungrily. She tilted her head back, eyes blind with tears, laughter in her mouth. His mouth was on hers, crushing hers, greedily satiating himself after the famished months of separation.

Long moments passed as they kissed and kissed again. Natasha leaned against him dizzily. Even now, with his arms about her, his tall body bending to hers, she could not believe that it was real. She trembled, burrowing into him, as though seeking the consolation she had lacked for so many months, trying to break through to the reality of his *living* body.

His arms tightened around her. "Darling," he said. "It's been so long. So long . . ." His hands were cupped around her head, her face raised to his. "You are so beautiful," he said. "I had forgotten how beautiful."

She was more beautiful than ever, but subtly altered. The marvelous innocence had gone, that other-worldly air. There was a strength in her face that had not been there before. Suffering had changed her. Yet when she smiled at him, her face was radiant.

She, too, was looking for the signs of change in him. Her fingers traced the pattern of his fine mouth, the hollowed cheeks, the lines of his face, hardened by weeks of privation. He, too, had suffered. There was a new strength in him.

"I can't believe it's really you," she said.

"It's really me," he smiled, drawing her toward a sofa upholstered in blue velvet. They sat down together, hands held in hands, looking deeply into each other's eyes.

"We shan't be parted again," Richard said, kissing her hands.

Her lips brushed his cheeks, her eyes huge and grave, absorbing him. "Hush," she said. "Don't speak of that . . . yet. We're together. It's enough for the moment."

Then his arms were about her, encircling her fiercely, as though he would never let her loose. His lips were on hers, kissing her with a rough yet tender passion. Her lips opened yearningly, soft and yielding. They clung to each other, their bodies shaking with the intensity of the desire that flared between them. Long moments passed.

His hands were at the lace at her neck, opening her dress, freeing her breasts from the confining material. She shivered at the touch of his hands on her silken flesh, stroking her breasts. She gasped at the remembered sensation as his lips kissed their delicate tips. The rosy nipples hardened.

Her skirts rustled softly as they fell from her. Soon her body lay beneath him, her bared flesh glimmering in the light of the oil lamp with a creamy luster. She looked to be carved from ivory, mysterious shadows danced beneath her breasts and between her thighs.

Between kisses and long languorous embraces, Richard stripped. Soon they were both naked. His body was lean and hard, darkly gold in the lamplight, his skin familiarly warm against her own, as he drew her to him. She felt choked with emotion as he crushed her against his naked flesh. She could feel his heart battering against his ribs. Her own heart fluttered beneath his touch. Her nipples burned as her breasts flattened against his chest. She moaned gently, giving her whole self to him. She had the impression that her body was ripening beneath his touch.

His tongue invaded her mouth, his hands skimmed her body with greater urgency. Then his full weight lay upon her; she shook beneath him. Her arms were about his neck, her legs opened to receive him. She weakened beneath him, feeling the hard length of his body driving into her.

He took her then. At first the unremembered pain of it dazed her. Then pain and pleasure merged, growing more intense with each powerful thrust of his body, until her own rose to meet his, borne up and sinking with an equal rhythm. A wild light grew in her eyes, breasts heaving, her fingers raking his strongly muscled back. At last the tears came; remembering the anguish of their parting, the aching void of the past months. Her love was with her, back at last, filling her body with the proof of his existence.

Richard's arm embraced her with a new tenderness. Her sobs were muffled against his chest. His lovemaking changed subtly. No longer impassioned, but full of concern for the delicate, shuddering creature that he now cradled in his arms.

After, lying together, he began to speak of the past few months, questioning her about her life.

"It must have been terrible for you," he said, kissing her fingers tenderly.

She reached up to kiss him full on the mouth, stopping the words. "Let's not talk of it," she said. "That's all behind us. Let's think only of the future. . . ."

"But I want to know," he insisted. "You've been lost to me for months, my darling. I want to know what your life has been like."

She shuddered. "Don't make me relive it, Richka. We're together. That's all that matters. We mustn't lose each other again."

"No, we shan't," he said. "This time I intend going to the top."

She looked at him questioningly, and he told her of how—in London—he had interested the Princess of Wales and the Duchess of Edinburgh in their cause. The princess had promised to write to her sister, Dagmar, the wife of the tzarevich. The duchess was even more important, since she was the tzar's favorite daughter. Both of them had been moved by his story, both of them had personally guaranteed their support.

". . . I would not be here now, were it not for their influence," he ended. "We have powerful friends on our side, my darling. You shall be restored to the tzar's favor."

But to his amazement, Natasha shrank away from him. She shook her head, dumbly, then said: "We shan't need them, Richka." There was a faint hardness in her voice. "I don't wish to be restored to the tzar's favor. Next week I shall be in Switzerland. It is all arranged. We shall meet in Zurich."

"But, Natasha—"

She laid a finger on his lips. "Darling, I can't trust them any more. I've learned so much about them in these past few months. We can expect nothing from them. It's best that I leave with my new friends. They are the only ones to have shown me kindness, the only ones I can trust."

"But who are they?" Richard asked.

Again she laid a finger on his lips. "I can't tell you, Richka. But we can trust them. It's all arranged. Only be at the border to meet me."

Richard began to protest. "I can't leave you in their hands," he said. "I am back now, and I must be responsible for you!"

She made to silence him with another kiss, but he said

quickly, "At least we must make one more effort. I don't want you to be cut off from your country, your people. If we have official backing—"

She shivered. *"If.* Your princess and your duchess are a thousand miles away. I tell you, Richard, we can't trust them!"

He held her close, she trembled in his arms.

"My darling," he said, "I don't want you to be an exile. I don't want you spirited away. You are no longer alone and defenseless. I am here. You shall come back to Petersburg. I'll find you a room until we can be married, or until you have a legal exit visa. And that you shall have, Natashenka. I promise you."

She began to protest, and it was his turn to silence her with a long and passionate embrace. "I don't want to lose you again, Natasha," he said. "Not even for a week. They can't hurt you now—"

She broke free of him. "Really?" she asked. "Do you really think they can't hurt me? Do you think Trepov will allow you to set me up in a room here? How soon do you think it will be before I am asked to spy on you again? They said I was a traitor for loving you, Richka. They won't change. There's nothing you can do here. It's best that I go out of the country. It's all arranged."

She began to explain the situation with such earnest clarity that—against his better judgment—he was half convinced. He was amazed at the change in her, her strength of purpose.

"I must go through with their arrangement," she insisted. "In one week's time, we shall be together in Zurich. Free! Richka, I want to be free!"

He weakened then, in the face of her determination and in the face of her argument. She had been through so much in the past few months. He could not condemn her to a further period of waiting.

"If only I could go with you," he murmured.

She smiled. "You shall," she said, placing a hand on her heart. "Here."

She shook her head as he started to protest again. "I must go alone, Richka. I have given my word on it. I must go back to Moscow, to my friends. In a week we shall be together."

Then, sweeping all argument aside, she threw herself into his arms. Her dark hair clouded his vision, her lovely breasts pressed against his naked chest. He took her in a long embrace, so that she cried aloud with rapture. For a moment, a long breathless moment, it seemed to her that their innermost selves had joined together and become one.

CHAPTER
THIRTY THREE

Natasha had given her performance for that night. As usual, she had run quickly from the stage, to disappear into the maze of passages behind the restaurant. Her performance had ended in the usual hush of delight, followed by crashing applause.

She was in her room, mending a tear in the white lace sleeves of her rose-colored gown. The material looked shabbier than ever, though the old granny had washed it lovingly every three days.

Tomorrow would be her last performance.

From down below, she could hear the faint rumble of voices and laughter, the twang of a balalaika, the metallic strumming of a mandolin. Sergei's customers largely provided their own entertainment. Occasionally she could hear them in wild outbursts of joy or grief, fueled by rye beer and spirits. These orgiastic outbreaks were brief, since Sergei soon put an end to them. His command over his customers never failed to amaze her.

. . . Now, she became aware of a sudden silence. It was so unusual that she raised her head, suddenly alarmed. There was a barked order from a pair of lusty lungs, followed by a muffled shot.

The rose-colored gown slipped to the floor as she leaped up, then stood straining to hear. Had she been mistaken? There was a silence from below, deep and unnerving, broken by a cry of pain and a few gruff voices.

Then footsteps scuffled along the passageway. There were cries near at hand. Heavy boots thundered up the stairs. Spurs jingled. Another shot. More cries.

Natasha stood by her chair, quivering like an aspen.

The door crashed open, falling back with a splintering of wood. Natasha grasped the back of her rickety chair to steady herself, her face pale, her eyes wide.

A man in the uniform of the gendarmerie stood framed in the doorway, huge, hulking, sinister, a pistol tilted in his black-gloved hand. He stepped into the room, to be followed by another gendarme. They ignored Natasha, but moved rapidly around the room, tapping at the walls, touching the moldings, sounding the panels.

The room was almost bare of furniture. The coarse coverlet draped over the thin iron bed offered no place of concealment. Natasha was clearly alone. She still held the needle and thread in her hand, the white cotton vibrating like a plucked string to where the rose-colored satin lay at her feet.

"Come!" The man with the pistol gestured with his free hand. Without a word, incapable of speech, Natasha followed them from the room and down the passageway to the crowded café.

The customers had all been herded between the bar counter and the platform on which she danced. A dozen armed gendarmes surrounded them. Sergei was among his customers. He stepped forward as she entered, but a blow from a truncheon forced him back. He stood holding his forearm, mouthing curses.

Natasha was pushed in among the others.

More gendarmes came from the backrooms. Between them came a number of youths and some girls. The men all had the look of students, scruffy and bearded, wild-eyed and flushed. The girls were modestly dressed in gray and black, as uniform as nuns. Natasha wondered where they could have come from. She felt amazed that so many could have been accommodated at the Eye without her knowing they were on the premises.

Her feeling of apprehension grew to an overpowering fear. Beside her, an old man began to shake in a sort of fit. He stared with terror at a policeman guarding the youths.

"They're from the third section!" he hissed between his toothless gums.

Natasha, shocked, looked again at the policemen. The

secret police? They looked no different from the others. How did the man know?

He gestured with his shaking hand, and whispered, "That's Saltykov—the bastard!"

Natasha glanced at the police captain, who was now conferring with the captain of gendarmes. A chill settled on her. Even she had heard of Saltykov and his reputation for relentless cruelty. She could hardly bring herself to raise her eyes and look at him. When she did so, she was amazed to see that he was a pleasant-looking man, with preposterous side-whiskers and mild blue eyes.

He was smiling directly at her. He had a small, cherubic, rather pretty mouth.

Natasha, Sergei, the students and the girls were separated from the customers and marched off under escort to a line of waiting carriages, black, hearselike affairs, pulled by three draft horses. They set off down the middle of the street, just as dawn glimmered in the east.

For over an hour they traveled without a word being spoken. Sergei had been placed in another carriage, and none of the women in Natasha's carriage looked at her. If they knew who she was, they did not show it. Natasha felt that they suspected her. Perhaps they thought that she was a spy put in among them to report their conversation.

At the police station there were armed sentries at the doors. She and the girls were led into a small room and told to take their places on a long wooden bench. The room was austerely furnished, painted an institutional green. A large table, with a wooden armchair, stood in the center of the room.

After two hours of sitting on the hard wooden bench, Natasha felt stiff with fatigue and weak with a growing dread. All her worst fears had been realized. They were guarded by two armed gendarmes. After another hour of waiting, an officer entered. He sat down at the table, a swaggering, unpleasant-looking man who appeared to have spent the whole night drinking. He looked half asleep and thoroughly bad tempered. He shouted and swore at each woman as he interrogated her.

At last it was Natasha's turn. Bemused, she did not respond immediately. It was a mistake. Rough hands seized her, bundling her toward the table.

The officer shouted at her. "Do you know the woman Zazulich?"

She stared at him, bewildered.

"The woman Zazulich?" he yelled. "Do you know her?"

"Yes. I mean no. She is the woman who shot General Trepov," Natasha answered, still bewildered. She had read about Vera Zazulich's attempt to kill the general—in retaliation for his having caused the death of a student.

"I asked you if you *knew* her?" the officer shouted.

"No. Not personally," Natasha said.

The officer glared at her. "Where are your papers?"

She had no alternative but to give him her legitimate papers. She was to have been given her false passport within a few hours.

The officer looked up in astonishment. "You are a dancer?"

"Yes."

"You were with the Maryinsky Theatre?"

"Yes "

"Unbelievable," the man said.

"Not if you know my story," Natasha answered, with the boldness of complete exhaustion.

"What were you doing at the Eye café?" the officer asked, looking amazed.

"I was dancing," Natasha answered.

The officer looked disbelieving. It was an impression that Natasha was to grow accustomed to in the next few days.

It was Scavronsky who brought the item in the *Telescope* to Richard's notice. The paragraph was devoted to the arrest of a number of "conspirators" in a small café-restaurant called the Eye. Mostly they were students of the university in Kharkov, suspected of being nihilists. The woman Zazulich was believed to have been a member of this group. It was possible that she had received her orders from them, possible that the committee had planned the murder in the back rooms of the Eye café, which was owned by a former serf, Sergei Nestyev.

The suspected terrorists would be examined by a special tribunal in the Fortress of St. Peter and St. Paul. They were being brought to the capital in an armored train.

Scavronsky paused in his reading.

"Natasha Ivanovna was among those arrested," he said. "It

says here, quite clearly, 'a former member of the Maryinsky Theatre . . .'"

"Let me see."

The light in the room dimmed around Richard. The lines of print ran together in a black line. The newspaper became a black oblong before his eyes. How could it be?

The count took a steadying hold on his arm.

". . . It can't be," Richard murmured. "It can't be."

"I'm afraid it is," Scavronsky said gently. "And, by a further irony, my dear friend . . . it grieves me to tell you this—but, by some terrible stroke of fate, Verchinin is to be a member of the special tribunal set up to examine them."

Richard swore. "Christ," he whispered. "Sweet Christ! How did she come into this? Natasha. My beautiful, innocent girl . . ."

He turned to the count, very pale. "I must see her. I must find some way to see her."

"How will that be possible?" the count asked, giving Richard the glass of brandy that he had poured. "The girl is in the fortress. The trial is to be a military one. There is no way that you could enter the fortress—except as a *prisoner*."

CHAPTER
THIRTY-FOUR

The other three members of the tribunal were already in the vaulted stone chamber when Prince Verchinin entered. He saluted them, and took his place. The room was so dark, damp and cold, that the figure of the sentry guard at the door appeared to be wreathed in mist. The feeble glow of a lamp above the table cast a sickly yellow light on the faces of the four men.

Verchinin looked spruce and imposing in his dark green

guard's uniform, though he was hideously pale. His hands moved restlessly—touching his pen, straightening a paper, fingering the collar of his tunic, fiddling with the hilt of his saber on its thin leather crossbelt. When Natasha was shown into the room he cast his hooded eyes downward, glancing at her covertly from beneath his heavy lids.

A tremor of shock ran through Natasha as she recognized him. Her white hands went to her throat. The color burned fiercely in her face and then died, leaving her ashen, almost gray. She wore a plain "home dress," a high-necked blouse and a single skirt of lilac with an overskirt of a darker mauve. She had been given an old-fashioned shawl-mantle of wool, heavily patterned in shades of beige and bronze. It was far too large for her, making her look absurdly young and fragile. Her black hair lay loosely about her face.

"Excellency!" she cried, as though about to throw herself at Verchinin's feet. The arm of the sentry guard restrained her, his fingers biting into the flesh of her arm. Verchinin looked away, his face taking on a purplish tinge.

"Be silent!" a voice commanded from the bench.

This was General Ionin. He was dressed in a plain black frock coat and striped silk tie. Around his neck he wore a medal on a gilded chain; it signified his chairmanship. His voice compelled obedience. Natasha stood quivering in the huge clasp of the guard. She would have sunk to the floor had it not been for the way that he held her.

In a corner of the room was a desk on which were placed the Gospels and a crucifix. Natasha was led before this desk and told to place her hands upon the sacred objects.

"Swear to tell the truth," she was commanded.

"I swear," Natasha whispered. She was taken back before the court.

"Natalia Ivanovna Petrova," Ionin said sternly. "There is little need for us to tell you why you have been brought before us. You are as well aware of the reasons as—"

"Indeed, that's not true!" Natasha cried. "I know nothing of your reasons!"

The lines upon Ionin's face hardened noticeably, but he remained calm. "We know that you have played no important part in this business," he said quietly. "But it is our hope that you will help us to lighten the punishment that your actions deserve."

"But I've done nothing . . . nothing!" Natasha protested.

He cut her short with a sharp gesture. "You have been an

associate of the innkeeper, Nestyev, for almost two months. Are you trying to convince us that you were ignorant of the true nature of that establishment?"

"Yes, I was," Natasha said dully. "I was unaware of its *true* nature."

"You did not know that the Eye café was a meeting place for anarchists and revolutionaries?"

"No, I swear it! I was amazed when I saw the policemen bring them into the restaurant."

"And you did not know that the building housed an illegal printing press?"

Natasha stared. "Printing press?"

"Are you saying that you never heard the sound of the press at work?" Ionin asked sarcastically. "It makes a very *distinctive* sound. The rhythmic sound of type dropping into the chest. Are you saying that you never heard it?"

"I heard many sounds," Natasha said. "The Khitrov market is a noisy place. Many people work there—shoemakers, tinsmiths, blacksmiths—"

She stopped. "Yes, I did hear it," she said, biting her lips. "But I didn't know what it was. Sergei said that it was a water leak in a back room somewhere. A ceiling had fallen in. . . ."

She stopped again, her hand flying to her mouth, aware that she had betrayed Sergei in her careless need to show that she was speaking the truth. "But," she faltered, "I didn't know that it was what you say it was. I can't be sure. It could have been the water dripping. . . ."

The general went on, as though she had not spoken. "During the time that you were there, you must have seen many 'incidents' at the café. You must certainly have knowledge of the more frequent customers. You must have seen those who were allowed to use the back premises. The students and their females."

He fixed her with his formidable eyes, their pupils as sharp and bright as nails. Natasha stared at him silently. She had stopped herself from trembling by a great effort of will. The soldier's fingers no longer encircled her wrist.

"No, I have no such knowledge, sir," she answered softly, amazed that her voice should suddenly sound so natural.

The general regarded her sternly. "Petrova, the truth alone will serve you here. I rely upon your good sense to withhold nothing from us."

"Truly, I know nothing, your excellency!" Natasha cried, now terribly afraid. For in a moment of chilling understand-

ing, she grasped that they would never believe her, and she
had no means of making them.

"Your highness . . ." She turned to Verchinin, who looked
away uneasily.

"Your highness, Sergei Nestyev took pity on me—when
others only sought to . . . to hurt me. . . ."

Verchinin flushed. He peered intently into the dark shadows, away from the girl's distracted eyes. The other men
regarded him curiously. The girl had made a definite appeal
to him, and to him only. There appeared to be some hidden
meaning in her words.

Verchinin forced himself to look at her. He was shaken by
the change in her. She looked like an apparition in the murky
light. "You must answer to General Ionin," he said sharply.
"He is in command here. You cannot claim my sympathy."
He turned to his colleagues. "This woman and I were once
partially acquainted, when she danced at the Maryinsky. I
am, as you may know, a lover of the ballet."

The other men looked surprised. One, Count Gortchakov,
half suppressed a smile. A decrepit, wrinkled old man, he
knew the prince's tastes better, and had seen him snore his
way through many an evening at the theatre.

Tears showed in Natasha's huge eyes. Once again she
wavered, clutching at the young guard for support. "I know
nothing, gentlemen," she said dully. "I am a dancer, that's
all. *Was* a dancer," she corrected herself. Her tears glittered
as she shook her head angrily. "Sergei Nestyev gave me
employment when nobody else would. I danced for him.
That's all I did."

Count Gortchakov leaned forward. His skin shone like
yellowing parchment in the light. He glanced sneeringly at
both Natasha and the prince, his eyes sliding maliciously
between the two. "And after?" he inquired.

". . . After?"

"After you had danced for his customers. What was your
relationship with this fellow Nestyev?"

Natasha colored faintly. "He was my friend, sir."

"Do you mean your lover?"

"No, sir. I mean my friend. Nothing more."

"You are asking this tribunal to believe that you were
employed solely as his *attraction?*"

Verchinin's face was suffused with blood. He was listening
intently, one hand at his ear.

"I only danced for him," Natasha said simply. "He made no other demands."

Verchinin's cheeks turned a muddier red. Ionin noticed this. He diverted Gortchakov from his embarrassing line of questioning.

"Petrova, we are waiting to hear that you are willing to tell us the names of those people who most frequented the café."

Natasha shivered. She turned beseeching eyes upon the prince, but he looked fiercely away. "I don't know, excellency," she said wildly. "How could I know? They were only faces to me. Men—and some women—who came to see me dance. The room was half in darkness."

"Were your dances *modest?*" Gortchakov asked, with another sly glance at Verchinin.

Natasha looked bewildered. "Sir?"

"They were not a lewd exhibition. You were decently dressed?"

Natasha fought down a hysterical desire to laugh. "I have worn less clothing at the Maryinsky, excellency," she said.

The general cleared his throat again, with an angry glance at Gortchakov. "Let us keep to the point, count," he said, then turned to Natasha.

"Are you seriously expecting us to believe that you lived for so long with this scoundrel and never suspected what was happening there?"

Natasha clasped her trembling hands together. She was filled with an unbearable anguish. In her confused state, she felt she had been betrayed by Sergei.

"Yes, yes!" she cried. "I lived there without knowing. I am a child in these things. I have too much trust!"

She began to sob helplessly. "He promised me that no harm should come to me. Oh, Sergei, Sergei . . . You promised . . ."

The general waited—with some patience—for the outburst to die away. Then he said calmly, even gently, "Natalia Ivanovna, no harm shall come to you here if you will tell us all that you remember."

Natasha wiped her eyes and stared about the room in a dazed way. Her eyes rested on the prince's face. He flinched. She looked at him as she would have looked at a snake that had bitten her.

"Well?" Ionin asked. "We are waiting."

But Natasha did not hear him. She had fallen into a dead

faint on the damp stone flags. Ionin gestured for her to be taken away. The young guard picked her up and carried her from the room.

Gortchakov gathered his papers together briskly. "We are wasting time, general. What we must do is flog the truth out of her."

"I shall do as my duty dictates, count," Ionin replied. He called for the next prisoner to be brought in.

Verchinin sat hunched in his chair. There was a heavy weight at the pit of his stomach, an acid taste in his mouth. The weight moved, and a sharp pain stabbed him. He could feel the pain as something palpable. It was as though he had swallowed some sharp-edged object—a coin no bigger than a kopeck.

He must get himself excused from the committee. He could not endure the sight of the girl again, her childlikeness, her helplessness. Pity for her was like an agony, pity for the days of suffering that awaited her. The accusation with which she had been charged stunned him. How was it possible that she had become involved with anarchists and such riffraff? She must have rejected all hope in society.

The knowledge of his own guilt in the affair overwhelmed him, consumed him. His tongue, his limbs, his mind, all seemed paralyzed. The room was unbearably dark, the voices around him maddeningly indistinct.

Gortchakov was asking, "Don't you think the girl should be put to the whipping post, prince?"

Verchinin swayed against the table. He steadied himself with a great effort. Dear God, he thought. How can *I* set myself up to judge *her*? She is as innocent as an animal. And I . . . I am totally responsible for her condition.

Winter sank through the earth, and suddenly it was spring, a lavish stream of warmth and light. Spring: mild, juicy, scented, abandoned. Peasants brought dripping masses of wildflowers to sell in the markets of St. Petersburg. The bird cherry blossomed, waxy and bridal. The windows were opened at last and fastened back for the summer. The streets were bright with sunbonnets and parasols.

It meant nothing to Natasha, awake through the long days in her cell. No ray of sunlight crept through the dust-laden windows to shine upon the icon set up in a corner of the room.

Though she thought of spring often, measuring its progress in the days she ticked off by scoring the wooden frame of her barred door. She longed for the freedom of the streets. The perfume of flowers haunted her imagination. Half dreaming, she passed her days in imaginary wanderings through the woods of Orienbaum and Peterhof with the shadowy figure of her Richka. The woods filled with the fragrance of lily-of-the-valley, the ground shining faintly with dog violets in the May nights.

How long was it since she had lain with Richard beside the carpet of wood anemones, her body dissolving in pleasure beneath his skillful fingers? How clear the image was. Other memories had faded like the silk rose that had crumbled between her breasts, but that day remained vividly in her mind, strong and intense—the sunlight dappling their bodies, glinting on the golden hairs of Richard's arms, turning the hair on his chest to a fleece of gold; the sunlight striking her own arm as she raised it, scattering the white skin with tiny points of color. Dazzling color all about her. Warm, bright tones. Her body dissolving in the full force of the light, but his—above her, against the sun—defined by it, yet hazed with gold.

Richard. His body so strong, so solid. His eyes gazing down at her out of the dark bronze of his face, shining like aquamarines, burning blue between gold-tipped lashes, then blazing with passion. The line of his lips coming down to meet hers, the full strong mouth. Her fingers touching his face: the strong arch of his brow, the hollowed cheeks, the cleft of his chin. His wide shoulders hunching as he took her in his arms. Her face against his warm skin, the damp hair of his chest. The clean sharp smell of his body. Her hands running down the length of his back, feeling the muscles tauten under her fingers. His back so smooth, his chest so rough. It had never failed to move her, this sharp contrast.

Her body arching to meet his. Falling back, her body weakening, her bones seeming to crumble, her veins filled with honey. Arm across arm, arm across breast. The sweet warm smell of grass, the blades tickling her back, then everything blacking out in the upward surge of passion. Losing herself totally, as her body opened to his . . .

Afterward, resting. Everything sharp and clear, only his body cool and remote. Her leg, touching his, might have been touching some distant star.

One day a ladybird had alighted on her naked breast, an enameled jewel. "That's a sign of good luck in England," Richard had said.

. . . Good luck. She shivered.

How long had she been in this terrible fortress? Twenty days? Only twenty? How would it be when the days became months? For she never doubted that she would be found guilty. With Russian fatalism she recognized the outcome already. Her story would never be accepted by the tribunal.

It was ironic. She had not lied, unless silence could be interpreted as a lie. She had said nothing that could incriminate Sergei or Oleg. She thought, perhaps, that if—or when—she was forced to lie, she could make falsehood sound like truth, but she could not, apparently, make the truth sound like the truth.

Over the days she schooled herself to accept the situation, the hardships and the suffering. What a trick fate had played on her. To be so close to freedom, to be with Richard, only to be cast back into this terrible darkness.

In brief wild moments of optimism, she knew that she had a great deal left to live for. Richard was alive, they could be together. He would somehow save her. He had spoken of his influence with the English royal family. He would somehow convince the authorities that she was innocent.

Yet what if he, himself, believed her guilty? The darkness of despair would overtake her again. Her moods oscillated wildly. Her only refuge was in the lovingly remembered scenes of her days with Richard. They would wander, hand in hand, through those far-off sunlit days.

She was left strictly alone in the first grim weeks. Only a narrow-faced woman jailer was allowed into her cell. Natasha was given a worn-out cloth and a wooden bucket filled with tepid water. She was ordered to "slop out." It was not a matter of hygiene, but a punishment. Nothing could have removed the grime of centuries from her cell. Over and over again, as the bitter eyes of the keeper watched her through the spy-hole, she was made to wash and wipe the floor until the water was icy cold and black. Her hands were red and raw, permanently cold.

Once a day she was given a bowl of greasy soup, with a hunk of dry bread. In the morning she received an equally greasy bowl of gruel. Sheer exhaustion eventually overcame her fear of the place. She would fall into a deep sleep and rise to consciousness through a series of warm sweet dreams.

They were hardly inseparable from the daydreams. The image of Richard was so strong in her mind, so real to her, that she would awaken expecting to find his arms around her, his handsome face buried in her hair. Her sense of loss on awakening was more terrible to her than anything else she had to endure, the days of loneliness, of consuming hunger, of continuous and senseless exercise, of a terrible inner emptiness.

Then, after three weeks, she was taken before the committee again, to the same dank room, with the lamp above the table casting more shadows than light. Her eyes sought out Verchinin, but he sat well back, rigid and remote, wishing to isolate himself from the proceedings and yet continue to do his duty. He would never meet her gaze. She saw no sign of mercy in his half-averted face, or in the faces of his associates.

They began to question her about the attempt on Trepov's life. Gortchakov shuffled his papers peevishly. "You were acquainted with General Trepov?" he asked.

"Yes," Natasha answered reluctantly.

"*How* were you acquainted?"

"I met him on three . . . I think on three occasions."

Gortchakov leered at her. "Was the general also a 'ballet-lover?'"

"I don't know, excellency."

"Then what was his interest in you?"

They must surely know? she thought confusedly.

". . . Well, Petrova?"

The count looked more interested in Verchinin's reactions than in her own. His eyes danced spitefully as he observed the prince.

Natasha drew herself up stiffly. "He wished me to spy upon an Englishman, Richard Greville. He was with the British embassy."

"The Englishman was a friend of yours?"

"Yes, sir."

"Only a friend?"

Natasha was silent, refusing to answer.

"The Englishman was your lover!" Gortchakov suddenly shouted. "You had a scandalous affair with the man!"

General Ionin turned to the count and spoke to him in a low voice, furiously. Gortchakov sat back in his chair, glowering at Natasha.

"And did you spy upon Richard Greville?" Ionin asked, glancing down at the papers on his desk.

". . . Yes," Natasha answered hesitantly. This was her first outright lie. She was finding it harder now to control her voice.

Ionin seemed to pick up the note of reluctance in her tone. He spent some moments reading.

"According to this report, your efforts were not overly successful."

Natasha remained silent, biting back a retort. If they already knew, why did they ask?

Ionin, as though reading her thoughts, said, "We are anxious to hear your side of the story."

"I did as I was ordered," Natasha replied sullenly. "If I was unsuccessful, it is because I had no talent for such work."

She flashed a bitter glance at Verchinin, who kept his eyes resolutely on the desk top. "I was trained to be a *dancer*," Natasha said.

All three men concentrated on the papers before them. The prince shuffled his agitatedly.

"General Trepov states here that he found you 'patriotically uninspired,'" Gortchakov began. But Ionin cut him off, gesturing irritably, as though to say this line of questioning was unfruitful. He turned to Natasha.

"What do you know of the ex-students Kravchinsky, Zheliabov, Kibalchich or Perovskaya?"

Natasha shook her head. "Nothing, excellency."

"You recognize none of these names?"

"No, sir."

"You have not heard of the *intellectual*, Kravchinsky?" Gortchakov asked derisively. "A man who boasts publicly that he will carry out the next assassination attempt *successfully*?"

Natasha hesitated. "I may have heard of him," she said. "But only from listening to people gossip . . . in the market . . ." She stared at her judges helplessly. "This has nothing to do with me. I was in nobody's confidence. I was only a dancer."

There was a deadly silence. Then General Ionin asked quietly, "You were in nobody's confidence, you say? Then you are admitting that the people among whom you lived had secrets to be shared?"

Natasha shook her head, thrown into disorder by her blunder.

Ionin leaned forward, fixing her with his piercing gaze. "If you tell us the truth, Natalia Ivanovna, it will be well with you. There is a room above, where you can see the sun. You shall go there when you are sensible. But, first, we must know the names of those you saw—or spoke to—at the Eye café."

"I met nobody!" Natasha cried. "I saw nobody! Only Sergei and his granny. Sergei offered me his protection. He kept the public from me."

"How did you meet Nestyev?"

"I went there, looking for work."

"You went to such a miserable place expecting to find work as a *dancer?*" Gortchakov asked.

"I went to many places—each worse than the one before," Natasha said, looking at Verchinin bitterly. He fidgeted with his pen.

"And he offered you work?"

"Yes."

"And his protection?"

"Yes!"

"Why did he offer you his protection?" the count asked, with a malicious glance for Verchinin, who scowled and retreated further from the light.

"I was destitute," Natasha said. "I could not find work elsewhere."

"And how did you come to be destitute?"

"You know why! Because I was dismissed from the Opera Ballet."

"Ah, yes," Gortchakov said, this time looking directly at the prince, who cringed away from the mockery in his face. "You were dismissed from the ballet, because you were a troublemaker. Did you entertain revolutionary notions even then?"

Natasha stared hard at the count, fascinated and repelled. His face was lit by an inane malice. How much did he really know about her? she wondered. How much of the truth had they discovered? The count knew, she felt sure, that the prince had played some part in her dismissal.

She was tempted to tell them her version of the facts. To throw herself at their mercy in that way. But some inner sense of caution made her pause. Somehow, she felt that Verchinin might find some way to help her if she kept his part in this business to herself. She could see that he was troubled. He looked his great age. In a sense, this must be almost as great an ordeal for him as it was for her. He must, she felt sure, have pulled a lot of strings to avoid this "duty." One thing was obvious. He was not there to exult over her misfortune. He looked as wretched as she felt.

But how could he help her? He was there to question her. Every man before her believed her to be politically involved with the terrorists. A feeling of utter desolation swept over her. There was no way out.

"I can tell you nothing," she said hopelessly. "I know nothing."

Gortchakov lost his temper. "You shall taste the whip, and we shall see what you shall tell us then!" he shouted. "Do you think you can defy us?"

Natasha shrank away from the stale smell of the guard's body. But when she spoke her voice was low and steady. "No, excellency. I have learned that men of your . . . eminence . . . cannot be defied. Or resisted."

Verchinin groaned, and fell back in his chair. His fingers clutched at his close-fitting collar. He began to choke, a rough, hacking sound like the barking of a seal. His face was mottled with purple, the skin a ghastly gray.

His colleagues turned to him in alarm. Spots of blood speckled the gold facings of his uniform. The immaculate cloth was wrinkled where he had pulled at it. His eyes turned upward in their sockets. His mouth fell open slackly, the dead weight of his tongue lolled against the back of his throat.

Reacting quickly, Ionin reached out and pulled the old man's jaw forward, releasing his tongue. The prince began to breathe again, sobbing for air, his lungs wheezing like a broken-winded horse. Then he collapsed into the general's arms.

Gortchakov rose. "Take the woman away!" he shouted. "Send for the medical officer!"

Natasha was led from the room. Behind her, she could hear the prince fighting strenuously for every breath.

A curious feeling of dread filled Natasha as she was marched back to her cell. Once the iron door was slammed behind her and its echoes died away, she sank upon the thin pallet bed and misery overpowered her.

What if Verchinin were to die? Or be removed from the committee? As long as he sat in judgment on her, she stood some chance of mercy being shown to her. It was obvious that the prince was consumed by a sense of his own guilt. Every time she had managed to look into his face she had seen the

signs of an intense inner struggle there, a deep suffering. He
knew that she was innocent of the charges brought against
her, she was the victim of his own selfishness. Although he
had given her no positive sign, she clung to the belief that he
would find some way to help her if he could, if only to ease his
own conscience. His own sense of honor demanded it—
surely?

He would bring the weight of his opinion to balance that of
his colleagues, perhaps even influence them in her favor.

But now? If he was to be taken ill? What hope had she?

Three days later she was taken up into the courtyard to see
a man flogged. This, it was believed, would break her.

The unaccustomed light blinded her for a few seconds as
she emerged into the day. Then, slowly, her vision cleared,
and the first thing that she saw properly was the figure of
Count Gortchakov sitting astride a black gelding. Ionin and a
fourth member of the committee sat together at an open
window, among a group of military men dressed in full
uniform.

The flogging block had been set up in the center of the
courtyard, a grim contraption in the shape of a huge triangle.
A dozen soldiers stood at attention around it, men of the
artillery, in green tunics with scarlet epaulets and red and
black facings. Natasha had a sudden memory of the ice ball
with the dazzling uniforms, whirling and turning.

She felt dizzy and steadied herself against the rough stone
wall. The heat of the sun on its surface caused her to cry out.
After long days in semidarkness, she had almost expected to
find cold and snow, not this warm welcoming sunlight.

Gortchakov rapped out a command. There was a shouted
order from the sergeant of artillery, a door opened in the far
wall and a man was dragged out from it, pulling and straining
against his guards. He was stripped to the waist, his arms and
neck were darkened from exposure, his torso pale from lack
of sun.

With a startled cry, Natasha recognized Sergei. His face
was deeply lined with suffering, gaunt and white. But he was
unmistakably Sergei.

He, too, gave a great cry as he saw her. Words formed on
his lips, but ended in a bloodied mumble as a blow from a
guard's broad hand crashed into his cheek.

"Proceed," Gortchakov called. He looked back at the girl,
his small eyes bright.

Sergei was hauled, struggling at every step, to the flogging block. His arms were drawn above his head and lashed to the apex of the triangle. His legs were pulled apart and tied at the ankle to the base, so that he straddled the wooden frame.

"Proceed," Gortchakov called out again.

The sergeant of artillery repeated his order and a sturdy-looking man stepped forward. He, too, was stripped to the waist. The sunlight rippled over his sinewy body as he flexed his muscles. His right arm was bound in leather at the wrist, and in his hand he held a scourge. Natasha shivered as he snapped it experimentally. It was a thin whip from which sprouted a dozen thongs. The sound alone caused her to fall back against the arm of her guard.

"Courage, miss," the man whispered unexpectedly, and—startled—Natasha steeled herself to face the horror of the next few minutes.

The flogger had stood back, taking his stance. He raised the whip, measuring the distance. Then the whip lashed through the air and met flesh.

The blow made every muscle in Sergei's back stand out. A dozen bright red lines showed clearly on his white skin.

The sergeant said impassively, "First stroke!"

Natasha survived four strokes. As the whip fell with slow, irregular blows, the impact of leather on flesh exploded like the retort of a dozen firecrackers. Muffled sounds broke from Sergei's mouth, his body writhed, the muscles standing out like knots on a tree.

Natasha tried to will herself not to watch, to close her mind to the scene before her. But she could only stare at the mutilated back, in a daze of horror. It was she, herself, who hung there, bruised and raw. The lash falling upon his bare flesh was cutting into her own shoulders. The tips of the whip, curling around Sergei's chest, nicked at her own naked breasts. The blood, flowing in thin streams down his rigid back, was hers. She found herself praying that Sergei would not scream. If he screamed, she would . . . would . . .

Sergei screamed—a sudden, loud, shrill cry, a cry that was torn from him. Natasha collapsed. Darkness bore her away.

Later, in her cell, General Ionin said, watching her carefully, "Well, Natalia Ivanovna, will you have the whip too? Or will you tell us what you know?"

Natasha moaned, still feeling weak and stunned. She caught at the table for support. "I know nothing. Nothing."

She laughed suddenly, shrilly as Sergei's scream, her eyes rolling wildly. "Don't you know the truth when you hear it, general? I was a dancer. Sergei gave me shelter. For all I know, he could have been the biggest criminal in Russia, but he was kind to me—kinder than your sort were . . . Did you expect me to starve?" She stopped, afraid of revealing more. "I was a dancer. Nothing more."

She sank back against the dank wall.

"Have you made a complete sacrifice of your life, too?" Gortchakov asked sardonically. "Like your fellow conspi. .-tors?"

He would have said more, but Ionin stopped him with a curt gesture. When he spoke, his voice was calmly reasonable, but his words roused Natasha from her apathy, bringing the fire to her cheeks, causing her to sway.

"Would you rather not be free altogether?" the general said. "Free to join your lover, the Englishman. Free to leave Russia, perhaps. He is here in St. Petersburg. He is anxious for you—willing, even, to sacrifice his own career for you. He has petitioned our master the tzar on your behalf. . . ."

To Natasha, it seemed that her heart had stopped beating, only to start up again violently, crashing inside her breast. Hope surged in her like some secretion suddenly released into her bloodstream.

Richard still believed in her, still wanted her, was trying to free her. Then hope abated. How could she trust them? They were trying to trick her into betraying her friends. How could she buy her freedom at the cost of other lives?

"I know nothing. Nothing . . ." she said dully.

CHAPTER

THIRTY-FIVE

Lord Loftus regarded Richard with a face as sour as that of the queen's portrait behind him. "I have had a message from the minister of the Imperial Court," the ambassador said, frowning. "Your request to see his majesty has been refused."

Richard started up angrily. "Has his majesty *personally* refused to grant me an audience?"

Lord Loftus looked at the letter with its imperial seal. "It's hard to say," he said. "It simply states that his majesty cannot be involved in this affair."

Richard swore. "The bastards! The damned bureaucrats! It is *they* who have refused my petition. I doubt if the tzar has even seen it!"

The ambassador's frown deepened. "I must say as your superior, Greville, that I am very displeased by your decision to approach the crown directly in this *crude* way. It is most incorrect."

"What would your excellency have preferred me to do?"

The ambassador gestured irritably, tapping the offending letter with his fingers.

"I would have preferred that you had come to me, man. Then I could have at least attempted to dissuade you—"

"I would not have been dissuaded," Richard replied. "I had to do what I could, as I could. I have been waiting for the Princess of Wales—"

The ambassador's pale eyes bulged. "You have approached her royal highness?"

"Yes, excellency. Twice. And the Duchess of Edinburgh.

They were both most sympathetic when I saw them in London—"

Lord Loftus banged the desk top with a clenched fist. "Greville, have you taken leave of all reason? You have asked two royal ladies to approach the tzar, to intercede on behalf of a woman who consorted with men who planned the murder of his most trusted servant."

Richard looked grim. "Trepov was shot by a demented woman—she was quite independent of any group—"

"That's beside the point."

"In any case, it is irrelevant. There is no evidence that Natasha 'consorted' with these men. Scavronsky has given me an account of the trial, he is a great friend of Ionin. All the evidence shows that she simply went to work for this man because she could find no other work."

"Scavronsky has given you a report of the trial?" Lord Loftus asked, astonished. "A military trial, closed to outsiders?"

"He has it from Ionin," Richard said wearily. "He feels that I should be informed—as far as it affects Natasha, that is, though he has revealed other details, inadvertently. . . . I'm writing it up."

The ambassador looked appeased, but still uncomfortable. "All the same, you should not have written to the tzar," he said. "You should have applied through the proper channels. Dammit, man, you know the procedures! And in these difficult times . . ."

Richard stood at attention before the ambassador, hands to the sides of his braided trousers. "Exactly, your excellency," he said quietly. "In these difficult times there is little latitude for etiquette." He bowed. "If your lordship will excuse me . . . ?"

His lordship cut him short. "No, I'm damned if I'll excuse you, Greville. You seem to have gone to pieces over this business. You must tell me what you plan to do next."

Richard looked grimmer than before. "I plan to cut a few more corners, my lord."

"What!"

"Forgive me, sir, but I can't tell you what I plan to do further. You must give me leave to act in this as a private gentleman."

The ambassador exploded. "If you act in this at all, Greville, it must be as a private gentleman—as, indeed, you have acted so far! I must tell you categorically that you can expect no backing from this embassy."

Richard bowed again. "I understand that, my lord. I am only sorry that the embassy has been drawn into it."

He indicated the letter on the desk top. Lord Loftus cleared his throat gruffly. He was—in his chilly way—fond of Richard.

"I shall, in the name of this embassy, officially disassociate myself from your actions," he said.

"Of course, sir. You can do little else."

The ambassador made some inarticulate noise, looking both disturbed and annoyed. "But good God, man!" he cried, exasperated. "Don't you realize that there's nothing you can do? Nothing! They will only resent any further outside interference. It could mean your post here."

"A small price to pay," Richard said steadily, apparently unmoved. He smiled, his smile terrible. "But in any case, my lord, there is something that I can do. I can appeal *directly* to the tzar."

"What?"

"I have just remembered an old Russian tradition."

Richard chose a pleasant afternoon when he knew that the tzar would be driving in the park at the imperial village of Tzarkoe Selo, some miles from the capital. He also chose a broad avenue that the tzar would use. Alexander was, fortunately, a creature of habit—which caused his protectors considerable problems.

The dead-straight avenue cut through a silent spring forest. There was little traffic and no pedestrians. Trails led—if they led anywhere at all—through a gloomy jungle of dead and leaning trees overshadowed by giant firs.

Richard waited as the silence deepened around him, a silence made more unnerving by his own heightened state of mind. Would the tzar come this way? How long must he wait? The silence grew harder to bear. It was unbroken by even the cry of a bird.

Richard straightened, listening. Raising dust as it came, a carriage appeared between the trees. It turned into the avenue and rolled steadily toward Richard. He nerved himself for what was to come.

Reaching into his pocket he drew out a paper. He calculated the distance, choosing his moment. As the carriage reached him, Richard suddenly darted forward and threw himself in the dust. He steadied himself from the force of his landing, kneeling in the appropriate posture of a supplicant, leaving just enough space for the coachman to bring the carriage to a halt. He had judged the distance nicely.

Richard was at once surrounded by the mounted guards who had followed the emperor's carriage at a discreet distance. Pistols were leveled at his head on all sides.

A footman leaped from the carriage and walked toward Richard. Between the ring of horsemen, Richard could see the figure of the tzar leaning forward, dressed in the summer whites of a hussar.

"What do you want with his majesty?" the footman asked.

"To present a petition," Richard said, offering the paper.

The footman bowed and took the paper from Richard's hand. He walked back to the carriage and handed the petition to the tzar.

Richard waited, not quite sure what to expect. He had thought that he might be called into the tzar's presence. But it was not to be. The tzar sat in his carriage, remote as a god. From where Richard knelt it was hard even to see whether the tzar had condescended to read the petition. He was accustomed to receiving them—often in this dramatic way.

But, if he read it, surely he must call him forward? He would be amazed by the fact that Richard was English and a member of a diplomatic mission. Wouldn't he be impressed by Richard's audacity, moved by his desperation? Richard remained on his knees, head bowed.

Then there was a shouted order from the carriage. The guards fell back from Richard, clearing a passage for the landau. With a jingle of harness and a soft slur of turning wheels, the carriage set off, passing Richard in uncanny silence and a haze of dust as he continued kneeling.

Richard looked up, hoping to catch a glimpse of the tzar, wanting to see from his expression how his petition had been received. But the tzar's face was turned away from him, intent on some distant prospect.

The horsemen clattered after their master. Richard was left kneeling in the dust, covered in a fine powder. His heart filled with a murderous rage.

CHAPTER
THIRTY-SIX

The tzar had read Richard's petition, and had been moved by it. He sent for Richard, calling him to the Winter Palace.

The palace was like a beseiged fortress. The approaches to the tzar's private rooms were guarded by a chain of armed sentries, stationed every five meters. Richard's pass was scrutinized at every door. This feeling of heavy surveillance continued even into the tzar's quarters. Richard, waiting in the anteroom to the cabinet, was aware of a score of eyes upon him. From every wall the Romanov dynasty stared at him—the heavily rouged and plastered faces of the women, almost Oriental in the early years, and the stove-browned faces of the men. Only in the last few generations had the faces taken on a truly European appearance, ending with the tall, blue-eyed Alexander II, the man he was about to see, the handsomest prince of his time.

When Richard was finally admitted into the tzar's presence, he was shocked by his appearance. The emperor sat hunched before his large mahogany desk, simply staring into space. Anxiety had turned him into an old man. His hair was gray, his shoulders stooped. Richard felt a moment of pity for the man. Nothing in his life had gone right for him. Everything he had touched had turned to ashes. The golden age his reign had appeared to herald had turned to dross.

Unable to look at the tzar, Richard looked about him. The room was small, furnished with magnificent bad taste, its rococo charm buried beneath an avalanche of modern trappings—patterned upholstery and paper hangings, japanned goods and papier-mâché. The desk at which the emperor sat was cluttered with a number of silver-framed daguerreotypes.

The portrait of his mistress, Princess Catherine Dolguruky, and their children were prominent among those of his legitimate family.

When Richard told his story to the tzar—with passion and urgency—the tzar's pale and mournful face settled into a frozen look. When Richard came to a halt, the tzar looked up wearily. He passed a thin white hand across his face.

"The lady has no lack of defenders," he said unexpectedly.

Startled, Richard waited for an explanation.

"I know your story is true," the tzar said. "Prince Verchinin last night sent his confessor to me with the same facts. He wished to confess his role in this sad tale. On his deathbed he has found himself to be a good Christian, and my good subject."

Richard caught his breath "The prince is dying?"

The tzar nodded, and rose stiffly. "I have arranged to visit him this evening." He stood by the carved desk, musing. "Perhaps God's foreseeing care is at work here. I see His hand in it."

"Your Majesty?"

The tzar made no answer immediately. When he did so, it was to say with a morose smile, "I am only sorry that your friend is not being tried in an open court, Mr. Greville. Our juries have a tendency to ignore the law and deliver their verdicts from the heart. The girl's story would touch their hearts as it has touched mine. She would undoubtedly go free."

Richard knew that the tzar was thinking of the case of Vera Zazulich. In court, her defending counsel had drawn a picture of a pure young girl giving her life to avenge a comrade. The whole court had wept in sympathy and Zazulich had gone free, to be smuggled out of the country. This was why Natasha and the others were being tried by a military court—out of the public eye. Richard, picking up a cue, protested that it would be scandalous for the main offender to go free and for lesser suspects to be punished.

"The woman Zazulich was wrongly liberated," the tzar said coldly. "Had she not been deliberately spirited away, she would have been rearrested."

"But, in any case, Majesty, Natalia Ivanovna is innocent. I can swear to that."

"That is for the interrogation committee to decide," the tzar answered. He looked at Richard sharply, a pure agony gleaming in his eyes. "*Par malheur*, mine is a country in a state of civil war," he said. "Open civil war. But, even in such a situation, every citizen knows that a murderer and her accomplices must not be allowed to go unpunished." He sighed. "It is not for myself that I fear, you understand, but for my people—for their safety."

Richard fought back his desire to speak out again. He saw that it would only aggravate the tzar, who had begun to wheeze from an asthmatic attack, always a sign of acute distress. The breath whistled in his lungs.

In any case, the tzar had already brought the audience to an end. He had turned to the bell rope and summoned an aide. Richard was shown out of the room.

"I shall interest myself in the case," the emperor said. "But I can promise you nothing further."

The tzar's carriage, with its escort of Cossacks, rattled to a halt on the hay-strewn cobbles before Verchinin's palace. The men surrounded Alexander as he strode up the flight of steps leading to the great front door. All the windows of the huge building were ablaze with light in honor of the tzar's visit. The prince could have been giving a ball instead of taking his leave of his master.

The door opened as the tzar placed his foot upon the first step. A liveried footman opened the door, but the tzar was ushered into the huge pilastered hall by the prince's nephew, his heir.

Verchinin's whole family had assembled to meet the emperor. They accompanied him up the sweeping shell of the staircase and along the brilliantly lit corridors to the prince's bedroom. A priest accompanied the tzar to the vast canopied bed. The feeble rays of a rushlight threw its immense shadow over the rest of the room. A brighter light burned before the enameled icon set in a gold shrine in one corner of the room. The Mother of God stared blindly out from a gold and silver heaven.

The emperor looked toward the image and crossed himself. The priest did likewise. Verchinin, from his bed, followed the tzar's movements and feebly attempted to cross himself. But the effort was too much for him and his hand fell with a dull thump onto his chest. His fingers twitched convulsively in the lace of his nightshirt.

The old prince lay upon his silken pillows, appearing hardly to breathe. His face was a lifeless white, the dyed hair a

lifeless black. Only his eyes burned with haunted feverish
intensity. He bowed his head feebly, half rising from the
pillow. The tzar put out a restraining hand.

"Sire, you came. . . ." the old man whispered.

The tzar sat on the velvet stool set by the bed and inclined
his head toward the dying man, to save his strength.

"I am come to relieve your mind, prince, not to exhaust
your body," he said.

He waited quietly for the old man to speak. Verchinin
gathered his strength, but his voice, when it emerged, was
little more than a murmur. "Sire . . . the holy one has told
you of my folly and my trouble. No, it is too late. I
suffer. . . . I shall suffer. It is a terrible burden . . . terrible . . . terrible . . ."

"The priest has granted you absolution for your soul's
peace," the tzar said.

The old man sighed, the sigh dying in his throat.

"Divine mercy is boundless," the tzar said.

The prince closed his eyes for a moment, but opened them
as he cried, "But I am not clean! Not while I . . ." Terror
shook him. For a moment the imprint of death showed clearly
on his face.

He has only a matter of hours, the tzar thought, taking the
old man's hand in his. "You have confessed your guilt," the
tzar said soothingly.

The prince fought for every racking breath. "Yes," he
whispered. "And my secret is safe, under the seal of the
confessional. . . ." The hooded lids drooped wearily over the
burning eyes. "But . . . human forgiveness. Is there to be no
human forgiveness?"

"Who shall forgive you, prince?"

Verchinin's eyes almost started from his head in his anxiety. "She, Natasha Ivanovna. She must forgive me, sire."

His head fell back upon the pillow. A trickle of blackened
saliva dribbled from his lips. The priest took a white silk
napkin and wiped the prince's chin. The tzar remained silent,
unable to find the words to comfort him. Verchinin's hand
crept over the satin coverlet and picked distractedly at the
tzar's sleeve.

"She is upon the threshold of life," he whispered. "Such
things are not to be forgotten when the verdict is brought.
. . . She has been wronged. How is the folly to be undone?"

He repeated this question to himself many times, his voice

growing increasingly weaker. Then he made a tremendous effort to control his thoughts and his tongue. "I am the friend of none who is your enemy, sire," he said clearly. "But she is not your enemy."

"If she is not, she will be found innocent," the tzar said calmly.

"I have seen her questioned," Verchinin insisted. "I know she has told the truth. There is nothing to find out now. A child could see that she spoke the truth, but Gortchakov is a brute and Ionin . . ."

Terror gleamed again in his burning eyes. "I would stake my soul upon her innocence, sire. She has never lied. The truth is written in her eyes."

His anguish affected the tzar strongly. He had known Verchinin all his life, and he knew that as far as women were concerned the prince had few principles. He had "loved" all women indiscriminately. One woman had amused him as easily as the next. In all the years, he had never seen the prince so moved, so eloquent of purpose. His exhausted voice still carried the strength of utter conviction—and desperation.

"I ask nothing for myself, my emperor," Verchinin whispered, the tears beginning to run down his furrowed cheeks. "That day is gone. I have confessed. My soul should be at peace, but my heart is in torment. The girl is innocent. She is the wronged one—by many, but by me above all. . . ."

He lay back upon the pillows, his waxen face shining with tears, his strength almost used up. The tzar continued to sit beside him. But now he sat with his head resting on his hand.

Suddenly, the old man's eyes blazed open. He looked beyond the tzar, into the monstrous leaping shadows of the room. He cried out, then fell back upon his pillows.

His hand sought for his sire's. He turned to the tzar, but his eyes looked blindly beyond him. God, it is coming now! the tzar thought, motioning for the priest to come forward.

"Promise me, my master. Promise that she will not suffer. . . . Ah, but she was a beauty!" They were his last words. He sank into a coma from which he never recovered.

CHAPTER
THIRTY-SEVEN

Natasha, in her cell, knew nothing but long days of twilight. She was permitted no occupation and the guard no longer came in to torment her. They kept her hands idle, presumably to teach her the full meaning of imprisonment. In fact, were it not for the fact that they still brought her food twice a day, she might have thought herself forgotten.

She imagined in the first days after witnessing the whipping that she might lose her reason. The silence and darkness seemed to grow about her. At times she would succumb to a frenzy and beat upon the door with her fists, or hurl herself against the granite wall.

Her sanity was saved from the time she decided to spend her days in training. The idea came to her when she awoke one night to find herself standing in the center of her cell, poised in the fifth position. She had been dreaming of the Imperial School in Theatre Street. It took moments for her to realize that she was not in the bright rehearsal room, but in her darkened cell. Wearily, she had climbed back onto the thin iron cot, chilled and oppressed. Then it came to her.

"But that's it!" she murmured. "I must have a dancing schedule. When I am free to go to Richard, I must be fit and strong!"

Over the past few days she had begun to believe that Richard was working for her release. There must be some reason for the delay in bringing her to judgment, some reason for their having ceased to harass her.

Starting from that day she had begun to retrain her body.

Slowly and awkwardly she found new sense of balance, not only for her body but also for her mind.

That night they brought her supper as usual, the boiling tea and the black bread that tasted of earth. When she had eaten it, she lay upon her cot, letting her head sink upon her arms, allowing herself to be carried away to the dream country of woods and meadows, alive with the music of birds, to walk for a time holding her dream lover's hand. With his voice and their laughter in her ears, her usual sleep was sweet, for in her sleep hope could be reborn.

But that night she dreamed of the theatre. She was alone upon a vast stage—the lights of the auditorium seemed a mile away. A river separated her from the audience, water filled the orchestra pit like a moat. The stage stretched endlessly away from her, leaving her small frail figure in a dreary waste.

The music sounded faintly at first, so faintly that she could not follow the beat. Her partner came up behind her. His arms encircled her waist. Slowly, she raised into the air, *en pointe*.

She was lighter than air, her movements had no sense of effort, her feet barely touched the stage. She was all things flying, blown by the wind, an extension of her partner's arms, nothing more. The strong arms grew tighter about her waist. Turning, she looked down, into the ghastly grinning face of Verchinin.

She was held in his grip; his hands nipped her waist. Then her body was glued to his, his hands played freely over her breasts. She was naked in his arms, her dress dissolving on her limbs. Lust smoldered in his eyes as he whirled her about, giddily. The music skirled harshly. She awoke, her body trembling violently.

The door had opened. Its creaking hinges echoed the wild skirling of the music. A sergeant of the gendarmerie stood before her, illuminated in the rays of a lantern. There were three other men with him, rough, military men in drab gray cloaks.

"Come with us," the sergeant said, beckoning her toward the door.

She began to tremble more violently, still held by the terrifying dream. She cringed back against the wall as though she would find protection there. Her body was shaking, vibrating with cold and terror. Uncontrollably, she shrank from the man's hold as he reached out for her.

"What is it?" she asked, shielding her eyes from the rays of the lantern.

"You must come with us," the man said stolidly. "Their lordships are waiting."

Natasha felt that she had lost the power to move. Her mind was numbed with dread. Two soldiers came to stand on either side of her. They seized her by the elbows, almost lifting her from the floor. Leaving the cell, the soldiers dragged Natasha along. Tremors of horror swept through her body. She tried to stand upright, to find her feet, struggling desperately to conquer her fear and regain some measure of dignity.

This was the end of it all. They had passed sentence. What would happen to her? Had Richard succeeded on her behalf? Would these men treat her so roughly if he had? Her mind refused to contemplate the next few minutes.

Her hands scraped against the rough stone walls as they turned the corners sharply. She scarcely noticed that they were bleeding. The toe of her shoe caught in the hem of her dress, tearing it, and her foot poked clumsily through, preventing her from walking properly even when they set her on her feet.

They left the dungeons and began to climb the long flight of steps that led to the council chamber. The mighty granite walls appeared to close in around her the higher they climbed. A sentry opened the door to the gloomy room and Natasha walked into it at the sergeant's side. She was suddenly calm, fatalistically calm. Whatever happened, her future had been decided, she knew. The thought gave her an unaccountable sense of peace.

Suddenly light dazzled her. Every lamp in the room had been lit. Torches burned in the wall sconces, candles flared in a dozen holders. After the tomblike darkness of the corridor, she was blinded for a moment. Then her vision cleared.

The room was full of men and smoke. Soldiers in the green uniforms of the artillery stood guarding a dozen men. Each soldier was heavily armed, each prisoner loaded with chains. Natasha noticed that she had been favored. She had never been bound. Did that augur well for her?

To her horror, Natasha recognized Sergei. She was amazed that she could still do so. The flesh had dropped away from his skull, his mouth gaped toothlessly, his lips were bruised and swollen. Gazing back at her without recognition, his eyes looked sightless.

A sound escaped another man, further back in the group.

It sounded indistinctly like her own name. She turned, and fell back, clutching at the sergeant for support. The lights blurred before her eyes, yet she did not faint, though she longed to lose consciousness.

Oleg Mikhailovich! It wasn't possible! This strange figure, head wagging, apelike, haggard and bald. He wriggled in his chains, his white hands and quivering legs were never still. It could not be Oleg. Please God, it could not be.

But he had recognized her. Now he turned away from her, like a small boy hiding his hurt. The pathetically helpless movement went through Natasha's heart. Oleg, who had been so splendid, was this gibbering wreck.

"Attention!"

The soldiers snapped into line, motionless and erect. The prisoners shuffled together nervously, physically exhausted, morally broken.

General Ionin rose from his place behind the imposing table, spruce and trim in his faultlessly cut uniform, his old shoulders well squared, a Man of Iron. Slowly and solemnly, he began to read out the sentences. One by one the men were condemned to spend their terms of hard labor in the mines of Siberia—three, five, seven years.

Natasha waited tensely until the men had been dealt with. At last the general turned his terrible nailed eyes upon her. She tried to stand without the support of the guard.

Ionin's voice rang out. "Our gracious master the tzar believes that your offense is not strictly punishable by a term of imprisonment, yet he thinks that you are unfit for freedom. He has given you the chance to redeem yourself by accepting a period of penance. . . ."

Natasha could hardly breathe. She was to be enclosed in a convent for an indefinite period. Every instinct in her cried out at the injustice of it as Ionin went on remorselessly, ". . . Arrangements will be made for you to enter the convent house of the Holy Virgin on the island of Sarema. You will not be a prisoner in the strictest sense, but you will be at all times guarded from the public. Your own conduct will decide the length of your stay on Sarema, but you will serve not less than three years."

Three years! And after? . . .

Dimly Natasha heard Ionin say that she was to make a public penance at the church of St. Basilius.

CHAPTER

THIRTY-EIGHT

"But this is monstrous!" Richard said when Scavronsky went to him with the news. "They are punishing her, knowing that she is innocent."

The count looked pained. "Richard, they still don't know that for certain. None of the men broke under interrogation —at least, none incriminated her."

Richard's hands were tightly clenched, his whole body rigid with contempt. "If they had found her guilty, they would have sentenced her as they did the other women. Instead—good God!—they have condemned her to worse. She can be shut away indefinitely. The men, at least, will be back in circulation within a few years. . . ."

"Only if they *survive*," Scavronsky said. "She will not know the world, it's true. But neither will she live in darkness and isolation. She will be fed, clothed, housed—loved, perhaps. She will have the consolation of her religion."

Richard paced the room, trying to contain the fury that threatened to burst inside him. "She will be *confined*. That's all I know or care about," he said. "Marked for a life for which she is unfit. A life she never asked for, and doesn't deserve." His eyes blazed with rage.

Scavronsky held up a white, well-manicured hand. "*Mon cher ami*, there is nothing that anyone can do now, except wait for her release, and pray that it will be soon."

Richard scarcely heard him. "I've stood by for too long," he muttered. "I must find some way to oppose it. I'll not have her delivered up into . . . into . . ."

"Into God's hands?"

Richard glared. "No! Not into God's hands. Into *their* hands!"

Scavronsky took hold of his arm, restraining him. "Richard, believe me, you must seal up your feelings in this matter. There is nothing more that you can do. If you make any scandal they will send you away."

Richard paused. "Send me away?"

"Yes."

Richard shook off the count's hand. "What will that matter?" he cried passionately. "Why should I wish to stay in this accursed country if I'm denied her? If *she* is in exile."

He stopped in his wild pacing. "If they *had* made it exile, I would have gone with her."

Scavronsky looked astonished. "You would go with her into exile?"

"For Christ's sake, Kolya. Of course I would. Happily."

He turned to face the count, filled suddenly with an unreasoning hope. "Kolya, would it not be possible for the tzar to change the sentence to one of banishment?"

"Quite impossible," Scavronsky said. "You don't know the mood of the government in this. They have been outraged by the attack on Trepov, and fear for their own skins. You must submit to their will."

"No, I won't!" Richard shouted. "I will not submit to their damnable will. I am not the tzar's subject."

The count moved uneasily. He looked toward the door of Richard's sitting room, as though expecting it to open abruptly and disgorge a troop of police agents into the room.

"But I am a subject of his majesty," he said. "Richard, I have tried to make you understand. The decision has been taken. You are powerless to fight them. You have no weapons."

Richard remained silent for a few moments, thinking furiously. Then he said, "Yes, I have. I have one weapon left."

The count looked skeptical. "Believe me, you have not."

"I have my tongue, Kolya," Richard said quietly. "There's not a newspaper in democratic Europe that wouldn't print my story if I should choose to tell it. It's easy enough to keep the covers on the truth here in Petersburg, but I can bring a charge against the tzar outside Russia. He has condemned a woman only half suspected of a crime, and a woman hideously treated by his own ministers. If I go back to England without her, some unpleasant revelations will follow."

The count regarded him with dismay. He rose from his

chair, fastening his tunic, tying his belt. "Richard, I can't stay to listen to this."

He fell silent, shocked, yet filled with a sense of shame at the actions of his people. Richard watched him without expression as the count straightened the creases in his dazzling blue and white uniform of a colonel of the Imperial Guards.

Watching Scavronsky smooth his uniform, an idea began to form in Richard's mind. He began to see the possibility of rescuing Natasha from her terrible future. He would not leave her to fade, wither or die on that desolate island. How long was a period of penance? It could be stretched indefinitely.

The house that Richard had been directed to lay on Vassilevsky Island. He went from the Neva along the eighth Street toward the Bolshoi Prospekt. It was a house on a corner, a tall blue granite building.

He found the name he sought on the panel listing the tenants, printed in a faded gilt Cyrillic. The nameplate was so old that it must be genuine, he thought. As he had been informed, the house-porter was nowhere to be seen. He climbed the stairs to the third floor and rapped on a huge mahogany door.

The room he was shown into was expensively furnished, with a vaguely oriental opulence—huge, ornate furniture of dark wood, heavy moldings, dark paneling, fussy plasterwork. A magnificent Bokhara carpet lay on the gleaming parquet floor. Three gilded lamps lit the room. It was a strange setting in which to conduct his business. He had expected a garret or a student's quarters.

There were two people waiting for him. One he knew—the "General," who had brought Natasha to him weeks before. The other was a woman. Or, at first sight, a girl.

He was startled by her appearance, little expecting to find a woman there at all, and certainly not one who looked so young and inexperienced. Her face—round and small with a childlike forehead—stood out sharply against the dark brown of her modest dress. She was far from beautiful, but very striking.

The girl looked back at him with equal distrust in her face. Her small mouth was tightly shut, as though she feared to say more than was needed.

The General took over the meeting. After pressing Rich-

ard's hand vigorously, he moved to the table, opened a bottle
of vodka and poured out three glasses. Then he replaced the
vodka in a cupboard, his expression saying that was to be the
extent of his hospitality. Tossing back his own vodka, he got
down to business.

"You need our help?" he asked.

Richard said that he did, and explained the situation.

"We are acquainted with your story," the General said,
when Richard had finished. He and the woman exchanged a
brief glance. Richard understood them to mean that they
knew the students who had been arrested with Natasha.
These two had, somehow, escaped the net.

But before he could question them, the young man
said, "We shall need to know exactly what you want from
us."

"And how much you are prepared to pay for our services,"
the woman said. "Our party is poor. It lives on contribu-
tions."

"I shall pay three thousand rubles," Richard said. "Half
down now, the rest on completion."

The young man nodded. There was to be no argument.

Richard pulled out a leather bag. It contained one thousand five hundred rubles.

"Now tell us what you need."

Neither the man nor the woman paid any further attention
to the money on the table once it had been produced. From
their attitude, Richard could see that the money in itself had
no personal significance for them.

Quietly, Richard outlined his plan. They listened with
careful attention, their faces giving no clue to their thoughts.
When he had finished, Richard waited for their reaction.
Even as he had spoken, he thought, his plan had begun to
sound melodramatic and unworkable. He expected them to
reject it or revise it.

But the woman said quietly, "It's a good plan. Outrageous,
but good. It has the strength of the unexpected."

Her praise was given grudgingly. He had the impression
that she admired the plan but despised the aim behind it.

"Can you help me to carry it out?" Richard asked.

The two exchanged glances. Neither appeared anxious to
commit themselves. The man was less noticeably enthusiastic
than the woman. Then he nodded. "We have the resources,"
he said,

"And the ability," the woman added. "You'll have no

cause to curse our 'Russianness.' We shall only employ disciplined people."

Richard caught the suggestion of strain between the man and the woman. She, he could see, was all for action. The man was more cautious.

Then the gleaming pile of rubles caught the General's eyes and he smiled. "I've little liking for heroics," he said. "And this seems a very 'heroic' gesture." He picked up the wash-leather pouch and poured out the rest of the money. He started to count it. "However, as my comrade says, we need money—and we have the organization behind us."

He began to discuss Richard's plan as he counted, amending the details slightly. Richard was impressed. The man had a clear, ordered way of thinking, and was cool and calm. He had an encyclopedic knowledge of St. Petersburg and the port, the escape routes, the shipping channels, all of which knowledge Richard needed.

Obviously, too, he had a link with police headquarters. He already knew a great deal about the fate of the prisoners. Natasha, Richard learned, had been moved to the house of detention. Already the policing around her was more lax. That the two had a direct link to police headquarters was proved by their knowledge of the military interrogation. Not a word of it had appeared in the press. Richard, himself, had been advised of the court's verdict only because the tzar had "magnanimously" allowed Scavronsky to relay the decision.

No doubt these people were intent on releasing the café owner and some others, Richard thought. The money on the table represented the backing for such a *coup*. It had now all been counted and stashed away.

The girl smiled at Richard—a disconcerting smile, tight and intense. "You do realize, Mr. Greville," she said, as the last ruble vanished into the interior of the gladstone bag, "you do realize that you have—technically—now become one of us? An 'illegal.'"

Richard said nothing.

Her pale blue eyes gleamed briefly. "Just to give money to our group is a capital offense. You have officially become a revolutionary."

She stared at him. He had thought her eyes extraordinarily evasive, but now they were direct enough. There was in them an expression of stubborn resolution. It shocked him slightly. There was something in this girl—a fanaticism—that chilled him. She would carry her cause to the point of bloodshed.

Her eyes passed contemptuously over his elegant business suit of lightweight gray cashmere. "You don't look like a man who relishes the thought of handing over money to the enemies of your class."

"I relish handing Natasha Ivanovna over to tyranny even less," Richard replied.

CHAPTER
THIRTY-NINE

On entering the church, Natasha felt drowned in a flood of light. The bulbous curves of the building threw back the light of a thousand candles. The public humiliation decreed by law was to be as brilliantly illuminated as any stage performance. The placard on her chest described her role, the painted words lurid in the mortifying light: "Friend of Traitors."

Everything about her seemed to be moving, she was enclosed by circling undulating forms. Lines twisted in all directions in a baroque frenzy. The elaborately gilded walls with their florid scrolls and twisting columns whirled before her eyes.

At times the church and its congregation dissolved into mere outlines, masses of indistinct shape. The service passed in a dreamlike sequence of visions. Priests, choristers and the fashionable ladies who had gathered to witness her penance, all disappeared and reappeared in a bewildering mosaic of movement.

Natasha was dressed in a simple blouse and skirt of dark brown worsted, a brown woolen shawl over her head. The women around her were a riot of silk and satin, profusely trimmed with flounces and cascades of lace frilling. They could have been dressed for a matinée performance at the theatre.

Her heart flapped like a bird in a bag. She could almost

hear it pounding as her pulses raced. Lights danced before her eyes. The tessellated floor writhed and jumped beneath her feet. It amazed her that she could continue standing at her place before the altar rail. She was insensible to the priests' voices raised in prayer, the chanting of the choir, the murmuring of the worshipers as they walked about, craning to get a better view of her. She scarcely noticed the rough scratching of the coarse shift that she wore beneath her blouse and skirt.

Beside the altar, in a fog of incense, the priest carried out his duties. He was superb, mitred, leonine, his hair flowed over his shoulders, his beard shone on his chest, the folds of his chasuble were as neat as joints of armor.

Natasha sighed. She was completely removed from everything, beyond humiliation even. She felt nothing. The slow solemn ceremony passed in a haze of incense. At first, coming from the grayness of the prison world, she had been dazzled by this golden scene, momentarily uplifted. But soon a terrible numbness had gripped her. Only once did she raise her eyes to look about the church, as though seeking the face of a friend.

Richard, watching from a far corner of the church, shrank back into the shadows, pulling his cloak around him. The sounds around him, too, meant nothing. Standing shoulder to shoulder in the packed church, with no air, but only the overpowering odor of incense mingled with heavy perfumes, he said his own prayers. Seeing Natasha after all this time, so pale and pitiful, he was surprised to find that he could still think clearly. She looked deadened by her experiences. The irons upon her wrists cut at his own hands.

For her sake, he was going to stake all on one mad attempt to save her.

Before the service ended, he had left to take his place outside. In the church square some nuns, collecting alms, were seated at little tables. Their faces, in their long black veils, were shrunken and lined. Richard shuddered, seeing them. God save Natasha from their living death.

He walked to where his *golubki* waited in the front row of carriages. The driver growled in his beard and pulled upon the reins. Driver and carriage had been provided by the General.

It was all arranged. The man at police headquarters had discovered the route the police would use to transport Natasha to the island of Sarema. To Richard, it seemed an omen that the tzar had chosen Sarema as Natasha's place of confinement. It was to the west, in the open sea, a bare two hundred miles from Stockholm and neutral territory.

He climbed into the *golubki* and gave the order to move off. They rode out to the port, taking every shortcut to the broad Ostrovsky Quay. The young man had worked out the route superbly, there was not a moment wasted on the journey.

The quay was deserted, except for a late fisherman carrying rod and basket, and a guard who stood upon the deck of a steam launch, the *Kolosso*. Clearly, the authorities were not expecting trouble. Natasha was the least important of their "politicals."

Richard climbed from the carriage and dismissed the driver. It rolled away into the gathering darkness, as Richard strode across the quay to the *Kolosso* and walked down its narrow gangplank to the deck. The sentry saluted him, grinning broadly.

The man looked confident enough. Richard returned his smile, tensely. He had only met the man the night before, at the final briefing. The guard was in fact an ex-student, with a round potato face, an amateur yachtsman.

Once on deck, Richard began to pace it restlessly, with short irregular steps. The business was far from over. Taking the launch had been the easiest part. So far things had gone as planned, but the curse of Russian illegals, Richard had learned, was in their inattention to details. He didn't doubt this man's physical courage or his stamina, only his temperament. His name was Sacha.

Richard removed his chesterfield overcoat, a very fashionable garment with velvet collar and silk facings. Beneath it, he wore the drab green uniform of an officer of the gendarmerie. Sacha handed him a wide-crowned cap with a varnished peak. Richard pulled it low over his forehead, tilting it over one eye. It transformed his appearance completely. He stood in the bow of the launch, a tall, military-looking man, wearing the insignia of a captain, totally convincing to the casual observer.

Everything had been anticipated and dealt with. The genuine policemen had been overpowered and stowed away on an empty barge, bound and gagged. It had taken only a matter of moments to seize the police launch, the plan had been so well thought out and executed. Richard smiled, remembering the startled face of the captain of gendarmes when he had realized that his vessel was being taken over, staring with glazed stupefaction at the revolver trained on his fat stomach, unable to believe that the immaculate figure of the "brother gendarme" he had allowed on board was an illegal. Who would have suspected a plot to release such an unimportant prisoner? Security had been minimal—an officer and three seamen. He had been given no special instructions. Now Richard was in command of the *Kolosso*. But the business could still go wrong. Some small matter they had overlooked could still obstruct them. Any delay, however slight, could prove disastrous.

He could hardly feel the brass rail gripped in his hand. His hand could have belonged to another man's body. Time passed. Richard stood in the bow of the launch trying to control the fierce currents of impatience that swept through him. He could have stood there half an hour, it could have been half the night. Then, at last, a distant sound reached him—the faint rattle of carriage wheels and the steady trotting of hooves.

He was alert at once. Natasha was here! The knowledge sent wave after wave of moist heat over his body. Suddenly his hands were sweating, the brass rail was damp within his tight grasp.

Natasha stood upon the quay. The fresh wind blew in her dark hair and cast a refreshing spray upon her tired eyes. The scene around her was less bewildering than her ordeal in the church, but she could still not fully realize it. She had been exhausted by standing for over four hours with no possibility of relief, in a state of suffocation.

My last appearance "on stage" in Petersburg, she thought caustically.

She saw a steam launch lying at the quayside. She heard its timbers groan as the swell lifted it against the granite wall. But her eyes were mostly on the brilliant streak of sunlight on the horizon. Out there, in the sea, lay the island which was to be all her world for . . . how long?

Long weary years.

Fatalistically she turned to the launch, to stand arrested. Her breath stopped. Her pulses fluttered, then her heart began to hammer in her breast as the shock passed: the tall man standing in the bow of the launch—for a second she had thought . . .

She almost called out his name. Then the man moved

away, and she checked herself in time. Her breathing eased.
She stood silent and wondering. Was it possible? Was this
really Richard? She closed her eyes in agony, driving from her
mind the wild thoughts that astonished and confused her. The
lights of the lanterns danced dizzily upon the white decks of
the launch when she reopened her eyes.

Her escort pushed her toward the gangplank. Her feet felt
for the narrow board and she allowed herself to be guided
into the cockpit. As her feet touched the deck, strong hands
seized her, drawing her toward the companionway. She was
led below, away from the tall man who had now come
forward to sign the transfer papers. She caught a glimpse of
the well-loved face, then the door closed upon her.

Above, a voice cried, "Let go!" There was another cry
soon after, and the boat seemed to leave the quayside in a
great leap. The screws whirred urgently, thrusting the launch
forward with forceful drives. Through a port window, Natasha saw the outline of the city, black on gray, recede to a
distant horizon. The lights of St. Petersburg, the dim shapes
of palace and church, were hidden in the deepening mist.

She sank down upon an upholstered bench. Her cape was
still buttoned around her shoulders. The saloon was in
darkness. Time appeared to be flashing by for her. The
tremendous vibration of everything around her, the rattle of
glass in the ports, the swirl of the sea against the glass, spoke
of high speed. Speed spoke of a bid for freedom.

Steps sounded on the companionway. She looked up
expectantly. The door opened and the tall man entered,
stooping in the low doorway, a dark shadow against the
darker blue of the sky. Spray shone in crystals upon his
oilskins.

He struck a match and lit the lamp that swung above the
mahogany table. The lamp flung mad shadows around the
room. Once again, Natasha was aware of the speed at which
they were traveling through the waves. She felt a tingling
sensation at the base of her neck, sweeping over her whole
body. Like a cat whose fur had been rubbed the wrong way,
she felt the same spark of electricity. She leaned forward.
There was a long silence.

"Natasha," the man murmured. Then more loudly, "Don't
be alarmed. It's me—Richard."

He turned around. Natasha rose from her bench, her hand
to her heart. A shock wave ran through her. A dozen

emotions battled within her. Then they had both crossed the small space that separated them. He grasped her firmly by the shoulders. She clung to him.

"Natasha," he said. "I'm sorry. Oh, my darling, forgive me. I would have let you know sooner, but I couldn't. It would have been too cruel if . . . if . . . we should not have escaped."

She stared at him, her eyes still glazed with shock. "Escaped?"

The word was scarcely more than a breath, its meaning less than the sound of her voice. "Are we really escaped?" she asked.

"Once we are past the fortress of Kronstadt," he answered.

Even as they spoke, they could see the faint lights of the island fortress flashing upon the horizon. As they stood watching, the walls and towers of the citadel shaped themselves against the lowering western sky, an image of power and sullen magnificence. It was a vast and natural wedge that most foreign ships must pass, the northern gateway to Russia and a tomb for her enemies.

Richard and Natasha clung to each other. Natasha shivered in his arms. She raised her face to his. They kissed. Then, when they stood back, she shivered again. "I can't believe it!" she said.

"It's true," he murmured, his face against her cheek. "We have traveled fourteen miles of a lifetime's journey together."

Grimly he reminded himself that they were out of the maw of Russia, but not yet free of her jaws. Their liberty could still be an illusion. They were still hemmed in by the forts and batteries of Kronstadt, by the tremendous walls that protected the town and harbor.

"I should like to go on deck," Natasha said. "I should like to feel the wind on my face, to see the stars shining."

"Come with me, my darling. We shall see the light of Tollboken fall behind us. . . ."

When she stood upon the deck with him, the wind blew with such freshness and the spray blinded her so that she could see nothing at first. She clung to Richard and he wiped the droplets of sea water from her face. Lights flashed on every side—the lights of warships, the lights of barracks, the red, green and white lanterns of the bastions thrusting out into the sea. They were sailing with death on their right hand.

Should his plan misfire, he would be entombed in the granite heart of the fortress, or down in the freezing waters of the Gulf of Finland.

They stood watching the long southern shore of the island as the waves crashed against the bow. The boat appeared to race against the tide. They were mesmerized by the sight of the massive guns that threatened them from the huge ramparts.

Richard waited to hear the boom of guns that would signal their flight. The minutes rolled by, as slack and easy as the waves that broke against their bow.

Then, at last, they saw the flashing light of the Tollboken tower, and, beyond, the open sea. The black line of the grim island began to lose its shape. The Tollboken beacon magnified and the lights behind it—strung over the water—began to vanish one by one. It was like watching the stars fade at dawn. The salt of the open sea was in their faces.

The light of Tollboken receded. Faded . . . There was nothing now but the dark line of the horizon merging with the sky.

"Well," Richard asked. "Do you believe me now?"

She caught her breath. At last reality flooded in. She was looking at Russia for the last time. She was saying good-bye to all that was familiar, much that was loved. A part of her was deadened by the realization. Tears threatened, but she blinked them away angrily. Above all, she was saying good-bye to tyranny, fear and despair, with Richard at her side.

"But . . . how?" she asked. "How did you make it happen?"

Richard laughed, the wind whipping the laughter away. "It's a long story, my love, and perhaps this is not the best time to tell it."

"*Please.*"

He drew her beneath the shelter of his oilskins and kissed her, a long, cool, lingering kiss, with the taste of saltwater in it. After, she stood within the haven of his arms, silent and trembling as he told her of how he had arranged her abduction.

"It was our old friend Grigory," he said. "I went first to him, and he introduced me to the man who brought you to me. He's smuggled a great many of the General's 'troops' out of Russia, it seems. I daresay he might have been your guide, had you not been taken."

His arm tightened around her as she shuddered. "The

General helped me capture this launch, and supplied our crew. I can't work out whether they're true politicals or just honest rogues. But, whatever they are, they seem quite unconcerned at the thought of returning to Mother Russia."

Natasha shivered again, silent for a moment, thinking of how much they all risked for her, but Richard most of all. Then she said, "It must have been very expensive to arrange."

Richard kissed her brow. "Worth every kopeck, my darling." He gazed at her earnestly. "I think they mean to use the money to release your friends."

"Thank God," Natasha whispered, remembering the broken figures in the council chamber.

Richard, feeling her remembered horror, held her close. After a few sheltered moments, she drew away from him and asked him to tell her more. Richard explained how, in the uniform he still wore, he had taken three similarly disguised men on board, flourishing a forged warrant. Once on board, they had quickly overpowered the gendarmes. It had been the work of a few minutes; the attack was so unexpected that the captain had stood staring stupidly throughout.

"What did you do with the real gendarmes?" Natasha asked.

Richard laughed.

"We bound them with their own ropes, manacled them with their own handcuffs, gagged them with their own scarves, and left them in the hold of an unused barge."

"And if they're found?"

"They won't be found until morning, my darling. Not until the morning shift of stevedores arrives."

Natasha was silent. She could not share in his laughter. She could only think that Richard had saved her from years of confinement. But at what cost to himself?

She turned to him again, clutching his coat. "It can't be true," she whispered. "I shall wake to find it all a dream, and I shall be back in my cell."

He stopped her mouth with a kiss. Her salt-rimmed lips parted beneath his. "You shall tell me tomorrow whether it's true or not," he said, "when we are in Stockholm. Meanwhile, there's supper to think of. And, after supper, rest. It's time that we lighted the saloon. You're tired, sweetheart."

She was about to tell him that her tiredness meant nothing —her whole body was beginning to come to life under the touch of his hands. Then a flame of light shot up from the shore of the distant island. They saw it reflected in the dark belly of the clouds. Faintly, over the sea, the boom of a gun rolled like an echo of thunder.

Richard started, and Natasha jerked within his arms. "They have fired a gun from Tollboken," she whispered.

Richard turned, staring into the darkness. "It's only a ship's salute," he said.

Natasha shuddered, thinking of the shadows again. A second gun fired from the ramparts of Tollboken. ". . . Richka, they *know*."

Richard gathered her into his arms, trying to conceal the feeling of terrible dread that had possessed him since the firing of the first shot. Natasha clung to him. He enfolded her in his arms, bending her head back to kiss her.

"Nothing will stop us, darling," he murmured. "We stand together for good or ill. As God wills."

"*If* God wills," she said, through her tears.

Again he stopped her mouth with a kiss. "You are going to be my wife," he said simply.

Sacha's grinning face appeared above the coaming of the engine room hatchway. "She's doing twenty knots, captain," he said, in a parody of a seaman's manner.

"She must do more," Richard said. "Spare nothing to get up more speed. Burn the ship, if need be."

"May as well be hung for a vandal as a thief," Sacha grinned.

His grin vanished as another shot reverberated across the water. All three turned toward the sound. "That's the gun at Menzikoff," Sacha said. "They've roused the garrison. We'll see the lights of their ships soon."

The grinning face disappeared. Within minutes, a thick smoke rolled from the funnel of the launch. She plunged with new spirit into the spuming waves that the fresh wind drove in from the Baltic. The water washed her bow and ran ankle deep over her flush decks. She had no lights except for the glow that hovered over her funnel or spread fan-shaped when the furnace door was opened. Every timber in her quivered at the heightened speed.

This was a race for liberty—perhaps for life. Out there, in the northern darkness, lay freedom and happiness. Behind them, where the great guns roared dully, were the prisons of Russia, the lash and the knout, the empty wasteland of Siberia.

CHAPTER

FORTY

Their course lay almost due west for a while. When they had been at sea for an hour or more they could no longer distinguish the lights upon the Finnish shore, nor the further lights of the villages on the Ingrian coast. The gulf broadened so quickly that they stood almost at once in a widening sea, in the channel of ships steaming to Russia or laboring to make Helsingfors.

Scudding white mists hid the moon fitfully. Storm clouds began to gather in the south and to beat up warningly. As they stood out to sea, the night grew bitterly cold and the wind whipped at their faces.

"Come, let's go down," Richard said. He had been held to the deck as though chained there by anticipation of the worst. "I've tasted no food since breakfast," he said, smiling down at Natasha. "And I could swallow little of that." He hugged her close. "I should be ashamed to keep you up here, after what you've endured today."

She clung to his hand, seeking the shelter of his side, not from the weather, but from her own fears.

"We'll have supper," Richard said cheerfully. "It will be time to think of other things when we see the lights of their ships."

"Do you think they'll follow us?" she asked.

He nodded. "They'll probably send a cruiser. But don't worry, my darling. This is a good fast craft. It is—after all—built for pursuit. As long as we have coal in our bunkers or wood to burn, we shall be safe."

They entered the saloon. The room glowed cheerfully in the light of the lamps. The ports were shuttered and the curtains drawn. A jug of hot wine stood upon the table. Richard poured out a glassful and gave it to Natasha. "Drink it at a draught," he ordered. "I want to see the color in your cheeks."

Even after an hour of standing in the lashing wind, her face looked drained of color. Her pallor appalled him. She took the glass. When she had emptied it, she fell into Richard's arms, raising her face to him and kissing him wildly.

"How can I tell you all I feel?" she murmured.

His arms went around her. He hid his face in her hair. It smelled of incense. Incense clung to her. It was in her hair and in her clothes. When she raised her face to his, he was shocked at the change in her. It was his first chance to see her at close quarters. God, how she must have suffered, he thought. Her high cheekbones gleamed through her skin, her eyes looked bruised. He felt overwhelmed by pity for her, shattered by it.

The door opened and a fat man with a sly, good-humored face hurried into the cabin and set a steaming dish upon the table.

"Thank you, Piotr," Richard said, and the man grinned. Natasha smiled shyly and thanked him. The man withdrew.

Richard and Natasha sat down to eat the rich stew of meat and cabbage. As they ate a new confidence came into their talk. For a brief while they were led away from the hour and the place. The shadows passed from their faces. It was possible, down there in the warmth and brightness of their cabin, to imagine that they were already safe and free—to imagine that they had come home.

Richard began to talk about England, to talk of the sunny fields of Sussex and the villages where they might honeymoon. He made no mention of his ruined career, yet a sadness lay behind Natasha's eyes. Life would no more be the same for him than it would be for her, she knew. The end would be a new beginning in every respect. As Richard's wife she would never dance again—at least professionally. The ballet was not respectable in England, and she would be in society. Yet would they stay in England? By marrying her, would Richard have lost caste himself? How would they change in this alien world?

The spell of the warming wine worked upon Richard so that he could easily tell himself that the reward was far greater than the sacrifice. His career was ended. He would be a marked man, a notorious man, though matters would be hushed up, he knew that. Neither government would seek an open scandal, but it would be the end of his diplomatic life.

He put all thought of the future from him. The present was too demanding. He loved Natasha, she loved him. That was all that mattered. She, too, had sacrificed herself. They had already endured so much, and hardship had made them stronger, united them more closely. She had proved herself in every way. All he wanted now was to take the pain and sadness from her eyes. Gently, he drew her toward him.

She came to him, so that lips were on lips, on cheeks, on eyes. At first they were awkward and clumsy with each other. They had to find each other again. Then something in Natasha began to flower beneath the intensity of his kisses. She was a woman again, a desirable woman. She stirred against him, soaking in each new sensation as his hands moved over her body.

Richard undressed her with a dozen sensuous delays. Loosening the lace at her neck, the belt at her waist, his hands slipped beneath her blouse, stroking her silken skin into new awareness.

He could feel her breasts swelling beneath the coarse linen shift. Its roughness shocked him into remembrance of her intended destination. Anger made him suddenly brutal. He tore at the offending cloth, ripping it away from her body. His arms went about her, crushing her to him fiercely.

How strangely frail her body seemed, and yet how strong still—her shoulders so straight, her breasts so firm, her stomach curving gently, the flesh resilient to his touch. Her waist tapered to the richly curving roundness of her hips. Her long shapely thighs narrowed to well-formed calves and slim strong ankles. How had she maintained herself so well during the long weeks of imprisonment?

As though reading his mind, she said, laughing softly, "I danced in my cell. It kept me sane."

He was filled with astonished pride in her, at her courage and resourcefulness. He swept her back into his arms, kissing her passionately, to lay her gently back upon the leather berth.

But she reached out for him again, her arms going about him as she raised herself. The lamplight gilded her body. Her body was like a mysterious landscape to him, familiar yet unknown. There were soft shadows between her breasts, deeper shadows beneath the mound of her belly and between her thighs

Lamplight, too, spilled over Richard. Breathlessly she watched the play of light on his long broad back, the deep-shadowed ridge of his spine. When he turned to her, the light sparkled on the golden hair that covered the taut muscles of his chest. His limbs seemed covered with a fine gold mesh. The muscles of his shoulders knotted powerfully. Her hands groped for him, pulling him against her.

Heat rose from her body to match his own. Their bodies came together. Suddenly all awkwardness and restraint was gone between them. She was avid for him, eaten up by her desire. Her loins yearned for him. "Take me," she murmured incoherently. "Oh, darling, I want you . . . I want you . . ."

His body came down on hers, clasping her to him, bringing her body into line with his, easing her onto her back with great care. Her legs parted beneath him, her pelvis thrust up to meet his violently. His hands moved over her nakedness, calming her and yet at the same time stimulating her tremendously, pressing her back against the leather cover.

"Gently," he murmured. "Gently, my darling . . ."

His shaft tilted against her legs. She could feel the hard smooth tip nudging against her parting lips. A delicious warmth spread between her thighs. Slowly, gently, he entered her with long deliberate strokes. His lips found hers. Soon she was sobbing beneath him, her body rising and falling, opening and spreading, in perfect rhythm to his measured thrusts. She could feel the long length of him deep inside her, slipping smoothly against the silken lining, lingering at the limit of each forward lunge. Ecstasy, like a tide, ebbed and flowed within her. Her cheeks were moist, her vision blurred with tears. How long was it since she had wept for happiness, she wondered. A slow, warm feeling swelled through her breast, an almost suffocating sense of joy, of triumph.

"We are *alive*," she exulted. "We have come through. I am not dead. I can still feel . . ."

All emotion had not died within her, as she had feared. It had only slept throughout the tedious weeks, months. Now passion overwhelmed her. Pleasure conquered her. They reached their climax together, slowly and magically. Their bodies described long swaying waves, arching and collapsing, her body pliable and yielding. Where his manhood throbbed and spent itself she was as softened as wax.

After, as they lay together, she laughed softly to herself. "What is it?" Richard asked.

"You'll think it foolish."

"No, I won't. Tell me."

She laughed again, looking up into his eyes shyly. "Well, when I was leaving the house of detention, a guard came to me—one of the kindlier ones. I was all packed to go—what there was to pack—and the carriage was waiting. She made me sit down for half a minute, to say a prayer before the journey, for luck. You know the custom." Natasha shuddered. "It seemed so cruel at the time. Considering where I was heading . . ."

She shuddered again, then broke into a smile, her face radiant. "But now . . ."

She pushed her head against his naked chest, entwining her arms around him. Richard kissed her, holding her tenderly, hushing her into serenity. Lying there, in Richard's arms, she could forget the past, the future, even the cabin they were in and the peril they faced. All could be forgotten save for the fact that she was in his arms. She lived in a present that was in itself an eternity, the eternity of realized love.

Three hours passed swiftly away. Richard lingered in the cabin because he knew that the deck might show him what he feared to see, the lights of the cruisers sent out in pursuit. The men would send for him when he was needed above.

The quiver of the boards beneath his feet, the jarring of the woodwork, spoke of high speed maintained, and of a smoother sea. If they could keep the *Kolosso* at this speed she might outsteam any vessel sent after her. But the real danger lay ahead—in the warships of Helsingfors and Revel that guarded the neck of the Gulf of Finland. The telegraph would already have warned them of the escape.

Was it madness to hope in the midst of danger? Despair whispered that the girl he loved was in his arms, but that he held her there for the last time. Perhaps . . .

Natasha read the thoughts in his face. She turned her head into his shoulder and they lay in silence for a while.

Then the door of the saloon opened and Piotr, still wearing his inane grin, showed himself at the door. "What is it?" Richard asked, half rising, pushing the lamp aside to hide Natasha's nakedness.

"It's about the *coal*, comrade."

"Then I'll come at once."

The door closed behind the grinning fat man, and Richard turned to Natasha. "You must sleep now, my love. Tomorrow you shall be in Stockholm, by sunset at the latest. You can begin to think of England then."

She raised her lips to his and clung to him with a new tenderness. She had caught the note of alarm in his voice. Piotr's artless explanation had not deceived her.

Richard released himself and hurried up to the deck. Dawn straggled in the eastern sky. Without a word, Piotr pointed away upon the port quarter. Richard turned to look. A gray cruiser had put out from Helsingfors and was searching the gulf. The telegraph had done its work.

Richard swore. "God help us," he said.

CHAPTER

FORTY-ONE

The launch stood out upon its course. Except for the vibrations of her screws and the buffet of the seas upon her arched bow, no sound followed in her wake. She cut through the gathering waves rather than breasted them. She rushed onward through the swell as though she was some living creature from the deep come up for breath.

The gray cruiser stood to the north. Richard and his two crew watched its path with excitement. The false dawn continued to befriend them. Except where the pale light showed above the eastern horizon, night still flowed upon the sea to the west. They were moving into sheltering darkness, but the sun trailed them.

"They're standing out for the south," Piotr said. He was at the wheel. "It'll be in their heads that we're heading for the German coast. Or perhaps to Gotland." He grinned irrepressibly. "We'll go by 'em yet, with a handful of luck."

Piotr and Sacha behaved as though this adventure was no more to them than an hour in a fog at the mouth of the Neva. The race from the quayside to the open sea had been a lark to them. Nor did the appearance of the warship hold any terrors for them. Instead they joked about the future and the fame that would be theirs when they were smuggled back into Russia. What a daring business this had been—to steal the tzar's property and spit in the imperial eye. None of the General's men had ever gone so far, or had been so successful. That is, if they made it to Stockholm. And, by God, they would! They would!

"We still have the heels of 'em," Sacha said. "We can still shake a fist at 'em."

But Richard shared little of their optimism. Too much was at stake. He had banked on a clear run of twelve hours before the genuine crew would be discovered. It was the most damnable accident that the police crew had been found so quickly. He wondered idly how it had come about. Some stray mongrel setting up a howl, a drunken tramp looking for a night's shelter in what he thought was an empty hold? The police had not managed their own escape, he felt sure of that. He had tied their bonds himself.

"She's running to the south, Piotr," he said gloomily. "But it will not be for long." He cursed. "She's turning about now."

Piotr touched the little wheel and spat emphatically.

"It's true, by God!" Sacha said. "But what of it, comrade? It'll be a pretty steady hand that picks us off in this light. And we've the heels of 'em when all's said and done."

"Aye, that's true," Piotr said. "Take my word for it, if they're hoping to take us afore they go off duty tonight, they won't finish this watch till the day of judgment."

Richard smiled. "You've a pleasant way of looking at things, gentlemen."

Piotr's grin almost split his face. "That's our good fortune."

He touched the wheel again and the little boat rose on the crest of a great wave before plunging into the shining darkness of the hollow. The warship went about. The dawn lay like a gate of light in the east. It gave promise of a clear sky later.

For an hour the *Kolosso* raced in half-darkness toward the distant sea of refuge. Then the sun's rays shot out from a cloud and lit up the waters with a shaft of light. Rippling like molten gold, the pool of radiance widened, flowing onward toward the little launch. It made jewels of the wind-tossed spindrift. It focused upon the black sails of a small fishing boat and struck the hull of a steamer, so that Richard could count the men upon her decks. Then the light rested full upon the *Kolosso,* its touch growing warm and greedy, fingering them as though it touched prey and would torment it.

No man spoke. Piotr's hand was firm upon the wheel.

"God, for another hour of darkness," Richard murmured, leaning spellbound against the shrouds, watching the light pursuing them.

"That's the *Eagle* out of Narva," Piotr said, pointing at the gray warship. "I could pick her out of a thousand. She carries four twelve-inch guns and a stern-chaser. Her speed's fourteen—in the book."

"To hell with the book!" Sacha cried. "The question is, what's her speed here, and when is she going to show it?"

Piotr's grin was diabolical. "She's going to show it now, friend. If you want to dance, here's the music."

A gun boomed out above the moaning of the wind, and its smoke hung for an instant like an envelope of vapor above the decks of the *Eagle.*

Richard turned, to find Natasha standing at his side. She slipped her hand into his and stood with him. She smiled up at him, trying to hide the fear that she felt. Richard's fingers tightened about her hand. His smile had much pity in it.

"I couldn't stay below, Richka. Not now that I *know.*" She gestured toward the distant ship moving slowly across the spuming sea.

"I didn't want you to know of it," Richard said. "I thought you would be asleep and wake where no one could harm you." She hugged his arm. "But now . . ."

"We shall dance, as Piotr says," Natasha said. She stared at the *Eagle,* then at their racing wake. "The *Kolosso* is very fast, isn't she?" she asked.

"Very. One of the fastest."

"Then, surely, we can still keep ahead," Natasha said. She looked over the sea at the cruiser, perceptibly nearer now. "I know we can. That ship looks so . . . so ill-shaped, like a dowager." She smiled, and patted the sea-stained brass of the *Kolosso.* "This ship is full of grace."

Richard took her face between his hands and kissed her. "My darling. If I had your heart!"

"And she's brought luck on deck with her, too," Piotr said. "We're leaving 'em behind!"

The ships were abreast now, a mile of sparkling seas between them, but the lumbering *Eagle* was no match for the little launch. The *Kolosso* forged ahead. She held her course unflinchingly, even when the *Eagle*'s guns sent flame across the water again and a shell fell hissing in the waves behind her. The launch steamed on, shaking the cruiser from her.

A second shot hissed across the sea and was swallowed up in a fountain of foam. It fell so close to the launch that the faces of the crew were drenched. It drew a curse from Piotr, though his grin was as fixed as ever.

Natasha sought the shelter of Richard's arms. She turned to him, her fingers entwined in his. "Richka, when shall we be in England?"

"In about four days time, sweetheart."

"And then?"

He placed his hands over her lips. "No plans," he said, with a smile. "I've no thoughts beyond now."

She nestled against him, murmuring. "Richka, my Richka. . . . You have no regrets?"

He kissed her full on the mouth, then kissed her eyes. "Regrets? With you at my side? Filling me with courage?"

She answered with a half caress and he led her to the poop, where they watched the wake glow with a phosphorescent brilliance. The *Kolosso* plunged into the widening sea, away from Russian shores and into Swedish waters.

All the pent-up gladness in Richard rose to his breast, swelling inside him. He clutched Natasha to him until their bodies were molded together. Dear Christ, he thought wildly. Has this really happened to me—that dull, prosaic fellow of a year ago? Is it truly all over? Can Natasha and I really look forward to living out our lives together? No more partings, no more sorrow . . .

How would they live? *Where* would they live? He had to start giving thought to it. Within a week he would be at home. There would be questions to which he would have to find answers. Thank God society in England was no longer so stuffy about "unsuitable" marriages. His mother might be difficult, but Natasha would charm his father. . . .

Time to think of such things later. He was holding the woman he loved in his arms. The strengthening sun was falling upon their faces, falling upon their future together. His arms closed around her, more fiercely protective. Her head rested happily against his chest.

She had pushed all thoughts of the future away. She could only live in the present, with the glorious certainty that she was free and with the man she loved. The future would be hard, she knew that. But, shared, what terrors could it hold to compare with those she had lived through already? She had come through. She laughed throatily, triumphantly, reaching up to caress Richard's stubbled cheek.

"Go below now," Piotr said. "We've outsteamed 'em, by God!"

They went below. The color had come again to Natasha's face, her haunted expression was beginning to fade. She was again something of the dark enchanting creature who had captivated him at the ball on the ice. When he looked into her bright eyes and heard the laughter bubbling up from within her, love came singing up to compel complete forgetfulness of everything else.

As Natasha had said: In this end was a new beginning.

ROMANCE LOVERS DELIGHT

ROMANCE LOVERS DELIGHT

Purchase any book for $2.95
plus $1.50 shipping & handling for each book.

___ **ROYAL SUITE** by Marsha Alexander. Fabulous success threatens the passion of new love.

___ **MOMENTS TO SHARE** by Diana Morgan. Her ambition might destroy the only man she ever loved.

___ **ROMAN CANDLES** by Sofi O'Bryan. In the splendor of the Eternal City she found a daring and dangerous lover.

___ **TRADE SECRETS** by Diana Morgan. Passion and power steam the windows amidst the world of publishing.

___ **AFTERGLOW** by Jordana Daniels. She had but one choice to make — glamorous romance or success.

___ **A TASTE OF WINE** by Vanessa Pryor. In lush vineyards, she took her first intoxicating sip of love.

___ **ON WINGS OF SONG** by Martha Brewster. In the glory days of opera, their voices mingled in passionate melody.

___ **A PROMISE IN THE WIND** by Perdita Shepherd. A peasant beauty captured by a ruling enemy, desired by a noble love.

___ **WHISPERS OF DESTINY** by Jenifer Dalton. While love bloomed in her heart, the seeds of war grew in her homeland.

___ **SUNRISE TEMPTATION** by Lynn Le Mon. Her defiant heart battled between the power of wealth and the pursuit of passion.

___ **WATERS OF EDEN** by Katherine Kent. She tasted the fruits of passion that grew wild in a lover's paradise.

___ **ARABESQUE** by Rae Butler. Two defiant hearts, one impossible love dared to challenge the might of a nation.

Send check or money order (no cash or CODs) to:
PARADISE PRESS
8551 SUNRISE BLVD. #302   PLANTATION, FL 33322

Name _____

Address _____

City_____ State_____ ZIP_____